Praise for Ann Cleeves

HIDDEN DEPTHS

'Nobody does unsettling undercurrents better than Ann Cleeves' Val McDermid

'*Hidden Depths* is another classic, traditional crime novel in a contemporary setting by Ann Cleeves . . . a skilfully crafted mystery' *Sunday Telegraph*

'Ann Cleeves improves with every book . . . *Hidden Depths* is a subtle, nuanced book and Cleeves draws her characters with care and compassion. The landscape of rural Northumberland is vividly evoked and Inspector Stanhope – overweight, fallible and driven by personal demons – is a terrific central character' *Tribune*

'A dark, interesting novel with considerable emotional force behind it' *Spectator*

'A nicely atmospheric read' *Time Out*

'Ann Cleeves deserves a lot more attention than she gets. Her plots are beautifully crafted; her characters are intense and deeply drawn. She's also a real mistress of setting, taking us right into the scene of the action. All of those qualities shine in *Hidden Depths*, one of her best . . . Cleeves never lets up on the suspense in this very complex puzzle . . . masterful storytelling' *Globe and Mail*

RAVEN BLACK

'*Raven Black* breaks the conventional mould of British crime-writing, while retaining the traditional virtues of strong narrative and careful plotting' *Independent*

'Beautifully constructed . . . a lively and surprising addition to a genre that once seemed moribund' *Times Literary Supplement*

'*Raven Black* shows what a fine writer Cleeves is . . . an accomplished and thoughtful book' *Sunday Telegraph*

'A fine and sinister psychological novel in the Barbara Vine style. Cleeves is part of a new generation of superior British writers who put refreshing new spins and twist on the old forms' *Globe and Mail*

HIDDEN DEPTHS

Ann Cleeves worked as a probation officer, bird observatory cook and auxiliary coastguard before she started writing. She now promotes reading for Kirklees Libraries and as Harrogate Crime Writing Festival's reader in residence, and is also a member of 'Murder Squad', working with other northern writers to promote crime fiction. In 2006 Ann was awarded the Duncan Lawrie Dagger for Best Crime Novel for *Raven Black*. Ann lives in North Tyneside.

Also by Ann Cleeves

ANN CLEEVES

HIDDEN DEPTHS

PAN BOOKS

First published 2007 by Macmillan

First published in paperback 2007 by Pan Books
an imprint of Pan Macmillan Ltd
Pan Macmillan, 20 New Wharf Road, London N1 9RR
Basingstoke and Oxford
Associated companies throughout the world
www.panmacmillan.com

ISBN 978-0-330-51659-4

1 3 5 7 9 8 6 4 2

A CIP catalogue record for this book is available from
the British Library.

Typeset by Intype Libra Ltd
Printed and bound in the UK by
CPI Mackays, Chatham ME5 8TD

Visit **www.panmacmillan.com** to read more about all our books
and to buy them. You will also find features, author interviews and
news of any author events, and you can sign up for e-newsletters
so that you're always first to hear about our new releases.

For the boys

Acknowledgements

Thanks to Helen Pepper for all her advice
on crime-scene management.

As ever, any mistakes are mine.

Chapter One

Julie stumbled from the taxi and watched it drive away. At the front gate she paused to compose herself. Best not to go in looking pissed after all those lectures she'd given the kids. The stars wheeled and dipped in the sky and she almost threw up. But she didn't care. It had been a good night, the first with the girls for ages. Though it wasn't the girls that had made it so special, she thought, and realized there was a great soppy beam on her face. Just as well it was dark and there was no one to see.

At the door she stopped again and scrabbled through the eyeliner pencils and lippy-stained tissues and loose change in her bag for her key. Her fingers found the scrap of paper which had been torn from a corner of a menu in the bar. A phone number and a name. *Ring me soon.* Then a little heart. The first man she'd touched since Geoff had left. She could still feel the bones of his spine against her fingers when they'd danced. It was a shame he'd had to leave early.

She snapped the bag shut and listened. Nothing. It was so quiet that she could hear the buzz of the evening's music as a pressure on her ears. Was it possible that Luke was asleep? Laura could sleep for

England, but her son had never seemed to get the hang of it. Even now he'd left school and there was nothing to get up for, he was usually awake before her. She pushed open the door and listened again, slipping her feet out of the shoes that had been killing her since she'd got out of the metro hours before. God, she hadn't danced like that since she was twenty-five. There was silence. No music, no television, no beeping computer. Thank the Lord, she thought. Thank the fucking Lord. She wanted sleep and sexy dreams. Somewhere on the street outside an engine was started.

She switched on the light. The glare hurt her head and turned her stomach again. She let go of her bag and ran up the stairs to the bathroom, tripping halfway up. No way was she going to be sick on the new hall carpet. The bathroom door was shut and she saw a crack of light showing underneath it. From the airing cupboard there came the faint gurgle of water which meant the tank was refilling. And wasn't that typical? It took hours of persuasion to get Luke into the shower in the morning, then he decided to have a bath in the middle of the night. She knocked on the bathroom door but there was no urgency about it. The queasiness had passed again.

Luke didn't answer. He must be in one of his moods. Julie knew it wasn't his fault and she should be patient, but sometimes she wanted to strangle him when he went all weird on her. She crossed the landing to Laura's room. Looking down at her daughter, she came over suddenly sentimental, thought she should make the effort to spend more time with her. Fourteen was a difficult age for a girl and Julie had been so caught up with Luke lately that Laura almost seemed like a stranger. She'd grown up without Julie noticing. She lay on her back, her spiky hair very black against the pillow, snoring slightly, her mouth open. It was a bad time for hay fever. Julie saw that the window was open and, although it was so hot, she shut it to keep out the pollen. The moonlight splashed onto the field behind the house where they'd been cutting grass.

She returned to the bathroom and banged on the door with the flat of her palm. 'Hey, are you going to be in there all night?' With the third bang, the door opened. It hadn't been locked. There was a smell of bath oil, heavy and sweet, which Julie didn't recognize as hers. Luke's clothes were neatly folded on the toilet seat.

He had always been beautiful, even as a baby. Much lovelier than Laura, which had never seemed fair. It was the blond hair and the dark eyes, the long, dark eyelashes. Julie stared at him, submerged beneath the bath water, his hair rising, like fronds of seaweed, towards the surface. She couldn't see his body because of the flowers. They floated on the perfumed water. Only the flower heads, not the stems or the leaves. There were the big ox-eye daisies which had grown in the cornfields when she was a kid. Overblown poppies, the red petals translucent now. And enormous blue blossoms, which she had seen before in gardens in the village, but which she couldn't name.

Julie must have screamed. She heard the sound as if someone else had made it. But still Laura slept and Julie had to shake her to wake her. The girl's eyes opened suddenly, very wide. She looked terrified and Julie found herself muttering, knowing that she was lying, 'It's all right, pet. Everything's all right. But you have to get up.'

Laura swung her legs out of bed. She was trembling, but not really awake. Julie put her arm around her and supported her as they stumbled together down the stairs.

They stood like that, wrapped up in each other's arms, on the doorstep of the neighbour's house and the silhouette thrown on the wall by the street light made Julie think of people in a crazy three-legged race. One of those pub crawls that students went in for. She leaned against the bell until the lights upstairs went on and footsteps came and she had someone to share the nightmare with.

Chapter Two

It disturbed Felicity Calvert that she'd become so pre-occupied with sex. Once, in the doctor's waiting room, she'd read a magazine which claimed that adolescent boys thought about sex every six minutes. Then she'd found it hard to believe. How could these young men lead a normal life – go to college, watch a film, play football – when they were so frequently distracted? And what of her own son? Watching James playing on the floor with his Lego, it had been impossible to imagine that in a few years he would be similarly obsessed. But now she thought that an interval of six minutes between sexual daydreams could be a con-servative estimate. In her case at least. For a while now an awareness of her body and its responses had been with her whatever she was doing, an uneasy, occasionally pleasurable background to the stuff of everyday life. For someone of her age this seemed inappropriate. It was as if she'd attended a funeral wearing pink.

She was in the garden picking the first of the strawberries. She lifted the net carefully, sliding her hand underneath between the mesh and the straw bedding. They were still small but there should be enough for James's tea. She tasted one. It was warm from the sun and very sweet. Glancing at her watch she saw it was almost time for the school bus. Ten more minutes and she'd have to wash her hands and walk down the lane to meet him. She didn't always go. He claimed he was old enough to make his own way to the house and of course that was true. But today he'd have his violin and he'd be glad to see her because she could help him carry his stuff. She wondered briefly whether it would be the old bus driver or the young one with the muscular arms and the sleeveless T-shirt, then looked at her watch again. Only two minutes since she'd last considered sex. The thought returned that at her age it was quite ridiculous.

Felicity was forty-seven. She had a husband and four children. She had, for goodness' sake, a grandchild. In a few days Peter, her husband, would be sixty. The bubbles of lust surfaced at random, when she was least expecting them. She hadn't talked about this to Peter. Of course not. He certainly wasn't the object of her desire. These days they seldom made love.

She got up and walked across the grass to the kitchen. Fox Mill stood on the site of an old water mill. It was a big house, built in the thirties, a coastal retreat for a ship owner from the city. And it looked like a ship with its smooth, curved lines, the mill race flowing past it. A big, art deco ship, stranded quite out of place in the flat farmland, with its prow pointed to the North Sea and its stern facing the Northumberland hills on the horizon. A long veranda stretched along one side like a deck, impractical here where it was seldom warm enough to sit outside. She loved the house. They would never have afforded it on an academic's salary, but Peter's parents had died soon after he and Felicity had married and all their money had come to him.

She put the basket of strawberries on the table and checked her face in the mirror in the hall, running her fingers through her hair and adding a splash of lipstick. She was older than the mothers of James's friends and hated the idea of embarrassing him.

In the lane the elders were in flower. Their scent made her head swim and caught at the back of her throat. On either side of the lane the corn was ripening. The crop was too dense for flowers there, but in the field which they owned, close to the house, there were buttercups and clover and purple vetch. The pitted tarmac shimmered in the distance with heat haze. The sun had shone without a break for three days.

This weekend it was Peter's birthday and she was planning what they might do. On Friday night the boys would come. She thought of them as boys, though Samuel, at least, was as old as her. But if it stayed like this, on Saturday there could be a picnic on the beach, a trip to the Farnes to see puffins and guillemots. James would love that. She squinted at the sky, wondering if she could sense an approaching cold front, the faintest cloud on the horizon. There was nothing. It might even be warm enough to swim, she thought, and imagined the waves breaking on her body.

When she reached the end of the lane there was no sign of the bus. She hoisted herself onto the wooden platform where once the churns from the farm had stood to wait for the milk lorry. The wood was hot and smelled of pitch. She lay back and faced the sun.

In two years James would move on to secondary school. She dreaded it. Peter talked about him going to a private day school in the city, to the school which he'd attended. She'd seen the boys in their striped blazers on the metro. They'd seemed very confident and loud to her.

'But how would he get there?' she'd said. This wasn't her real objection. She didn't think it would be good for James to be pushed. He was a slow and dreamy boy. He'd do better working at his own pace. The comprehensive in the next village would suit him better. Even the high school in Morpeth, where their other children had been students, had seemed demanding to her.

'I'd take him and bring him back,' Peter had said. 'There'll be lots going on after school. He can hang on until I've finished work.'

That had made her even less favourably disposed to the plan. The time that she had with James when he arrived home from school was special. Without it, she thought, he would be lost to her.

She heard the bus growling up the bank and sat upright, squinting against the sun as it approached. The driver was Stan, the old man. She waved at him to hide her disappointment. Usually three of them got off at this stop – the twin girls from the farm and James. Today a stranger climbed out first, a young woman wearing strappy leather sandals and a red and gold sleeveless dress with a fitted bodice and full, swirling skirt. Felicity loved the dress, the way the skirt fell and the exuberance of the colours – the young today seemed to choose black or grey even in summer – and when she saw the woman help James off the bus with his bags and violin, she was immediately drawn to her. The twins crossed the road and ran up the track to the farmhouse, the bus drove off and the three of them were left, standing a little awkwardly, by the hedge.

'This is Miss Marsh,' James said. 'She's working at our school.'

The woman had a big straw bag strung by a leather strap over her shoulder. She held out a hand which was very brown and long and bony. The bag slipped down her arm and Felicity saw that it contained files and a library book.

'Lily.' Her voice was clear. 'I'm a student. This is my last teaching practice.' She smiled as if she expected Felicity to be pleased to meet her.

'I told her she could come and stay in our cottage,' James said and set off up the lane, unencumbered, not caring which of the adults carried his things.

Felicity was not quite sure what to say.

'He *did* mention I was looking for somewhere?' Lily asked.

Felicity shook her head.

'Oh dear, how embarrassing.' But she didn't seem very embarrassed. She seemed to be remarkably self-assured, to find the incident amusing. 'It's been such a nightmare travelling from Newcastle every day without a car. The head asked in assembly if anyone knew of accommodation. We were thinking of a B&B or someone wanting a paying guest. And yesterday James said you had a cottage to let. I tried to phone this afternoon but there was no answer. He said you'd

be in the garden and to come anyway. I presumed
he'd discussed it with you. It was hard to say no . . .'

'Oh yes,' Felicity agreed. 'He can be very insistent.'

'Look, it's not a problem. It's a lovely afternoon.
I'll walk into the village and there's a bus from there
into town at six.'

'Let me think about it,' Felicity said. 'Come and
have some tea.'

There had been tenants in the cottage before, but
it had never quite worked out. In the early days they'd
been glad of an extra source of income. Even with the
money from Peter's parents the mortgage repayments
had been a nightmare. Then, with three children
under five, they had thought it might house a nanny
or au pair. But there had been complaints about the
cold and a dripping tap and the lack of modern convenience. And they hadn't been comfortable having
a stranger living so close to the family. They'd felt
the responsibility for the tenant as an extra stress.
Although none of them had been particularly trouble-
some, it had always been a relief to see them go.
'Never again,' Peter had said when the last resident, a
homesick Swedish au pair, had left. Felicity wasn't
sure how he would feel about another young woman
on the doorstep, even if it was only four weeks until
the end of term.

As they sat at the table in the kitchen, with the
breeze from the sea blowing the muslin curtain at
the open window, Felicity Calvert thought she probably would let the young woman have the place if she
wanted it. Peter wouldn't mind too much if it was for
a short time.

James was sitting beside them at the table, surrounded by scissors, scraps of cut paper and glue. He was drinking orange juice and making a birthday card for his father. It was an elaborate affair with photos of Peter taken from old albums and stuck as a collage around a big 60 made out of ribbon and glitter. Lily admired it and asked about the early photographs. Felicity sensed James's pleasure in her interest and felt a stab of gratitude.

'If you live in Newcastle,' she said, 'I suppose you wouldn't want the cottage at weekends.' She thought that would be another point to make to Peter. *She'd only be here during the week. And you work such long hours you wouldn't notice she's around.*

The cottage stood beyond the meadow with the wild flowers in it. Besides the garden, this was the only land they owned. Viewed from the house the building looked so small and squat it was hard to believe that anyone could live there. A path had been trampled across the field and Felicity wondered who had been here since the grass had grown up. James probably. He used it as a den when he had friends to play, though they kept the building locked and she couldn't remember him asking for a key lately.

'Cottage makes it sound more grand than it is,' she said. 'It's only one up and one down with a bathroom built on the back. The gardener lived here when our house was first built. It was a pigsty before then, I think; some sort of outhouse anyway.'

The door was fastened by a padlock. She unlocked it then hesitated, feeling suddenly uneasy. She wished she'd had a chance to look around the building before inviting the stranger in. She should have left Lily in the kitchen while she checked the state of the place.

But although she was aware at once of the damp, it was tidy enough. The grate was empty, though she couldn't remember cleaning it after her youngest daughter and her husband had been here at Christmas. The pans were hanging in their place on the wall and the oilskin cloth on the table had been wiped down. It was pleasantly cool after the heat in the meadow. She pushed open the window.

'They're cutting grass at the farm,' she said. 'You can smell it from here.'

Lily had stepped inside. It was impossible to tell what she thought of the place. Felicity had expected her to fall in love with it and felt offended. It was as if an overture of friendship had been rejected. She led the woman through to the small bathroom. Pointing out that the shower was new and the tiles had recently been replaced, she felt like an estate agent desperate for a sale. Why am I behaving like this? she thought. I wasn't even sure I wanted her here.

At last Lily spoke. 'Can we look upstairs?' And she started up the tight wooden steps which led straight from the kitchen. Felicity felt the same uneasiness as when she'd paused at the door of the cottage. She would have liked to be there first.

But again, everything was more in order than she had expected. The bed was still made up, the quilt and extra blankets folded neatly at its foot. There was dust on the painted cupboard and dressing table, on the family photographs which stood there, but none of the rubbish and clutter which usually remained after her daughter's stay. A jug of white roses stood on the wide window sill. One of the petals had dropped and she picked it up absent-mindedly. Of course, Felicity thought. Mary has been in although I never asked her. What a sweetie she is! So unobtrusive and helpful! Mary Barnes came to clean twice a week.

Only when she was closing the padlock behind them, did Felicity think that the roses couldn't have been there for more than a few days, and Mary, an unimaginative woman, would never have thought of a touch like that without being prompted.

They stood for a moment outside the cottage. 'Well?' Felicity asked. 'What did you think?' She caught a falsely cheerful note in her voice.

Lily smiled. 'It's lovely,' she said. 'Really. But there's such a lot to think about. I'll be in touch, shall I, next week?'

Felicity had intended offering her a lift, at least as far as the bus stop in the village, but Lily turned away and walked off across the meadow. Felicity couldn't bring herself to shout or run after her, so she stood and watched until the red and gold figure was lost in the long grass.

Chapter Three

Julie couldn't stop talking. She knew she was making a tit of herself, but the words spilled out, and the fat woman wedged in the Delcor armchair that Sal had got from the sales last year just sat there and listened. Not taking notes, not asking questions. Just listening.

'He was an easy baby. Not like Laura. She was a real shock after Luke. A demanding little madam, either asleep or crying or with a bottle in her gob. Luke was . . .' Julie paused trying to find the right word. The fat detective didn't interrupt, just gave her the time to think. '. . . restful, peaceful. He'd lie awake all day, just watching the shadows on the ceiling. A bit slow talking, but by then I'd had Laura and the health visitor thought that was why. I mean, she was so bright and taking up all my time and sucking my energy, that Luke had got left out. Nothing to worry about, the health visitor said. He'd catch up as soon as he started nursery. Geoff was still living with us, but he was working away a lot. He's a plasterer. There's more money in the south and he went through one of those agencies, ended up working on Canary Wharf . . . It was a lot to cope with, two kids under three and no man around.'

Then the woman did respond, just nodding her head a touch to show that she understood.

'I started him at the nursery at the school in the village. He didn't want to go at first, they had to drag him off me, and when I went back an hour later he was still sobbing. It broke my heart, but I thought it was for the best. He needed the company. The health visitor said it was the right thing to do. And he did get used to it. He used to go in without screaming, at least. But all the time looking at me with those eyes. Not speaking but the eyes saying, "Don't make me go in there, Mam. Please don't make me go."' Julie was sitting on the floor, her knees pulled up to her chin, her arms clasped around them. She looked up at the detective, who was still watching and waiting. It came to her suddenly that this woman, large and solid like rock, might once have known tragedy herself. That was why she could sit there without making those stupid, sympathetic noises Sal and the doctor had made. This woman knew that nothing she could say would make it better. But Julie didn't care about the detective's sadness and the thought was fleeting. She went back to her story.

'It was about that time Geoff came home from London. He said the work had dried up, but I heard from his mate that there'd been some row with the foreman. He's a good worker, Geoff, and he won't be pissed about. It was a difficult time for him. He was never one for sitting around and he was used to making big money. He put in a new kitchen for me and did up the bathroom. You'd never believe what this place looked like when we first moved in. But then the cash ran out . . .'

Sal had made tea. In a pot, not with bags in the mugs as Julie always made it. Julie reached out to the tray and poured herself another cup. It wasn't that she wanted one, but it gave her time to sort out what she wanted to say.

'It wasn't a good time. Geoff wasn't used to the kids. When he was working in London, he had only one long weekend a month at home. Then it was a novelty for him being there. He'd make a fuss of them, bring presents. We were all on our best behaviour. And every night he was out at the club drinking with his mates. When he came back for good it couldn't be like that. You know what it's like. Baby clothes drying on the radiator and toys all over the floor. Mucky nappies . . . There were times when he lost patience, especially with Luke. Laura would giggle and play up to him. Luke seemed to be in a world of his own. Geoff never hit him. But he'd shout and Luke would get so scared you'd think he *had* been battered. I used to shout all the time but they knew I never meant it. They'd get their own way anyway. It was different with Geoff. Even I got scared.'

She was silent for a moment thinking of Geoff and his temper, the gloom which lingered over the house after one of his outbursts. But she couldn't keep quiet for long and the words started again.

'Luke was no bother in the infants' school. He even seemed to like going. Perhaps he was used to it, because the nursery was in the same building. He had a lovely teacher in the first class, Mrs Sullivan. She was like a grandma to them, sat them on her knee when she was teaching them to read. She told me he had problems – nothing serious, she said – but it would be best to get him checked out. She wanted him to see a psychologist. But there was no money, or the waiting list was too long and it never happened. Geoff said the only thing wrong with Luke was that he was lazy. Then he left us. He said we got on his nerves. We were dragging him down. But I knew fine well that he'd been having a fling with a nurse from the RVI. They ended up living together. They're married now.'

She stopped again for a moment. Not because she'd run out of things to say, but because she needed to catch her breath. She thought Geoff had known all along that there was something wrong with Luke. You could tell by the suspicious way he'd stare at him when he was playing. He just didn't want to admit it.

It was eight-thirty in the morning. They were still sitting in her neighbour's house, in Sal's front room. Outside the postman walked past, staring at the cop standing by her front door. The kids further down the street were chasing and giggling on their way to school.

The fat woman detective leaned forward, not pushing Julie to continue, more showing her that she was content to wait, that she had all the time in the world. Julie sipped the tea. She didn't tell the woman about the way Geoff had looked at Luke. Instead she moved the story on a year.

'The tantrums started when he was about six. They came out of nowhere and you couldn't control him. Mam said it was my fault for spoiling him. He wasn't in Mrs Sullivan's class then, but she was the only one at that school I could really talk to, and she said it was frustration. He couldn't explain himself properly and he was struggling with his reading and writing and suddenly it all got too much for him. Once he pushed out at this lad who was teasing him. The lad tripped and cracked his head on the playground. There was an ambulance and you can imagine what it was like waiting to pick up the bairns that afternoon – all the other mams pointing and whispering. Luke was dead sorry. He wanted to go and see the lad in the hospital, and when you think about it, it was the other lad who'd started it with his teasing. Aidan he was called. Aidan Noble. His mam was all right about it, but his dad came round to the house to have a go at us. Mouthing off on the doorstep so the whole street could hear.

'The head teacher called me in. Mr Warrender. He was a short plump man, with that thin sort of hair that doesn't quite cover the bald patch. I saw him in town the other day and I didn't recognize him at first – he's taken to wearing a toupee. He wasn't nasty. He made me a cup of tea and that. He said Luke had behavioural problems and they weren't sure they could cope with him in school. I showed myself up. Started crying. Then I told him what Mrs Sullivan had said about it being frustration and if they'd pushed for Luke to see a specialist earlier on then he might not have worked himself up into such a state. And Mr Warrender seemed to listen because Luke did see someone. They did tests, like, and said he had learning difficulties, but he should be able to stay in school with some support. And that was what happened.'

Julie paused again. She wanted the fat woman to understand what it had felt like, the relief of knowing that the tantrums and the moodiness weren't her fault. Her mam had been wrong about that. Luke was special, different, had been from the beginning. Nothing she could have done would have altered the fact. And the woman seemed to know how important that had been because at last she allowed herself to speak.

'So you weren't on your own.'

'You don't know,' Julie said, 'how good that felt.'

The woman nodded in agreement. But how could she know, when she'd never had children? How could anyone know, if they hadn't had a child with a learning disability?

'I could put up with people talking about us and the whispering at the school gate about the special help he was getting, because it was out in the open and most people were dead kind. There was a classroom assistant who came in just to help him. And Luke did all right. I mean, he was never going to be a genius, but he tried hard and his reading and writing came on, and some things he was good at. Like, anything to do with computers he took to really quickly. They were good years. Laura had started school too and I had some time to myself. I got a part-time job in the care home in the village. My mates couldn't understand why I enjoyed it so much, but I did. It made me feel useful, I suppose. Geoff was never very interested in seeing the kids, but he was OK about money. I mean, nothing exciting ever happened, no holidays or wild nights out, but we managed.'

'It can't have been easy, though,' the detective said.

'Well, maybe not easy,' Julie conceded. 'But we

coped. Luke started getting into bother again when he moved to the high school. Other kids saw he was an easy touch and took advantage. Set him up to act out in class. He was always the one that was caught. He started getting a reputation. You must know how it happens. You must see it all the time. The police were called when he was caught thieving from a building site. Plastic drainpipes. What would he want with those? Someone had offered him a few quid to take them, but it wasn't that. He wanted people to like him. All his life he'd felt left out. He wanted friends.'

You could understand that, couldn't you? Julie thought. She didn't know how she'd have managed without her friends. The first trouble with Geoff and she'd be on the phone to them. Sharing her worries about Luke when he'd been ill. And they'd be straight round with a bottle of wine. Keen for the gossip of course, but there for her.

'He did have one special friend,' she went on. 'A lad called Thomas. They met up when Luke started at the high school. He was a bit of a scally. In and out of trouble with the police, but when you talked to him you could see why. His dad had been in prison for most of the time he was growing up and his mam never seemed to bother with him much.

'I'd never have chosen Thomas as a friend for Luke, but he wasn't a bad lad, not really. And he seemed to like spending time in our house. In the end he was almost living with us. He was no bother. They'd be up in Luke's room, watching videos or playing on the computer, and while they were there they weren't thieving, were they? Or taking smack like a lot of their mates. And they got on really well. Sometimes you'd hear them laughing at some daft joke and I was just pleased that Luke had a friend.

'Then Thomas was killed. Drowned. Some lads were messing about on the quayside at North Shields. He fell in and couldn't swim. Our Luke was there too. He jumped in and tried to save Thomas but it was too late.'

Julie paused. Outside a tractor and trailer with a load of bales went past. 'Luke wouldn't talk about it. He shut himself in his room for hours. I thought he just needed time, you know, to get over it. To grieve. He stopped going to school, but he was fifteen by then and he wasn't going to get any exams, so I thought I'd just let him be. I'd talked to the lady who runs the care home and she said she might be able to find some work for him there when he was sixteen, helping in the kitchen. He'd come to work with me a few times and the old folk really took to him. But I should have realized he needed help. It wasn't normal the way he carried on, but then our Luke never really was normal, was he? So how could I tell?

'He stopped washing and eating and he was awake all night. Sometimes I'd hear his voice, as if he was talking to someone in his head. That was when I got the doctor. He got him taken into St George's. You know, the mental hospital. They said he was very depressed. Post-traumatic stress. I hated visiting him in there, but it was a relief not to have him at home. I mean, I felt guilty thinking like that, but it was true.'

'When did he come home?' the fat woman asked. Her first question.

'Three weeks ago and he seemed better. Really. I mean, still sad about Thomas. Sometimes he'd burst into tears just thinking about him. And he was still seeing the doctor at the outpatient clinic. But not crazy. Not mad. This was the first night out I'd had in months. I really needed it, but I wouldn't have gone if I hadn't thought he'd be all right. I never thought he'd do something like that to himself.'

The woman leaned over and took Julie's hand, covered it in her great paw.

'This wasn't your fault,' she said. 'Luke didn't commit suicide.' She looked at Julie to make sure that she'd taken that in, that she really understood. 'He was dead before he was put into the bath. He was murdered.'

Chapter Four

They were sitting at the table in the kitchen eating breakfast and already it was sunny, the sunlight bouncing off the yellow crockery on the dresser, reflected onto the ceiling. Peter was buttering toast and talking, complaining about a record he'd sent to the British Birds Rarity Committee, which had been rejected. Felicity seemed sympathetic without giving the conversation her full attention. She'd had a lot of practice. When he was a young man Peter had been convinced that he was destined for greatness. He'd been described as the best young scientist of his generation. Now, close to retirement, he had come to realize that the natural history establishment did not recognize his abilities. He expressed his disappointment in a way Felicity considered churlish and ugly – there were snide comments about other staff in the department, their lack of rigour, and he dismissed other birdwatchers as chasers after rare birds, saying that they didn't appreciate the importance of covering a local patch. Felicity understood the background to his disillusion. She wished with all her heart that his talent would be recognized. How wonderful it would be if he found a spectacular rarity close to home. Or was given promotion within the university. But his complaining irritated her. Occasionally she found herself wondering if he really was the great man she had believed him to be when they married. Then she would look at him, at the anxiety and sadness in his face, and feel disloyal. She'd stroke his face with her finger or kiss him while he was still in the middle of a sentence, shocking him into a sudden grin which made him look twenty years younger.

'What time are the others arriving?' he asked, breaking into her thoughts. He sounded excited. The gloom seemed to have lifted. She thought he was more excited about seeing his friends than he was about her. She never had that effect on him any more.

Felicity had been wondering about Lily Marsh, the student teacher, about whether she would accept the offer of accommodation. Felicity realized that they hadn't discussed money. Perhaps that had been the problem, why Lily had run off in that way. Perhaps having seen the cottage, very picturesque, if a little primitive, Lily had thought the rent would be beyond her. She was only a student after all. Felicity wondered if she should send a note to school with James, something welcoming but very precise, mentioning a sum which wouldn't put the young woman off. She'd been composing the letter in her head when Peter spoke.

She turned her thoughts to the matter in hand. Peter's birthday meal. A ritual. The same three friends invited each year. 'I've told them dinner at eight, with a walk to the lighthouse beforehand.' The walk to the lighthouse was a ritual too.

She heard the postman's van down the lane and then the flop of envelopes onto the hall floor. She left

Peter to his toast and went to collect them. All the letters were for him. She recognized the children's writing on three of the cards. She set the letters on the table in front of him. He put them into his brief-case without opening them. He always did that, always saved them to open at work. She'd wondered once if he had something to hide, in a moment of fantasy imagined another wife, a secret family. But it had just become a habit. He did it without thinking.

As he shut the briefcase, he stood up. There was a flurry of activity; Peter had promised James a lift up the lane to the bus and stood at the bottom of the stairs shouting for him to hurry. There were bags to be picked up and the packed lunch was almost forgotten. Felicity realized the note to Lily Marsh had never been written. She almost shouted to James as he ambled towards the car. *Tell Miss Marsh to give me a ring about the cottage.* But Peter would want to know what it was about and she couldn't hold him up now. Besides, he might disapprove of the idea. She would need to sell the plan to him when things were less fraught. She put Lily Marsh out of her mind. At last the car drove off and the house was wonderfully silent.

She sat over another coffee and made a list for the farm shop. She had planned the weekend meals already in her head. There was a cake of course, already baked and iced. It was a pity the three older children lived too far away to share it. For dinner tonight she'd made a daube of beef, rich and dark, slip-pery with olives and red wine. It stood in the pantry and needed only to be reheated. Now she changed her mind. It was too hot for beef. If Neil at the farm had a couple of chickens, she'd do that Spanish dish with quartered lemons and rosemary and garlic. It would be much lighter, beautifully aromatic and Mediterranean. Samuel would like that. She could set a long table on the terrace under the veranda and they'd eat it with plain rice and a big green salad, and make believe that they were looking out over orange trees and olive groves.

Occasionally, when she talked to other mothers, who rushed in and out of her house to drop off their sons, or to pick up hers, she wondered if she was missing out by not having paid employment. They seemed astounded when they found out she was at home all day. But what could she have done? She hadn't had much of a life before her marriage. She had no qualifications, few practical skills. Besides, Peter depended on her being there, calm and rested, to look after him when he came back from the disappointments at work. Certainly he needed her to be no competition. Imagine if she had become a successful lawyer or businesswoman, if she had started to win awards in her own right! The idea made her smile.

The farm shop was cool, the door into the yard open, letting in the smell of cows and grass. She was the first customer. Neil was still filling the fridge. The huge wooden board, the cleaver, the long pointed knives were still clean. He weighed the chickens and packed them into her bag.

'They're not free-range.' He knew Felicity would be interested. 'But barn-reared, not battery. You'll taste the difference.'

'That was a wonderful piece of pork I had from you last week.'

'Ah,' he said. 'It's all in the cooking, Mrs Calvert. And in the growing. I only cut it up.'

Another ritual. Like Peter taking his letters to work every day and the same three friends being invited for his birthday. This exchange passed between them every week. He carried the veg box out to the car for her and winked as he had added a few extra links of sausage for free into her bag.

'I hear it's a special birthday for Dr Calvert.'

She wondered, as she always did, how the butcher could possibly know all her business.

When she unlocked the door the phone was ringing and she ran inside, leaving everything on the drive. It was Samuel Parr.

'I wondered if there was anything you'd like me to bring tonight. A pud?'

'No,' she said. 'Really. Nothing.'

She found herself smiling. Samuel always put her in a good humour. He, too, was always at the back of her mind.

Later, when the chicken was cooking and the house was full of the smell of lemon and olive oil and garlic, the phone rang again. Felicity was sitting outside with the paper and another cafetiere of coffee, enjoying the last hour of silence before she had to drive into Hepworth. James had chess club after school and she'd arranged to collect him. A heat haze covered the fields towards the sea and in the distance the lighthouse seemed to shimmer, insubstantial. When she heard the phone she hurried inside. Her feet were bare. The flagstones on the terrace were so hot that they almost burned and the tiles in the kitchen were cool. The contrasting physical sensations on her feet excited her, made her suddenly catch her breath.

She had been certain it would be one of the children calling, but when she answered the line went dead. She dialled 1471 and was told that the caller had withheld his number. That had happened several times recently. She wondered if she should mention it to Peter. There had been a couple of thefts in the area. Perhaps the phone calls were to check if the house was empty. But she knew she would not tell Peter. Her life's work was to protect him from unpleasantness and worry.

She finished her coffee, looking out towards the sea. A bath, she thought, using some of that expensive oil she'd bought in Fenwick's on her last trip to town, to relax her before the guests descended.

Chapter Five

'Do you fancy a bit of a walk?' the fat detective said. She stood up and Julie thought how strong the muscles in her legs must be to get all that weight off the seat in one go. Looking at her, you'd think it would take a crane to shift her, one of those huge cranes that towered over the river down at Wallsend. And it wasn't only her body that was like that, Julie thought. The detective was a strong woman. Once she was decided on something nothing would shift her. She found the idea somehow comforting.

'I thought you might like a bit of fresh air,' the woman said.

Julie must have looked at her bewildered, the way Luke would look at you sometimes, when he didn't quite get what you were talking about.

'They'll be coming to remove Luke's body in a bit,' said the detective gently. Her name was Vera. She'd told Julie that when they'd first started talking, but Julie hadn't remembered it until now. 'No doubt the neighbours will be gawping. I thought you might want to be out of the way. Or perhaps you'd rather see him off. It's up to you.'

Julie thought of the body submerged by water and felt sick. She didn't want to think of that.

'Where would we go?'

'Wherever you like. Nice day for a walk on the beach. You can bring Laura.'

'Luke used to like the beach,' Julie said. 'One summer he went fishing. My da gave him an old rod. He never caught anything, like. But it kept him out of mischief.'

'There you are, then.'

They'd put Laura to bed in Sal's spare room. The detective went upstairs with Julie to ask the girl if she'd like to come out with them. Julie thought Vera was nosy. She'd met people like her before. People who were greedy for other folks' business. Perhaps that's what it took to make a good detective. Now, she thought Vera wanted to find out about Laura. If they went out for a walk together, she'd make Laura talk about herself. She'd think the girl had been neglected, that Julie had given all her time to Luke.

Laura was still asleep. 'I don't want to wake her,' Julie said quickly. 'We'll leave her here with Sal.'

'Whatever you think's best, pet.' Vera's voice was comfortable, easy, but Julie could tell she was disappointed.

She didn't see anyone staring as she walked out of Sal's front door to Vera's car, but she knew fine well everyone was looking. Any drama like this in the street and Julie would have been just the same, in the front bedroom, her nose to the nets. Any drama that she wasn't playing a central role in.

Vera parked the car behind the dunes at Deepden. On one side of the track was a small nature reserve. A wooden hide looking over a pool and a couple of walkways built from planks. In the distance a bungalow, where birdwatchers stayed, the garden so overgrown you could hardly see the house. On the seaward side a stretch of grass, spattered with small yellow flowers, and then the range of dunes. They'd brought the kids here a few times when Geoff had been in the mood to play happy families, and they'd loved it. Julie had a picture in her mind of Luke, aged about eight, caught in mid-air just after leaping off one of the sand hills. Perhaps there was a photo and that was what she was remembering. She could see it quite clearly. The frayed cut-off denims, the red T-shirt, his mouth wide open, part fear, part delight.

Despite the sunshine there weren't many other cars parked there. Thursday morning and the kids still at school, it was only the active retired and their dogs who had the chance to enjoy the weather. Julie had a sudden thought.

'I'm supposed to be at work. The nursing home. Mary'll be expecting me.'

'Sal phoned her first thing. Mary got someone else to cover your shift. She said she sends her love.'

That made Julie stop in her tracks, caused a small landslide as the fine dry sand dribbled past her feet. Mary Lee, who owned the home, wasn't a sentimental woman. It wasn't like her to talk of love.

'Have you told my mam and da?'

'Last night as soon as I arrived. They wanted to come over. You said you'd rather be on your own for a bit.'

'Did I?' Julie tried to remember, but last night was all a blur. Like that time they'd gone on Bev's hen party and she'd ended up in casualty with alcohol poisoning. That same nightmare sense of unreality, jagged images and flashing shadows.

She walked on and they reached the highest point of the dunes, began to slide down towards the beach. She'd taken off her trainers and had them tied by the laces and slung over her shoulder. Vera was wearing sandals and hadn't bothered to take them off. In the car she'd put on a huge white floppy hat and dark glasses. 'The sun doesn't agree with me,' she'd said. She looked a bit mad. If Julie had bumped into her in St George's on the way to visit Luke, she'd have put her down as one of the patients. No question.

They were at the southern end of a long sweep of beach, about four miles long. At the northern end it swung into a narrow promontory where the light-house stood, almost lost to view in the haze.

'It can't have been easy, living with Luke,' Vera said.

Julie stopped again. There was that salt breeze that you only ever get by the sea. Three tiny figures right in the distance: two old gadges and a dog run-ning after a ball, just silhouettes because the light was so bright.

'You think I killed him,' she said.

'Did you?' Because of the hat and the glasses, it was impossible to tell what the detective was think-ing.

'No.' Then the words, all those words that had been spilling out of her since she'd found the body, dried up. She couldn't explain that she would never ever have done anything to hurt Luke, that she'd spent the last sixteen years protecting him from the world.

She opened her mouth, felt as if she were choking on dry sand. 'No,' she said again.

'Of course you didn't,' Vera said. 'If there was any chance you'd done it, I'd be talking to you in the police station, tape recorder on and your lawyer sitting in. Otherwise the court wouldn't accept what you'd told me as evidence. But I had to ask. You could have killed him, you see. He'd not long died when you got home. Physically it was a possibility. And usually the murderer is a family member.' She paused and then repeated, 'I had to ask.'

'You believe me, then?'

'I've told you I do. You *could* have killed him. If he'd wound you up and you couldn't cope any more. But you'd have told us. Besides, you really believed he'd killed himself. When I arrived you thought he'd committed suicide and you were blaming yourself.'

They were walking on the hard sand that the tide had just left behind. Julie rolled up her jeans a couple of turns and let the water cover her feet. The detective couldn't follow her without getting her sandals wet. She looked out to sea so Vera couldn't tell she was crying.

'Someone killed him,' Vera said. Julie could hardly hear her. Although the sea was too calm for waves there was still the sucking sound when the tide pulled back. 'Somebody strangled him, then took all his clothes off. Someone ran the bath and lifted him inside and scattered those flowers on the water.'

Julie wasn't sure if she was supposed to answer, so she said nothing.

'Did you have the flowers in your house?' Vera asked.

Julie turned to face her. 'I never have flowers in the house. Laura has hay fever. They make her eyes stream.'

'What about the garden?'

'Are you joking? Nothing grows in our garden. My da comes and cuts the grass for us, but we don't bother with any plants. There's only room for the washing line out the back.'

'So the murderer brought the flowers with him. We'll say it's a *him* just for convenience. Most murderers are men. But we'll keep an open mind all the same. Why would he bring flowers? Does it mean anything to you?'

Julie shook her head, though something was picking away at her brain, some memory.

'They brought flowers to the place where Thomas was killed. They threw them onto the river. The people who lived on the estate where his mam stayed. I mean, even people who didn't know him or knew him and didn't like him. To say they were sorry, like. To say they understood what a waste it was. Him losing his life because of a few lads horsing about. Luke went too. I bought some daffs for him from Morrisons.'

'Flowers for remembrance and sorrow,' Vera said. 'Universal.'

Julie wasn't sure what she meant by that.

'Are you saying whoever murdered Luke was sorry for it?'

'Maybe.'

'But if you were sorry – sorry in advance, like, if that's what the flowers were for – why kill him? It's not like anyone forced him to break into my house and kill my son.'

'No one did break in,' Vera said.

'What?'

'There's no sign of a forced entry. No broken window. Nothing like that. It looks as if Luke let him in. Or Laura.'

'It will have been Luke,' Julie said sadly. 'He'd be taken in by anyone. He'd give to every lad begging on the street if he had the money. Anyone coming to the door with a story, he'd let them in. Laura has more sense.'

'Did Laura and Luke get on?'

'What are you saying?' She was angrier than she'd been when she thought the detective was accusing *her* of murder. 'Laura's a lassie, just fourteen.'

'There are questions that have to be asked,' Vera said. 'You're not daft. You understand that.' She paused for a moment. 'You realize I'll have to talk to her. She's not in a fit state yet, but when she's ready. It's better that I know how things were between them before I start. Is it possible, for example, that Luke confided in her? If he was worried about anything, would she know?'

'They weren't that close,' Julie said. 'It wasn't easy for her having a brother like that. He always got all the attention, didn't he? I tried to make her feel special too, but he was the one I worried about. It must have been embarrassing for her when she got to the high school. Everyone knew he got into bother. Everyone calling him names. That didn't mean she'd have wished him any harm.'

'No,' Vera said. 'Of course not.'

Two teenage lads ran down the dunes onto the beach. They were scallies, you could tell just by looking at them, kicking sand at each other and swearing. They were about the same age as Luke, probably bunking off school. Julie pressed her lips together hard to stop herself from wailing.

'Which taxi did you use from town last night?' The question came out of the blue. Julie knew Vera was trying to distract her and was grateful.

'Foxhunters, Whitley Bay. We booked it in advance. The driver dropped Lisa and Jan off first. I was last stop.' She paused. 'He'll confirm my story. I was only in the house minutes before I was banging on Sal's door. If he went to the end of the road to turn round, he might even have seen me on the doorstep.'

'I'm more interested in whether he saw someone else in the street. Did you see anyone?'

Julie shook her head.

'Take a bit of time,' Vera said. 'There might be something. See if you can rerun it in your head like a film. Talk me through it. From the taxi pulling up.'

So there on the wide and empty beach, with the gulls screaming over her head and the tide sucking at her feet, Julie shut her eyes and felt the dizziness that had hit her when she first stepped out of the taxi. 'I was drunk,' she said. 'Not fall-in-the-gutter drunk, but not really with it. Everything spinning. You know how it is?' Because she was sure that Vera had been drunk in her time. She'd be a good person to get drunk with.

'I know.' She gave Julie a minute. 'Did you hear anything unusual?'

'Nothing at all. I noticed how quiet it was. Usually there's traffic on the main road through the village.

It's always there so you don't hear it. Last night there was nothing. Not when I was opening the door.' She frowned.

'But later? When the door was open?'

'A car started up in the street.'

'Could it have been the taxi, turning round?'

'No. This was the ignition being switched on, the engine revving. It's a different sound, isn't it, from a car that's already running?'

'Quite different,' Vera said.

'It must have been parked down the street, near the junction with the road into town. That's the direction the sound came from.'

'So you'd have passed it in the taxi on your way in?'

'Must have done.'

'Don't suppose you noticed it? A strange car? Not belonging to one of the usual residents?' Her voice was so studied and casual that Julie knew it was important.

'Nah,' she said. 'I wouldn't have done.' But she shut her eyes again and concentrated. They'd come over the humped-back bridge and she'd leaned forward to tell the driver to slow down because they were nearly there. *There's a nasty right-hand turn just on the corner.* And at the same time she was pulling her purse out of her bag, so there wouldn't be that embarrassing last-minute fumble for payment. Lisa and Jan had already given her more than their share so she knew she had the cash. There'd been nothing coming in the opposite direction and the taxi driver had pulled into her street without having to stop. And there had been a car. Almost on the corner. Parked outside the bungalow where Mr Grey lived. She'd wondered about that because Mr Grey hadn't driven since he was diagnosed with Parkinson's and everyone knew his only son lived in Australia. She remembered because she'd wondered if the car might belong to the doctor, if there was some emergency. And she'd looked to see if there were any lights on, thinking of the gossip she could pass on to Sal. But the house had been dark. And anyway it had been a small car. Not the sort a doctor would drive.

All this she told Vera.

'I don't know what make it was.'

'Never mind, pet. It gives us something to work on. One of your neighbours might have seen it.'

The scally boys were throwing a football around, bouncing it hard in the wet sand, so muddy spray flew all over their clothes. Their mothers will kill them, Julie thought.

'Home,' Vera said. 'Are you ready?'

Julie almost said she never wanted to go home.

'Laura will be awake. She'll be needing you.' Vera stamped away towards the sand hills, leaving Julie no option but to follow.

Arriving back in the street, it was as if she was seeing it for the first time. Part of her was still on the beach with the sound of the gulls and all that space. Hard to think of this as home. A cul-de-sac ending in reclaimed farmland. Once there'd been the slag heap from the pit, but now there were fields all the way to the coast. Old folks' bungalows on one side of the street, each with a ramp to the pavement and a hand rail. A row of semis on the other, council once but all privately owned now. Julie thought: Would this still have happened if we lived somewhere else?

Vera asked her to point out the exact place where she'd seen the car the night before. She tried her best but her heart wasn't in it. All the time she was thinking of things she might have done to avoid the loss of her son. She could have moved, or not gone out with the girls, or had Luke put into a special school, a boarding school where he'd have been properly looked after.

Vera pulled up carefully right outside the house. There was still a policeman on the doorstep, but Julie knew that Luke had gone.

Chapter Six

When Vera arrived home that evening, there was a buzzard sailing over her house. The rounded wings were tilted to catch the thermals and the last of the sun caught it, so it shone like polished wood, carved in a totem. The buzzards were only just returning to this part of Northumberland. Common in the west of the county, the keepers here had shot them to buggery, stamped on eggs, put out poisoned bait. Vera knew there was a keeper on a neighbouring estate with murdering tendencies. Let him try, she thought. Just let him try.

Inside, the house was stuffy and untidy. She'd not been home for twenty-four hours. She opened windows, picked up mucky clothes from the bedroom floor and shoved them in the washer in the lean-to. Then she wondered if there might be anything in the freezer worth eating. Since the death of her father Vera had lived alone and knew she always would now. There was no point considering whether she could have survived a relationship. There had been someone once who'd kept her awake at nights dreaming, but nothing had come of it. It was too late now for regrets. Which didn't stop her, late at night, with a whisky in her hand.

She took a beer from the fridge, flipped off the top with an opener and drank it straight from the bottle. Even when she hadn't bothered to buy in food there was always booze in the old station master's house. She drank too much. Too regularly at least. Emotionally dependent, she told herself. Not addicted. She carried the beer with her back to the lean-to and ferreted in the chest freezer. Her father had stored the animals and birds for his taxidermy in there; she could do with a smaller freezer now. In the bottom she found a plastic tub of venison stew. The venison had been donated by the same keeper who hated raptors, but she'd accepted it without a qualm. Here in the hills you had to keep up a pretence of liking your neighbours. You never knew when you'd need a tow out of a ditch on a snowy day. She'd spent a wet Sunday afternoon cooking the venison, using lots of root vegetables to keep it moist, bay leaves from the garden and red wine. She'd thought it had all been eaten and finding a portion gave her a brief moment of joy, an uncomplicated pleasure of the kind you rarely experienced as an adult.

All the time she was stamping around the house, she had the Armstrong case at the back of her mind. Like an actor, she was feeling her way into the characters, living them. She already had a sense of Luke Armstrong. Julie's words had brought him alive for her, and anyway she'd met boys like him before. Mostly she'd bumped into them in police cells or Young Offender Institutions. The system had failed them, as it would have failed Luke without a mother like Julie to fight on his behalf. Luke had been a boy who had struggled. Everything had been difficult for him – school, relationships and the boring stuff of everyday life. He would have seen the world through a fog of misunderstanding. He hadn't ever quite made sense of it. He would have been an easy boy to manipulate. A few kind words, the prospect of a simple treat and he would have welcomed a stranger as a saviour. Vera could have understood if he had died in a pub brawl. She imagined him wound up and wound up and then lashing out with the frustration of a toddler. Even a street shooting would have made some sort of sense. He would betray without meaning to and a death like that could be a scrappy mistake or a message to others.

But this murder made no sense at all. The way Luke had been lovingly laid out in the bath, with perfumed oils and flowers, almost implied respect. It made Vera, who was more imaginative than her appearance suggested, think of sacrifice. A beautiful child. Ritual and reverence. And then there was surely a literary reference. O level English had been a long time ago, but the image was a striking one. Ophelia's suicide. And how many of Luke's scally friends and contacts had read *Hamlet*?

She had no idea yet what Laura was like. Her mother said she was bright and gobby. Was it credible that the girl had slept through the whole thing? The strangling, the bath being run. Had the murderer even known she was there?

Vera tried to imagine what might have happened. Someone was standing on the doorstep with a bunch of flowers. Did Luke let him in? Did he know him? Then what? The Crime Scene Investigators hadn't been prepared to commit themselves as to where the murder had taken place. At the bottom of the stairs? If that was the case, had Luke been carried up to the bathroom? Vera couldn't picture it. It didn't make sense. So perhaps the murderer had asked Luke to let him use the bathroom and Luke had shown him upstairs. Then the murder must have taken place in the room next to Laura's. Vera shivered slightly, imagining the girl still asleep while the boy was dying so close to her.

She ate her meal on a tray, sitting by an open window. Her immediate neighbours were ageing hippies in search of the good life. They had a smallholding, a couple of goats, one cow for milking, half a dozen hens, a small flock of rare-breed sheep. They had no use for pesticides, despised agri-business and their hay meadow was overgrown with weeds. Vera could smell the hay. There was a flock of twites feeding off the seed heads. She'd opened a bottle of Merlot and was a couple of glasses into it. She felt happier than she'd been for months.

Recently most of her work had been routine, boring. This was different and a challenge, something to pick over when she spent the evening on her own, something other than a gloomy play on Radio 4 to occupy her mind. God, she thought. I'm a sad old bat. She did feel some guilt in taking such a delight in a bonny lad's death. She liked Julie, thought she couldn't have done any better by the boy. But none of that stopped her relishing the case, the unusual details of the crime scene. She had few other pleasures in her life. She sat by the open window until it was dark and the wine bottle was almost empty.

*

The next day she brought her team together and she talked about Luke as if she'd known him.

'You'll have met the sort. A bit slow. You'd speak to him and you'd not be sure he'd understood. Say it again and you'd still wonder if he was any the wiser. Not a nasty lad, though. Soft-hearted. Generous. Good with the old folks in the home where his mother works. On the edge of trouble. Not bright enough to get into bother on his own account, but not bright enough either to stay away when his friends dragged him into it. And then only petty stuff . . .

'Luke witnessed a drowning. Joe has the details and will pass them round. It might be a coincidence of course, but it's the best lead we have at the moment.' She paused. 'The only lead.'

On cue Joe Ashworth played paper monitor, dishing out sheets of A4. Vera wondered suddenly if she treated him too much like teacher's pet. Did he resent it? Trouble was, he was one of the few members in the team she could trust absolutely to get things right. Perhaps that said more about her than about them.

She continued. 'The lad who drowned after the scrap on North Shields quayside was Thomas Sharp. One of *the* Sharps. Notorious family and we'll all have heard of them. Father is Davy Sharp, at present serving three years in HMP Acklington. There was no prosecution after the accident – it seems generally to be accepted as horseplay which got out of hand. It's possible of course that none of this is relevant, but ask around. Was Luke involved with people his mother knew nothing about? Is someone trying to send a scary message here?'

She paused again. She liked an audience, but preferred it if the listeners were responsive. No one answered. 'Well?' she demanded. 'Has anyone heard anything?'

They shook their heads. They seemed stupefied, too well fed, too hot. The room was airless, but she was surprised by their lack of excitement. Wasn't this what they'd joined up for? It didn't occur to her that she scared the pants off most of them, that even the ones who shouted their mouths off in the police canteen were too timid to commit themselves to an opinion which she might consider foolish.

'The crime scene,' she said. 'You'll have heard by now it was a tad unusual. The boy was strangled, then placed in a bath of water. Flowers had been scattered over his body. Luckily Julie didn't empty the bath when she saw Luke. The CSIs spent hours scooping out the water and saving it. There might be something. They're analysing the bath oil. We might even get a hair from the murderer if we're lucky. But we can't rely on that. We need to find where the flowers came from. Were they picked from fields and gardens in the village or did the murderer buy them? We need to know exactly what they were, then get someone to go round all the local florists checking that out. They didn't seem to me the sort you'd get in a standard bouquet. Mostly wild flowers, I'd say. So where were they picked? Is there a local botanist who can help? Joe, can you find out from the university?'

She didn't wait for him to answer. 'The more

important question is why. Why the gesture? It seems a risk, an unnecessary fuss. It's almost as if the killer wanted to draw attention to himself, make a grand spectacle. Julie was out for the night in Newcastle, but no one knew exactly what time she'd be back. She must almost have walked in on it. Laura, the sister, was in the house throughout. Fast asleep as it happens. Her mother says she could sleep through a bomb dropping. Is that significant?'

A hand rose tentatively. Vera liked a responsive audience but she could be as cruel to interrupters as a stand-up comedian to unwelcome hecklers. She was gracious to this one.

'Yes?'

'Does it mean the murderer knew the family? Knew that Laura was a heavy sleeper and that Julie was out for the night? She didn't often go out, did she?'

Vera nodded in approval. 'Maybe. Or that he'd been watching the place for a while, waiting for an opportunity.'

Another hand. 'Yes?'

'Could it have been the sister? A row that got out of hand?'

Vera considered for a moment. 'You could imagine them fighting,' she said. 'A lad like that. It must be a nightmare having him as a brother, especially the age she is. That age you want to be the same as everyone else, don't you? Last thing you need is a loony in the family. She could have drowned him too. If he was in the bath, it wouldn't take a lot of strength to push him under. But he was strangled and then put in the water. I can't see a fourteen-year-old girl doing that. She's a skinny little thing. Nervy. I don't think she's hiding anything, though. Where would she get the flowers from? The mother confirms there were none in the house. I think we can forget the girl unless anything else comes up. Everyone agree?'

There were a few half-hearted nods. Vera continued. 'The father, though, is a different matter. It sounds as if he always found it hard to cope with Luke. He and Julie separated years ago, but he's kept in touch with the family. Nothing formal. He calls in when he feels like it. The kids go to his house occasionally. If he killed the lad, it would explain why there was no sign of a break-in. Of course Luke would open the door to him. Julie says the boy always wound him up. You could think of a scenario when he was provoked to murder, to strangling.'

'You'd have the same problem explaining the flowers, though,' Ashworth said.

'Maybe. Unless he was clever enough to realize he'd be a suspect and knew that sort of elaborate staging would make us look elsewhere. All the more reason to get some details on the flowers. If they were available in the village, he could have picked them after the murder.'

Ashworth was sceptical. 'He'd have to be pretty cool. Dream up the theatricals, go out for the flowers, let himself back into the house. Surely someone would have seen him.'

'You'd have thought so, wouldn't you? Has there been any joy from the house-to-house? Was anyone seen in the street?'

She thought that later in the day she would go back to the village herself. Not that it was appropriate for her to be knocking on doors. Not according to her boss. Her last appraisal had mentioned an unwilling-ness to delegate. Her role, he said, was strategic, the management of information. But she liked to get a feel for what was going on in the neighbourhood. Not everyone was very good at that.

She looked at the blank faces, waiting for someone to reply. Is it any wonder, she thought, that I'm not keen on delegating?

At last Ashworth spoke. Teacher's pet again. Though she guessed they called him a lot worse than that when she wasn't around. 'No one saw anything unusual, according to the team who did the house-to-house.'

'What about the car Julie remembers seeing in the street on Wednesday night?'

He looked at his notes. 'It definitely wasn't there at nine o'clock apparently. A woman was bringing her daughter home from Guides. She says she would have remembered.'

No one else spoke. There was a moment of silence. Vera was sitting on the edge of a desk, as fat and round and impassive as a Buddha. She even closed her eyes for a moment, seemed lost in medita-tion. They could hear distant noise from the rest of the building – a phone ringing, a hoot of laughter. She opened her eyes again.

'If this wasn't the father playing silly buggers,' she said, 'we have to consider what was going on at that crime scene. It was like a work of theatre. Or one of those art installations. Dead sheep. Piles of elephant crap. The sort of art where the meaning's more impor-tant than what it looks like or the skill that's gone into making it. We need to know what this artist was *saying.* Does anyone have any ideas?'

They looked back at her, rather like dead sheep themselves. And this time she couldn't blame them. She didn't have any ideas either.

Chapter Seven

It was Friday afternoon and the traffic on the dual carriageway leading from Newcastle to the coast was heavy. People had left work early to enjoy the sun. Windows down, music loud, the weekend had already started. Luke Armstrong's father lived just off the coast road in one of the sprawling new housing estates on the outskirts of Wallsend. Vera knew it wasn't her job to talk to him. She should leave the legwork to the rest of the team. How would they learn otherwise? But this was what she was good at. She pictured Julie Armstrong holed up in Seaton with her daughter and her memories, and she thought she wasn't going to leave this to anyone else.

The house was a red-brick semi. It had a small patch of front garden, separated from the neighbour's with a lavender hedge, a block-paved drive, integral garage. The developers had squeezed every inch out of this land which had once held three collieries, but the estate was pleasant enough if you didn't mind communal living. It had been designed around lots of small cul-de-sacs so children could ride their bikes safely. Trees planted in the gardens were starting to mature. There were hanging baskets outside the houses, spotless cars on the drives. Nothing to sneer at, Vera told herself.

She hadn't been sure Geoff Armstrong would be in. When she'd phoned there'd been an answering machine, but she hadn't left a message. She'd just as soon catch him unprepared. She drove slowly down the street looking for the right house. It was three o'clock and the younger children were coming out of the primary school on the corner. Mothers waiting in the playground looked pink and dazed after an afternoon in the sun. Vera was standing on the step with her finger on the bell, when Armstrong walked into the drive. He was holding the hand of a little girl only just old enough to be at school. An ad-man's dream cute kid – blonde curls, freckles, huge brown eyes, dressed in a regulation red gingham frock.

'Yes?' he said. Only one word, but spoken with that undertone of aggression which had scared Julie.

Before she could explain, the front door opened. A slight woman was framed in the doorway. She was wearing a dressing gown, blinked out at the sunlight, but wasn't embarrassed to be caught like that. She knew she still looked good.

'Kath works nights,' Armstrong said angrily. 'I finish early on Fridays so I can fetch Rebecca. That way Kath gets an extra hour in bed.'

'Sorry, pet.' Vera spoke to the woman, not to him. 'No one said.' She held out her ID so they could both see. 'Can I come in?'

They sat in the small kitchen, leaving Rebecca in the lounge with juice, a biscuit and children's TV. Kath put the kettle on then excused herself to get dressed.

When Vera apologized again for waking her, she waved it away.

'It's impossible to sleep in when the weather's like this. Radios in the gardens and the kids playing out. Anyway, this is important. Poor Luke.' She stood for a moment in the doorway, then went upstairs. They heard her progress: footsteps, a cupboard being opened, the shower.

They sat on tall stools next to the breakfast bar. Vera thought they must look ridiculous. Two overweight gnomes on toadstools. 'Did Luke spend a lot of time here?' she asked.

'Quite a lot, before he was ill. More than Laura. I thought she'd be excited when Kath had the baby. A little sister. But she seemed to resent her. Luke was better with Rebecca even when she was tiny.'

'He hadn't been here since he left hospital?'

'No. Kath wanted to have him over to stay last weekend, but I wasn't sure . . .'

'You were worried about your little girl?'

'Not that he'd hurt her, like. But that if he behaved strange, she wouldn't understand.' He paused. 'I never handled Luke well when I lived at home. Pride, Kath says. I wanted a boy who was strong, competitive, good at games. Like me only better. I suppose I was ashamed because he was different from other lads.'

Vera thought he'd changed since he left Julie. Kath must be a civilizing influence. Or maybe she'd just taught him how to talk a good game.

'You used to lose your temper with him.'

He looked up, shocked. He was a bereaved father. She wasn't supposed to talk to him like that.

'It was a bad time,' he said. 'I'd lost my job, no

money, Julie and me weren't getting on. Lately I'd been trying to understand him better. Then that lad he was knocking around with drowned and it freaked Luke out. No one could get through to him then.'

'Did you visit him in hospital?'

'Kath and I both went. I'm not sure I could have faced it on my own. First few times you could tell he was really doped up. I mean, I'm not sure he knew we were there. But even then he looked scared. He jumped whenever anyone came up behind him. When he got better we took him out for an afternoon. A pizza and a bit of a walk round Morpeth. He was more chatty then, but still very nervy. He kept saying it was his fault, that lad drowning. We got to the bridge, you know over the river by the church, and he really lost it. Shaking, crying. We'd only just got him calm when we arrived back at the hospital.'

'Did he say *why* he was scared? Did anyone blame him for the boy's death?'

'He was never able to explain himself very well even before the breakdown. We asked, but questions only made it worse.'

'You'd been to see him a couple of times after he came out of hospital?'

'Yes, and he seemed better. He didn't like to leave the house, Julie said. But he was more himself.'

'His sister will have been glad to have him home.'

Armstrong leaned forward across the breakfast bar. His hands were hard and callused, the nails very short. 'Aye, perhaps.' He paused, seemed to study his fingers. 'But it wasn't easy for her. She found it hard to get on with Luke at times. Maybe she's got too much of her father in her to make allowances. Maybe she was just fed up with him getting all their mother's attention.'

They heard a door shut upstairs, more footsteps and Kath appeared. She was wearing her uniform and had put up her hair.

'Is it OK? Or would you rather talk to Geoff on his own?'

'Come away in,' Vera said. 'I'm just about to get to the hard bit. Could do with a woman's common sense. Stop your man flying off the handle.'

'What do you mean?'

'I need to ask you both what you were doing when Luke was killed. That doesn't mean I think you had anything to do with his death. But I have to ask. You do understand?'

'Of course,' she said.

'Geoff?'

He nodded reluctantly.

'I was at work,' Kath said. 'The gynaecology ward at the RVI. There were three of us on. It was frantic. A couple of emergency admissions from A&E. I didn't even have time for a break. Geoff was here all night, babysitting Rebecca.'

'Do you always work nights?'

'I have done since I went back after Rebecca. It suits us. Geoff's self-employed. Most of his work comes from a builder in Shields, Barry Middleton. Geoff does all his plastering and joinery. Barry's well thought of and the work's regular, but Geoff can suit himself pretty well, fit it in round the family, school holidays. He has Rebecca ready for school in the morning when I get in and Fridays he picks her up. It's almost her bedtime when I leave for the hospital in the evening. Neither of us gets much of a social life, but it means Rebecca sees plenty of us.'

'Did your daughter wake up the night Luke was killed?'

The question was directed at Geoff, but it was Kath who answered again. 'She never wakes up! She's a miracle. She's slept through since she was six weeks. Once she's in her bed you don't hear from her till seven the next morning.'

There was an awkward silence. Almost as she spoke Kath realized the implication of her words. 'But he wouldn't leave her,' she cried. 'You've seen what he's like with her. He'd never go away and leave her on her own.'

'Geoff?'

'I didn't leave her,' he said. She knew he was controlling his temper, to prove to her and to Kath that he could, that he didn't lose it any more. 'I couldn't even go to the end of the road without imagining things. That the house was on fire. That she was sick. I wouldn't do it. Anyway, I could go to see Luke any time. Why wait till the middle of the night?'

'Right, then,' Vera said. 'Now that's out of the way, we can move on.' Though it wasn't out of the way. Not really. He could have got someone in to sit with Rebecca. Or if he was desperate enough he could have left her whatever he claimed in front of his wife. She'd get the team chatting to the neighbours tomorrow. Check if anyone was called in to babysit, or if anyone saw his car moved from the drive. She took a breath. 'Do you have any idea who might have wanted to kill Luke? Julie said he had no enemies, but a mam always thinks her bairn can do no wrong. I need something to work on here. Somewhere to start.'

From the living room they heard the little girl singing along to a rhyme on the television. Vera didn't know much about children but thought it must be unusual to get one this undemanding. It was a very different household from the one in Seaton where Luke had grown up. This was calm, ordered. The family lived by routine. Julie needed a bit of drama in her life to get through the day. Vera kept her eyes fixed on the adults, waiting for them to speak.

'Luke could wind you up,' Armstrong said. 'He didn't mean to. He just didn't understand what you were saying to him. You'd ask him to do something and he'd look at you like you were the daft one for expecting him to catch on. I can imagine that getting him into bother. Some of the people he mixed with, they were used to being treated with respect.'

'Like the Sharps?'

'Maybe.'

'Did the Sharps blame Luke for their son's death?'

It seemed Armstrong needed time to think about that. 'I don't mix with them,' he said at last. 'I wouldn't know. They're not famous for their patience, though, are they? And our Luke would have tried the patience of a saint. If one of them had asked him what happened that night Thomas died, Luke wouldn't have been able to answer. He'd get stressed, flustered. The words wouldn't come out and he'd just end up staring. Like I said, that would wind you up. Even if you didn't believe Luke was responsible, it would still make you mad.'

'Not mad enough to go round to his house and strangle him,' Kath said.

Armstrong shrugged. 'I can't think of anyone else who'd want to kill him.'

'Did Luke ever talk to you about the accident?'

'Not the accident itself,' Kath said. 'He came here soon after it happened. He talked about all the flowers that had been thrown into the river afterwards. How pretty they were. He'd gone with Julie and seemed really moved by it. There was a picture on the front page of the *Chronicle*. He brought it for me to see.'

Rebecca appeared at the kitchen door. She stood shyly, curious about the stranger.

'Do you mind starting on the tea, Geoff?' Kath said. 'I need to get ready for work.'

She followed Vera towards the front door. In the kitchen Geoff had switched on the radio and he and Rebecca were singing along to a pop song.

Vera had dozens of questions. She wanted to know how Kath and Geoff had met. What had she seen in him? How had she seen the potential doting father under the loutishness and the anger? But that was probably just prying and none of her business and she contented herself with a single comment. 'I was told your man had a bit of a temper,' she said. 'No sign of that now.'

Kath paused for a moment, reaching out towards the door handle. 'He's happy,' she said. 'There's no reason for him to get angry any more.'

Vera thought that sounded a bit glib. Too good to be true. But she didn't push it. She had an appointment, someone else to see.

Chapter Eight

Lying in the bath, the window open a crack, the water deep and very hot, Felicity found herself brooding on the past. She wasn't given much to introspection and wondered what might be the cause of it. Peter's sixtieth birthday perhaps. Anniversaries occasionally had that effect. Or a menopausal moodiness. Meeting Lily Marsh had unsettled her. She was jealous of the young woman's youth and vitality, the firm skin and flat stomach, and she had envied her independence.

Felicity had married too early. She'd met Peter at a party. She was an undergraduate, only six weeks into her degree. Her parents had tried to persuade her to apply to a university a bit further from home, but she'd been daunted enough at the prospect of a hall of residence. She needed the security of the vicarage only an hour away, an escape route. Her father was a priest, mild, relaxed about theology, but strict on kindness. In fact, she'd taken to university life, the friendships and the late nights and especially the men. She saw that she might be attractive to them. They quite liked her shyness, perhaps they even saw her demure demeanour as a challenge. But she wasn't sure how she should respond to them. She wandered around, bewildered and a little lost. Alice in an academic wonderland.

So, she was at this party in a student house in Heaton. There were bare floorboards and Indian cotton pinned on the walls, unfamiliar music and the heavy smell of dope which registered without her knowing what it was. It was very cold, she remembered, despite all the people crowded into the room. They'd had the first severe frost of the autumn and there was no form of heating. Outside, the soggy fallen leaves were frozen in heaps on the pavement.

Whatever had Peter been doing there? It really wasn't his thing at all and beneath his dignity anyway to fraternize with undergraduates. But he was there, dressed in corduroy trousers and a hand-knitted woollen jumper, completely anachronistic, as if he'd wandered out of a Kingsley Amis novel. He was drinking beer from a can and looking miserable. Although he'd been out of place in the student party, he had been a familiar figure to Felicity, a familiar type at least. There had been lonely men in the parish, attracted to the church because, surely, there they would not be rejected. The last curate had been terribly shy. Her mother had made fun of him behind his back, and the middle-aged spinsters in the village had taken to competing for his affection with lamb casseroles and spicy gingerbread.

But when she started talking to Peter, Felicity had discovered that he was nothing like the weedy young Christians she'd met at summer camp, or the amiable curate. He was abrupt and arrogant and quite sure of himself despite the bizarre clothes.

'I'd arranged to meet someone,' he said angrily. 'But they've not turned up. A complete waste of time.'

Felicity wasn't sure whether the person who'd failed to materialize was male or female.

'I've papers to mark.'

Then she realized that he wasn't a mature student. He hadn't looked thirteen years her senior. She was immensely dazzled by his status. She had always been attracted to men in authority, liking the idea of someone else taking control, of educating and informing her. She had so little experience of men and was convinced she would do everything wrong. Better let someone who knew what they were about lead the way.

She asked haltingly about his work and he began to talk about it with such energy and fire that she was enthralled, though she didn't understand a word. They moved into the hall where the music wasn't so loud, and sat on the stairs. They couldn't sit side by side because they had to leave room for the people stumbling up to the bathroom, so he sat above her and she took a place at his feet.

The conversation wasn't all one way. He asked about her and listened when she described her home and her parents. 'I'm an only child. I suppose I've been very sheltered.'

'This must all come as rather a shock,' he said. 'Student life, I mean.' She didn't like to say that actually she was enjoying the noise, the chaos and the freedom of university. He seemed taken with the idea that she was vulnerable and it seemed rude to contradict him. He was even tolerant of her religious faith, as if it was appropriate for someone at her stage of experience. As if she were a six-year-old who had confided a belief in the tooth fairy. 'Even I agree that not everything can be explained by science,' he said and that was when he first touched her, stroking her hair as if he wanted to reassure her that she wasn't making a fool of herself. Not really. And she was grateful for his understanding.

They left when the party was in full swing. He offered to walk her back to the hall of residence. They took the bus into town and then walked over the Town Moor. It was bitterly cold, everything white and silver, mist caught in the hollows and coming from their mouths. There was a swollen white moon. 'It looks too heavy,' she said. 'As if it should crash to earth.'

She expected then a brief sermon on gravity and the planets, but he stopped and turned towards her, taking her face in his gloved hands. 'You are delightful,' he said. 'I've never met anyone like you.'

Later she realized that was probably true. He had been to a boys' school, then straight to university and all his energies had been taken up with his academic work. Perhaps he had dreamed of women, perhaps they had haunted him, diving into his consciousness once every six minutes. Certainly he must have had sexual encounters. But he hadn't allowed himself to be distracted. Until now. When they walked on he put his arm around her shoulders.

Outside her hall he pulled her to him and kissed her, and he stroked her hair, not gently this time, but with a violent, rubbing motion which made her feel how frustrated he must be. This pressure on her hair and scalp was the only expression of desire he allowed himself. She felt the contained passion stinging and fizzing inside him like electricity.

'Can we meet for lunch?' he asked. 'Tomorrow?'

When she agreed she felt as if *she* was in control. She was the one with the power.

As he walked off, a friend wandered up. 'Who was that?'

'Peter Calvert.'

The friend was impressed. 'I've heard of him. Isn't he supposed to be brilliant? Almost a genius?'

He took her to Tynemouth for lunch, driving her there in his car. She had expected they'd go somewhere in town, somewhere close to the university. The car and the hotel restaurant full of businessmen again set him apart from her student friends. It took very little to impress her. Afterwards they climbed the bank to the priory and looked down over the river to South Shields. They walked along the bank of the Tyne and he pointed out a Mediterranean gull. He'd been wearing binoculars. She had thought that was odd because his subject was botany. She hadn't understood then the nature of his ruling passion.

'Do you have to be back?' he asked. 'A lecture?' He took her hand in his, drew on her palm with his finger. The sun was shining and today he had no need of gloves. 'I don't want to lead you astray.'

'Don't you?'

He smiled at her. 'Well, perhaps. Come and have tea with me.'

His flat wasn't far away, in North Shields, an attic overlooking Northumberland Park. Two elderly sisters lived in the rest of the house. One of them was in the small garden when they arrived, raking up leaves from the lawn. She waved in a friendly way, then went back to her work without taking undue interest in Felicity. The flat was very tidy and Felicity imagined that Peter had cleaned it specially. It was full of books. A large-scale Ordnance Survey map showing the area of his field study had been pinned to the wall and the way in was blocked by a telescope on a tripod. There was a living room with a cramped kitchen and a bathroom off and a door which she presumed must lead to the bedroom. The door into the bedroom seemed to hold a fascination for her and while Peter was making tea she found her eyes drawn to it. It was panelled and the grain of the wood showed through the white gloss paint. It had a round brass knob. She wondered if the bedroom was also tidy, if he had changed the sheets in expectation. She would have sneaked a look but he came in, carrying a tea tray. There were cups and saucers which didn't match and slices of fruit loaf, buttered.

Later that afternoon they went into the bedroom and made love. Her first time and nothing to write home about, of course. There was a lot of fumbling with a Durex, which he seemed as uncertain about how to use as she was, and they must have got the whole thing seriously wrong, or there had been an accident, because she found out soon after that she was pregnant. It must have been that first time. Later they became more proficient. The sex got better too. Even that first afternoon, though, she had a glimpse, an inkling of something wonderful, and that was more than she had expected.

She took Peter to meet her parents soon after, before she realized she was pregnant. It was a damp, raw day and, although it was only lunchtime, as they drove through the trees they could see the lights on in the living room, and a fire. 'It was always like this when I came home from school,' she said. 'Welcoming.' He never talked much about his parents. They were in business, rather driven. He made her feel as if her attitude to her family was sentimental and unreal.

Her mother had made a thick vegetable soup because it was Felicity's favourite and home-made bread. After lunch they took coffee and chocolate cake and sat by the fire. Peter had been very quiet at first. It was as if he felt out of place, much as she did in the university. He was feeling his way. Now, sitting by the fire, he seemed to relax. Felicity seemed unnaturally tired. She listened to the conversation as if she was half asleep. He was talking about his work and her father was asking questions – not out of politeness, Felicity could always tell when he was simply being polite – but because he was interested. That's good, Felicity thought. They get on. Then she must have fallen asleep because she woke with a start when a log fell and a spark cracked and spat onto the hearth rug. Her mother smiled indulgently and made a comment about wild parties. Felicity felt the same exhaustion in the first stage of all her pregnancies.

Marriage was Peter's idea. Her parents put no pressure on them. Indeed, they seemed unsure about the wisdom of such haste. 'You have been together for such a short time.' They would probably have supported her through an abortion if that had been her choice. Peter asked to speak to her parents alone. There was another trip to the vicarage and the three of them talked in the kitchen while she dozed once more over a book in the living room. She felt altogether that the matter was out of her hands. She lacked the energy to make a decision.

On the way back to Newcastle, she asked Peter what had been said. 'I told them I wanted to marry you the moment I set eyes on you.' She thought it was the most romantic thing she had ever heard and the wedding went ahead.

Felicity was so caught up in her memories that the sound of a door closing downstairs made her start with surprise. The bath water was tepid. She climbed out and wrapped a towel around her, went out onto the landing and shouted downstairs. .

'Peter! I'm up here.'

There was no reply. She looked over the banister but there was no sign of him. She walked down the stairs, still wound in her towel, leaving a trail of damp footprints. The house was empty. She told herself she must have imagined the noise of the closing door, but a sense that the house had been invaded remained with her for the rest of the day.

Chapter Nine

Acklington Prison was up the coast and almost on Vera's way home. It hadn't been easy to arrange to visit Davy Sharp this late in the afternoon. Mornings were the time for official visits – solicitors, probation, police – and prison routine was rigid. It had taken called-in favours and tantrums on the phone before they'd agreed. She parked and walked to the gate. There was a heat haze over the flat fields towards the sea. Everywhere was quiet. Still the sun was shining and she felt the sweat greasy on her forehead and her nose just in the time it took to get to the building. The gate officer greeted her by name, though she didn't recognize him. He was friendly and chatted about the weather as she handed over her mobile phone and signed herself in.

'If it doesn't break soon, there'll be trouble,' he said. 'The heat gets to them. It's a nightmare in the workshops. Someone will kick off soon and we'll be lucky if there's not a riot.'

She waited in an interview room while they fetched Davy Sharp. All the heat of the day seemed trapped in the small square space and the sun still streamed through a high window. In winter, she knew, the prison was freezing, the wind blowing straight from Scandinavia. She struggled to focus. She'd talked to Davy Sharp before. He could be sullen and uncommunicative, or charming. She thought of him as an actor or a chameleon. He could play whatever part he needed. It was always hard to know how to respond to him. Important to recognize that he was cleverer than he made out. And all the time her thoughts came back to beer, straight from the fridge, the condensation running down the outside of the glass. She'd had the picture in her head since leaving Geoff Armstrong's.

There was the sound of boots in the corridor outside, keys on a chain, and the door was opened. Davy wore a blue-and-white-striped shirt, blue jeans, trainers. He slid across the threshold without a sound. It had been the officer who'd made the noise. He stood, weighing the keys in his hand, then nodded in her direction, not really looking at her, not speaking. Vera could tell he was resentful about the disrupted routine, at being forced to unlock the prisoner, walk him here from the block, while all the other officers, his mates, were in the office, drinking tea, having a laugh. He moved outside, sat on an upright chair, stared into space. She shut the door, was aware of the smell of hot bodies, hoped it came from Davy and not from her. She took a packet of cigarettes from her bag, offered him one. He took it, lit it quickly, inhaled.

'You'll know why I'm here,' she said. They all had TVs in their pads now, he'd have seen the news, even if word of Luke's death hadn't got back to him in other ways.

'That lad who was a friend of our Thomas. Is that it?'

She didn't say anything, tried to banish the picture of the pint glass from her mind.

He leaned forward. Already the cigarette was half smoked. He knocked the ash into the foil ashtray. He was a thin, nondescript man. If you met him in the street you'd walk past without a second glance. It was an advantage. He'd grown up in a family where thieving came as second nature. Infamous. In Shields mothers said to kids who misbehaved, 'You carry on like that and you'll end up like the Sharps.' He specialized in credit-card fraud. It suited him that people couldn't remember his face. Vera never had any idea what he was thinking. Yet he couldn't be that good at what he did. He'd spent a third of his adult life in prison. Perhaps he was more comfortable inside.

He looked up at her, eyes narrowed. 'You don't think we had anything to do with that?'

'Luke blamed himself for your lad's death. I wondered if maybe you blamed him too.'

'It was an accident.' He stubbed out the cigarette. She saw his hand was trembling, wondered if that was part of his act too. She slid the packet across the table towards him, waited until he'd shaken the next one out.

'Did you ever meet Luke?'

'Not while Thomas was alive.' He gave a little smile. 'I haven't been home much recently. They let me out for my lad's funeral. I met the Armstrong boy there. Thomas had spoken about him, though, when he came here on visits. It sounded like they were real mates. Two of a kind maybe. Not the sharpest tools in the box. That was the impression I got from wor lass. We were pleased he'd taken up with the Armstrong boy. We didn't want Thomas following me into this game. He'd never be any good at it and he'd never survive a place like this.'

'Did you speak to Luke at the funeral?'

'Aye. Just a few words. They wouldn't let me stay on for the beer and sandwiches.'

'What did he say?'

'That he was sorry. That he'd tried his best to save Thomas. You could tell he meant it. He looked a real mess. He cried like a baby throughout the service, could hardly spit out the words when he was talking to me.'

'Was his mam there?'

'Big blonde lass? Aye. Thomas had talked about her too, said how good she was to him. I thanked her.'

'You were inside then, when Thomas died?'

'On remand.'

'But you must have tried to find out what happened.'

'I talked to a few people.'

'And?'

'For once your lot got it right. The lads had been drinking, horsing around. Thomas fell in. Like I said, an accident.' He paused. 'I wish there was someone to blame. But there isn't.'

'Did Thomas have any other friends?'

'Not really. There were kids he played with when he was younger, an older lad in the street who looked out for him, but Luke Armstrong was his only real mate just before he died.'

They sat for a moment in silence. Outside the officer must have shifted on the uncomfortable chair. They could hear the keys on his belt clinking.

'Is that it?' Sharp said at last.

'Have you any idea who might have wanted Luke Armstrong dead?'

He shook his head. 'No one I know would strangle a boy.' Vera knew that wasn't true but let it pass.

'He wasn't working for you? I mean, you weren't using the boys?' She was thinking something menial; maybe he'd given them a few quid to run messages.

'I told you, I'd never met Luke Armstrong until I saw him at my son's funeral and I didn't want Thomas caught up in my business. Besides, I wouldn't trust either of them. Not even to fetch me a bag of chips. Too unreliable.'

'Just seems a coincidence. Both of them dead. Couldn't be someone's trying to send you a message?'

'Coincidences happen,' he said grimly.

She looked at him sharply, tried to tell if there was anything behind the words, but his face was impassive.

'You could put the word out,' she said. 'Let people know you've got an interest.'

At first it was as if she'd not spoken. He continued to stare ahead of him. Then he gave an almost imperceptible nod. 'I'll do that.'

'And you'll let me know if you hear anything?'

He nodded again.

She felt she was missing something, that there was one question still to ask. They sat for a moment looking at each other. She wondered if she should mention the flowers scattered on the bath water where Luke had been found – might that have some meaning for him? But they'd managed to keep that out of the news and she didn't want it to become public knowledge. At last she pushed the packet of cigarettes across the table to him without a word. She waited until he'd slipped them into the pocket of his jeans, then opened the door and called to the officer.

'OK. We're finished here.'

While she was waiting at the gate to be signed out, she tried to picture Sharp's face, some expression she should have picked up, some message he might be trying to convey. But she couldn't do it. In her memory the features were a blur. She wasn't even sure if she'd select him out of an identity parade.

She'd switched off her mobile before handing it over to the gate officer. Walking back to the car, she turned it on. No messages. No missed calls. They were no further forward than the night Luke had died. She'd parked the car in the shade and the sun was lower now. She switched off the air conditioning and opened the windows. Away from the coast the roads were quiet and as she climbed into the hills she felt her spirits lift. At home there was a fridge full of beer and tomorrow she'd come to the investigation fresh and rested.

Her phone rang just as she'd parked outside the old station master's house. She didn't hear it at first, because the Edinburgh train was roaring north. Virgin not GNER. A flash of red. It rang again when the train had passed.

Chapter Ten

James loved chess. Clive, one of Peter's friends, had taught him, and perhaps because he considered it an adult pastime he'd been passionate about it ever since. It made him feel grown-up. Peter didn't often have the patience to play with him, but James always beat Felicity now. She waited outside the school, looking occasionally at her watch. She'd told him to make sure he came out on time, because she had the special meal to prepare, but still he was the last one to cross the playground. I should be pleased, she thought, that he's so laid back.

All the way home he talked about the game he'd been playing and she had to interrupt him to ask about the student who'd come to look at the cottage.

'Did Miss Marsh say if she wanted to live there?' she asked just as they turned into the lane which led to their house.

'No,' he said, so vaguely that she could tell he was still thinking of other things. 'I didn't see her today.'

She thought that was probably the end of the matter. It was a shame. It might have been fun to have the young woman as a neighbour just for a few weeks, until the end of term. Then she had to pull right into the hedge, because a Land Rover was turning out of the lane, and she forgot all about it.

Felicity had expected that Peter would arrive home early that night, but in fact he was later than usual. She had started to feel a niggle of concern; the road from town was a notorious accident black spot. But he arrived before that could develop into serious anxiety and relief made her affectionate. She took him into her arms and kissed his neck and his eyelids and followed him upstairs, sitting on the bed while he changed. Then they heard cars on the drive and she had to run down to greet their guests and the hall was suddenly full of male voices and laughter. She was pleased Peter had friends. There was nobody at the university he met socially. And she had always liked the boys, the courteous Samuel, the shy Clive, the lecherous Gary. She liked the taut bodies, fit from walking over the hills, and the way they admired her. She knew they thought Peter was lucky to have her. Clive especially adored her. She was flattered when he followed her around the room with his eyes. She liked to see him flush when she paid him attention. Yet when the four of them were together she couldn't help feeling excluded. The men had nothing in common except an interest in natural history, but that passion was all-consuming and she couldn't share it.

They were very polite to her. Samuel had brought her the script of his latest short story. 'I thought you'd be interested. You know I value your opinion.' She kissed them all in turn, enjoying the momentary touch of her hand on a muscular shoulder, a strong back. When Samuel's dry lips touched her cheek she had a shiver of excitement.

'Go through to the garden,' she said. 'I'll make you tea.'

But Peter, who was in an excitable mood, said they didn't want tea. They wanted beer, and they all followed her into the kitchen to fetch it, getting in her way when she wanted to prepare the meal. Peter was loving every minute of it. Felicity wasn't sure about Samuel – it was hard sometimes to tell what he was thinking – but the rest of them *were* true believers as far as Peter was concerned. They thought he was the cleverest man they knew, that he'd been overlooked at work because of politics. His records were only rejected by the Rarities Committee because of petty jealousies. This was their chance to show him how much he was appreciated by them. How devoted they were. And he blossomed under their attention, became charming and generous. He poured drinks for them and held court.

At that point she sent them on to the lighthouse ahead of her. She felt trapped by them, that she couldn't breathe. 'Go on,' she said. 'I'll just lay the table and I'll catch you up.' Usually she could cope with them en masse like this, enjoyed having them in the house, but today it was too much for her.

Samuel offered to help, but she refused him too and stood at the kitchen door to wave them off, a straggling, laughing line, her son bouncing around them like an untrained puppy. She watched until they'd climbed the stile and were out of sight and she was sure she had got rid of them.

She laid the table on the terrace, taking her time,

polishing the glasses with a tea towel when she took them from the tray, though they were straight from the dishwasher and there was no need. The sun was still warm, but the light was softer now. She poured a large glass of white wine from the bottle left in the cooler, chose one of the chairs at the long table and looked out over the garden.

At last she felt she should join them. She had promised. But she wouldn't follow them over the stile and along the edge of the cornfield. After collecting James from school, she'd changed into a simple linen dress. It was sleeveless and full length. Slit down one side, it allowed her to walk but not to climb with dignity over fences. She would take the path through the meadow, along the bank of the stream. It would take a little longer, but she knew they wouldn't return immediately from the lighthouse. James would want to poke around in the rock pools for crabs. The adults would humour him and then they would sit in the soft evening light and talk. By the time she reached them they would only just be ready to leave.

She set off towards the meadow then returned and checked that she had locked the house. Beyond the cottage the field dipped towards the burn. In winter, the land here was marshy and occasionally it flooded. A public footpath ran along the opposite bank and there was a simple plank bridge to join it. As she passed the cottage she checked the door. She still couldn't quite convince herself that she'd imagined the intruder in the house. It was locked. It occurred to her that this might have been another argument in her campaign to persuade Peter to let Lily live there; it would be a deterrent to thieves to have the place occupied. Close to the burn the grass was shorter in irregular patches. It looked as if someone had taken a scythe to it, but she couldn't imagine why anyone would. She stood for a moment in the middle of the bridge, looking down at the water. She'd heard that otters were back in the area and, though she had no idea what signs she should watch out for, she always stopped here, hoping to catch a glimpse.

Here, the burn was freshwater still, and very placid. There were cows in the field, released from evening milking. They'd softened the bank and she left the footpath briefly to avoid the mud. There was a small wrought-iron gate with a drop latch, and beyond that the character of the landscape changed. The grass was cropped by rabbits. There were scratchy bushes of buckthorn and bramble. The bed of the burn was sandy and it was shallow and wide and smelled of salt. The lighthouse was straight ahead of her. Although she couldn't see the others she fancied she heard them, a burst of laughter which could have been Gary, James shouting for attention. She looked at her watch. Already it was eight-thirty. Peter usually hated eating late, but he wouldn't mind so much tonight. She knew he would be enjoying himself.

She found them in the watch tower, which stood on the seaward side of the lighthouse. Once it had been a coastguard lookout. Now birdwatchers used it to watch for seabirds. They were sitting on the bench in a row, looking out over the bay. Although it was the wrong time of the year for seabirds, the watch tower pulled them in. Other men relaxed in the pub, but this was where they felt most at home. As she climbed the wooden steps she heard desultory conversation. She waited, silent, listening.

'What is it with sea watching?' Gary said. 'I mean can anything be more chilled? It's like Zen, or something.'

Felicity smiled to herself. What would Gary know about Zen? He knew about sound systems and rock music and acoustics. But Zen?

For a moment nobody answered. Clive leaned forward, his attention caught by something on the horizon. He had an old pair of binoculars which his mother had bought for him when he was about twelve, but his vision was legendary.

Then Peter spoke. Pedantic, as if he was in front of a class of students. Weighing every word.

'It's about possibility, isn't it? Possibility and chance. The random nature of the universe. We can sit here for four hours and see nothing but a few Manx shearwaters. Then the wind changes. A weather front shifts. And suddenly there are more birds than we can count.'

Clive moved in his seat. He lowered his binoculars. Felicity thought he was going to say something profound. Sometimes he did. But he just called two puffins going north and went back to staring out to sea.

Felicity climbed on into the tower. James jumped off the bench and came up to her, pulling a face. She could tell he was bored and restless.

'Can we go home now?'

'Go and have a look at the rock pools. As long as you don't go too far . . .'

Samuel stood up too. 'Why don't we all start back? It must be dinner time.'

She smiled at him. He could be such a kind man. 'It's a lovely evening. And Peter's birthday. Let's enjoy it for a while.'

When James started screaming her first thought was that the noise would make Peter irritated and he was in such a pleasant mood that that was the last thing she wanted. James did like drama. He'd probably found a live crab or a jellyfish stranded by the tide.

'Don't worry,' she said. 'I'll sort him out. And then perhaps we should start back.'

When the screaming continued she found herself panicking, imagining a dreadful accident, that he'd slipped and cut himself on a sharp rock, broken a limb. At first she couldn't see him. The noise was disembodied. It was as if her son had disappeared into thin air and that only added to her panic. She scrambled across the rocks, felt the seam of her dress rip as she slipped. Then she came upon him, found herself looking down on him. There was a deep gully with a shallow pool at the base and he was standing there, apparently unharmed.

Felicity saw the flowers first. They were scattered across the surface of the water close to the edge where her son stood, mouth open, rigid. There were poppies and buttercups, ox-eye daisies and pink clover. Someone must have waded in and placed them carefully on the surface. That, at least, was how it seemed to her. There was no breeze. She didn't think the blossoms could have drifted so far if they'd been thrown from the bank. They formed an irregular circle. Then she saw, in the middle of them, the blue cloth of the skirt and the corn-coloured hair. The pool was so shallow that the body lay just under the surface, and the water lifted the flimsy fabric and stirred the hair. But the gully was deep and the whole scene was in shadow. It was like looking at a painting a long way away.

'James,' she said. 'Climb back. Darling, come here to me.' She didn't think she'd be able to make it down and most of all she wanted to stop him screaming. Her voice seemed to wake him from a spell and he turned and clambered back towards her. She took him in her arms, looking over his head at the figure in the pool.

If Lily had been wearing the peasant dress of the previous day, Felicity might have recognized her, but she was convinced that this was a stranger. She stood, her arms clasped around her son, frozen. She knew there were things you should do. She'd seen the medical dramas on the television, doctors thumping on the chest and breathing into the mouth. But all that seemed beyond her. Small and ridiculous objections came into her head. *If I was wearing jeans I'd try. If I had on sensible shoes.*

Then the rest of them turned up. And they seemed no more able to act than she was. She had a horrible temptation to laugh at the four of them peering down into the bowl of rock. Then James pulled away from her and looked up into her face.

'Mum,' he said, his voice quite controlled now, just a little unsteady as if he was struggling for breath. 'What's Miss Marsh doing in the pond?'

And that was when she saw quite clearly that it was Lily.

Chapter Eleven

They were all sitting at a long table on the veranda at Fox Mill. It was dark and the scene was lit by fairy lights, which Felicity must have strung up along the outside of the house earlier in the day, and one fat candle, almost burned down now. Gary was feeling seriously weird. He thought this could be a stage set. Opera. The whole evening had that sense of melo-drama. He could imagine some fat lass wandering in and belting out a tune, arms outstretched towards the dark garden. He sometimes did the sound for opera at the City Hall. Bits of it he quite enjoyed, but it was so over the top that you could never pretend it was real, could you?

He was drunk. He'd made an effort to cut down lately. It wasn't like the old days, just after Emily had left him. Then, the only time he was properly sober was when he was out birding. But tonight he had an excuse. Peter's birthday. And being involved in a murder. He pictured the body, spread out like a star-fish just under the water, covered with flowers. It made him think of a collage, something you might see hanging on the wall in the Baltic Art Gallery in Gates-head. Bits of net and lace cut into pieces, seaweed and shells. Beautiful. If you liked that sort of thing. He reached out and topped up his glass from a bottle of red, pleased that his hand didn't shake and none of it spilled.

Felicity served the meal and it was amazing, just as it always was. A big pot of chicken smelling of lemon and herbs. He didn't know anyone else who could cook like her. Since he'd met up with Peter, he'd thought this was what he wanted – not just the food, of course, but the family, the wife. That was what he'd imagined when he'd proposed to Emily. Now he wondered if it was all too good to be true. It was as though they were part of a show. The Calvert family at home. I could do the sound, he thought, and imagined clipping the mic into the top of that simple black dress she was wearing. Her skin would still be warm. He'd be close enough to smell her perfume, the shampoo she used. He thought they'd all had dreams about Felicity, especially when she was younger. Even now they all fancied her. Sometimes he caught Clive staring at her, his mouth slightly open. He wondered if Clive had ever had a woman. Gary had offered to take him into town a couple of times, but Clive always refused. Perhaps he preferred fantasies of Felicity to the real thing.

It was late to be eating, even for him and he was used to meals at strange times. They'd had to wait for the police to arrive at the lighthouse, explain who they were, give their names and addresses. Then there'd been the walk home. Across the table from him, James, Felicity's son, was almost falling asleep over his food. The boy roused himself at one point to talk about the dead woman.

'What do you think happened to her?'

'I don't know,' Felicity said. 'Some dreadful accident.'

Gary knew that wasn't true. All the adults knew it was no accident. The flowers showed this death had been intended.

'If she'd come to live in the cottage,' James said sulkily, 'she'd have been able to help me with my homework.'

Gary didn't know what lay behind that comment and was too pissed to work it out. Felicity persuaded James to bed then. She put her arm around him, almost carried him into the house, and the men were left alone. Somewhere behind them a tawny owl screamed in the tall oaks up the lane. The dark shadows of bats flew in and out of the light. Other occasions, other birthdays, this was the time Gary loved best. The four of them sitting together after the meal, relaxed in a way he could be with no one else, sometimes quiet, sometimes following a conversation about old glories or making plans for the future – trips abroad, the definitive book about the county's birds. Tonight, though, there was an awkwardness. It was as if the dead young woman lay on the table between them, dripping seawater and demanding to be remembered.

'What did James mean?' Samuel asked. 'Was the dead woman going to come and live here?'

'No!' Peter said. 'It was just the boy being foolish.'

And they lapsed again into an uneasy silence.

Then Felicity came back and cleared the table. She brought out a plate of cheese and offered them coffee. Peter opened another bottle of wine. She took her place beside him. Samuel returned to the dead woman and how James had known her, but this time the question was directed at Felicity.

'Her name was Lily Marsh,' she said. 'She was a student teacher at James's school.' She was about to continue but was interrupted by a shout so loud that it made them all start. Gary could feel his pulse racing, wondered if he was old enough for a heart attack, thought again that he should drink less. He wasn't ready to die. Not now.

'Hello! Anyone at home?' The voice was deep and brusque. Gary wasn't sure if it came from a man or a woman. A figure appeared at the French window that gave on to the veranda. A woman. Tall and heavy, but wearing a skirt. She'd switched on the light in the room and she was silhouetted in front of it. 'You shouldn't leave your front door on the latch like that,' she continued in the grumbling tone of a teacher talking to idiots. 'Even when you're home, you never know who might walk in.'

They all stared at her, still shocked. She stepped down towards them until she'd reached the table. The candle shone upwards onto her face. She paused before she spoke again. Gary thought this was someone else who liked a drama.

'Inspector Vera Stanhope. Northumbria Police. Senior Investigating Officer in the case of that lass you found tonight.' She pulled out the chair where James had been sitting and lowered herself cautiously onto it. It was a director's chair with a wooden frame. The canvas creaked. Gary watched closely, expecting a ripping, tearing sound. Perhaps she was expecting it too. This was a woman who'd be able to carry off farce. But the canvas held and Vera continued cheerfully, turning to Felicity. 'I understand you knew her. The young woman who died, I mean. Weren't you just saying . . .'

Felicity answered, hesitating at first. She kept looking at Peter. Gary wasn't sure what that was about. She repeated the sentence she'd begun before Vera Stanhope's dramatic entrance.

'Her name was Lily Marsh. She was a student teacher at my son's school, the primary in Hepworth. She turned up here yesterday, on the bus with him. It seemed that James had said she could live in our cottage until the end of term. Without consulting us, of course.'

'You didn't tell me,' Peter said.

'There was nothing to tell. She looked at the cottage and left.'

'You'd said she could stay, then?' Vera Stanhope asked.

'I don't think either of us came to a decision. I couldn't even tell if she liked the place. She said she'd think about it.' Felicity turned to Peter. Gary could tell she was willing him not to make a scene, not to get all arrogant and pompous. Gary loved Peter to bits, but he could do pompous better than anyone he knew. 'Of course if the girl had decided she was interested, I'd have discussed it with you before deciding whether or not to rent. James really liked her.'

'Had any of the rest of you met this Lily Marsh?' The woman stared around the table at them. Gary thought she could make you feel guilty even if you'd done nothing wrong. 'Seems she was a bonny lass. You'd not forget her in a hurry.'

There was a murmured denial, shaken heads.

'Take me through finding the body. The boy found her first, then you went to look. Was there anyone else about?'

Clive raised his hand from the table. As if he was still a kid, Gary thought. A shy nervous kid. 'There was a family on the flat bit of grass by the burn. A father and two boys, I think. Playing football.'

'Any cars parked next to the lighthouse?'

Clive answered again. 'A people carrier. One of those big Renaults. Maroon. I don't remember the number, but registered last year.'

'Why would you remember something like that?'

'I notice things,' Clive said defensively. 'Detail. It's what I'm good at.'

'What were you doing in the watch tower anyway? It's hardly the right time of year for sea watching and the tide was right out.'

'What do you know about sea watching?' The words came out before Gary could stop them.

She looked at him, laughed. 'My dad was a bit of a birder. I suppose you pick it up. It seeps into the blood. He took me to the coast sometimes. Really, though, he was happier in the hills. He was a bit of a raptor freak.' She paused. 'Is that what brought you all together? The birding?'

'Aye.' Gary wondered if she really wanted to know and how he'd explain it. He'd always been interested in birds. Since seeing an old copy of *The Observer's Book of Birds* in the school library when he was ten, it had been a sort of obsession or compulsion. Music had done it for him too, but not in the same way. Music had been social, something to do with friends. At first the birding had been a secret passion. He'd started off collecting eggs in the park. Then at high school he'd met up with Clive Stringer. They had nothing else in common and now he couldn't remember the chance conversation that had brought them together. He must have made some remark which had given his interest away. Usually he was careful about what he said. He wouldn't have wanted what he did at weekends to be general knowledge in school. He had a reputation to keep up. It had been a revelation that someone felt the same way as he did about the natural world. He and Clive had started to go out birding together. Places they could get to on the bus. Seaton Pond. St Mary's Island. Whitley Bay Cemetery.

And one day, sitting in the hide at Seaton, waiting for a Temminck's stint to emerge into view, they'd met Peter Calvert. The famous Dr Calvert, who'd written papers for *British Birds* and had once been the chair of the Rarities Committee. He was dressed in black, a suit, a tie, a white shirt. Not the usual birding gear. Perhaps he'd seen them staring and thought it needed explaining. Perhaps that was why he started talking to them. He'd said he'd just been to a funeral. The wife of his best friend. Everyone else had gone back to the house for drinks, but he couldn't face it. Not yet.

Then he'd suggested that they might become trainee ringers. Casually. Not realizing that for them it was the most exciting suggestion in the world. There was another trainer, he'd said. Samuel Parr. He'd look after them. It was Sam's wife who'd just died and he'd need something else to focus on. Besides, they could do with some new blood in the Deepden team. After that Gary and Clive had spent most of their weekends up the coast at the Deepden Bird Observatory, sleeping on the bunk beds in the dorm at the cottage, waking at dawn to set nets and ring birds. They'd all become friends.

Gary realized the detective was still staring at him. 'Well?' she said. 'What were you doing in the watch tower if you weren't sea watching?'

'There's always a chance,' he said, 'that something good will fly past. But we'd gone for a walk. It's Peter's birthday. We do it every year.'

'A ritual?'

'Yeah. Kind of.' Gary wondered why someone else couldn't join in the conversation. Why had they left it to him?

Vera continued to look at him. She had her legs stuck out in front of her, big, rather grubby feet in sandals.

'What's your name, pet?'

'Gary Wright.'

She took a notebook out of a big, soft, leather handbag, flipped a page, looked at the squiggles written there. But Gary thought that was just for effect. She knew the facts already, had probably worked out who he was as soon as she'd sat down at the table.

'You live in Shields?'

He nodded.

'You're sure you didn't know the lass? Only it seems to me you're a bit of a party animal. You've got a history. A couple of cautions for drunk and disorderly, a conviction for possession.'

Gary looked up, suddenly sober. 'That was years ago. You've no right—'

'This is a murder investigation.' Her voice was

sharp. 'I've every right. Are you sure you never came across her?'

'I don't remember her. The town's full of students.'

'You didn't meet her while you were working?'

'I don't mix business and pleasure.' He couldn't understand why she was picking on him, felt an irrational panic. The mellowing effect of the wine had quite left him. 'I'm serious about my work.'

'Tell me about that.'

'I'm a sound engineer. Self-employed. It could be anything from an opera gig at the City Hall to the Great North Run. There are a couple of bands I do the sound for and I go on tour with them.'

'Glamorous.'

'Not really. Folk clubs, small arts centres. The same mediocre musicians singing the same boring songs. A night in a Travelodge before unloading the van somewhere equally forgettable.' Until he'd started talking he hadn't realized just how much he'd come to dislike it. He reached a decision he'd been hesitating over for a week. 'I'm giving it up. The freelance work. I've been doing quite a lot of work at the Sage Music Centre, Gateshead, and now they've offered me a permanent job. Regular wages, holiday pay, a pension. Suddenly it seems quite attractive.'

'So you're going to settle down? Why now?'

'Age,' he said. 'I suppose that's it. The late-night curries in small towns have lost their appeal.'

'Not a woman, then?'

He hesitated for a moment, then thought: What business is it of hers? 'No, Inspector,' he said. 'Not a woman. Certainly not Lily Marsh.'

He wondered if the use of the name was a mistake. Did that imply previous knowledge? But Vera Stanhope let it go and turned her attention to the others gathered at the table. Gary was relieved that he'd had to go first. He took a drink from his glass, surprised to find it still almost full. Now it was his turn to be the audience. Vera was about to speak when her phone rang. She got up, walked away from them to take the call and stood at the end of the veranda in complete shadow. They began to talk among themselves to prove that her conversation was of no interest to them, but when she returned they fell silent.

'Sorry, folks,' she said cheerfully. 'I'll have to go. Don't worry, though, I've got all your addresses. I'll catch up with the rest of you another time.'

But she stood there, not moving.

Felicity stood up. 'I'll just see you to the door.'

'Are you interested in how she died?' Vera asked, looking at them all.

'I thought suicide,' Felicity said, shocked. 'It was all so dramatic, so arranged.'

'She was strangled,' Vera said. 'Hard to manage that by yourself.'

They stared back at her, silent.

'One last question. Does the name Luke Armstrong mean anything to any of you?'

Nobody replied.

'I'll take that as a no, then, shall I?' she said irritably. 'Only he was strangled too. Not so far from here.' She looked at them, waiting for someone to answer. 'And the cases have certain things in common. I don't want you talking about this. Not to anyone and certainly not to the press. I hope you understand.'

Still there was no response and she followed Felicity into the house. Watching, Gary, who'd had one or two brushes with the law, thought he'd never come across police like her.

Chapter Twelve

Vera Stanhope drove back to the crime scene. It was a bugger to work, the Crime Scene Investigator said. They just didn't have the time to deal with it properly. The body had been found at low water. They had four hours before that stretch of the shore would be covered completely. And though it was mid-summer the light had started to go almost as soon as they arrived.

Vera parked by the lighthouse and saw that they'd almost finished. The body had been removed and the sea had slid up the gully and covered the pool. She wondered if they'd managed to retrieve all the flowers, imagined them floating out into the North Sea, tangled in the propeller of the DFDS ferry.

Billy Wainwright, the CSI, was still there, loading his bag into his boot. He was a pale, thin man and seemed not to have aged in the twenty years that she'd known him. She thought now that he had one of those faces which always look boyish. She got out of her car and wandered over to him. Even now, in the early hours, the air was heavy and mild. The beam of the lighthouse swept over their heads.

'Anything unusual?'

'A young woman. Strangled. Laid out in a public place in broad daylight. Flowers scattered over her body. Pretty unusual that, I'd have thought. What more do you want?'

'Would it have been broad daylight?'

'Must have been. Think of the tide. And anyway she can't have been there long. The place would have been crawling with people during the day, with the weather we've been having. I know it's a weekday and not school holidays, but all the same the sun always brings people out to the coast. My guess is she was put there not long before she was found.'

Not that public, Vera thought. You had to be right on the lip of the gully before you could see in. Getting her there, though. That would be quite a different matter. Someone must have seen that. And the killer must have wanted her seen before the tide washed all his elaborate stage set away. How would he have felt if James Calvert hadn't got bored and gone exploring?

'Do we know how long she'd been dead before she went in?'

'Sorry, you'll have to wait for the PM for that. John couldn't really do much at a scene like this. By the time he arrived we had to be thinking of moving her.'

'Are they doing it tonight?'

'I hope not. At least until I've had time for a pizza. I was just sitting down in front of a vindaloo when I got called out. I'm bloody starving.' Billy's appetite was a standing joke. He was as thin as a bean pole, but voracious. She pondered briefly on the injustice of genetics. 'We might leave it till the morning,' he went on. 'I'm waiting to hear from Wansbeck.'

On cue his phone buzzed. He walked away from her to talk. There were rumours he was having a fling with a new young pathology technician at Wansbeck

General and Vera, who was a great one for gossip and saw it as a tool of the trade, tidied away the information about the whispered conversation to pass on to Joe Ashworth. Her sergeant would pretend he didn't want to hear, but she knew he'd be interested. She wondered how Joe was getting on. They'd tracked down Lily Marsh's parents to a village just outside Hexham and Joe had volunteered to tell them that their daughter was dead. He'd said he didn't want just anyone doing it. He was a father himself. He couldn't come close to understanding what it must be like to lose a child, but thought he'd make a better fist of it than some in the team.

Wainwright finished his conversation and came back to her. Even in the dark she sensed a studied nonchalance which made her want to tell him not to be a muppet. He was a married man. Happy enough, she'd thought. The young technician was lonely, playing games with him. Then she told herself it was none of her business and she was hardly a candidate for relationship counsellor.

'John would like to do it soon,' he said. 'He's tied up later in the morning. Say an hour?'

'Fine. I'll be there.'

She stood, leaning against the bonnet of her car, listening to the waves breaking beneath the watch tower, until he'd driven away.

Her mind drifted back to the group sitting outside that strange white house which seemed so out of place in the Northumberland countryside. She'd gone to visit them because she'd had nothing better to do while the scene of crime team was working. They'd found the body, they'd all be together for the night and after that they'd disperse. The PC first at the scene had established that much. She thought she'd catch them while they were still in the area, check if they'd seen anything odd. She'd been hoping, she supposed, for the description of a car similar to the one Julie had seen in her road the night Luke was killed. But they'd caught her interest. It wasn't just that there was a connection to the dead young woman. Or that the men reminded her of her father, sitting in the kitchen at home with a bunch of cronies after an illicit raid on the raptors' nests in the hills. Something about the conversation had made her feel they'd need closer looking into. A smugness which irritated her and had something of a challenge in it. She tried to work out which of the individuals had so got under her skin, but couldn't pin down the source of her unease. In the end she got into her car and followed Wainwright down the track to the road.

John Keating, the pathologist, was an Ulsterman in his fifties, with a bluff, no-nonsense attitude which scared some of her younger officers. The only time she'd seen him show any emotion during a post-mortem was when he was investigating the death of a three-year-old child. And talking about a rugby match to a Welsh sergeant. He'd played when he was younger, still had a squashed nose. He made her coffee in his office before he changed for the autopsy.

'What were your first impressions?'

'She was strangled,' he said. 'But you'll have gathered that.'

'Similarities with the Armstrong lad?'

'I didn't have time to do a great examination in the field. Imagine your worst nightmare for a crime scene and this was it. A few hours later and the body would have been washed out to sea.'

'Then we'd never have seen the flowers, might not even have linked it to the Seaton case.' She came back to the point which had troubled her at the lighthouse. 'Is that what the murderer wanted? Was it a private ritual? Or did he gamble on the body being found earlier?'

'Hey! Don't ask me. I deal with dead bodies not live minds.'

She watched the post-mortem through the glass screen, not because she was squeamish but because she was conscious of her size and was always worried that she was in the way. There were so many people gathered around the stainless-steel table – the technicians, the photographer, Billy Wainwright.

They unwrapped the corpse from the polythene sheeting and to the flash of continual photography they began to undress Lily Marsh. They removed the blue cotton skirt and the embroidered white shirt. Vera saw she was wearing matching white bra and pants. But hardly virginal. The bra was deep cut, lacy, revealing. The pants had little red-silk bows at each side, a red-silk crotch. While Billy Wainwright bagged each garment, Keating gave a commentary, glancing at her occasionally to check that she'd noted the significance of what he was saying. 'There was little disturbance to the clothing. No apparent sign of sexual assault.'

Unless he dressed her afterwards, Vera thought. Let's wait for the results from the vaginal swabs before we come to a decision. But there'd been no evidence of sexual assault on Luke and she was already certain that the cases were linked.

Keating continued. 'No bruising. No lacerations. Can we have photographs of the eyes and lids, please. Note the petechiae.'

Vera had already noted them, had seen them at the crime scene – the pinpoint haemorrhages caused by obstruction of the veins in the neck. The classic sign of strangulation.

'Not manual strangulation,' Keating was saying. 'No finger marks. See the line around the neck. It hasn't broken the skin, so not wire, unless it was plastic-coated. Fine rope, perhaps.'

And that too was the same as in the Armstrong case.

She watched as he continued his external examination, saw Billy take all the samples – a trace of lipstick left even after her submersion in seawater, fingernail scrapings, a clip of pubic hair – but her mind was buzzing with theories and ideas. What could connect these two very different young people? Keating began his dissection and still her thoughts were racing.

When it was over, she sat with him again in his office. Outside, it was just getting light. Soon the hospital staff on early shift would be arriving. There was more coffee. Chocolate biscuits. She realized she was starving. She couldn't remember the last time she'd eaten.

'I don't think there's much else I can give you,' he said. 'There's nothing to suggest she was assaulted before she was strangled. She'd been sexually active, but not recently. No pregnancy and she'd never had children.' He paused. 'She had all that ahead of her. Such a shame.'

'She didn't struggle,' Vera said. 'Did she know the murderer?'

'Not necessarily. He could have surprised her.'

'It could have been a woman.'

'Oh yes,' he said. 'Physically a woman could have done it.'

But Vera could tell he didn't really believe in a woman as a killer. He was a chivalrous and old-fashioned man. Women who missed the opportunity of childbirth were to be pitied. I suppose, she thought, that he pities me.

Chapter Thirteen

The press hadn't yet tracked down Lily Marsh's parents, or if they had they were showing more than their usual restraint. The young police officer waiting with them said there'd been no phone calls, no visitors apart from the rector from the village church and Mrs Marsh's sister.

'I don't think it's sunk in yet,' he said. 'The way the mother talks, it's as if the girl's just gone away for a while and will turn up any time.'

The couple were more elderly than Vera had expected. Phyllis had been forty-four when Lily was born and her husband five years older. 'We'd given up, Inspector. It was like a miracle.'

Almost hope for me, then. But Vera knew she'd never have children. And the aching for them had almost passed anyway.

Lily's parents lived in a neat semi. They'd lived there since they were married. Phyllis explained this as she made them tea. 'It's all paid off. We thought it would be something to leave to our daughter. We've no other savings.' For the second time in a week Vera was listening to a bereaved mother talking too much, fending off thoughts and memories with words. When Vera and Joe arrived, the husband, Dennis, was in the small greenhouse in the back garden and they let him escape back there once they'd introduced themselves. Phyllis greeted Joe Ashworth like a friend, but Dennis was finding it harder than his wife to hold himself together. He had a blank, wild look on his face. 'I'll come out and chat to you in a bit,' Vera said, 'when I've had my tea.'

Through the window of the small living room they saw him perched on an upturned box, staring into space.

'He's always had trouble with his nerves,' Phyllis said. Vera thought she caught the hint of accusation in her words. Now, when she most needed support, her husband was falling apart, still making demands on her.

The three of them sat clutching cups and saucers. Phyllis apologized for forgetting the sugar, though none of them took it, and jumped up to fetch it from the kitchen. She was a small, energetic woman, in her late sixties. She wore her hair in a tight white perm. 'I was always worried that one of us would die before Lily was old enough to be independent,' she said. 'It never crossed my mind that she would go first.' She had to talk about Lily being dead, otherwise she wouldn't believe it.

Everywhere in the room there were reminders of her daughter. She kept getting up to point things out to them. The certificates for ballet and tap dancing, for piano. 'She got as far as grade five then she stopped taking lessons. Too much school work. But she was still a lovely little player. She was going to start it up again. She said it would be useful in teaching.' There were photos on the mantelpiece, the window sill, the upright piano. Lily at a birthday party, aged five or six, grinning out over a cake shaped like a hedgehog. The official school photos. By the time Lily was fourteen she was already so attractive she'd turn heads in the street. Even with a school sweatshirt and no make-up. That was something she had in common with Luke Armstrong. They were both physically beautiful. In all the chat, Vera was listening out for anything else which might provide a connection, but it seemed there was nothing. Then, in an enlarged, framed photo hung on the wall, there was Lily in her hired cap and gown on graduation day, head thrown back, a wide smile.

'It looks as though she was enjoying herself there,' Vera said. 'Did she like being a student?'

'She loved it,' Phyllis said. 'Every minute. I was so glad for her. Not that I wanted to let her go, of course. I missed her something terrible. But there was nothing much for her here. No brothers and sisters. Hardly any young people left in the village. And her father with his moods . . . He wanted her to live at home, travel in every day on the bus, but I knew that wouldn't do. I said to him, "Be grateful that she didn't end up in Kent or Exeter." They were universities on her list. "It's time she had some freedom." He saw sense in the end.'

'Did she work while she was at college?' Vera asked. 'Most students have to these days, don't they?'

'She worked in the holidays. Saturdays in term time. She got a flat in town with a couple of other lasses. In West Jesmond. A lovely flat. I wasn't sure how she could afford it, but apparently it belonged to one of the other girls' dad. He'd bought it, like, as an investment and rented it out to them. We helped her out as much as we could. Dennis got a bit of redundancy from the slate works when that closed so we had some savings.'

'Where did she work in the holidays?' Vera asked.

'In Robbins, that posh frock shop near the Monument.'

Vera nodded to show she knew the one Phyllis was talking about. She'd never been inside but she'd looked in the window. All tailored linen and crisp white blouses. Jackets £250 a shot.

'I'd hoped she might find somewhere in Hexham, one of the hotels maybe. Then she could have come home for the summer at least. But, like she said, she had to pay rent to keep her place and she'd never find wages as good as Robbins' out here. Besides, she always liked to dress well. She had style even when she was little. And she got discount on the clothes she bought from there. She brought me some lovely birthday presents . . .' Her hand started to shake, her cup rattled in its saucer. Ashworth stood up and took it from her. Phyllis pulled a tiny cotton handkerchief from her sleeve and began to weep. 'We thought she would come back now,' she said, still talking through the tears. 'She's a country girl, really, and there are lots of village schools crying out for teachers. I had this picture. Her married to a nice lad. Living local. Somewhere I could get to on the bus, at least. A grandchild before I get too old to enjoy it.' She took a deep breath. 'Take no notice of me. Nonsense.' She paused again, stifled a sob. 'Just you find out who killed her.'

Vera nodded imperceptibly to Ashworth to take over the questions. He had more tact in his little finger than she had in her whole body. She'd already put together her own picture of the family. An only child growing up with ageing parents, an overprotective mum, a moody dad. No wonder Lily hadn't come home in the holidays, had salved her conscience by buying cut-price clothes from Robbins for her mam's birthday. Who could blame her? But Vera needed details and Ashworth would get them out of Phyllis, without shattering her fantasy of Lily as doting daughter.

'When did you last see Lily?' he asked. 'It'll have been hard for her to get away from college much, I suppose. It's an intensive course, the PGCE. Demanding academically and then there's all the teaching practice.'

Just the right line to take, Vera thought. No implied criticism of Lily. Any of that and Phyllis would clam up.

'She was over for the Easter weekend,' the woman said.

'You had a good time?'

'Beautiful. It was just like old times. She came to church with me on the Sunday. It was one of those breezy, sunny days. All the daffs out.'

'You've not managed to see her since then?'

'She wanted to come over for the Whit half-term,' Phyllis said quickly. 'But she had an essay to write. She had to stay near to the library.'

'Of course.' Ashworth smiled. 'Her final term. She'd have been snowed under.' He paused. 'How did she seem at Easter?'

'Canny. She'd got the teaching practice she was hoping for. A little village school up the coast. You could tell that was the way her mind was working. She was looking for the right experience to get her back this way.'

And Vera saw this was where the dream had come from. The nice lad and the grandchild. The house just down the road. Lily had let slip some comment about her teaching practice and Phyllis had conjured up all the rest.

'I don't suppose she brought anyone home with her that time? A boyfriend?'

'No. I always said her friends would be welcome, but she was always on her own.'

'Did she mention a lad? A bonny lass like her, there must have been someone . . .'

'I didn't like to pry,' Phyllis said.

'Of course not.'

'They're very secretive at that age, aren't they? They'll tell you nothing.'

'You've been in touch since Easter, though? On the phone?'

'I phone every week. Sunday. It's cheap rate then. You couldn't expect her to phone us, the budget she's on.'

'Did you call her landline or mobile?'

'Mobile. That way she wouldn't have to stay in specially.'

'How did she seem?'

'Really well. Happy. Excited, even.'

'Do you know why she was feeling so good? Or was she always like that?'

'Not always, no. We all have our bad days, don't we? I thought afterwards about what might have made her so cheerful. I asked her if she'd sorted herself out a job for September. "There are things in the pipeline."

That's what she said. It sounds daft, but you could hear her smiling as she said it. I thought perhaps she'd applied for something locally. Near home, I mean. Maybe even got an interview. But she didn't want to say anything. Not to get our hopes up, like. In case we were disappointed.'

There was a moment of silence. In the greenhouse Dennis Marsh took a tin of tobacco from his jacket pocket and began rolling a cigarette. Phyllis frowned. She probably thought roll-ups common, something not to be done in front of guests. Not even when your daughter's just died.

Ashworth leaned forward, caught her attention again. 'Did Lily ever do a teaching practice in Whitley High?'

'No, she was a primary specialist. She didn't do high schools.'

'So she'd never have taught a lad called Luke Armstrong? Never mentioned him at all?'

'Why? Is he the one that killed her?' The words were spat out, so loud and so fierce that she shocked them both.

'No,' Ashworth said quietly. 'Nothing like that. He was murdered too. There are certain similarities.'

Vera left them then. Phyllis was making more tea, just about holding herself together with ritual chat, warming the pot, finding biscuits. She'd have liked Joe Ashworth as a son-in-law, Vera could tell. She might even have been thinking that as she prompted him to take another fig roll. There was a glass door from the kitchen into the garden and Vera went out through that, closing it behind her, shutting out the conversation, knowing she was a coward, but not able to bear it any more.

Dennis must have heard her approaching, but didn't look up until she appeared at the open greenhouse door. She pulled up a plastic garden chair and sat just outside, facing him. He had the drawn, defeated face of men she'd seen in the cells or sleeping rough. Phyllis would save him from that, at least. She'd make sure he washed and shaved, cut his fingernails, wore clean clothes.

'Tell me about Lily.' Vera planted her feet firmly on the grass.

'I should never have had a bairn,' he said.

She felt like saying she'd always believed children were pretty overrated herself, but thought that wasn't what he wanted to hear.

'I don't suppose anyone thinks they make a good job of it, bringing up kids.'

'I can't even look after myself.'

'Lily seemed to have turned out all right. University. Going into teaching.' Vera caught the cheerful tone of the social worker in her voice, hated herself for it.

'She was never happy, though,' he said. 'Not really. Not even when she was at school.'

'What was she like at school?'

'Bright,' he said. 'Oh yes, always top of the class in the little school. And when she started her A levels they put her down for Oxford.'

Vera was surprised Phyllis hadn't mentioned that, but understood why it hadn't come up when he continued speaking. 'Then she didn't do as well in her exams as they'd been expecting. There was this lad, I don't know, she was obsessed by him. Thought she was in love with him. Couldn't concentrate, it seemed. Got A levels, but not the grades she needed for Oxford.'

'It happens,' Vera said. 'Teenage girls . . .'

'It wasn't normal, though,' he said. 'Not a normal crush. She was fixated. Stopped sleeping. Stopped eating. I thought she was ill. She needed special help. Phyllis wouldn't see it.'

Vera said nothing.

'I knew,' he said. 'I recognized it. I've been in and out of mental hospital over the years. Not so much now that they've sorted out the drugs, but I had my first breakdown when I was Lily's age. Too much of a coincidence, isn't it? She must have got that from me. She got her mother's brains. My madness.'

'Do you remember the name of the lad she fell for when she was at school?'

He frowned. 'My memory's not so good. I blame the ECT but it's probably just age.'

She waited, hoping it would come to him. She didn't want to bring this up with Phyllis, cause her even more pain.

'Craven,' he said. 'Ben Craven. A nice enough lad. Not his fault.'

'What happened to him? Did he go on to university?'

Dennis shook his head. 'I don't think I ever knew.'

'You said you had a couple of spells in hospital, Mr Marsh. Where did you go?'

'St George's. That place in Morpeth.'

The first link between Luke Armstrong and Lily

Marsh, Vera thought. Tenuous, but something at least to work on.

'And Lily? Do you think she ever went there for treatment? Once she left home, maybe? Not as an inpatient. You'd have heard about that. But to one of the outpatient clinics?'

'I told her to go,' he said. 'I gave her a card with the name of my doctor on it. But I don't know if she took my advice.' He made a brave attempt at a smile. 'You know what it's like. Two women in the house. They weren't going to take any notice of me.'

Chapter Fourteen

'So what have we got here?' Joe Ashworth said. 'Some nutter who thinks it's OK to go round strangling nutters?'

They were in the car on the way to Newcastle. They'd arranged to see Lily Marsh's flat and to talk to the two students she'd shared with.

'Maybe.' Vera was thinking it was all too elaborate. Some game. Some clever bastard pulling their strings. 'But forget the window dressing. The flowers on the water. If we had two murders this close, same cause of death, what would you think?'

'I'd still think it was a nutter.'

'Serial killer?'

'Perhaps.' He was cautious, surprised she'd used the word even to him. *Serial killer* meant the press going wild, hysterical politicians, and that was the last thing she'd want. It wasn't something to speak of lightly.

'But if it wasn't random, if it wasn't some psychotic who'd taken against attractive young people?'

He took a moment to think. 'The second murder could be to cover up the first. I mean, we know that Lily Marsh was around in the area. She worked in Hepworth. What's that? Six miles from Seaton where

Julie Armstrong lives. If we can place her in Seaton at the time of Luke's murder, we'd have a reasonable explanation. She saw something, heard something. Or she was acquainted with the killer, guessed. Confronted him.'

'You're thinking a boyfriend?'

'Maybe. It's odd that the parents don't seem to know anything about him.'

'So what do we do now?' Vera shut her eyes as Ashworth drove too fast round a bend and had to brake sharply. A tractor was coming in the opposite direction. He didn't swear, it wasn't his style. She did, under her breath.

'Make the link,' he said, when he'd pulled into the hedge to let the tractor past. 'Find out where she was the evening of Luke Armstrong's murder. Talk to all her friends. Her tutors. The people she worked with.'

'Nothing difficult, then.' Vera stretched and yawned. 'A piece of piss.' Before he could answer she fell asleep.

She woke when they pulled up outside the house, lucky to find a parking place. It was Saturday morning; shoppers saved paying for city-centre parking by leaving their cars in West Jesmond and taking the metro into town. The flat was the ground floor of an Edwardian terrace; a bit grand, she thought, for a student place. There was blue-and-white tape around the door and Billy Wainwright was inside. She called to him through an open window.

'You're OK to come in,' he said. 'We're just about

finished. I'll soon be away to my bed. The search team will be in any time.'

They all stood for a moment inside the front door. Billy seemed tired but too wired-up to relax, fidgeting with the clasp on his case.

'What can you tell me, Billy?'

'There's no sign she was killed here. No break-in. No evidence of a struggle in her room. Apparently the lasses she was sharing with were out for the evening. They're at a friend's house up the road now, if you want a chat.'

'You'll have had a look in the bathroom?'

'Of course. There were a few hairs in the drain, but I'd bet a year's salary they belong to the tenants. There's nothing to connect this place with the Luke Armstrong scene.'

'Bath oils?'

'Plenty. We'll get them tested, but I couldn't recognize anything that smelled like the water when we fished the Armstrong boy out.' He yawned. 'If you're going to be here for ten minutes, I'm going. Like I said, the search team is on its way. The victim's room is the last on the left.'

When he'd gone Vera and Joe stood for a minute in silence. The hall was cool. The floor was tiled, the ceiling high.

'Not your usual student gaff,' Joe said. He pushed open a door into the living room. They looked in at the stripped wooden floor, cast-iron fireplace. There was a sofa with a terracotta loose cover, an upright piano. Everything very tidy, spotlessly clean. 'I couldn't afford a place like this on my salary. How do

they manage it? And I thought students were supposed to be mucky.'

Vera had moved on to the kitchen, which looked
like something out of the style magazines she dipped
into at the dentist's. She opened the fridge. A box of
eggs, a couple of bags of salad, some natural yoghurt.
In the door two bottles of white wine. French.

There were three bedrooms, two at the front overlooking the small garden and the street, one, Lily's, at
the back. Vera saved Lily's until last. The front bedrooms were in keeping with the rest of the house. So
tasteful Vera had an urge to hang a Boots print on the
wall or stick a cheap and nasty vase on the window
sill. She'd always thought of the places she looked at
in the magazines as fantasies, hadn't believed they
actually existed. They weren't the sort of rooms she
visited often through work.

Lily's room was different. It was the smallest in the
house, smaller even than the bathroom. The furniture
was less grand; perhaps it had been left behind by the
previous owners when the flat was sold. There were
net curtains at the window, which looked out onto
a yard where the bins were kept. Inside, a single bed, a
desk and computer, a post-war utility wardrobe like the
one in which Vera still kept her clothes. One wall was
covered with cheap, bare-wood shelving, holding
paperback books. Vera pulled on latex gloves, but stood,
looking around, not touching anything. The room was
so small that Ashworth stayed in the doorway.

'A diary would be good,' Vera said. 'An address
book.'

'Wouldn't she keep that on the computer?'

'More than likely. We'll wait for the experts to do

that for us.' The search team, specially trained. They'd not want her mauling through the evidence before they had a chance to do it properly. She opened the desk drawers. There were ring folders, envelope files, on the desk she saw a library card for the university and another for Northumberland Libraries. Exactly what you'd expect in a model student's room. But this was like no student's room Vera had seen. At least in the other two bedrooms there were personal touches. Family snaps, birthday cards, party invitations. Lily had lived in this room for nearly three years, but it contained nothing of her. No photos, no posters. It could have been a room in an anonymous, cheap B&B. She opened the wardrobe door and at last she caught a flavour of the dead woman.

The first impression was of colour. A rack held amber beads, a turquoise silk scarf with a silver thread running through it, long red satin gloves. She pulled out hangers holding a loose velvet jacket, blackberry-coloured, a dress in swirls of blues and greens, skirts in bright cotton prints. On shelves there were folded blouses, lacy underwear. Nothing cheap.

'So,' Vera said. 'She liked to dress up.' She looked at the labels at the necks of the jacket and the blouses. 'Some of it from Robbins,' she said. 'But not all of it. She wouldn't have got these at discount. She must have spent all her spare cash on clothes.'

And that, in the end, was all they learned about her. Nothing else in the room gave a clue to her life. They waited in the kitchen for the search team to arrive, not speaking, glad when they heard the van pull up in the street and they had an excuse to leave.

Chapter Fifteen

Lily's flatmates were staying with a friend who lived in the same road. Another big house, this time on the corner, with a garden at the back. It didn't seem to be split into flats. A student house, maybe. Vera rang the bell, hit it again when there was no response. She was about to ring it a third time when there were footsteps and the door opened. The young woman standing in the doorway was tiny, with chopped blonde hair, the build of a ten-year-old, eyes expertly made up to look enormous.

'I'm sorry,' she said. 'Annie's out.'

'I'm not looking for Annie.' Vera flashed her warrant card and walked in without waiting to be asked. 'It's Emma and Louise I'm after. Lily's friends.'

The woman seemed flustered. 'Of course. Sorry to keep you waiting. Annie's taken her daughter to ballet. Lou and I were having a late breakfast in the garden. After hearing about Lily, then camping out here, neither of us slept very well. Come on through. I'm Emma.' Not a local voice. Southern. Rich.

She was wearing leather flip-flops and tripped ahead of them, talking all the way. Not a student house after all. No beer cans or loud music, unsafe wiring or peeling wallpaper. A family lived here.

There was a small bicycle propped against the wall in the corridor, a child's paintings on the kitchen notice-board. But still wealthy. If Annie was a single mother she wasn't struggling financially.

'Is Annie a student too?' No reason for needing to know, but Vera had always been nosy.

'No. She's older than me. She lectures. On the course Lily was taking, actually. She's a sort of cousin of mine. Her husband works away a lot and when we were flat-hunting, we thought it would be nice if we could find somewhere close.'

'Very convenient,' Vera said, wondering what it was about this woman she disliked so much.

'Yes.' Emma turned briefly then led them out onto a flagged patio where four wooden chairs stood around a table. The garden was small, surrounded by a high wall. Blackbirds were calling somewhere in the ivy.

Emma continued talking. 'This is my flatmate, Louise. Lou, it's the police.'

Louise seemed still to be wearing pyjamas. Her feet were bare, her hair unbrushed. She nodded to them, played with the croissant flakes on her plate.

'I'll just put on some more coffee,' Emma said.

Vera sat down heavily. 'Not for us, pet. This isn't a social call. We've not much time. We just wanted to talk about Lily.'

'Of course.'

'How long have the three of you been living together?'

'Well, we met up in the first year. Same hall of residence, though we were all doing different stuff. Lily was into English, Louise did languages and I'm a medic. That's why the three of us are still here when most of our friends have left. Our courses last longer than the standard three years and Lily was doing a PGCE. We shared a kitchen then, got on OK, decided to move in together.'

'How could you afford to live in a road like this, like?' Emphasizing the accent, playing the dumb cop. It never hurt if they underestimated you.

'Well, it was down to my dad, actually. He thought he might as well buy somewhere. Thought it would be a decent investment. We'd pay enough rent to cover the mortgage. I mean, it's still not cheap, but when you look at some of the places other students live . . . My parents are great. They give me an allowance.'

'But Lily didn't come from that sort of background, did she? How did she keep up with the rent?'

Emma shrugged. 'She never said. I think her dad was made redundant at the end of her first year and gave her something to start her off. She didn't pay as much as us, because her room is a bit smaller. And she worked on Saturdays and in the holidays.'

'Tell me about her. Living together that long, you must have known her as well as anyone.'

For the first time Emma seemed lost for words. It was Louise who answered.

'Nobody knew her very well.'

'But three lasses together. You must have confided in each other.'

'Not really. Not Lily.'

'There'd have been nights out in town, a few drinks. She'd let down her hair then.'

'I don't think Lily ever let go in that way, Inspector. She was very controlled, very focused.

Ambitious, I suppose. Something to do with the background she came from. She worked much harder than the rest of us.'

'Was she ever ill?'

'Nothing serious. A cold, throat infection. Just like the rest of us.'

'You never worried that she might be depressed? Keeping herself so isolated.'

'No. I don't think she was that isolated. She just didn't include us in the rest of her life.'

'Where were you both last night?'

Louise answered. 'It was my birthday. We went out for a meal. A whole gang of us.'

'What about Lily?' Vera asked. 'Were you expecting her to be there too?'

'I asked her of course, but I wasn't surprised when she didn't turn up. It wasn't really her thing.'

Why not? Did you make her uncomfortable with your confident voices and your parents' money?

'Did she have a boyfriend?'

There was a silence. The women flashed a glance at each other. 'We think she must have done,' Emma said at last. 'There were nights when she didn't come home. But he never came to the flat. At least, not when we were in.'

'And she never talked about him?'

'Not to us.' Emma paused. 'Look, Inspector, in some ways Lily was a model tenant. Thoughtful, tidy. That's why I wanted her to come in with us in the first place. But we were never friends. Not really. I can't think of any reason why anyone would have wanted to kill her. But I wouldn't know. Her life was a mystery to us.'

*

It was lunchtime and Vera brought the team together, bought in sandwiches, proper coffee, doughnuts. Anything to keep up the energy levels. After the catnap in the car she felt on top of the world, but she knew the younger members didn't have her stamina. Still, they were a bit more alert now. A second body. A bright young woman. Somehow that made the case more exciting. They hadn't been able to get worked up about a lad with a learning disability, but a pretty student and suddenly they were buzzing. She told herself she was too cynical for her own good.

She filled them in on the visits to Lily's parents and the flat, walking backwards and forwards at the front of the room, in and out of the light streaming in from the windows.

'The lasses she shared with are camping out at a neighbour's house until the search team has finished. Of course we asked if Lily was at the flat on the night Luke Armstrong was killed. She wasn't there. It wasn't unusual for her to stay out. That's why they presumed she had a boyfriend.'

'Didn't they ask about him? They must have been curious.' This was from Holly Lawson. Eager, fresh-faced, looked like a sixth-former. 'I mean, you might say you respected someone's privacy, but really you'd want to know. Wouldn't you?' She looked around her.

'You're probably right. Go back and talk to the flatmates,' Vera said. 'You might get more out of them. You're nearer their age.' She took a sip from the cardboard cup. The coffee had been OK at the beginning of the meeting, but it was already cold and she could feel the grounds on her tongue. She set the cup on the table, went up to the windows and pulled the blinds to keep the worst of the sun out of her eyes. The room seemed suddenly gloomy, the people in it blurred shadows.

'I think we'll have to bite the bullet and have a news conference,' she said. 'I don't want anything about the scene to get out. Not the flowers. Not the cause of death. The last thing we need is a copy-cat killer. I told the group who found the body that if they speak to the press they'll have me to answer to. But someone must have seen the corpse being carried from the car park to the rocks. There's that stretch of grass to cover and there's usually someone there. Dog walkers. Parents with young kids. We'll get the press liaison people to set it up.

'Now, what have you got for me?' Vera had landed on the desk at the front. Like a teacher. She wondered what sort of teacher Lily would have made.

'We've found someone at the university to look at the flowers,' Holly said. 'A Dr Calvert. Senior lecturer.'

'No.'

'Sorry?'

'Peter Calvert. He won't do. He found the second body. At least, his son did. He was on the scene immediately after. We can't use him.'

'Oh God, I should have realized. I tracked him down yesterday, before Lily Marsh was killed.' She blushed, stammered, waited for Vera to let fire the sarcasm. But Vera was feeling kind. She was thinking about Peter Calvert. It was probably a coincidence. It didn't take a botanist to scatter flowers on a dead body. But if they were looking for someone who liked to play games, it could be seen as a calling card, a signature.

'Get someone else,' she said. 'Not from Newcastle University. Try Northumbria or Sunderland. There must be another botanist somewhere in the north east. And check out what Dr Calvert was doing the night Luke was killed. Just to show we're tying up all the loose ends.' She remembered the scene on the veranda she'd walked into the night before. Four men sitting at the table. One woman. About the same age as her, but elegant, made-up. Desired. An interesting group, she thought again. 'On second thoughts, you can leave Dr Calvert to me.' It would be an excuse to go back. 'Can't trust you lot with the gentry.'

They smiled, not bothered. One less job for them and whoever heard of a university lecturer as a murderer?

She turned back to the group. 'Who's been checking out Geoff Armstrong's alibi?'

'Me.' Charlie Robson. Charlie was older than her. She thought he must be up for retirement soon. He didn't like working for a woman, but he'd had to get on with it.

'Well?'

'First I had a word with the guy he does most of his work for. Barry Middleton. Small builder. Does kitchens, bathrooms, loft extensions. He's known Geoff for years, even before he started passing work his way. He says Geoff always had a temper on him. One of those people who could take offence if you looked at him the wrong way. There were a couple of scraps on site. He lashed out at a foreman when he was working in London. That's why he turned up back here without a job. But apparently he changed completely when he remarried. Now he's a real family man, according to Barry. Devoted to Kath and the little girl. He'd even started to build bridges with Julie.'

'That's what he said to me.' But do I believe it? Vera thought. Do I believe people change that easily?

'I went onto the estate this morning,' Charlie went on. 'Geoff and the family were leaving just as I got there. Looked like a trip to the beach. They had towels, a picnic.'

'Very domestic,' Vera said.

'They didn't see me. I had a word with the neighbours. Everyone said the same. They're a lovely family. He's a bit quiet. Doesn't go to the pub or the club. Stays in to mind the bairn while the wife's at work. But nobody had a word to say against him.'

'What about Wednesday night? Did anyone see him leave the house?'

'No, and one couple is certain they would have done if he'd taken his car out. They were having a barbecue, had invited a few friends round. They'd even asked Geoff. They only live a couple of doors down the street and thought he could keep calling back to check the little girl was OK. He didn't go in the end, said he didn't like leaving Rebecca. But they were out in the garden all evening. It's on the corner and they'd have seen if he left. That's what they reckon.'

Vera was pleased they could count Geoff out of the investigation. She imagined the three of them on a beach somewhere. Tynemouth, maybe. Kath laid out on a towel catching up on some sleep, Geoff keeping the girl amused, holding her hand as she jumped the waves, building sandcastles, buying ice cream.

She must be going soft in her old age. She thought he deserved a second chance.

She realized the team was waiting for her to go on. 'Let's leave Geoff Armstrong, then. Unless anything else comes up. I want someone to talk to Luke's consultant. Find out if Lily Marsh was treated at St George's too. She probably wouldn't be an inpatient. Her flatmates would know about that. She might have gone to a clinic, though. We know her dad had a history of mental illness. It's an outside chance but worth following up. And I'd like you to check out Lily Marsh's finances. Bank account, credit cards. All that. The way it looks, she was living way beyond her means. Did she have some other income? A rich lover, maybe. And we need to trace the lad she had the crush on when she was at school. His name's Ben Craven. He could still be living locally.'

She thought there'd been enough talk. They all liked talk. Talk and coffee and buns saved them having to go out there and mix it with real people.

She stood up, made sure she had their attention. 'The first priority is to make some link between the victims. Something that places them together, a person they have in common.'

They sat, staring up at her.

'Well, go on, then,' she said, raising her voice, teacher again. 'You're not going to find it in here, are you?'

Chapter Sixteen

It was Saturday and the sun was still shining, but at Fox Mill there were no preparations for the picnic Felicity had been planning as an extra celebration for Peter's birthday. Everyone had stayed the night and they ate a late, subdued breakfast in the kitchen. The four men seemed preoccupied and washed out. Perhaps they were suffering from a collective hangover. Even James was unusually quiet and mooched back to his room to watch children's television.

She was glad when the guests left before lunch. Peter tried to persuade them to stay, but they must have realized she wanted them out of the house. Today even Samuel was no comfort. In the afternoon Peter locked himself in his office. He had a grand project. A book about the effect of weather on the movement of seabirds. One of the larger natural history publishers had expressed a vague, polite interest, but no firm offer had been made. They'd have to see the completed work, they said. Peter's theories had grown more complex as he analysed the material. There were days when she thought she would never see it finished.

Felicity went into the garden and began weeding the beds at the front of the house. She enjoyed the methodical, mindless activity, the instant result. There was the sound of a car in the lane. She ignored it at first. Walkers sometimes parked on the verge before setting off on the footpath to the coast. Then she could tell it had turned into the drive and she straightened, pulling off her gloves, tucking her shirt back into her jeans, preparing to meet the visitor. She had thought it might be Samuel. He would have realized she was upset. It would be like him to think the matter over and come back to check that she had recovered. She was already planning the words she would use to him, the apology for being so crabby, so inhospitable. The lie. *You know I didn't mind you being here. It was the others. Just too much.*

But it wasn't Samuel. It was a car she didn't recognize. She felt a sudden disquiet, then saw the big female detective from the night before struggle out from the driver's seat. There was the moment of quiet superiority she always felt when she saw a woman of around her own age who had let herself go. The detective's face could even be attractive if she made more effort. Her clothes were shapeless, her hair badly cut. Did she really not care what she looked like? Felicity couldn't understand it. Somehow it made Vera Stanhope invulnerable. *She*'d always enjoyed being admired. She couldn't imagine not caring what other people thought.

'Inspector.' She checked that her hand was clean and held it out. The woman took it with a brief, sharp grip, but her attention was on the garden.

'This is lovely,' she said. 'It'll take a lot of work.'

'Oh,' Felicity knew she was being flattered but was

still pleased. 'We have help, of course. An elderly man from the village.'

'Of course,' the detective said.

Felicity heard the sarcasm, wasn't sure how to respond.

'Can I help you?'

'Just a few more questions. You know how it is. Things come up.'

How can I know how it is? Felicity thought. I've never found a body before.

'Your friends have gone?'

'Yes, they had to get away. I think Gary is working tonight.' She felt awkward standing there, grubby and unprepared.

'What do they do? Gary told us, but what about the others?' Vera had moved into the shade of the house and Felicity followed.

'Samuel's a librarian. Also a rather fine writer. Short stories, mostly. Clive works as an assistant at the Hancock Museum. The natural history section.'

'Does he? I loved it in there when I was a kid. My dad used to take me. It had a smell all of its own. I haven't been there for years.' Vera seemed lost for a moment in the memory. 'Is your husband at home?'

'He's in the office,' Felicity said. 'Come through.'

'Is he working too?'

'On his research, yes.'

'I understand he's a botanist. That must be useful when it comes to gardening.' The voice was jolly, impressed. Felicity didn't know what to make of it. She decided not to explain about the seabird book. It might be considered a hobby, not work at all, and she wanted the detective to take Peter seriously.

'We often stop for tea at about this time. Perhaps you'll join us? I'll give Peter a shout.'

Felicity wouldn't have been surprised if the detective had insisted on disturbing Peter in his office, but it seemed she'd decided to be conciliatory.

'Why not? I'm gasping.'

'We could sit outside, make the most of the sunshine.'

'I'd rather not, pet. I have this allergy. Direct sunlight. Makes me come out in lumps and blotches.'

So they sat up to the kitchen table. Felicity had made to take the tea things through to the living room on a tray, but Vera had touched her arm to stop her. 'Eh, we don't want any fuss. I'm more the hired help than visiting gentry.'

Felicity knew the detective was playing with her and wasn't quite sure how to take it. She just nodded her agreement, sliced the scones she'd fetched out of the freezer the afternoon before and spooned homemade jam into a pot. When Peter came out from his office, Vera had her mouth full, and spattered crumbs over the table as she tried to speak. Felicity wanted to say to Peter: *Don't be taken in by this woman. She wants you to believe she's a clown. She's brighter than she looks.* But she could tell that Peter had already dismissed her as a fool. As she choked and coughed and swilled tea, he raised his eyes to the ceiling.

At last the pantomime was over and Vera began to speak.

'I got interrupted last night,' she said. 'There are a few questions. You'll understand. Formalities.'

'Of course.'

'You work at the university, Dr Calvert? Miss

Marsh was a student there. On the post-graduate education course. You're sure you didn't know her?'

'What did she take for her first degree?'

'English. She did that at Newcastle too.'

'However, I never met her, Inspector. My subject is botany. Our paths never crossed. I'm afraid it must be a coincidence. Her teaching our son, enquiring about accommodation and then our stumbling across her like that on the shore.'

A random occurrence, Felicity thought. Like sea watching. Like birds flying past just when you're there to see them. Except, of course, it wasn't chance which connected the birders and the birds, as Peter had described it in the watch tower the night before. They took steps to make sure they were there at the right time. They listened to the shipping forecast every night to hear which way the wind was blowing. They consulted tide tables.

'The girl was murdered,' Vera said suddenly. 'Strangled. But you know that already. I told you last night. Something that elaborate, staged, you'd think it'd be easy to find out who did it. They'd leave traces. A jilted lover, maybe.' She paused. 'Jilted. That's an old-fashioned kind of word. And it seemed like an old-fashioned sort of crime, at first. Something from a gentler age. Looked peaceful, didn't she, lying there. The flowers. But there was nothing peaceful about her dying. I can't believe she wanted to go.'

Felicity felt tears in her eyes. As if, somehow, she was being held responsible. She was pleased that Peter seemed moved too, that he kept quiet.

The detective continued. 'And there are other complications. There was another victim. A lad was

killed two days earlier. Name of Luke Armstrong.' She
looked at them both. 'Are you *sure* you don't know the
name?'

'You mentioned him before,' Felicity said. 'And I
saw it on the local news. He came from Seaton.'

'What I didn't tell you was that he was put in a
bath. Covered with flowers. Like I said last night, it
could hinder our investigation if something like that
became common knowledge. But you do see what
I'm saying. It's not simple any more. A jilted lover
isn't going to kill a sixteen-year-old boy as a sort of
practice run. Why take the risk? Far too elaborate. I'm
looking for links here. The mother's name is Julie.
Julie Armstrong.'

'Wasn't that woman Gary was raving about called
Julie?' As soon as the words were out of her mouth
Felicity regretted them. It was such a stupid thing to
say. Why point the inspector in the direction of Gary,
who wouldn't hurt a fly? She could feel Peter glaring
at her and tried to rescue the situation. 'I mean, it's a
really common name. I'm sure it doesn't mean . . .'

'Why don't you tell me anyway, pet?'

'He met this woman, that's all. Some gig he was
doing the sound for. A local band in a pub in North
Shields. That place with the view over the river.
Bumped into her in the bar after. They got talking and
found out they'd been to school together. You know
how it is.'

'I'm not sure I do. Why don't you explain?'

'He talks a big game, Gary. I mean, to hear him,
you'd think he had women all over the country. But
since his fiancée left him, I don't think he's had a real
girlfriend. He loved Emily, really loved her. When she

went off with someone else, he was devastated. I just got the impression that he clicked with this Julie. He hoped to meet her again.'

'Did he say any more about her? Like whether she had kids?'

'No, nothing like that.'

'What about you, Dr Calvert? Did he talk to you about this woman?'

'I'm sorry, Inspector. It's not really the sort of thing men talk about.'

'Isn't it?' As if she was genuinely surprised. 'Well, I can ask Gary about it, can't I? Get it straight from the horse's mouth.'

Felicity thought that the ordeal was over then. Vera Stanhope licked her finger, swept up the remaining pieces of scone from her plate, drained her teacup.

'What were you both doing on Wednesday night? Late. Between ten and midnight.'

Felicity looked at Peter, waiting for him to answer first.

'I was here,' he said. 'Working.' He looked at his wife. 'I was still in my office, wasn't I, when you got in?'

'And what were you up to, Mrs Calvert?'

'I was at the theatre,' she said. 'The Live, down on the quayside. It was the work of a young local playwright. I've seen some of his stuff before. It's very evocative. I think it's important to support new writing.' She stopped talking, realizing she was saying too much.

'Were you on your own?'

'No, I went with a friend. Peter doesn't enjoy the

theatre very much. Not that sort of play, at least. I was there with Samuel Parr. You met him here last night.'

'Of course,' Vera said. 'Samuel the librarian.' Felicity expected some sly comment, but none came. 'What time did you arrive home?'

'It probably was nearly midnight. We had supper after the show and it's quite a trek from town.'

'Thanks for that, then.' This time Vera did get to her feet. 'I'm sure you understand why I had to ask. I'll let you get back to your work, Dr Calvert.'

Felicity walked the detective back to her car. The sun was covered by a thin layer of mist, but it didn't look as if it would lead to rain. Gardening would be more pleasant now that it was a bit cooler. She didn't think she would go back to it, though. A bath, she thought. That would relax her. Then she remembered what the inspector had said about Luke Armstrong being found in the bath and the image of a body, strewn with flowers, flashed in front of her eyes.

Vera stood by her vehicle. Felicity started to walk back into the house.

'Just one thing, Mrs Calvert. Would you mind if I had a look at the cottage? The place you showed Lily Marsh the day before she died.'

Felicity had a moment of revulsion. She didn't want to be in the space where she'd been close to Lily Marsh, close enough to see the stitching on the hem of her skirt as she walked ahead of Felicity up the stairs. Then she told herself that was ridiculous. She'd have to go into the cottage sometime. Why not now? Better, surely, to humour the detective than antagonize her.

'Of course. I'll just get the key.'

They walked through the meadow to the cottage door. Inside, it was all as it had been since her last visit, except the roses in the bedroom were dead. Felicity took them from the jug to take to the compost heap, held them carefully because of the thorns. Vera followed her down the stairs, but then she seemed reluctant to leave.

'This was the last time anyone saw her alive,' she said. 'Last time anyone will admit to, at least. She didn't go into school on Friday. We talked to the head teacher this afternoon, finally tracked her down.' She looked sharply at Felicity. 'And that's not for public consumption either.' She looked out of the window. 'What a beautiful place. You'd have thought she'd have jumped at the chance to stay here.'

'I wondered if she thought she wouldn't have been able to afford it.'

'What rent were you going to charge?'

'I don't know. I hadn't really considered it.'

'Didn't she ask?'

'No,' Felicity said. 'She just said she'd think about it. Then she ran off.'

Chapter Seventeen

Julie was back in her own home. Her mother opened the door to Vera, pulled her close for a conspiratorial whisper.

'We've asked her to stay with us for a while, but she says she'd never face coming back. So I've moved in to keep an eye. Just for a week or two.'

Vera nodded, walked on into the house, kept her voice low too.

'What about Laura, Mrs Richardson? How's she?'

'Eh, I don't know. Not eating. Keeps to herself. I've asked if she wants her friends round but she says not.'

'Is she in now?'

'Aye, she's in her room.'

'I'll just go up for a quick word. I'll see Julie on my way out, if that's all right. Would you mind telling her I'm here?'

Laura was lying on her bed, curled on her side, a magazine beside her. It was open but she didn't seem to be reading. The window was shut and the room was hot. It was at the back of the house, looking out over a paddock, where a couple of tired ponies cropped the parched grass, and then a field of arable. Vera had knocked at the door and walked in without waiting for an answer.

The girl looked up. 'What do you want?' She was skinny, angular. Fourteen but no figure to speak of. Her hair was cut short and spiky. Eyes that glared at you. A rash of freckles across her nose which made her seem younger than she was. Soon, Vera thought, she might become an interesting beauty. Now she was sullen, miserable, lonely. There'd been a time when Vera had been desperate for children. The longing had come on her suddenly, when she was in her late thirties, shocking her with its intensity. It had been more potent than her dreams of men and sex. Just as well it never happened, she thought now. I could never have coped with someone like this.

'I'd just like a chat,' she said. 'Now you've had a chance to think about things.'

'I don't know anything about what happened that night. I was asleep.'

'I wanted to talk to you about that, pet. Are you sure you didn't hear anything? A knock on the door, voices, a scuffle. You might have heard, thought it was Luke and his mates larking about. Nothing to feel guilty about if you did.'

'I don't feel guilty.'

'Because I find it hard to believe you slept through all that.'

'I sleep like a stone,' Laura said. 'Ask Mam.'

She glared at Vera, who felt out of her depth. She would have pushed another witness, but this was a young girl who'd just lost her brother. 'Still,' Vera said. 'You might be able to help. I need to talk about Luke's mates, what he got up to, who he mixed with. You'll have a better idea about that than your mam.'

'No, I won't.' Aggressive. As if Vera was crazy even to consider it.

'He didn't talk to you, then?'

'No.' That tone again. The one teenagers did when they really wanted to wind you up. Sneering. The voice that made you want to slap them. 'I didn't want him to.'

'You didn't get on?'

Laura pulled herself up onto her elbow. 'I've had all the lectures, OK? From Mam and Nan and the teachers at school. I know it wasn't his fault, the learning disability. I know I'm a bitch. But I couldn't stand it. Everyone pointing at me, knowing I was his sister. Sniggering behind my back when he did something stupid. As if I could help it. We didn't *not* get on. I just wanted him out of my life.'

She realized the implication of what she'd said as soon as the words came out, but wasn't going to show she was sorry. She sank onto the bed and turned her back on Vera. Vera knew something of what she was going through. When she was a kid, people had sniggered about her too. She'd lived on her own with a mad father. No mother. No one to iron the school uniform or bake cakes for sports day. No one to take her to the hairdresser's or explain about periods. Just Hector, who spent his spare time prowling the hills looking for raptors' nests, who seemed to care more for his egg-collecting friends than his ugly daughter. But it wouldn't help if she talked about that to Laura. Young people saw the middle-aged as a different species. How could Vera's experience mean anything to the miserable girl lying on the bed?

She reached out and touched Laura's shoulder.

'Eh, pet, it's not your fault. And you might be able to help without realizing.'

The girl turned onto her back, stared at the ceiling.

'I didn't know any of his friends.'

'What about Thomas Sharp?'

'He's dead.'

Vera kept her voice even. The team back at Kimmerston would be astonished, she thought, that she could be this patient. 'But you must have met him when he came to the house.'

'Sometimes.'

'What did you make of him?'

There was a silence. Vera wondered if she'd pushed too hard.

'He was OK,' the girl said at last. 'Better than the others Luke had knocked around with. A laugh.'

She liked him, Vera thought. Fancied him, even. Had anything gone on between them? Furtive groping behind her mother's back? What had Luke made of that?

'It must have been a shock when he died.'

'It was dreadful.'

'Did you go to his funeral?'

She shook her head. 'Mam wouldn't let me take the day off school. She says I'm the only one with brains in the family and I have to use them.' She paused. 'I went with them to the river, though, when they took the flowers.'

'Did Luke ever tell you what happened when Thomas drowned?'

'He said he should have saved him.' The answer came back loud and angry.

'Do you think he could have saved him?'

'I don't know. Maybe. If he hadn't been such a daft sod. If he'd made more effort.' She started to cry, not for her brother, but for his friend.

'Do you know anyone called Lily Marsh?'

'I don't know any old ladies.'

'Why do you think she's an old lady?'

'It's an old lady's name, isn't it? Lily.'

It's the name of a flower, Vera thought suddenly and wondered why she hadn't realized before. Does that mean anything? Did Luke have any middle names? Something floral? Were there any male names connected to flowers?

Laura was getting restive, curious despite herself. 'Who is she anyway?'

'Not an old person,' Vera said. 'A student teacher. Did she ever work in your school?'

'Nah.' Laura picked up the magazine and pretended to read it.

Vera saw she'd get nothing more out of her today. 'I need to talk to your mam now,' she said. 'If you think of anything give me a ring. I'll leave my card here on the window sill.'

Julie was sitting in her front room, staring at the television screen. Saturday teatime. Daft celebrities getting families to do daft stunts. Despite the heat she was wearing jogging pants and a sweater. When she saw Vera she jumped up and switched off the television, embarrassed perhaps to be caught doing something so normal. The room was the same size as Sal's next door, but more cluttered. There'd be reminders of Luke everywhere – his clothes would still be in the plastic laundry basket next to the ironing board, his favourite video in the pile on the floor.

'Sorry about the mess,' Julie said. 'You know . . .'

Vera nodded, happy to accept the excuse, but she knew it would always be messy. Probably messier than it was now, because Mrs Richardson was here, keeping on top of things. Julie wouldn't be one for a tidy house. Not like Kath on the prim estate in Wallsend.

Mrs Richardson hovered just inside the door. 'Tea, Inspector?'

'Champion.' If I have more tea, I'll drown, Vera thought, but she didn't want the mother listening in to this. She sat on an armchair covered by a puce chenille throw, beckoned for Julie to sit down again too.

'It's about Gary,' she said. 'Gary Wright.'

Julie moved her head very slowly until she was looking at Vera. 'What about him?'

'You do know him?'

'Not really.'

'Tell me.'

'I was with him the night Luke was killed. I mean, not *with* him, not like that. We never left the club. But dancing together, having a laugh.' She snapped her mouth shut as if the thought of laughter was obscene.

'That wasn't the first time you met him?'

'No, a few weeks ago I was in the Harbour Bell with my mam and da. Sunday afternoon. Just before they let Luke out of hospital. Laura was spending the day with a friend. Da likes his music. If you let him, he'll bore you for hours about the old days. The Animals. The clubs in town where he used to go in the sixties. The Bell has live music on Sunday afternoons and there was a band he wanted to hear. I'd had my dinner at theirs and went just for the ride. I had a good time. Gary was doing the sound.' Julie's voice tailed off. She looked straight at Vera. 'You know, that could have been months ago. Years. It feels as if everything has changed. It's me I'm talking about but it's like I'm describing a different person.'

'I know,' Vera said.

'Gary made me laugh,' Julie went on. 'At first you could tell he was just showing off. Telling stories about his work. The musicians he'd done the sound for. You could tell he'd come out with the same stuff to anyone. Any woman, at least, aged between fifteen and fifty.'

Even me? Vera thought.

'Then we just clicked. We found out we'd been to the same primary school, started chatting about the people we could remember. Mam had to come and get me in the end. She was worried we'd miss visiting time at the hospital. She was coming with me to see Luke.'

'And you arranged to meet him in town?' Vera said.

'No. It wasn't a firm arrangement. Not really.' But Vera could tell it had been firm enough for Julie. Special. 'He just asked if I ever got into town, and I said, hardly ever. Then I remembered Jan's birthday and how the girls had asked me to go with them. So I said I'd be there. That night.'

Vera could imagine how that had been. The mother listening in. Julie keeping her voice casual, but making sure he'd made a note of the date, the places the girls always went. *Not the Bigg Market. We're a bit old for that.* She'd have been looking out for him all night. And he'd turned up. She'd have felt like a sixteen-year-old, giddy, triumphant. And she'd arrived home to find her son strangled, scattered with flowers.

Mrs Richardson appeared from the kitchen, a mug in each hand. Vera accepted hers, then tipped most of the contents into the compost of a sad umbrella plant when the woman went to get biscuits. Julie, staring at the blank television screen, didn't notice.

'A great cup of tea,' Vera said, slurping the dregs. 'Just what I needed.' Now the two women sat, looking at her. Perhaps they could tell she had something else to say. 'There's been another murder. A young woman. A student. She was called Lily Marsh. Does the name mean anything to you?'

They shook their heads. They didn't really care about the death of a strange woman. Luke was all that mattered to them. Vera found a space for the mug on the coffee table. 'I wanted you to know,' she said. 'It'll be in the press. And it might make it easier for us to find Luke's killer. It'll give us more to go on.' That was the theory, at least. She stood up. 'I'll be off now, Mrs Richardson. If there's any news, I'll be in touch.'

Julie got up from her chair too. 'Why did you want to know about Gary?'

'No reason, pet. Just routine.'

At the door Vera stopped. 'Did Luke have a middle name?'

'Geoffrey,' Julie said. 'Like his dad.'

Nothing floral, then. No connection there.

As Vera walked into the street she could sense the eyes behind net curtains; the neighbours would wait until she'd driven off before getting on the phone to share the latest rumours.

Chapter Eighteen

One time, he wouldn't have admitted to living in North Shields, Gary thought. Certainly not if he was chatting up a woman, trying to impress. People from outside had a picture of it. All charity shops and boarded-up buildings, Wilkinson's and Poundstretchers the only stores doing business. Even now, if you waited at the metro, you'd share the platform with teenage mothers and gangs of lads who skipped off the trains whenever the ticket inspector arrived. But it was changing. Now if he said he lived in Shields people nodded, understanding. It was the sort of place where people in his business might live. Still not quite respectable, but interesting. There were new apartments, bars and restaurants on the Fish Quay. A couple of writers had taken up residence. House prices in Tynemouth were so high that people had crossed the boundary, blurring the edges. There was no shame to living in Shields these days. Sunday's Quiz Night at the Maggie Bank pub was full of lecturers and social workers. Gary had been a regular once, but only bothered going now to catch up with old friends. Even though he could score on the music round, he had no chance of winning.

He lived in a newish development on one of the

steep streets between the Fish Quay and the town, a four-storey block of flats, with a Gothic stone Methodist chapel on one side and a carpet warehouse on the other. He'd bought it soon after he split up from Emily; thinking back, he couldn't remember much about moving in. He'd been pissed when he signed the contract, swore at the estate agent about something that had irritated him. Clive had helped him carry the few bits of furniture they couldn't get into the lift up the stairs, organized Northern Electric to get the power on, even made the tea. That was the sort of friend he was. He never made a fuss but was there when he was needed. Gary hoped he'd act the same way if the circumstances were reversed, but he wasn't sure. Now the flat felt more like home than anywhere he'd lived since he was a kid. It would be a wrench to leave.

That morning, he'd given Clive a lift back from Fox Mill. In the car, they'd talked about the dead girl in the pool, tuned the radio to the local BBC station in case it had made the news. Gary had done most of the talking. Clive hadn't said much, but then he never did. Perhaps that's why they got on so well: Gary liked a ready-made audience. At school Clive had been a loner. He still didn't have any other friends. Only Gary, Samuel and Peter. The discovery of the body headed up the news, but there were no details. Nothing about the way she was found or the flowers. Not even her name.

Gary wandered out onto the balcony and looked over the town and down to the river. Upstream the ferry was sliding away from the South Shields jetty. He had his phone with him and leaned on the rail to dial. He was on the top floor and there wasn't too much noise from the street. He was about to press the buttons when the intercom buzzer sounded and he went inside to see who was waiting in the lobby. He wasn't sorry to have to put off his phone call. He still hadn't decided quite what to say.

'It's me, pet. Vera Stanhope.' The detective of the night before. He thought he'd answered all her questions and her presence threw him. At one time he'd have been able to take this in his stride. He'd had the confidence to talk himself into any event, out of any bother. Now, it wasn't so easy. But he couldn't leave her there, waiting.

'Come on up.' Keeping the voice light, to show he had nothing to hide.

He checked his appearance in the long mirror. Habit. Reassurance. Like spending a fortune on the right haircut, a decent pair of shoes. Then he opened the door of the flat and stood there, waiting for her to appear. He couldn't hear the lift and was wondering if she'd been called away on more urgent business, when she appeared at the top of the stairs, wheezing, heaving for breath.

'I don't like lifts.' The words came out in quick accusing pants, as if she was blaming him for living there. 'I'm never quite sure they'll carry my weight.' And he realized her appearance was something she was sensitive about. She'd have been bullied at school and the only way to deal with it would have been to get the jibe in first. Surprised that last night he'd been intimidated by her, he leaned back against the door and let her walk into the flat ahead of him.

Inside, he watched her checking out the flat, saw

it through her eyes. It would be tidier than she'd expect. He had lots of electronic equipment but it was all boxed and stacked on shelves along one wall. He didn't mind a bit of mess but he didn't like chaos. Against the same wall stood a long desk with a PC and printer, a pair of headphones, a pile of audio magazines. In the middle of the room a sofa and coffee table. In the corner a TV and DVD player. A couple of enlarged black and white photos on the wall. One of the river in the centre of town. Dusk. Looking through all the bridges to the Blinking Eye. But there was nothing really personal, he thought. Nothing to give himself away. He'd allowed himself to keep one photo of Emily, but it was on his desk, small, nothing flashy. The inspector wouldn't notice that.

'Sit down,' he said. 'Tea? Coffee?'

Her face was red with the effort of climbing the stairs. He didn't bother with the lift either unless he had heavy gear, but didn't even have to catch his breath when he got to the top. He told himself not to be such a smug bastard. She was an overweight, middle-aged woman. Hardly competition.

'I don't suppose you've got a beer, have you?' she said. 'I'm not fussy, pet. Whatever you've got in the fridge.'

He found himself smiling. Despite himself he couldn't help liking her. He brought out two cans of lager, a glass for her. She lowered herself carefully onto the sofa. He sat on the floor, legs stretched in front of him, felt her looking him over.

'Your file says you're thirty-five,' she said. 'You've not worn badly. If I was guessing, I'd say five years younger.'

'Thanks.' He was annoyed at himself for feeling flattered. It was an odd thing for her to say, an odd feeling to have her eyeing him up. It occurred to him briefly that women must feel like this all the time.

'This place must have set you back a few quid.' She looked out towards the window. 'A view like that.'

'Not really. I bought it from new six years ago. Everyone thought I was mad moving to Shields. I'd make a canny profit if I sold it now.'

'Live here on your own?'

'Yes.'

I'm not so sad, he wanted to say. Not really sad, like Clive. I was engaged once. To Emily. The love of my life. We were going to live together in a tidy flat in Jesmond. And since then there've been women. Not living in, maybe. Not real girlfriends. But I've never gone without for long. And now there's Julie.

She tugged at the ring pull on the can. He slipped a look at his watch. He still had that phone call to make.

'Expecting someone?' she asked.

'No,' he said quickly. 'Nothing like that. Is this about that student who died? I thought you'd finished with me last night.'

She made him wait until she'd taken a mouthful of beer, straight from the can, not bothering with the glass he'd set on the table in front of her. 'I'm going to ask you a question,' she said. 'You've heard it before. This time I want you to think about it.'

He was about to interrupt, to tell her she was wasting her time, that he knew nothing about the student's death. But she waved her can at him to stop him speaking and he did. She had a way of getting what she wanted. Again she waited until she was sure she had his full attention. 'Does the name Luke Armstrong mean anything to you?'

'No. I told you last night.'

'I said think about it.'

They looked at each other in silence. Gary shook his head.

'He has a mother by the name of Julie. A sister called Laura. Perhaps that jogs your memory.'

He froze, his beer almost to his mouth. 'Julie's son,' he said at last.

'Aye, Julie's son. The lad who's been ill.'

'I didn't mean to mislead you, Inspector.'

'You did, though.'

'I never met him. Julie talked about him. I know he'd been having a rough time. But the name didn't really register. I still think of her as Julie Richardson.' He looked up at her. 'He's dead?'

'Murdered,' she said. 'Didn't you see it in the press?'

'I don't read the papers much. I listened to the radio on the way back from Peter's this morning. It mentioned Lily Marsh, but not the boy.'

'We're not encouraging the media to make a connection.'

'And he was killed in the same way as Lily Marsh?'

'Not exactly. But there are similarities.'

'Oh God,' he said. 'Julie will be devastated. She said he wasn't an easy kid, but I could tell she was crazy about him. I mean, she said she loved both her children, but Luke was special. He needed her most. I don't know what to do. I was just about to phone her when you arrived. I was expecting her to phone me.

She said she would. I thought she'd changed her mind about wanting to see me again. Now I understand.' He paused. 'I don't suppose she'll want to hear from me now.'

'Typical man,' Vera said, speaking to herself. 'A woman's lost her son and all he can think about is getting his leg over.'

'No!' he said. 'I didn't mean it like that. I meant maybe she could use a friend. But probably not me. I mean, she'd be better off with someone who's known her longer, wouldn't she? I'd just be in the way. What do you think?'

'Eh, pet, I'm a detective, not a relationship counsellor.'

He looked straight at her. 'How is Julie?'

'Her son's just been murdered. How do you think?'

He stood up and walked towards the balcony. The door was still open. A couple of herring gulls screamed and squabbled outside. He knew it was pathetic, but he felt sorry for himself. He wasn't really thinking about Julie at all.

Vera heaved herself to her feet and followed him out. 'You do know he died that night you were out with her?' she said.

Gary turned, apparently horrified. 'Wednesday?'

'Aye, she got home from the night in town and found him.' She paused, narrowed her eyes. 'Some people might say it was a bit of a coincidence. You were chatting up the first victim's mother just before he was murdered and came upon the second soon after.'

'I'd never met either of them,' he said. 'Honestly.'

'Tell me how you got together with Julie,' she

said. 'I mean, were you set up? Some friend saw her, maybe, thought you were her type. Someone pulling your strings?'

'No, nothing like that. Why?'

'Probably no reason,' she said. 'I was just looking for a connection. It crossed my mind it would be a way of keeping tracks on her. Someone bringing you together would have inside information. But I've never been a great one for conspiracy theories.'

Gary found himself telling the inspector about the meeting anyway. He wanted to tell it. It was like one of those stories which become family legends, told to grandchildren. They stood together, leaning on the balcony rail and looking down into the street. 'It was a chance meeting. Pure chance. I saw her in the other bar. At least I heard her first, heard her laugh. She's got one of those laughs. You know, infectious. Then something about her was familiar. I'd not seen her since we left primary school, but I recognized her. Amazing, really, after all that time. And suddenly it hit me. That was what I wanted. To get together with someone like that. Someone who could laugh like that. I've always gone for younger women. Lookers, you know. But they've never stuck around. Thinking of settling down with someone, I suppose it was all part of getting old. Like taking the permanent job at the Sage after swearing I'd never stop being self-employed.'

She listened impassively. 'Aye,' she said. 'That's how Julie told it. But she kept to the facts. Left out the soppy bits.'

'She told you about me?'

Vera left the question unanswered. 'Did you tell anyone you were going to meet her that night?'

He couldn't stop himself grinning. 'All my close mates. I don't really do secrets.'

'All the people who were with you when you found Lily Marsh, they knew beforehand that you planned to meet up with Luke's mother on the Wednesday night?'

'Probably. I'd chatted to Felicity about Julie. Then there was a Bird Club meeting on Monday evening. All the lads were there. We went for a pint afterwards. I wanted their advice – how to play it. I probably bored them to death.'

'I didn't think men were supposed to talk about things like that.'

'Yeah, well. I never did the strong, silent thing.'

'And the others? Do they get touchy-feely too?'

'We're close.' Gary was suddenly serious. 'Nothing wrong with that.'

'I should go,' she said, but she didn't move. He could tell she was drawn to the view from the balcony.

'Did Julie tell you what triggered Luke's illness?' she asked.

'Some mate of his drowned . . .'

'Down there,' she said. 'Just off the Fish Quay. You didn't hear anything about it?'

He shook his head.

She wandered back into the room, stopped by the desk, nodded to the photo of Emily. 'Who's that, then?'

He felt himself blush, couldn't help it, thought she must be some sort of witch to go straight for the picture. 'An old friend.'

She stood for a moment looking at the picture.

'Strange-looking lass,' she said almost to herself. 'Pretty enough, if you like them anorexic.'

She was letting herself out of the door when he called her back. 'What do you think I should do about Julie? Should I phone her?'

She paused for only a second. 'Not my call, pet.'

Chapter Nineteen

Monday morning Gary woke up to the sound of his pager. He'd set it so it made a noise only when there was a mega alert, when an exceptionally rare bird had been seen somewhere in the country. It was six o'clock, but this time of year and this far north it had already been light for more than an hour. He slept with the pager on the floor next to his bed and scrabbled to reach it, pressed the buttons, screwed up his eyes to read what it said. He didn't travel all over the country to see rare birds any more, but there was still the rush of adrenaline.

It was a moment before he could take in the information. *Marmora's warbler. Deepden Nature Reserve. Northumberland.* His patch. The place where he and Clive started ringing with Peter and Samuel. The only place that had provided any retreat from thoughts of Emily. Then there was the intense stab of envy. *It should have been me. I should have been the person to find it. And if not me, then one of the others.* Really, it should have been Clive, he thought. It mattered to him more than any of us. Clive never really talked about his mother, but you'd been able to tell it was only the weekends at Deepden that had kept him sane. He supported the place long after the rest of them had moved on.

Those thoughts were at the back of his mind, but he was already out of bed with his mobile in his hand. He was the only one with a pager. The others pretended to despise the whole concept. They were into natural history, not ticking rare birds. He dialled Peter's number first. If they were any sort of gang, Peter Calvert was the leader and, though he pretended to be above keeping a list, he wouldn't want to miss out on this. He'd been part of the group which had founded Deepden in the sixties.

Peter listened to Gary's gabbling then swore under his breath. 'I've got a lecture at ten. Still, if it's showing well and I can get it straight away . . .' And Gary knew he would go for it, lecture or not. 'I'll phone Sam,' he went on. 'He should have time to go for it before work.' Gary thought Peter was the only one of them to get away with calling the writer Sam.

He ended the call then pressed the button again for Clive's number. There was no question that Clive would go. He'd throw a sickie if he had to, stay the night at the obs and look again the next morning. But he'd need a lift. By the time Clive answered, whispering, because of his dreadful mother asleep in the next room, Gary had his binoculars round his neck, his scope over his shoulder and he was already down the first flight of stairs.

Gary had heard the tale about the start of the Deepden Observatory hundreds of times. When he was a kid and they'd gone there every weekend, the older observatory members had explained it. Sitting in front of the fire after a day's ringing, drinking whisky or beer, they'd relived the triumph of raising the money to buy the cottage off the elderly woman who owned the place, the planting of the garden, the digging of the pond, the cutting of mist net rides through the undergrowth. The grand opening of the observatory which had attracted everyone of any importance in the field of natural history. Perhaps once all the work had been done, the excitement had passed, because even then they'd spent more time drinking tea in the cottage than going out into the field. Now a new generation of birders camped out in the two dormitories, staggered back late at night after a lock-in at the Fox and Hounds in Deepden village and found the rare birds.

The four of them had stopped going regularly a few years before. It had been a statement. A stand. Gary was already more attracted to sea watching and had been a sporadic visitor even then. He couldn't quite remember what the disagreement had been about. Some matter of politics within the Observatory Trust. Or Peter not feeling he'd been treated with the respect he deserved. Peter had resigned as chairman and the other three had supported him. The weekend ritual of staying in the cottage ended abruptly. It was harder on Clive than the others. He had no life at all. Unless he had an alternative existence which he kept quite secret, and Gary wouldn't have put that past him. They still visited of course, but it was strange to turn up as an outsider.

Clive was already waiting on the pavement outside his mother's bungalow. 'We should have gone there yesterday when we left Fox Mill.' His first words, before even saying hello, before getting into the van.

And all the way on the drive north he was tense, hunched up in the passenger seat, his shoulders rigid. Gary talked about Julie, about her lad being killed. They all talked to Clive because they knew he could keep secrets.

'It must be a nightmare,' he said. 'Imagine what it must be like, losing your son like that! And for her daughter. She was asleep in the next room when it all happened.'

Clive didn't say anything. He only moved when Gary's pager flashed its red light and then he read out the updated news on the warbler.

The observatory was a quarter of a mile inland, the first patch of cover for migrating birds once they hit the coast. The house was a low bungalow, built before the war as a holiday retreat, with an acre of garden which now formed the reserve. It had been the location that had made it so special. The bungalow itself wouldn't have been out of place in any seaside town – a squat, rather mean building of brick and white stucco, made a little more attractive now by the clematis which grew around the porch and which was just coming into flower.

They'd driven east from the A1, down a narrow lane, the rising sun in their eyes, through an ugly village and then down a dirt track. The observatory was at the end of the track and when they arrived there were already half a dozen cars pulled into the verge. Gary recognized Peter's Volvo and the sporty little Volkswagen which Samuel had recently bought. Clive was out of the van before Gary had the engine switched off and was heading through the wooden gate into the garden, leaving him to follow and shut it after them. The garden was an oasis in the flat, bare land which surrounded the house. Inland, there was a vast stretch of open-cast mining, a moonscape of rocky ridges and pits; already huge lorries with fat tyres crawled over it. Between the house and a line of dunes which marked the coast, cattle grazed in a long narrow field.

The garden had been designed to attract birds and insects. They'd dug up the lawn and replaced it with a pond. Now vegetation had grown up all around it and over it, so the water was hardly visible. There were the flat shiny leaves of water lilies, a patch of reeds. Where once there had been herbaceous borders, there were huge spikes of buddleia for the butterflies and bushes which in autumn would produce berries to pull in the thrushes.

The mist nets were unfurled, meaning a group of ringers was staying. They must have found the Marmora on their first round of the nets. Behind the house there was a small orchard which had been planted when the house was built and it was here that the group of birdwatchers stood.

The Marmora's warbler had been seen on the top of a hawthorn hedge which marked the boundary of the reserve. The birdwatchers stood in the dappled shadow thrown by the apple trees, binoculars raised, looking. From a distance it was impossible to tell if the bird was there or if people were searching for it. By the time Gary arrived Clive had his tripod set up and was staring through the scope.

'It disappeared into the bushes ten minutes ago,' he said. 'Nobody can tell me exactly where it went in.' He sounded murderous.

Gary thought they'd all have been talking when the warbler flew off. On the other side of the group he could see Peter and Samuel, smiling and chatting. Once you'd seen a bird there was a release of tension and you relaxed your concentration. He stared into the hedge, felt his guts as a hard knot of anxiety. He didn't enjoy this sort of birdwatching. It was too stressful waiting, knowing the bird had been there. Not knowing if it still was. Since Emily, he hadn't been able to handle stress. He preferred sea watching. That was the most relaxing experience he knew, sitting in the watch tower next to the lighthouse. There was nothing you could do to make the birds fly past, so no point getting anxious. Now, as he felt his heart beat faster, he tried to control his breathing and wondered if he'd been right to come.

'There it is.' Clive, still bent over the telescope, spoke so quietly that only Gary could hear. 'About four metres in from the fence, on the bare branch just below the top.' And then Gary was on to it and it was filling his scope. He could see the inside of the bill when it began to call and the colour of its eye. Mind-blowing. Only the sixth British record and it was here in Deepden. Worth falling out of bed at six in the morning and the tension of the drive.

Around him other people had picked up his excitement and they were looking at it too. Then the bird disappeared behind the hedge again and they were all standing around grinning. Some people started wandering off, talking about bacon sandwiches and work. Clive remained focused, though, and when the bird reappeared, further away on a dead tree by the lane, he was the person to find it.

Peter Calvert was full of it. You'd have thought he'd found the bird himself.

'Every year we get at least one *British Birds* rarity. A reserve this small. And when we started they all said we were wasting our time.' Gary thought with amusement that he was still claiming credit for something that had happened forty years before. It didn't bother him, but he could see why the man got up some people's noses.

'I've got to go,' Peter said. 'I'm giving a lecture this morning. Can't disappoint my students. Are ·you coming, Clive? I can give you a lift into town.'

And though you could tell Clive would have liked a bit longer with the bird, he twisted the legs on his tripod and followed Peter to the car. Peter was still his hero. Gary thought he'd have run into a burning house if Peter had given the order. Outside in the lane cars were still arriving. One of the observatory committee was standing at the gate with a bucket, demanding money before he'd let people in.

Samuel and Gary went into the house. They were still paid-up observatory members, so no one could stop them. Once inside the door, Gary was taken back to the time when they'd been regulars. It still smelled of wood smoke in there, though it must have been months since the fire had been lit. Wood smoke and the waterproofing you rubbed into Barbour jackets and leather boots. They made tea, stole a couple of soft biscuits each from the tin in the cupboard and sat outside on the rusty wrought-iron chairs by the pond.

'What did you make of that business on Friday night?' Samuel asked.

It took Gary a moment to realize he was talking

about the girl by the lighthouse. 'That business' seemed an odd way to describe the discovery of a body.

'I don't know. That detective turned up at my flat on Saturday. The big woman who was at Fox Mill. The lad who died in Seaton was Julie's son. She was with me in town on Wednesday night, then she went home and found him. It must seem a strange coincidence, but she appeared to believe me when I said I didn't know anything about the girl.'

Samuel took a moment to speak. Gary had read a couple of his stories. It always shocked him that Samuel, so good-humoured, so ordinary, could write stuff like that. Stuff that haunted you, so you'd wake up in the night with the pictures still in your head. It was impressive, but a bit scary.

'You didn't know Lily Marsh, did you?' Samuel said at last.

'No! I'd never seen her before.'

Samuel seemed pleased by the answer. 'Perhaps we should start coming back here,' he said. 'Show them how it's done.'

But Gary thought Deepden had too many memories for him, of how he'd nearly lost it when Emily had left him. He'd needed the place then and the three good friends who'd held him together. But now, he thought, it was time to move on. Although he didn't have to be in the Sage until the afternoon, he told Samuel he had to get off to work. He went back into the house to drop off his mug, then he went to his van. The lane was so jammed with cars that it took him nearly half an hour to turn it round.

Chapter Twenty

It was Monday morning. Vera woke up as she always seemed to these days with a faint hangover, a sense that she hadn't slept properly. Her window was open and her neighbours' cockerel was drowning out every other sound, seemed to be living somewhere just behind her eyes. She realized she was an object of curiosity to the couple who owned the smallholding. They'd moved from the city and had made an effort to get on with her, had this ridiculous notion that country people had a wisdom about nature, saw it as almost mystical. Then they found out Vera was police and she could tell they thought they should disapprove. They'd gone on marches, saw the police as the enemy. Vera didn't bother one way or the other. Except occasionally she dreamed about strangling the cockerel.

She shut the window and went to the kitchen to make tea, ignoring the pile of dirty plates in the sink. The first sip of tea and she was already engrossed in the case, her mind buzzing, the guilt about her drinking forgotten. The cockerel dismissed. This was what she was made for.

Today she was planning a trip to Newcastle, the big city. That was how she'd seen it when she was a girl and still thought of a visit to town as an adventure. She collected Joe Ashworth from home on her way through. She knew she wasn't fit to be let loose on the academic world on her own. She was too loud and brash and she'd end up offending someone. Joe lived in a small estate on the edge of Kimmerston. He too had grown up in the city and this was all he'd ever dreamed of: a new house, professional neighbours, a family. His wife was pregnant again, nine months and uncomfortable. When Vera turned up she'd just emerged from bed, huge belly and swollen tits wrapped in a cotton dressing gown, bleary-eyed. Joe was giving his daughter breakfast to the background noise of Radio 2. The little girl sat in the high chair beaming, while Joe spooned in Ready Brek on a plastic spoon. More happy families, Vera thought. There was all that talk of family breakdown, but wherever she went there were people making a go of it. Making her feel inadequate and depressed.

She'd phoned Peter Calvert at home on Sunday night and made an appointment to meet him at the university. She wanted to see him away from his ideal home and his ideal wife. She used the flowers as an excuse. 'It would be useful for us to know where they might have been collected. It will take time for the forensic people to release them. You saw them, at the second crime scene at least. It could give us a head start . . .'

And he'd been delighted to be asked. She could tell that. 'I understand you're an expert,' she said and had almost heard him purring.

They arrived at the university a little early and he was at the end of a lecture. They stood at the back of the theatre, listening. Vera didn't take in what he was saying, just watched him perform. She'd been sent on a course once. Body language. She tried to remember what the psychologist had said about it, but nothing of it came back to her. What she could tell now was that Peter Calvert liked the young women. There were a couple of pretty lasses sitting a couple of rows from the front. They wore frilled muslin skirts and lacy tops you could almost see through, and he seemed to be directing his words straight at them. When one of them asked a question he complimented her on making an intelligent point and gave a little frown, to show he was taking her seriously. But maybe all sixty-year-old men would be the same, Vera thought. No harm in looking, even if you did make a fool of yourself. She didn't mind looking at young men, though she tried to be discreet.

Calvert still seemed to be in a good mood when he took them into his office. He fiddled with a filter coffee machine which stood on the window sill.

'I can only offer you black, I'm afraid. I don't take milk myself. Though I could probably borrow some from a colleague. You wanted to ask about the flowers.'

'Informally,' Vera said quickly. 'Not as an expert witness. We'll deal with that later if we need to. But speed is important at this point in an enquiry.'

'Of course.'

'You did see the flowers when your son found the body?'

'Yes. I mean, my first priority was to move James away. He was upset enough as it was. Bad enough to come across something like that. Even worse when we found out he knew her. So I didn't have time to study the blooms in detail, but of course I noticed them.'

'What did you make of them?'

'There seemed to be a mixture,' he said. 'Some wild flowers, the sort you'd find in a hay meadow. Poppies, ox-eye daisies, buttercups. The rest garden flowers. Perennials. I didn't see anything exotic or unusual.'

'Not the sort of thing you buy in a florist, then?'

'Oh no. Nothing like that. Picked. And fairly recently. Or kept in fresh water. They hadn't wilted. At least I don't remember them looking dead or tired.'

'Were there any you'd have in your own garden? I was thinking you could show us. We can look them up in a book, but it wouldn't be the same. And it might trigger your memory.'

'I'm not sure,' he said easily. 'You'd think I'd know, but Felicity is the gardener. You're very welcome to come round and have a look. Any evening you like. We're usually both in.'

'And you're absolutely certain you can't tell us anything about Lily Marsh?'

'Positive, Inspector. As you can see, this is a big community. Our paths never crossed.'

There was a knock at the door. A young man stuck his head round. 'You said you wanted to talk to me sometime today, Dr Calvert. Is this a good time?'

'Ah yes, Tim. Just give me a minute. If you've finished, Inspector . . . This close to the end of term everything's pretty hectic. There are some students I have to see.'

Vera thought this was too convenient. She wouldn't have put it past Peter Calvert to arrange the meeting with the student so the interview with the police didn't drag on. That didn't mean he had anything to hide, of course. He could just be an arrogant bastard who thought his time was too precious to waste on catching a killer. She smiled sweetly and led Ashworth out of the room.

Along the corridor there was an open-plan office where three middle-aged women sat in front of PCs. There were plants on the shelves, photos of grandchildren. They seemed to be having an intense conversation which had little to do with the university. Vera thought these might be people who enjoyed gossip as much as she did. She tapped on the open door and walked in, leaving Ashworth lurking outside. The room fell silent, but she thought they were curious, not hostile.

'I wonder if you can help me. My name's Vera Stanhope. I'm heading up the investigation into the murder of one of your students.' That had them gripped, as she'd known it would. It would keep them talking through until the lunch break. 'Dr Calvert's been giving us some expert advice. He's with a student and I don't want to interrupt him. I was wondering if one of you looked after his diary. I need to check a couple of dates, see when he's next free.'

A plump, motherly woman with grey hair waved her hand, like an excited child at the back of the class with the answer to a difficult question. 'That's me, for my sins. Marjorie. Marjorie Beckwith.'

Vera beamed. 'He updates it on the PC, I presume.'

'He's supposed to,' Marjorie said indulgently, 'so the rest of the department knows what he's up to, but he's not one for following guidelines, I'm afraid.'

And she reached to a shelf behind her and handed a black, hard-back book to Vera. It was that easy. Vera took it to an empty table, sitting so she had her back to the room and flipped through the pages. The day of Luke's death, Peter Calvert had attended a meeting of the department in the morning. At five o'clock he'd planned a tutorial with two students. There were no names, only initials. The entry had been scored through with two lines and someone had neatly written *cancelled* in the middle of them. The following Friday – the day of Lily's murder – he had a lunch appointment. No name. Just *12.30–2.00 lunch out, unavailable*. Presumably that was for Marjorie's benefit. The rest of Friday was clear. Vera flipped back the pages. It seemed the lunch appointment was a regular feature.

'I was thinking of meeting up with him on Friday afternoon,' Vera said, turning the diary a week on, seeing the page was empty. 'There's nothing here. He doesn't have a regular commitment? A lecture?'

'Oh no,' Marjorie said. 'Dr Calvert never lectures on Fridays.' She looked up, eager to help. 'Shall I make you a provisional appointment?'

'No thanks, pet. I'll give him a ring later in the week if we need his assistance.' Vera put the book back on the shelf, gave a little wave to the three women and returned to where Joe was still keeping watch in the corridor.

'Well?'

'He was free both afternoons. The Wednesday before Luke's death and the Friday before Lily's. He cancelled a tutorial at five o'clock on the Wednesday.'

'So he had the opportunity,' Ashworth said. 'Along

with fifty per cent of the population of the north east. But there was no motive. No connection, even. So far as we know he hadn't ever met the victims.'

Vera was going to say she didn't care. She didn't like the man. But she couldn't face a lecture from Ashworth about detachment and objectivity so she let it go.

Outside, it was still hot. There were students lying on the grass or sauntering into town in the shade of the Gothic buildings. They had more than an hour to kill before the next appointment and Vera had a sense of time passing, time wasted. She got on the phone to Kimmerston but there was no news. Holly had arranged to meet Lily's flatmates later in the afternoon and Charlie was trying to prise information out of her bank. They had a news conference set up for the following day and local plods would be at the lighthouse in the afternoon to ask regular walkers if they'd seen anything. The press officer would take the news conference. Vera was pleased. Those occasions always made her feel like a performing bear. She switched off the phone.

'Coffee,' Ashworth said. 'And a bun. I didn't have time for breakfast.' He could sense her frustration, knew food might calm her for a while. Vera thought he treated her as he did his daughter; he was distracting her before she threw a tantrum.

He sat her in the shade of an umbrella, on one of the seats set out on the pavement, while he went inside. The cafe was close to the university and seemed full of idle students. A couple of young women approached her table and she glared at them, hoping to frighten them off. Then she recognized them. They were the lasses from the lecture theatre, the ones Peter Calvert had been performing for.

'Sorry,' she said. 'No problem. You're welcome to join us. Let me move my bag.'

They looked at her uncertainly. As if she were a dangerous dog, she thought. Were the young taught any manners these days? Didn't they know they should be polite to their elders? Then Ashworth turned up, all soft words and smiles, and she realized why she'd come to rely on him.

'Let me buy you a coffee,' he said. 'You're students, right? I remember what that's like. Especially at the end of term when the loan's run out.'

One of them laughed. 'My loan disappeared a week after we started.'

'I'll get them,' Vera said and she went inside to buy the extra drinks, leaving him to tell a story which would pull them in.

When she returned, carrying a tray, they were laughing, easy together. He could have been a student too, though she knew fine well that he'd never stepped foot inside a university.

They introduced themselves. Fancy southern names which she couldn't remember five minutes after they'd told her. Camilla? Amelia? Jemima? It didn't matter. Ashworth would have made a note of them.

'This is Vera,' Ashworth said. 'My aunty.'

They sipped their frothy coffee and looked at him with pity. A duty day out, they thought. A treat for her birthday. Or maybe he was taking her to an outpatient appointment at the RVI. Vera gritted her teeth and let him get on with it.

'So you do botany,' he said. 'A mate of mine did that a few years ago. What's the lecturer called, the famous one? Calvin?'

'Peter Calvert. He likes to think he's famous but it's years since he published anything.'

'You don't like him?'

'He's a creep. Like, he's *really* old, but he still comes on to you.'

'Yeah, and everyone knows he's got a wife and four kids. I mean, you'd think someone in his position would have a bit more dignity. The whole department knows what he's like. But some people play up to it. You know, flirt, in the hope of getting extra marks.'

'Just flirt?' Ashworth asked, keeping his voice light. Like he was cracking a joke.

'God, you'd have to be *really* desperate to go any further. Can you imagine him touching you? God, you'd just throw up.'

'There was that rumour,' the other said. 'You remember, at the beginning of the term. Someone saw him out in town with a much younger woman. It got round that he was having an affair with a student.'

'Oh?' Ashworth said. Not really interested. Just being polite. I've taught you well, Vera thought.

'It was probably just a story,' the student said. 'No one got any details. And we tried hard enough to find out what was going on. I mean, it could have been anyone. His daughter, even. It certainly wasn't one of us. Not a botanist.'

And they floated off to the sound of the bangles clinking on bare brown arms, soft twittering voices.

Chapter Twenty-One

Joe seemed happy to sit there in the sun, nursing his fancy coffee until it was time to meet Clive Stringer, but Vera was impatient and restless. 'I'm going to see if I can track down Annie Slater, the woman who put up Lily's flatmates the night she died. She was one of Lily's tutors. And they lived in the same street. I'll see you at the museum.'

And before he could argue or offer to come with her, she'd gone. She'd had enough of Joe Ashworth acting as her minder. She felt like a naughty kid bunking off school and wondered if her male colleagues ever had the same response. She found Annie in a staff common room, standing by the pigeonholes, reading a sheaf of mail. Lily's flatmates had talked about her children; Vera thought she'd left motherhood until the last minute. She was mid-forties, well preserved. Her hair was very black, cut in a severe bob and her lipstick was very red. She took Vera into a small office and frowned at her. 'I haven't got long. I've a meeting in ten minutes.'

'It shouldn't take long. Just a few questions about Lily Marsh.'

'Yes,' she said. 'Poor Lily. It was a shock. One hears about these things happening, but it's seldom to a person one knows.' Vera thought the shock seemed well hidden. Her attention was still caught by one of the papers in her hand.

'Would she have made a good teacher?'

Annie hesitated for a moment, focused for the first time on the conversation. 'I'd probably describe her as competent but uninspired. And that's more than I could say for most of the students in her group. She worked very hard, prepared the lessons, related OK to the kids, but I didn't think her heart was in it. I couldn't see her still being a classroom teacher in twenty years.'

'Did she ever seem depressed or anxious?'

'I didn't notice anything, but then I probably wouldn't. This is a short course and there's not much contact time. You'd be better talking to her friends about that.'

I would, pet. But I'm not sure she had any.

'How did she end up doing her teaching practice in Hepworth?'

'She requested it. She said she'd read the school's Ofsted report and thought she'd get a lot out of a placement there. I was pleased that she was showing some passion for teaching and tried to wangle it for her.'

'How was she doing?'

'Well. I had a chat with the head teacher a couple of weeks ago. She said Lily was making a real effort to build relationships with the kids. Before that, I'd felt her teaching had been a bit mechanistic. I was pleased.'

'Did you know anything about her private life?'

Annie Slater looked up then, apparently astonished by the idea.

'Of course not. We were never in any sense friends.'

'You lived in the same street, you socialized with her flatmates.'

'That's rather different. There's a family connection to Emma.'

You moved in different circles. Vera had been at the wrong end of snobbishness, could sense it a mile off. Perhaps that's what prompted her to persist. 'You'd not heard any rumours, then, about Lily having a relationship with one of the staff here?'

'I don't listen to university gossip, Inspector.' Which wasn't any sort of answer at all. She turned back to the letter and left Vera to find her own way out.

Vera met up with Joe outside the Hancock Museum. They had to wait until a crocodile of small school children had been shepherded inside by teachers and parents. There was a dinosaur exhibition – reconstructed skeletons, models which moved. The adverts had been all over the city; tyrannosaurus heads leered out from posters on buses, the metro and shop fronts. The children were unusually quiet, overawed by the building, the thought of enormous beasts, *Jurassic Park* come to Newcastle.

Vera and Ashworth followed them in and stood in the lobby, enjoying the coolness of the museum, when Clive Stringer arrived to collect them.

'Great, isn't it?' Ashworth said, watching the children disappear into the gallery. 'Hooking the kids while they're so young.' A couple of years, Vera thought, and he'd be bringing his own lass here.

'I don't know.' Clive blinked uncertainly behind thick round spectacles. 'I don't really deal with the public.'

His kingdom lay behind a wooden door, opened by a swipe card. There was a series of high-ceilinged rooms, rows of dusty cabinets. There seemed to be few other staff around. He led them into a workroom. It reminded Vera of the place in Wansbeck General where John Keating had performed the post-mortem on Lily Marsh. There was a long table in the middle, deep sinks at one end, the smell of chemicals and death. Though everything here was older, wood and enamel instead of stainless steel, and it didn't have the scrubbed, sterile feel. The windows were so dirty that the light seemed filtered through them.

On a board lay the corpse of a black and white bird. Beside it a scalpel, wads of cotton wool, small metal bowls. Another sort of dissection.

'Isn't that a little auk?'

'Yes. First winter. It was blown inland during those gales last November and found dead in a garden in Cramlington. The householder brought it in. I've had it in the freezer since then, but I want to do a cabinet skin.' He looked at Ashworth, saw he didn't understand the term. 'We preserve the skin for research, not display. It's kept here at the museum, a resource for students and scientists.'

Vera's father, Hector, had been an amateur taxidermist. He'd worked on the kitchen table in the old station master's house. He hadn't bothered with cabinet skins, though. He claimed his interest was about science, but Vera had known he was deluding himself even then. He'd prepared mounted birds, always moorland species. Usually the object of his attention was a bird of prey, a trophy for whichever game-keeper had killed it. That was art too in a way, she thought. At the end of his career the activity was illegal, but that had never bothered Hector. If any-thing, it had increased his pleasure and excitement. He'd been an egg collector too. When he died Vera had set fire to the whole collection. A huge bonfire in the garden. She'd drunk his favourite malt whisky and realized she wasn't grieving at all. She'd just felt relief that he'd gone.

'How long have you worked here?' Ashworth was asking Stringer.

'Since I left school.'

'You don't need a degree to do something like this?'

'I started as a trainee.' He paused. 'I was lucky. Peter knew the curator and put in a word for me.'

'That's Dr Calvert?'

'Yes.'

'You've known him for a long time?'

'Yes, he was my trainer when I started ringing. I was fifteen then.'

'Ringing?'

'The study of migration. Birds are caught in nets or traps and small metal rings are put on the legs. If they're caught again or found dead, we can tell where and when they were first ringed.'

'And Mr Parr and Mr Wright are ringers too? That's how you met?'

'We don't ring so much now. I'm the only regular

at the observatory up the coast at Deepden and I don't go so often. The rest have other lives. More exciting lives. But we're still friends. We still go birdwatching together.'

'Sea watching?' Vera asked, joining in the conversation for the first time.

Clive gave something approaching a smile. 'Gary's the passionate sea watcher. The right time of the year he'll spend hours in the watch tower. I say it's because he's so idle. He doesn't mind the waiting. He says it's a form of meditation.'

'It must have been a shock, coming upon the body on Friday night.'

'Of course.'

'But perhaps not so much for you as the others,' she said. 'You work with corpses every day.'

'The corpses of birds and animals. Not young women.'

'No. Not attractive young women.' She paused a beat. 'Do you have a girlfriend, Mr Stringer?'

When she'd first seen him at the mill, she'd thought he looked like an overgrown, prematurely balding schoolboy. Now he blushed, furiously, and the image came back to her. She felt almost sorry for him.

'No,' he said. 'I don't have a girlfriend.'

'Are you gay?'

'No.'

She looked at him, waiting for him to speak.

'I find it difficult to approach women,' he said at last. 'I suppose I'm shy. And I don't socialize much. I live with my mother. She was widowed when I was a baby and now she's not very well. I'm all she has.'

Vera wanted to tell him to get out and get a life while he still had a chance. But it wasn't her place.

'Does Dr Calvert have a girlfriend?'

Clive stared at her, horrified. 'What do you mean?'

'A mistress. A lover.'

'Of course not. He's married to Felicity.'

'This might come as a bit of a shock, pet. But some married men do commit adultery.'

'But not Peter. You've seen them together. They're happy.'

They put on a good show, Vera thought. That's not the same thing at all.

But she smiled at him. 'Aye,' she said. 'Maybe you're right.' She nodded towards Ashworth for him to take over the questions.

'Were you working last Wednesday?'

'Yes, until four-thirty. I start at eight and I'm supposed to finish at four, but it's usually half past before I leave.'

'What did you do then?'

'I went home. I called at the supermarket on the way. We had a meal together. Mother usually goes to bed early. Around nine. After that I stopped up and watched television. I'd videoed a documentary on the rain forest. Mother tends to talk through programmes which don't interest her.'

'You didn't go out?'

'No.'

'You seem to have a very clear memory of what you did that night,' Vera said.

'I do have a good memory. I told you on Friday night, I'm good at detail.'

'Do you drive?'

'I can drive. I mean, I passed my test and I hold a driving licence. But I don't enjoy it. I'm always aware of the potential danger. And I have a conscience about the environment. Greenhouse gases. I decided a couple of years ago to do without a car. Public transport's quite good into the city centre. And I have a bike.'

Vera could tell Clive was uncomfortable. Although the building was gloomy and cool, he'd started to sweat. He fidgeted with the scalpel on the board in front of him. She told herself not to read too much into it. This was probably the longest conversation he'd had with anyone other than his mother for years. When he was with his friends, he'd be a listener not a talker. Now, she kept her voice easy, gossipy. His mother would probably enjoy a good gossip.

'Did Gary tell you about his new woman?'

The change of tone in the question seemed to surprise him and he took a moment to answer. 'He told us all about it.' He paused. 'It wasn't unusual. There's always some new woman in his life. He's mad about all of them. For about a week. None of them stay.'

'He said this one's different,' Vera said.

Clive smiled again. Like smiling was something he did about once every six months. 'That's what he always says. Ever since Emily left he's been looking for someone to replace her.'

'Emily?'

'They were engaged. She dumped him.'

'Did you know Julie, the latest girlfriend?'

'No. He doesn't take me out on his dates.'

'Her son was the lad who was murdered,' Vera said. 'Strangled. Like Lily Marsh.'

'I'm sorry.'

'I don't suppose you know a family called the Sharps?' she said, not really expecting a response.

'Davy Sharp lives in our road. When he's not in prison.'

'You came across the boy, Thomas?'

'I saw him about. My mother looked after him sometimes when he was a baby. She took a shine to him. He was there sometimes when I got home from work. Not recently, of course. Not once he was old enough to fend for himself.'

'She must have been upset when he died.'

'Yes, we went down to the river. She'd seen the flowers on the water on the news and wanted to see. To pay her respects.' He paused. 'There wasn't much to look at when we got there. The tide was on its way out. It had carried the flowers out to sea.'

They sat in silence. Through the open window came the sound of a siren, shouted voices.

'Tell me about these mates of yours,' Vera said at last. 'Gary, Peter and Samuel. They are your mates? Only you don't seem to have much in common. Except the birding.'

'We're close. Like family.'

'With you and Gary as brothers and Samuel and Peter as mummy and daddy?'

'Don't be ridiculous!'

She knew she was pushing him, wanted to see if he ever lost that control. He was very flushed.

'OK, then,' she said. 'So they're not really like family. Tell me why you get on so well together, what it is that's kept you together over all these years.' She was really interested and it showed. She wasn't sure about friendship. She had colleagues, the people she'd grown up with, who lived close to her in the valley. But no one she felt any obligation to, no one she had to put herself out for. She thought it could be a two-edged sword, friendship. You'd end up giving more than you got.

'Partly it's the birding,' he said. 'People outside don't understand. They think you must be geeky, weird. But it's more than that. Although we're very different, we trust each other. I feel supported by them.'

She gave a chuckle. 'Eh, pet, you've lost me now. That sounds like something from a women's magazine.'

He shrugged. 'I wouldn't expect you to understand.'

'What about Friday?' Ashworth asked. He gave the impression that he too was irritated by Vera's comments and questions, that he didn't want to be here all day. 'What did you do before you went to Fox Mill for dinner?'

'I met Peter for lunch.'

'Another birthday celebration?'

'No, nothing like that. We meet most Fridays. Just a pint and a sandwich. When we were more active ringers that's when the weekend would start. I work flexi so I could take the time off, we'd have lunch then Peter would give me a lift up the coast to the observatory. The others would join us later. We don't go out so much now, but still have lunch when we can.'

Vera thought sadly that it was probably the highlight of his week. Lunch with an ageing, self-obsessed man who only wanted an admirer.

'How was Dr Calvert?'

'Fine. Like always. Looking forward to the week-end.'

'What did you talk about?'

'I'm not sure . . .'

'You must remember. You have a brilliant memory. Detail. It's what you do.'

'He's writing a book. We talked about that.'

'And after lunch?'

'I went home to spend a couple of hours with my mother.'

'What about Dr Calvert?' Ashworth said. 'Where did he go?'

'Back to the university. At least, I presume that's where he went. He didn't say, but he walked off in that direction.'

'How did you get to Fox Mill?'

'Gary gave me a lift.'

'He picked you up from home?'

'No, he was running late and coming straight from work at the Sage, so we arranged to meet in town. I got the metro.'

He picked up the scalpel again, turned over the dead bird on the board, ran his finger over the skull. 'Really, I should be getting on with this. I don't understand the need for all these questions. I was there when a body was found. That was all. I'd never met either of the victims.'

Vera looked over at Ashworth to see if he had anything else to say. He shook his head. 'We'll leave it at that, then,' she said. 'For the time being.'

'I'll show you out.' Clive dragged his attention away from the little auk, walked ahead of them down the corridors, through the dust caught in shafts of sunlight from the long windows. He opened the door which separated the staff territory from the public domain, hesitated as if reluctant to go further. Vera stopped too and faced him.

'Would you tell us if you suspected one of your friends of committing these murders?'

He answered immediately. 'Of course not. I trust them. I know that if they've done something as appalling as commit murder, they must have a good reason.'

He turned and walked away, leaving Vera and Joe staring after him.

Chapter Twenty-Two

Felicity wandered back from the garden. She was holding a colander of beans for supper, too many she realized. There would be only the two of them this evening; James had arranged to be out with a friend. In the kitchen she had a moment of unease as she imagined herself and Peter, sitting at opposite ends of the table, eating dinner. She wasn't sure what they'd say to each other. She imagined Lily Marsh there too. A beautiful ghost, coming between them.

It was ridiculous the effect the death of a stranger was having on her. She told herself not to be hysterical. But this life she'd spent years creating – the house, the garden, the contented family – suddenly seemed very fragile. She had a picture of Vera Stanhope shattering it with her loud, intrusive voice, her big feet, the heavy hands slammed against the table. With her questions, Vera would wreck it all.

She glanced at the clock on the kitchen wall. There were pictures of birds instead of numbers and their calls marked the hours. It was a joke present from Clive to Peter for one of his birthdays. She hated it but Peter had insisted on putting it up. It would soon be two o'clock. There were at least four hours before Peter would be home. She ran upstairs, changed from trousers into a skirt, put on lipstick and a splash of perfume. As the wren finished calling she snatched up the car keys from the hall table and almost ran outside.

She had never visited Samuel at work. She wasn't even sure where he would be. Certainly, she thought, he would disapprove of this unplanned meeting. He kept his life in separate boxes. But she couldn't stay at home fretting. She had never made demands before. He would understand that the pressure was intolerable.

She drove along the straight, narrow roads, impatient when she had to slow down for a tractor. It was an old car, without air conditioning, and she had the windows open. The sun shone hot on her arm and shoulder. In the town she slid into a parking space in the street next to the library. Now she sat for a moment thinking again that this trip had been a terrible mistake. Samuel was a clever man. If he'd thought it sensible for them to meet, to discuss strategies, he would have suggested it. He would consider this a rash, foolish gesture. In the end her desire to see him made her give up on reason. She shut the windows and got out of the car. She was a member of the library after all. She had every right to be there.

Inside the building it was cooler. A couple of students and an elderly man were hunched over their public-access computers. Behind the desk was a thin, rather untidy young woman in crumpled linen trousers and a white cotton blouse. She caught Felicity's eye and smiled at her. She looked familiar. Felicity thought vaguely that she might be the daughter of one of her book group friends.

The book group had brought her and Samuel
together. She loved the company of the group, the
excitement of trying a book new to her, and when she
had been a member for a year, she had persuaded him
along to give them a talk. A real published author. The
group had read his most recent anthology beforehand
and hadn't known quite what to make of it. The stories were so depressing, they said. Well constructed but
twisted and rather horrible. One woman said they
gave her nightmares. Generally they preferred happy
endings. When he visited, though, they were more
positive. They sat him in the big armchair in front of
the fire. They were meeting for this session in the
home of a large, capable woman who worked as a
physiotherapist. Her husband was a surgeon and the
room was quite grand. Green walls covered with
paintings, large, old furniture. It was February, cold,
and the curtains were drawn against the chill weather
outside. The audience was wholly female. They drank
white wine from tall glasses. Samuel had charmed
them, speaking as if their opinions were important to
him. He talked about the structure of the stories.
These days people were obsessed about character, he
said. Character was important, that was a given, but
anyone could write faithfully about people like themselves, or people they knew. He was more interested
in ideas. His themes were reflected in the construc-
tion of his plots. He wasn't so interested in portraying
reality, but in creating a world where the most
unlikely events were possible.

'It's the only way one has to play God,' he said.

One woman asked if that made him more like a
poet than a novelist. He smiled, delighted, and said

perhaps it did. Felicity had thought it all went way above her head. She worried about what she might say to him when they were alone.

'But wouldn't you make more money writing real, long books?' This came from a farmer, who read voraciously but understood nothing of literary snobbery. She never bothered with reviews or award lists. There was a moment of silence. The other women were afraid that he'd been offended. But it seemed that question had pleased him too.

'If I wrote a novel I'd get caught out,' he said. 'I'm not that good an author. I can't keep going for more than five thousand words.' He turned towards Felicity, giving her a look of complicity. The light from the fire caught his face. The women in the room laughed. She could tell that they all admired him.

Felicity had given him a lift to the book group and it had been arranged that she would take him home. In the car he suggested they go for a drink and she agreed. It was the least she could do. Her standing in the book group had changed because she'd introduced him to them. The pub was crowded and noisy, not the sort of place either of them would usually have chosen. Perhaps they landed there because it was so anonymous. They had a small table to themselves, crushed into a corner.

The announcement came out of the blue. He took her hands in both of his and said he thought he loved her. At first she couldn't believe he was serious. It was a joke. He was a great one for games. Nothing could come of it, he said. He was Peter's friend. Then she saw he was deadly serious and she was very flattered, moved. How noble and honourable he was! In the pub car park, which looked out over bare, open hillside, she reached up and kissed him. Droplets of mist clung to his hair and his jacket.

Later, back at his house, she asked, 'Aren't you going to invite me in for coffee?' She knew exactly what she was doing, had already considered which underwear she was wearing, remembered that she had shaved her legs that morning. He had hesitated for longer than she expected. Perhaps his friendship to Peter was so strong he would refuse. But at last he nodded, held open the door for her, took her hand once they were inside. That had been five years ago. They had been lovers ever since. Very discreet. There were no phone calls which couldn't have been overheard, no emails which might not have been read. They met every few weeks, usually in his neat little house in Morpeth. This was quite different from the public friendship – the trips to the theatre or the ballet. Nothing intimate ever took place on those outings.

Even after all this time, she didn't consider the relationship as an affair. There was nothing romantic about it – no flowers or presents or candlelit dinners. She knew Samuel felt a continual guilt. He never talked about love after that first meeting. And she had never once considered leaving Peter. He needed her. She saw the delight and excitement Samuel gave her as a wage, her dues for living such a boring and unadventurous married life, for keeping the Calvert show on the road. She knew it wasn't the way women usually looked at things, but couldn't see why they couldn't all maintain a civilized friendship. At least, she had thought that until Vera came blundering in with her questions.

Now Felicity wandered around the library shelves, as if she was having difficulty choosing a good read. She couldn't see Samuel, but that didn't mean he wasn't working here. He was a manager, would have an office somewhere behind the door which said STAFF ONLY. He would be there, or in a meeting with his staff, or out of the region altogether on a trip to one of the big library suppliers to select books. She encouraged him to talk about his work in the little house in Morpeth when they drank tea together before they separated. She was always fascinated by other people's working lives, and when she lay in her afternoon baths she imagined him sitting at his big desk, or chairing a meeting in his precise and authoritative way. It excited her that none of his staff could possibly guess what he did on his days off.

She was preparing to ask at the desk if he was in the building when he appeared through the STAFF ONLY door. He was carrying a briefcase and seemed to be on his way out. He was wearing an open-necked shirt and a pale linen jacket, a concession, she supposed, to the weather. Usually when they met up, if he'd come straight from work, he wore a tie. He dressed very well and cared what he looked like. At first he didn't see her. He was smiling at the young girl behind the counter. Felicity felt a stab of physical discomfort which she realized was jealousy. She wondered if he took other women to his house on his free afternoons.

Then he turned and saw her. He gave no indication that they knew each other. He said to the young woman, 'I'll be in Berwick for the rest of the afternoon. But if anyone phones, tell them to call back tomorrow. This is an important meeting. I don't want interruptions.'

Felicity caught up with him outside. He was walking down the pavement towards his car. If she hadn't hurried after him, perhaps he would have driven off without giving her the chance to talk to him.

'I'm sorry, Samuel. I had to speak to you.'

He must have heard her footsteps following, but he affected surprise.

'I really do have a meeting in Berwick.' He frowned, seemed more nervous than displeased.

'Just ten minutes.' Now that she was here, she wasn't sure what she wanted from him. Reassurance, she supposed, that everything would continue as normal.

He agreed to meet her in the Little Chef on the A1 and was already there when she arrived, apparently engrossed in the menu. Even walking towards him she sensed he was frightened, that he needed reassuring more than she did. The place was almost empty. The windows were all open and the traffic noise came in from outside. They ordered tea from a sweaty youth, stared at each other.

'You know something,' she said suddenly. 'Something about the girl. Lily. Had you met her?'

'No. Nothing like that.' But he was blustering, not at all his usual controlled self. This wasn't like one of his stories. He couldn't make the plot work out.

'The boy, then. Luke Armstrong. You'd heard about him?'

'I think Gary was going out with his mother. That woman he was talking about. She was called Armstrong. I'm sure she had a son. It's a link.'

'I told that detective Gary was seeing someone called Julie. He wouldn't kill anyone!'

'Of course not. But they don't believe in coincidences.'

It seemed a tenuous connection to her. A woman called Armstrong who had a son. How many Armstrongs were there in the phone book? Samuel must know more than he was letting on.

The waiter came back with their tea. As he lowered it to the table, liquid slopped onto the tray. He paused, expecting a reaction from them, anger, complaint, but they sat in silence until he left them again.

'I was worried that detective would find out about us,' Felicity said.

'How could she?' But she saw that the idea had occurred to him too. Perhaps that was why he seemed so uneasy, so unlike his usual urbane and confident self.

'I wondered if perhaps we should tell her, in confidence,' she said. 'That way she would know it could have no bearing on the girl's murder.'

'Of course it has no bearing!' His voice was impatient. She imagined he might speak in the same tone to a foolish library assistant. She felt tears come to her eyes.

'We know that.' She tried to sound reasonable. 'But Lily Marsh came to Fox Mill the day before she was murdered. You can imagine the police jumping to conclusions, building up a scenario. What if we were together that afternoon and she saw us? That might give us a motive for killing her.'

She waited, expecting another angry response, but he smiled. 'You should write fiction,' he said. 'A creative imagination like that. We weren't together, were we? Not in the afternoon. I was at work all day on Wednesday. Book selection, then Library Management Team. I'd be able to prove it. We only met up in the evening to go to the theatre. Besides, James was there with you when the girl was at your house.'

'Yes,' she said. 'He was.'

Samuel looked around the room. There were no other customers now. The staff were at the counter, engrossed in conversation. He reached across the table and took her hand. 'How can anyone know?' he said. 'We've been so careful. I'd hate it to come out. It would seem so squalid. How could people understand?' He pulled away from her and leaned back in his chair. His voice was still very low and she had a struggle to make out the words. 'I couldn't bear it if Peter found out. I'd die.'

Chapter Twenty-Three

When they'd finished with Clive Stringer, Vera took Joe home. She could tell he was fretting about his pregnant wife and his daughter. But she couldn't settle. She called into the police headquarters at Kimmerston and raged around the building, demanding action and answers. Holly was out, but Charlie was there, hunched over his desk, staring at the computer screen. His waste bin was overflowing – empty Coke cans, burger cartons, greasy chip paper. She remembered hearing that his wife had recently left him for a younger man. Like Vera, he probably didn't have much to go home to.

'Nothing unusual about Lily Marsh's bank account,' he said. 'She had a bit more money this year because they get a grant for doing the post-graduate teaching course, but she still spent pretty much up to her student overdraft limit. No mysterious payments to suggest a rich boyfriend. She was paid direct into her account by the dress shop, but it wasn't a fortune. Better than the minimum wage, but not by much.' He paused. 'Something a bit odd, though. I can't tell how she paid her rent. Not by cheque and it wasn't covered by standing order. No regular withdrawals of cash either.'

'Maybe she had a different account,' Vera said. 'Building society. Internet account. Perhaps there's a statement in that material we recovered from her flat. Get onto it, Charlie. She was living beyond her means. She should have been massively in debt. But she wasn't. Something doesn't add up.' And she stamped away without giving him the chance to complain.

She set off for home then, but she knew she'd only start drinking as soon as she got in. She was in that sort of mood. A large whisky before she scratched together a meal and downhill from there. Passing the Morpeth turn-off she decided to call on Samuel Parr. She'd have seen them all, then. The whole group. The four birdwatchers who claimed they had nothing to do with the murders except being present when the body was found, but who seemed tangled up with the case all the same. Gary, who had fallen for Luke Armstrong's mother. Clive, who, as a kid, had known Luke Armstrong's best friend. And Peter Calvert, who worked at the university where Lily Marsh had been a student. In the north east there were a lot of small communities, all interlinked. There were always going to be connections. Perhaps it was of no significance, but she couldn't ignore it. And where did Samuel Parr fit in?

He looked as if he had not long arrived home. When she rang the bell of the small stone house, he answered immediately. He'd been standing in the hall. Perhaps he'd just shut the door behind him. There was a briefcase at the foot of the stairs. He wore a linen jacket, slightly crumpled.

'Is this convenient?' she asked. Samuel Parr was a minor local celebrity. She'd looked him up. His stories had been read on Radio 4. He'd got an OBE in the people's honours for service to libraries. She'd best treat him with a bit of respect. At first, at least.

'Yes, of course, Inspector. Come in. It'll be about that business on Friday night. Dreadful.' He took off his jacket and hung it on the banister. 'I'm late home. A meeting in Berwick. Awful traffic on the A1.' He was tall, bony and his hair was very short.

She remembered hearing one of his stories. She never bothered much with television, but the radio was on all the time at home. It had been a domestic tale. A man and a woman in a loveless marriage. A stranger in town who had become a lover. The ending had been horrific and quite unexpected. The couple had collaborated in killing the lover. They needed the stability and routine of their marriage more than the excitement of love or of loss. Vera tried to remember what they had done to the body. She knew it had been disturbing. Not explicit in the description of the violence, but so chilling, that it had haunted her for days. So chilling perhaps that she'd forced it out of her mind and the details wouldn't return. Now, looking at this quiet, middle-aged man, she found it hard to believe he had dreamed up the tale. She thought she should get the anthology out of the library. See how the story had ended.

'I always indulge in a glass of wine at this time of the evening. Can I tempt you?'

She thought he was playing up to the stereotype of the librarian. Surely he didn't talk like that while he was in the watch tower and the skuas were streaming past in a northerly gale. Then he'd shout and swear like the rest of them.

'Thank you,' she said.

'I only have red, I'm afraid. I live alone, so I just buy to suit myself.'

'You never married, Mr Parr?'

'I'm a widower.' There was a pause. 'Claire, my wife, committed suicide.'

'I'm sorry.' She'd always thought suicide the most selfish act.

'She'd suffered from depression since before I knew her. I didn't understand how desperate she was. Of course I'll always blame myself.'

He'd led her into a long narrow room, which covered the width of the house. He opened a window and let in the song of a blackbird, the smell of cut grass. He turned his back on her to stand at a Victorian sideboard and open the wine. She couldn't make out if he was as calm as he seemed. She wanted to ask how his wife had killed herself. Had she drowned? It wasn't a question to ask over a glass of Australian Shiraz, and anyway she'd be able to find out. There'd be a coroner's report. And where had she been treated for depression? On the wall, there was a photograph of a woman, her head thrown back, laughing. Claire? It seemed to be the only record of the woman in the room.

He turned now and held out a large glass of wine to her. She nodded at the picture. 'She was very pretty.' He didn't answer.

She took the wine, sat on a scarred leather Chesterfield, waited for him to speak. He told stories for a living. Let him go first.

'It was a terrible shock, finding the young woman's body,' he said. 'Hearing James scream, my first response was irritation. I never felt any desire to have children, even when Claire was alive. I know we should encourage them into the library, but really my attempts are half-hearted. They're so noisy. Such a nuisance. Then when we saw that young woman, her hair floating to the surface, her dress . . . I was reminded of a Pre-Raphaelite painting. The muted colours in the shadow. Perhaps it was because we were looking down at her, seeing it at a distance.'

'It looked staged,' Vera said. 'Posed, like a model for an artist?'

'Yes.' He looked up, surprised that she'd understood him so easily. 'It wasn't just that someone wanted her dead, it was that a point was being made.'

'You didn't recognize her?'

'No.'

'And now, having had time to consider, you're sure you'd never met her?'

'She didn't look like a real woman,' he said. 'I can't be certain I'd know. But the name means nothing to me.'

'We found a Northumberland Libraries ticket in the belongings in her flat.'

'I don't know all our borrowers, Inspector.'

'Why would she join if she lived in Newcastle?'

'If she worked in Hepworth, she might find our branch there more convenient than the city library. It opens only a few hours a week, but it's very close to the school. Perhaps she just wanted to access her emails.'

'Would you be able to tell us what she borrowed recently?'

'Is it important?'

'Probably not,' Vera said. 'But I'd be interested to know. Curiosity . . .' She grinned at him. 'Probably something writers and detectives have in common.'

'I couldn't tell you now, even if I went into work. Our system will be shut down for the day. I could look tomorrow and let you know if there any books outstanding on her ticket. I can't do more than that.'

'Do you think you can tell what people are like from what they read?'

He laughed. 'Absolutely not. Many of our readers are gentle old ladies, who adore the most gruesome American thrillers.'

Vera found that she was enjoying herself. It was the wine, but he was good company. Easy. She'd been expecting someone restrained and dull, but now he seemed more relaxed too.

'What got you into birding?'

'A good teacher,' Samuel said. 'He took us on field trips. I grew up in a suburb of the city and it was a revelation to visit the hills. I suppose I have a romantic response to natural history rather than a scientific one. I enjoy beautiful things.'

'Dr Calvert takes the scientific approach?'

'Yes. We went to the same school. He's a few years older than me, but we met in the Natural History Society. Separated for university, but we've been friends ever since. He was into science; I loved reading.'

'Why did he do botany? Why not zoology?'

'He says he prefers to have birdwatching as a pleasure, not a chore.'

'Did you know that Gary had a new girlfriend?'

The sudden switch in conversation didn't seem

to throw him. 'I knew he'd fallen for someone.' He paused. 'It couldn't have been the murdered girl, you know. That was the sort of woman he'd usually have gone for. But his latest conquest was different, I think. Someone older, someone he'd gone to school with. We laughed at him, asked if he was growing up at last. He's in his thirties, but he's always played the part of wild adolescent in our group.'

'The new woman in his life is called Julie Armstrong. She's the mother of a lad who was strangled in Seaton the Wednesday before Lily Marsh died.' She looked up. 'Hadn't you heard? You're such close friends, I'd have thought one of them would have told you. The others know.'

'They might have tried to phone,' he said. 'I've been in meetings all day and I've only just got in.'

'If Gary is the wild adolescent, what part does Clive play?' She realized she'd finished her wine and put her glass on the table. She wondered if he'd offer her another, if she could accept it and still be under the limit.

Samuel thought for a moment. 'Clive's an obsessive,' he said. 'A brilliant birder. The best of us by far. He reads field guides like I read fiction, but he remembers every word. He's not wonderful company in the pub. He doesn't make us laugh. Not like Gary. Not like Peter even, if he's on form. But he finds the birds for us. He reminds us what brought us together in the first place.'

'Where were you on Friday before you arrived at Fox Mill for the birthday party?'

He looked at her over his glass. 'Am I a suspect,

Inspector?' He wasn't angry. He seemed to find the idea amusing.

'I need to rule out anyone involved with the victim, even peripherally.'

'I wasn't. Not while she was alive.' He set down the glass. 'I'm sorry, Inspector, I shouldn't take this lightly. You're entitled to ask your questions. I was working on Friday afternoon in the library in Morpeth. I took some time back and left early. At about four o'clock. Then I came home. I was re-drafting a story. I wanted it finished to take with me that evening.'

'A present for Dr Calvert? Something you'd written specially for his birthday?'

'Nothing like that. Peter never reads fiction. Felicity enjoys my work. And I value her opinion. I wanted her to look at it before I sent it off to my agent.'

Vera wanted to ask what the story was about, but could see that it probably wasn't relevant. Perhaps she just wanted to prolong the interview so she wouldn't have to return to an empty house.

'Can anyone confirm that you were here? Any phone calls or visitors?'

'I'm afraid not. And I never answer the phone when I'm writing.'

'Perhaps a neighbour saw you leave for the party?'

'You can check, Inspector, but I'd be surprised. This is a neighbourhood where people mind their own business.' He smiled. 'Some more wine, Inspector? Just half a glass as I know you're driving.'

She was tempted, but she shook her head and stood up. She wondered why he was being so pleasant to her. Men seldom bothered to make an effort with her and Samuel wasn't flirting exactly, but he wanted her to like him. Was that habit? He worked with eccentric middle-aged women. Perhaps he'd developed it as a management style. Or did he have some other reason for wanting her onside?

He walked with her to the door, shook her hand, and stood in the small front garden while she opened her car door. Driving away she felt she'd been in a small way seduced by him. He'd controlled the conversation. Things had gone just as he'd wanted.

Chapter Twenty-Four

Gary had been thinking all day about going to see Julie. The idea had got into his head and he couldn't get shot of it. It was a bit like those annoying bits of music that run in a loop in your brain. That Comic Relief song a few years ago, for instance. You try to replace it with something better, but the effort just makes it worse and the crap song gets louder and louder, so you can hardly think straight.

He'd been doing a technical rehearsal at the Sage, in the small space. He was working from the sound desk in the body of the hall. The artist was a poet, who spoke and sometimes sang with a band behind her. Usually when he was working, he couldn't consider anything but getting the sound spot on. The Sage was tremendous for large orchestras, but something small and intimate like this, it was tricky to get the balance right. The band was good, bluesy and moody, and he wanted to do them justice. Though poetry wasn't at all his thing he caught himself listening to the lyrics. Perhaps it was because the artist reminded him of Julie. She didn't look like Julie – she was black, for one thing, and younger – but there was a warmth about her and she was big and she laughed a lot. So all day he'd been wondering about Julie and how he could get in contact with her, and whether that would be a good idea or just gross.

He had a few hours free between the rehearsal and the performance. It would be a late-night gig, attracting people mellow from the bar and the arty crowd who didn't have to get up in the morning. He walked down the steps towards the river, the heat hitting him after the air-conditioned building. You'd never think Gateshead could get this hot, he thought. Gateshead should be a biting east wind and sleet. At the top of the bank the Ferris wheel turned slowly. Looking back, the Sage was lit up, so you could see the two halls inside the outer skin of glass. He thought they looked like two great ships. The large hall was like a liner, with rows of decking, number two like a snub-nosed tug. He'd been intending to wander across the footbridge and into town to get some food, but suddenly changed his mind.

He ran back up the steps to the car park and then he was in his van, the engine running, driving north. He wanted to see her house. It didn't mean he'd come to a decision about seeing *her*. He could drive down the road, turn round and come straight back. But that would be better than nothing.

Then he remembered them all in the pub after the Bird Club meeting, him talking about Julie and Peter mocking him. *My God, how romantic the young are these days. All moonlight and flowers.* And Gary, driving down the Heaton rat runs, avoiding the worst of the town traffic, knew that was what Julie had come back to on the night her son had died. Moonlight and flowers. That was what the inspector had meant when she said Luke's murder had been similar to Lily's. It had been posed in the same way.

He knew where Julie's house was. He'd looked up her address in the phone book. It was only a quarter of a mile from where she'd lived as a kid. He'd grown up in the village too, though the other end, on the new private estate, which wasn't new any more. It felt strange coming back. He'd come down the main road from Whitley every day on the bus when he was in high school. Memories came flooding into his head, at last pushing out his concern for what Julie would make of his turning up on the doorstep. Loud lads shouting on the top deck, throwing bags around. Him easing his arm round Lindsay Waugh's shoulders, nibbling her ear lobe, while she blushed bright scarlet and everyone cheered. And sitting next to Clive, on their way to a green-winged teal on the River Blyth, pretending not to know him, because he was such a nerd and a geek, and what would Lindsay and the others say if they'd known Gary was a birder too.

Without realizing it, he was in the village and turning into Julie's street. It was six o'clock and the kids were out playing. A couple of mothers sat on the doorsteps watching them. Since Luke's death he supposed this was how it would be. He was aware of their staring. A stranger in the street. If they hadn't been there he would probably have gone to the end of the road, sat in the car, lost his bottle, and driven away. But they made him defiant. And cautious. He was Julie's friend. What was wrong with paying his respects? Besides, one of them would probably have made a note of his registration number by now. If he drove straight off they'd be on to the police reporting a suspicious character, claiming they'd frightened him away.

So he parked up right outside the house, and without looking at the staring women he walked up the path and knocked on the door. Standing there, he thought he should have brought something with him. A gift. But what? Not flowers. How insensitive would that be! Wine, perhaps; but then that would imply that he was gatecrashing a party. He stood, his hands slid into the front pockets of his jeans, because he didn't know what else to do with them. Sometimes, after too much Stella and a vindaloo, he had this nightmare. He was standing on the stage at the City Hall in front of a full house, fiddling with a mic, the sound all wrong. Stark naked. That was how he felt now.

The door opened. It was a young girl in school uniform. Sort of uniform. White shirt, short black skirt. No tie. He wondered if he'd got the wrong house, then remembered that Julie had another child, a daughter. He scrabbled in his mind for a name. Laura. But before he had a chance to call her by it, a middle-aged woman scurried out from the back. She had a pair of oven gloves dangling from one hand and the air of an ineffective bouncer. 'Laura, pet, I told you to let *me* open the door.' The girl paused for a moment, staring at him, then she shrugged and disappeared upstairs.

The older woman turned to Gary, more aggressive now. 'Who are you? We're not talking to reporters. The police'll be back in a minute.'

'I'm not a reporter. I'm a friend of Julie's.'

The woman stared at him. She had very small eyes, fierce.

'Julie's not up to seeing anyone.'

He was about to give up, almost relieved. He could leave a message. That way at least Julie would know he was thinking about her. Then there was a voice, hardly recognizable. 'Mam. Let him in. I want to see him.'

The woman paused for a moment then stepped aside. Once he'd walked past her into the house, she shut the door loudly on the prying neighbours.

He went through into the living room, noticed in passing how untidy it was, wondered if it was always like that. Considered briefly if he'd be able to live in such mess. It was certainly nothing like Fox Mill, which had always been his ideal home. The windows were covered by thin white blinds which kept out the worst of the sun and the prying eyes. They made the room shadowy. It was hard to make out detail. Then he saw Julie, curled on the sofa. He sat beside her, took her hand. The woman stood in the doorway, anxious and protective.

'I was just getting dinner,' she said. She was almost growling, the words coming from the back of her throat.

'It's all right, Mam. He's a friend.'

'I'll be in the kitchen.' That was directed to Gary. A warning and a threat. She glowered at him and left the room.

'Sorry about Mam,' Julie said.

'Don't worry. I'd be just the same if I was here looking after you.'

She gave a brief smile. He stroked the back of her hand.

'I'm so pathetic,' she said. 'I can't do anything. I just sit here all day.'

'You couldn't be pathetic. Never.'

'I should be strong for Laura.'

He thought he could hear the echo of her mother's words in the phrase. He didn't know what to say. He wasn't sure what he thought of Laura, skinny and long legged. There was something about her which reminded him of Emily and he found that disconcerting. Behind the blinds the window was open. The bairns in the street were playing a skipping game, chanting. He hadn't heard anything like it recently. It was years since he'd seen girls skip. Perhaps one of the guardian mothers had taught it to them, dredging the rhyme out of her memory. It took him back to Seaton primary school, running round the playground with Julie Richardson, playing kiss chase on the green when nobody was looking. Perhaps she was having the same thoughts, because she joined in with the words.

'. . . *I never should, play with the gypsies in the wood.*'

She stopped suddenly. Outside, the rhyme continued without her.

If I did, she would say . . .

'I feel so stupid,' he said. 'Just sitting here. Nothing to say. Helpless.'

She squeezed his hand. 'No,' she said. 'You're helping. Honestly.'

'I wasn't sure whether I should come.'

Then she did something unexpected. She pulled him down to her and kissed him. A real deep kiss, pushing her tongue into his mouth, against his teeth, down his throat. He held her tight against him, felt her breasts soft against his chest, the beginnings of desire. Despite himself. Knowing that nothing could happen. Not with her daughter and mother in the house. Not while she was so screwed up. But singing inside, because in the end it would work out. All those dreams he'd had about her since meeting up with her again. Luke wouldn't get in the way of that.

He pushed her gently away from him, stroked her cheek, bent and kissed her hair at the parting, where he could see the darker roots. She was crying.

'Oh God,' she said. 'I'm sorry.'

He knew he shouldn't feel like this. He should be sad because she was sad. 'Nothing to be sorry about.' He kept his voice serious, low. Low voices were sexy, weren't they? 'Do you want to talk about Luke? I mean, I never met him, but if you want someone to talk to . . .' Behind her back he twisted his wrist so he could see his watch. He had to be back at the Sage for eight-thirty.

'No,' she said. 'I've done nothing but talk about Luke for days. To the police, Mam, my mates. I wanted to forget about him. Just for a minute. I wanted to see if I could.'

'Could you?'

'Not really.' She smiled. Not quite the old Julie smile. 'But I enjoyed trying.'

There was a noise at the door. He was expecting her mother again but it was Laura. She stood just inside the room, staring at them. Gary moved along the sofa so there was some distance between them.

'Laura went to school today,' Julie said, in a horrible, bright voice. 'I thought that was dead brave. How was it, pet?'

'All right. The teachers were nice. There was an assembly about it. About Luke and that. They said I didn't have to go.'

'Did you?'

'Nah. But I waited outside and I could hear what they were saying. It was all crap. I mean, it wasn't like they were talking about Luke at all. You wouldn't have known it was him they were talking about.'

'Nice, though, for them to remember him, to pay their respects.'

Laura looked as if she was about to say something rude and dismissive, but she kept her mouth shut.

'This is Gary,' Julie said. 'He's an old friend. We were in the primary together.'

It was as if Laura hadn't heard. 'Nan says tea's nearly ready.'

Gary stood up. 'I should get off.'

'Why don't you stay?' Julie said. 'Have something to eat with us?'

But he could tell she was back in coma mode. She was just going through the motions.

'I'm working tonight,' he said. 'A gig at the Sage.'

He started towards the door. He wondered if she'd rouse herself from the couch to see him out, but she seemed lost in thought again. It was Laura who opened the door to let him out. The kids stopped their game to stare and the women on the steps looked up from their magazines. He expected the girl to be intimidated by the attention. He found it difficult to handle himself. He wanted to shout at them: *What do you think you're looking at?* He thought Laura would shut the door on him immediately and hurry inside. But she didn't. She was still standing there while he got into the van and drove away.

Chapter Twenty-Five

Tuesday morning. Vera had called the team together for an early meeting. Charlie looked as if he'd slept at his desk; certainly he hadn't shaved. Joe had Ready Brek down the front of his shirt. Only Holly seemed awake and alive. Looking at her, so fit and bonny, Vera felt a horrible, destructive envy. Even when she was young, she'd never looked like that. When she arrived they were all sitting round a table. Joe was talking about Clive Stringer.

'What about him?' she said, coming in at the tail end of the conversation.

'If we're looking for a nutter, he's pretty weird.'

Is he? Vera thought. She'd grown up with several odd young men like that. Loners, obsessives. Acolytes of her father.

'I mean, he spends all day with his hand up a dead bird's bum, no friends apart from the group at Fox Mill, no girlfriend.'

Vera wondered if Joe would describe her as a nutter. She didn't have many friends either.

'What's his motive?' she asked.

'I don't know. Maybe he came on to Lily and she rejected him?'

'We'd need some proof that they met. And that doesn't explain Luke.'

'Envy, then? They were attractive and young. Perhaps that was enough for him.'

'There's no evidence,' she said. 'Nothing. And he doesn't have transport.'

'He has a driving licence. Nothing to stop him borrowing a car.'

'Who from?' Vera demanded. 'You said yourself he has no friends.'

'He could steal one, hire one.'

'Aye,' she conceded. 'He could. Check the car-hire places. They'd remember him.'

'We should talk to his mother too.'

'Of course,' she said, only just keeping her temper. 'But we'll keep an open mind.'

Joe shut up then and she had the sense that he was sulking. He thought she'd worked with him long enough to realize he'd not need telling that. Quite often he was the one who had to keep her on track.

'All right,' she said. 'What else have we got?' Implying, give me something useful. Not speculation or prejudice. She kept her voice calm. This wasn't a time for panic, though they should have a suspect by now. As they sat she was aware again of time passing, the possibility that these were random killings with no understandable motive, that they'd find another beautiful young person drowned and dressed in flowers.

Charlie shifted in his chair, cleared his throat in a way that reminded Vera of winos in doorways about to spit. It made her want to gag.

'I've found out where Lily's rent came from.'

'Where?'

'A building society account in her own name. The North of England. There was a passbook in the stuff the search team found in her room. She got a cheque made out from that once a month.'

'What went into it? Her wages from the dress shop?'

'Nah, I told you. They were paid direct into her current account.' He leaned back in his chair. Vera wanted to scream at him to get on with it. 'She paid in five hundred pounds every six weeks or so.' He paused again. 'Cash.'

'Where would she get that sort of money?'

He shrugged. 'Maybe she did a bit of high-class soliciting on the side. Some students do. So I understand.'

Another occasion there might have been sniggers. *How would you know about that, Charlie?* But they must have realized Vera wouldn't appreciate the humour.

Vera thought of the clothes in Lily's wardrobe, the expensive lingerie, the clothes that had the air of fancy dress. 'I suppose it's possible. Take a photo to some of the likely hotels in town. See if anyone recognizes her.'

Holly raised her forearm from the table. A polite student with a point to make.

'Yes?' Vera hoped her impatience didn't show.

'Or she could have a rich lover . . .'

'Any evidence of that?'

'I spoke to her flatmates.'

'They told me there *was* no one.' Vera could tell she sounded defensive, couldn't stop herself. 'At least, if there was, they knew nothing about him.'

'They were embarrassed to admit they listened in to one of Lily's phone calls. There's an extension in the kitchen. It only happened once. They were just desperate to know what was going on. I knew they would be; I mean, it's only natural, isn't it? I pushed them on it a bit. Lily was ringing out. They picked up the kitchen phone and listened in.'

'And?'

'No details,' Holly said. 'Nothing useful, like a name. Not even proof that she was having an affair with him. They think she must have suspected they were listening because she ended the call very quickly.'

'What *did* they get?'

'An older man. Educated, well spoken. An arrangement to meet for dinner.'

'That could have been anything. A relative. Colleague. Boss from the shop.'

'It doesn't sound like a relative,' Joe said. 'If there'd been anyone like that in the family you'd have thought Phyllis would have mentioned him. Bragged, like.'

'I don't suppose they did anything useful,' Vera said. 'Like follow her and see what he looked like.'

Holly grinned. 'Nah. They were tempted to book a table in the same restaurant, but they're well-brought-up lasses. Thought it wouldn't be right to spy on her.'

'I hate well-brought-up lasses,' Vera said.

'Luckily the women she worked with in the dress shop weren't so picky.'

Vera smiled slowly. She thought perhaps she could take to Holly after all. 'What did you get from them?'

'Nothing exciting,' Holly admitted. 'I mean, nothing really useful. But confirmation that the meetings with the older man weren't about a family connection or to do with work. She did talk a bit more freely with the girls in the shop. I think she felt more easy with them. She liked the idea of sharing the posh Jesmond flat with the classy southerners, but they didn't have much in common.'

'Tell me.'

Holly pulled out a small notebook, covered with her open schoolgirl writing. A swat wanting to impress.

'About six months ago she came into work wearing a new ring. Opal and silver. Antique. She said it was a present. He'd bought it when they were out for the day in York. It was the first time they'd spent the night together—'

Vera interrupted. 'Did they get the name of the hotel?'

'No. But one of them could remember what Lily had said about it. "That's the great thing about going out with someone a bit older. They know how to do things properly." They asked her how old he was, but she wouldn't say. "You wouldn't understand." One of them asked if he was old enough to be her father. She hadn't answered but she'd laughed so they guessed he probably was.'

'They never saw him?'

'No. Like I said, nothing really useful.'

'Oh believe me, pet. There's plenty useful here. Dig out the ring. Charlie, is it in the stuff the search team brought in?'

'I don't think so.'

'Check again. I don't remember seeing anything like that in the flat, but it must have been there. Then someone can have a fun day out in York, visiting the antique shops and the jewellers. Unless her mysterious lover paid for it by cash, we've a reasonable chance of tracking him down. And let's have someone on the phone to all the decent hotels.'

'Isn't it obvious?' Joe said.

'What do you mean?' Vera turned on him.

'We heard from Peter Calvert's students that he was having it off with a younger woman.'

'We heard there was a rumour going round,' she said. 'Nothing definite and no proof. And even if the rumour was true there are a fair few bonny young students in Newcastle for him to choose from. Doesn't mean it was Lily Marsh.'

Besides, she thought, Peter Calvert isn't the only older man floating around the edge of this case. There's Samuel Parr. Lily had a Northumberland Libraries ticket, could have bumped into him too. And if I had to choose between Peter Calvert and Samuel Parr, I know which one I'd go for every time. And the elaborate crime scenes were much more Parr's style. But she didn't say anything to the team. She kept her suspicion to herself. A private pleasure. A possibility to surprise them at the end of the case. If she turned out to be right.

She realized they were looking at her, waiting for

her to continue. 'Well?' she demanded. 'Anything else?'

Joe leaned across the table towards her. 'I've tracked down Ben Craven.'

She knew the name should mean something to her, but it didn't. He watched her. She could tell he was pleased with himself. *You're getting a bit smug for my liking.*

'The lad she was passionately in love with when she was in the sixth form. The one she got so obsessed about she messed up her A levels.'

'Of course,' she said as if she'd known all along. Fooling no one. 'What's he up to now?'

'He went away to university. Liverpool. Did a social work course. Moved back to the north east last summer. Guess what he's doing now?' He looked at them, savouring the moment, before answering his own question. 'He's a psychiatric social worker at St George's. The hospital where Luke Armstrong was treated.'

'Did he work with Luke?' Vera wasn't in the mood for games.

'I don't know. I haven't had a chance to talk to him.'

'Don't. Not until I've had a chat to Julie. We don't want to frighten him away.'

Why hadn't Joe told her this as soon as he'd found out? She felt like demanding an explanation. But this wasn't the place. Not in front of the others. He's getting complacent, she thought. Cocky. He thinks he can take me for granted.

Perhaps he sensed her anger, because he became

apologetic. 'I spoke to his mum only just now. Just before the meeting.'

I take him for granted too, she thought. Think of him as family, expect more of him than I should.

'Samuel Parr's wife committed suicide,' she said. 'I want the background, how she died. Charlie, can you look into that?'

He nodded and scribbled a note on a scrap of paper.

'Anything from the lighthouse? Anyone remember seeing a murderer with the body of a young woman under their arm?' She knew it wasn't funny, but it was getting to her. The nerve of the killer. The cheek of him.

'Nothing useful yet. Someone said Northumbria Water were working there for an hour. I'll check if their guys saw anything.'

'Well,' she said brightly. 'We've all got a lot to get on with . . .'

Charlie cleared his throat again. The ball of phlegm seemed constantly stuck in his gullet. 'There is something else. Probably nothing.'

'Spit it out, Charlie!' Thinking, as soon as the words came out: *But not literally, pet. No, not that.*

'I found this in the middle of all the papers we got from the search team,' he said. 'And I thought, with the flowers, like, it might be important.'

He held it in a clear plastic bag. A piece of cream card, A6 size, and, stuck to it, a pressed flower. Yellow, delicate. Some sort of vetch? Vera thought. There'd been a craze for pressing flowers when she was a kid. One of the teachers had started them off. You stuck the flower between blotting paper and weighed it down with heavy books – there'd been plenty of those in Vera's house – but she'd never much seen the point. Clearing out the house after Hector had died she'd come across one of her attempts among the pages of one of his field guides. A primrose, picked, pressed, then forgotten for more than thirty years. It had gone onto the bonfire with the rest of the crap.

'Anything written on the back?'

Charlie turned over the plastic bag. XXX in black ink. A row of kisses. It could have been a card made by a child for a mother. But this was something different, Vera thought. A love token?

'Was it in an envelope?'

'No, just like this.'

'No chance of DNA, then.'

'It suggests Peter Calvert, doesn't it?' Joe Ashworth said tentatively.

'Maybe.' She found it hard to imagine the arrogant lecturer taking the time and effort to make the card. Wouldn't it be just the sort of thing he'd sneer at? 'Perhaps Lily did it herself, but never got the time to send it. Or it could have been preparation for something she was planning to do with the kids in her class. Get it to forensics. They might give us something on the glue.'

She was still sitting at the table after the rest of them had gone. She poured the last of the coffee from the Thermos jug, took her time over drinking it. She couldn't get rid of the feeling that someone was playing with her. She was a piece in an elaborate board game. Real murders weren't like this. They were brutal and mucky. Unplanned usually, always ugly.

She tried to remember Julie Armstrong, staring at the telly in the front room at Seaton, Dennis Marsh hiding in his greenhouse; tried to persuade herself that she wasn't enjoying every minute.

Chapter Twenty-Six

The doctor had given Julie tablets to help her sleep. Every night she thought they weren't going to work, then sleep came in an instant. It was like being smashed over the head, a sudden unconsciousness. For the first time, that morning she remembered dreaming. She woke abruptly as she always did with the pills. It was early morning. She could tell by the noise of the birds and because there was no traffic in the street. The curtains were thin and the light came through them; it was sunny again.

Her first waking thought was of Luke, as it had been every morning since he'd died. The picture of him lying in the bath, the heavy scent, the condensation running down the mirror over the sink. But she was immediately aware too that he hadn't been the subject of her dream. It had been a sexy dream, the sort of daydream she'd conjured up after Geoff had left, when she'd thought she'd never have sex with a man again. In this dream, she and Gary were walking along a beach at night. There was a heavy moon just above the horizon, the sound of waves. The sort of thing you'd read in a cheesy magazine, one of those mags for old ladies which her mam took on coach trips. But then the dream shifted and they were in the dunes, making love. She remembered the weight of him on top of her, the sand rubbing against her back and her shoulders, his tongue in her mouth. Now it was like the memory of a real event, not a dream at all. Lying in bed she put her right hand on her left breast and believed it still felt tender, as if it had been pressed and squeezed. She started to move her hand down over her stomach and between her legs, then stopped herself. There was a shock of guilt. What was she doing? How could she even consider sex at a time like this? What sort of mother had she been? She should have sent Gary away the day before. What had possessed her to let him into the house?

She looked at the alarm clock by her bed. Nearly six o'clock. She zapped the remote and the portable TV on the chest of drawers came to life. She dozed, watching the moving pictures, not listening to the words, until her mother came in with a cup of tea and a pile of post. She could tell there were more cards. All her friends sending messages of support, telling her how sorry they were. She knew what they'd be like. Pictures of crosses and churches and lilies. She hadn't been in a church since they'd had Laura baptized, wondered what it was about dying that brought out the religion in everyone. She hadn't been able to face opening the mail and added the new envelopes to the mound of unopened post by the bed.

All morning she struggled to banish thoughts of Gary. Her mother seemed to sense she was more unsettled today and tried to distract her. Or perhaps she thought Julie had had enough moping around and it was time she pulled herself together. She wasn't given to sentiment and was easily irritated. She got

Julie up for breakfast, then set her to making a packed lunch for Laura to take to school. When the girl was out of the house and Julie was still sitting at the kitchen table, staring into space, she brought the bundle of letters and cards down from the bedroom.

'These need answering, Julie. You can't just ignore them. That'd be rude.'

Julie had been wondering where Gary was today. She had his number, hadn't she? She could phone him. She had this fantasy that he would come and collect her, take her to work with him. There'd be a dark room, flashing lights and a rock band. Really loud music which would blow away all the other thoughts from her head. The thumping of a bass which she'd feel vibrating through her body. Then the guilt hit her again and, as a sort of penance, she sat as her mother told her, a mug of milky coffee at her elbow, and began opening the cards.

When the doorbell rang, she felt her pulse racing. Gary had come back. Her mother was upstairs making the beds but she shouted down, 'Don't worry. I'll get it.' And Julie stayed where she was and made herself breathe slowly, telling herself over and over again that it was wrong to be thinking about a man at a time like this. Then she heard Vera Stanhope's voice, loud enough that you'd believe the whole street could hear, and she felt like bursting into tears.

Vera came into the kitchen and sat beside her. 'Sorry to interrupt again, pet. Just a few more questions.'

Then she noticed what Julie was doing, saw the one opened card on the table. 'That's bonny. Did it come today?'

And for the first time Julie looked at the image on the card. No church this time. It was one of those classy handmade things which cost a fortune. A pressed flower on thick cream card. She was going to pick it up to look at the message on the back, but Vera stopped her, physically stopped her by putting her great paw over Julie's hand.

'Humour me, pet. This might be important. Was it delivered today?'

'I'm not sure,' Julie said. 'I haven't been able to face opening them. They've been arriving since Friday.'

'Still got the envelope?'

'Aye, it's there on the table.'

She watched, dazed, while Vera took a pen from her pocket and flipped the envelope over so she could see the postmark and the address. She couldn't think what could be so important, didn't really care, stared out of the window at a tractor driving round and round a field in the distance.

'This isn't addressed to you,' she heard Vera say. 'It's addressed to Luke.'

Then she did look at the envelope, which was white, not cream, and didn't seem to belong to the card.

The writing was in black ink, in capitals. LUKE ARMSTRONG, 16 LAUREL WAY, SEATON, NORTH-UMBERLAND. No postcode.

She looked up at Vera. 'That's wrong,' she said. 'This isn't Laurel Way, it's Laurel Avenue. Laurel Way is round by the school.' Still she couldn't understand what the fuss was about.

'It was sent on Tuesday,' Vera said. 'First-class

stamp. If they'd got the address right it'd have got here on Wednesday.'

'If it'd arrived on Wednesday, Luke would have opened it. No way would I have opened a letter addressed to him. I might not have done it today, if I'd realized. I just assumed it was for me.' She watched Vera sitting there, frowning. 'It came with the others on Friday. Must have done. Is it important?'

'Probably not, pet. Let's just see what they had to say. Don't suppose you've got a pair of tweezers I could borrow?'

Julie went upstairs to fetch them, glad of the action. Her mother was in the bathroom. Julie could hear the sound of water, then the hiss of the spray cleaner. Every day her mother cleaned the bath, bent over it, rubbing away so you'd think the colour would come off on the cloth. It didn't make any difference. Julie still hadn't felt she could use it. But the bathroom door was shut so at least she didn't have to explain what was going on. Back in the kitchen, Vera held the card carefully with the tweezers and turned it over. The back was blank.

'Maybe some sort of joke,' Julie said.

'Aye. Maybe. But I'll take it away with me, if you don't mind. Get it checked out.'

Julie had a fleeting moment of curiosity, but it passed. Really, what did it matter what the inspector was up to? She flicked on the kettle to make Vera coffee. When she returned with a mug in her hand, the card and the envelope had disappeared.

'You said you had some questions?' She had no interest, just wanted to get this over as quickly as possible. Why? So she could return to her fantasy world of mindless heavy metal and a boy she'd first chased around the playground when she was six? She opened the biscuit tin and pushed it across the table. Vera took a chocolate digestive and dipped it in her coffee, bit it quickly just before it dropped.

'Did Luke have a social worker?'

'There was someone who came round when he first started having problems at school. Nosy cow.' Julie hadn't thought about her in years. She'd gone in for long cardigans and flat shoes, thick tights in strange colours. She'd had a mole on the side of her nose. In her head, Julie had called her *the witch*. 'I can't remember her name.'

'Anyone more recently?'

'I didn't need a social worker. I managed fine.' She looked at Vera suspiciously. 'And I don't need anyone sticking their oar in now. It's bad enough having my mother around the place.'

'I know you're managing,' Vera said, in a way that Julie knew she meant it. 'But we're looking for connections between Luke and the lass that was killed. It might help us find out what happened. Did you talk to one of the hospital social workers?'

'I don't think so. But it's possible. I mean, it's not like a real hospital where the nurses wear uniform and you can tell who everyone is. They all looked the same. Doctors, nurses, psychologists. All so young you'd think they were just out of school. They had name badges, but I never bothered looking at them. My head was so full of crap I knew I'd never remember. And every time I went, there was someone new.'

'This was a young man,' Vera said. 'Not long out of

university. Name of Ben Craven. Does that mean anything?'

Julie wanted to help. She wanted to make Vera smile, to please her, but when she thought about those visits to the hospital everything was a blur. All she could remember was the smell – stale cigarette smoke and old food – and Luke's huge haunted eyes. 'I'm sorry,' she said. 'He could have been there. I don't know.'

'But he never came to the house?'

'Oh no.' Julie was quite sure about that. 'He never came to the house. Not while I was here.'

'If someone came while you were at work, Luke would have mentioned it?'

Julie considered that. 'I'm not sure,' she said. 'He wouldn't keep thoughts for very long in his head. He couldn't pin them down. He wouldn't mean to keep it a secret, but it just might not occur to him.'

'Might Laura know?'

'Luke was less likely to talk to her than to me.'

There was a silence. She could tell the inspector wanted to get off, but after resenting Vera turning up, now she was reluctant to let her go. 'If you have any news,' she said, 'you will come and tell me? Straight away?'

Vera stood up and took her mug to the sink to rinse it.

'Of course,' she said. 'Straight away.' But she had her back to Julie while she was speaking and Julie wasn't sure she could believe her.

Chapter Twenty-Seven

Felicity saw James onto the school bus and walked slowly down the lane towards Fox Mill. Since Peter's birthday nothing concrete had changed. She still washed and shopped and cooked every night. She made sure James did his homework and over dinner she asked Peter if he'd had a good day at work. She lay beside him in bed.

She'd tried the night before to talk to him about the dead girl. Through the open window came the smell of the garden, but underneath cut grass and honeysuckle was an imagined hint of the sea. In her head she was taken back to the watch tower, to the clean salt air, the seaweed and the flowers floating on water.

'Do you think they know yet who killed her?' she asked.

She was lying on her back, staring up at the ceiling. She knew he was still awake, but he took so long to answer that she wondered if he was pretending to be asleep.

'No,' he said at last. 'I don't think they have a clue. They came to talk to me today. That woman inspector and a younger man.'

'What did they say?' She turned so she was facing

him, could just make out the shape of his face. At one time she would have reached out and stroked his forehead, his eyelids, his neck. His lips and inside his mouth. She'd loved the intimacy of his skin on her fingertips. Now, not even their feet were touching.

'They asked if I could identify the flowers. I'm not sure . . . That could have been an excuse.'

'They can't think that one of us had anything to do with it.'

'No,' he said easily. 'Of course not.' And he'd gathered her into his arms as he might have done when they were first married. A father comforting his child. She'd lain quite still, pretending to be comforted.

Walking down the lane, in and out of the shadow thrown by the elders, she thought that while on the surface everything seemed the same, in fact it never would be. Immediately after the idea came into her head she dismissed it as melodramatic nonsense. The trouble was that she had nobody to talk to about it. Of course she'd told her friends about finding the body, in fact over the last couple of days she'd described the incident so often – on the telephone, in different kitchens over mugs of coffee and glasses of wine – that she was no longer quite sure what was true. Had she embellished it slightly for effect? But what she couldn't share with her friends was the suspicion, right at the back of her mind, that someone she knew might be a murderer. Just as she had confided in none of her friends about her relationship with Samuel.

In the empty house, she thought what she needed was company. Peter's birthday had been ruined by the murder. She should organize a party, a barbecue, bring the boys back to do it properly. But she recognized an edge of desperation in the plans and knew that if she did go ahead with them the evening would be horrible, worse than the last time. A failure. Then she thought she would invite her daughters to stay, with their partners and families. They could have a grand family celebration. At least in her role as mother and grandmother she felt secure. She would talk to Peter that evening. It would be something to discuss. It would fill the deadly silence over dinner.

When Joanna, her youngest daughter, came to visit she and her husband always stayed in the cottage. It was a tradition which had started when Joanna first went to university. She'd come back one weekend with a group of friends and Felicity had thought they'd cause less fuss there. They could stay up all night drinking and listening to music without disturbing Peter or keeping James awake. Now Felicity decided she would prepare the place for their stay. She put cloths, a dustpan and brush, dusters and polish into a bucket and walked through the meadow to the cottage. Her mother, kneeling on cold stone to polish pews on which nobody would ever sit, had talked about the therapy of cleaning. She would put the theory into practice.

She hadn't been in there since the weekend, when Vera Stanhope had asked to see inside, and nobody had stayed since Christmas. Despite the weather it smelled damp and musty. She hadn't noticed it so strongly before. Perhaps that had put Lily Marsh off renting. Perhaps that was why she had rushed off without giving Felicity an answer. She propped the door ajar with a pebble and opened all the windows. With the door open the mill race seemed closer. As she worked she could hear the water outside.

She stripped the bed and put the sheets and pillow cases in a pile at the foot of the stairs, dusted the chest of drawers, polished it with beeswax. Then she stood on a chair to clean the bedroom window, lowering the sash so she could reach outside. Her mood was lifting already. She caught herself humming the snatch of a song which James had brought home from school. She fetched a broom from the cupboard in the kitchen and swept under the bed, pushing the dust ahead of her over the bare wooden boards into a pile. She gathered the pile into the dustpan, realized she hadn't brought bin bags with her and carried it carefully downstairs.

She washed the tiles in the bathroom, scrubbed the top of the oven and inside the kitchen cupboards, brushed more dust into a pile. Then she decided she needed coffee. There was a jar of instant in the cottage and some powdered milk, but she deserved better than that. She left the cottage open to air and went back to the house. The long grass was feathery against her bare legs as she walked across the field.

She put the kettle on and checked the phone. One message. It was Samuel. Bland and distant as he always was. *Perhaps you could phone me back if you have a minute. Nothing urgent.* But even that contact thrilled her. She thought he wanted to meet, imagined walking into the house in Morpeth, him greeting her. She dialled his direct line. No answer. She was disappointed, but pleased too. She'd try again later and it would be something to look forward to. Delayed gratification. She poured the coffee into a Thermos mug. She thought she would take it to the cottage, drink it sitting on the step looking out over the water. She recognized how childish the morning had been. Mary Barnes would have spring-cleaned the cottage a few months ago, would do it again if Felicity told her Jo was coming to visit. This morning she'd been behaving like a little girl playing house. At the last minute she remembered she'd need a bin bag and went back to fetch it.

Drinking the coffee she thought of Samuel, his long bony spine and his slender back. Behaving like a girl again, she thought. Really, it's time I grew up. But she smiled to herself. She went back into the cottage and closed the windows. She flushed the toilet to wash away the bleach. She scooped up the dust in the pan and tipped it into the bin bag. And saw something glittering. She set down the pan, stooped and picked the object out. A ring. Very attractive. Blue-green stones in an oval silver setting. An art deco design. Vaguely familiar. It must belong to one of the girls, she thought, pleased to have rescued it. Joanna probably. It was the sort of thing she'd love. How careless of her not even to realize it was missing.

It wasn't until she was back at the house, in their bedroom, on the wicker chair next to the phone, preparing to call Samuel again, that she remembered where she'd seen the ring. It had been on Lily Marsh's finger. Felicity had noticed it when Lily had reached out to help James with his violin after they'd got off the bus. She'd coveted it secretly even then. It must have been loose on the young woman's finger, slipped off sometime during the guided tour. Felicity set it on the bed. The quilt was of thick white cotton and the ring looked magnificent against it. She was tempted to keep it. She slipped it onto her own middle finger. It fitted perfectly. Who would know? Since her friendship with Samuel, all sorts of wickedness seemed more possible. She relished the idea of behaving against type, against the expectations of her family and friends who would have described her as a very *good* person. With the ring still on her finger, she dialled Samuel's number. He answered immediately.

'Parr.'

'It's Felicity. Returning your call.' She always identified herself though she knew he must recognize her voice. Even when there was nobody to overhear they maintained the pretence that there was nothing between them but friendship. Until they were alone together in his house.

'It was good of you to get back to me.' He paused. 'How are you?'

'Well,' she said. 'You know . . .'

'And James?'

'Oh he's fine too.'

'I wondered if you'd heard any more from the police.'

'They went to see Peter at work yesterday.'

'The inspector came to me too. At the house.' Felicity felt a moment of disgust. It was almost sacrilegious, that big, ugly woman sitting among Samuel's lovely things. He continued, 'I'm not entirely sure what she wanted.'

She didn't know what to say to that and found herself coming out with the inconsequential information which was still at the front of her mind. 'I've just found a piece of jewellery belonging to Lily Marsh. A ring. It was in the cottage. She must have dropped it while I was showing her around.'

'Have you told the police?' She was surprised by the urgency in his tone.

'No, not yet.' She kept her own voice light, playful. 'It is *very* pretty.'

'You can't think of keeping it!' He was shocked. 'You must tell them. Straight away. If you don't, they'll think you have something to hide.'

'It can't be that important. They know she was in the cottage.'

'All the same,' he said. 'They'll see it as evidence.'

'All right. I was only teasing.' She thought he could be very high-minded and preachy.

'And I was only thinking of you.' This was as intimate as he got on the phone and she was surprisingly moved. 'Please phone Inspector Stanhope. Now.'

'All right.'

'Promise?'

'Yes,' she said. 'I promise.' Then, 'Are you free this afternoon?'

'No, I've got a meeting.' She couldn't tell whether he was telling the truth or whether he was still nervous about them being together. Perhaps he imagined the inspector knocking at his door, demanding to be let in, while they were making love. How he would hate that, being caught when he wasn't entirely in control. She thought that her relationship with Samuel was something which had also been quite changed by the discovery of Lily Marsh's body.

'I must go,' he said. 'I'm wanted on the desk.' He ended the call without properly saying goodbye.

She sat for a moment, looking out of the window at the lighthouse shimmering in the heat haze, then picked up the telephone again to speak to the police.

Chapter Twenty-Eight

Vera arranged to meet Ben Craven in a day centre for psychiatric patients. He spent one day a week there meeting the clients who'd been discharged from hospital. It was on the edge of a coastal town which had once been famous for its docks. Now, it's only claim to fame was as the drugs capital of the north east.

On the way, she stopped at the library in the town centre, a Gothic red-brick building, with a clock tower and a huge painting in the lobby of a ship in full sail. She found a collection of Samuel Parr's short stories on a shelf marked LOCAL AUTHORS. She wasn't sure what he'd think about being displayed in that way. Was it an honour? Or did it mean he wasn't good enough to go on the shelves with the real writers? She stood browsing for a moment, but couldn't find the story she'd heard on the radio. In the end she decided to take it out anyway. When she handed over the book and her ticket the library assistant said, 'Such a lovely man. He came here to give a reading last year. He's one of our staff, of course.'

That made Vera think of her last conversation with Samuel Parr. He'd said he'd tell her what Lily had been reading. Still curious, but also interested what Parr's response to the request would be, she decided to follow it up. Sitting in the car she phoned Morpeth Library and asked to speak to him.

'Ah yes, Inspector. Let me just check the system. What was the name? Lily Marsh?'

What are you playing at? she thought. Of course you remember the girl's name. You found her body.

'There are no books outstanding on her ticket, Inspector. I'm afraid I can't help you.'

She switched off her phone, feeling unreasonably disappointed.

The psychiatric day centre had once been a nursery school and, walking in, Vera had the uncomfortable feeling that everyone here – even the staff – had regressed to early childhood. In one of the rooms an art class was taking place. The patients wore red aprons to protect their clothes, they used thick brushes and bright acrylic paint. In another, there was some sort of music lesson with tambourines, cymbals and a couple of glockenspiels. But everywhere was the smell of cigarette smoke. She'd never bothered much if other people wanted to kill themselves, but could feel this in her throat and lungs and she knew she'd have to change her clothes to get rid of the stink. She had to walk through the common room to find the social worker. The chairs were arranged in small groups, but nobody seemed to be talking to anyone else. Everyone was smoking. A thin woman was talking under her breath. Some long story about her rent and the council hounding her. The other people in the room ignored her.

Craven had a small office at the end of a corridor. His door was open and she saw him before he noticed her. He was sitting at a desk hitting computer keys with a speed she'd never master. Her first thought was that he looked good. He was the sort of young man you'd notice in the street, follow with your eyes just for the pleasure of seeing him move. Tall, blond, muscular. A tan to show off the eyes. He was squinting at the screen but she knew they'd be blue. He must feature in the fantasies of many of his female clients. No wonder Lily Marsh had fallen for him. What a couple they would have made.

He heard her approaching and looked up.

'Yes?' Just one word but that gentle, patronizing tone professionals use to mad people. A smile to make her feel at ease. He thought she was a patient. She wondered if she spoke to witnesses like that. Like they were children.

'Vera Stanhope,' she said. 'Inspector. We've got an appointment.' Brusque enough for him to feel awkward. A silly power game, which she'd usually despise.

He reached out and shut down the computer, stood up in the same movement, held out his hand.

'Inspector. Tea? Coffee?'

'No, thanks,' she said.

'Is it about one of my clients? Perhaps we should get my boss to sit in.'

She ignored that. 'Look,' she said. 'Is there anywhere else we can go to talk? Maybe get some lunch?'

'Do the mentally ill make you uncomfortable, Inspector?'

'Don't be daft, lad. I've worked with more loonies than you've had hot dinners. And I don't just mean the offenders.'

He smiled and she thought he might be human after all. 'I usually take a break around now.'

They walked out into the street. On the other side of the road was a narrow stretch of dune then the sea. In the distance a power station in the process of demolition. He led her down a terrace of double-fronted Edwardian houses, still stately despite their surroundings, and into a pub. The Mermaid. A carving like a ship's prow over the door. At night time they probably dealt drugs here, like everywhere else in the town, but now it was quiet, restful. A couple of old men with pitmen's wheezes playing dominoes in one corner. A middle-aged couple at a table eating steak pie and chips.

Craven ordered orange juice and a sandwich. She went for a half of Workie Ticket and a burger. Standing at the bar to pay, she looked at him, caught in the dusty sunlight, until she realized she was staring and turned away.

'Luke Armstrong,' she said, as soon as she sat down. 'Does the name mean anything to you?'

'Isn't that the lad who was killed in Seaton?'

'You knew him, then?'

'No, I never worked with him. But I heard other staff in the hospital talking. Gossiping. That's how I know he'd been an inpatient at St George's. I don't think he was ever referred to the social work department.'

'You didn't see him in hospital?'

'I might have done in passing while I was visiting someone else on the ward, but I certainly don't remember. Look, you really would be better talking to my boss. She'd know if there was any social work input with the family.'

'What about Lily Marsh?' Vera said. 'You *did* know her.'

He sat in complete silence. Still as a statue. Gilded by the sunshine. A bit of art she'd have in her house any day, she thought, only half as a joke.

'I haven't seen Lily since I was eighteen.'

'You heard she'd died too?'

'My mother phoned at the weekend,' he said. 'She told me there'd been some sort of accident. Lily was drowned. Up the coast somewhere.'

Vera wondered if that was the story Phyllis had spread round their village when she'd first been told of her daughter's death. Did she think it was shameful to be a murder victim? Not quite nice? It wasn't a fiction she'd be able to sustain for long.

'Lily was strangled. Just like Luke Armstrong.'

'You're saying the two deaths are connected?'

Bright too. Not just a pretty face.

'We don't get that many violent deaths in this part of Northumberland,' she said, not hiding the sarcasm. 'Not in one week anyway.' Then, watching him. 'You don't seem very shocked. It's a nasty business. You were very close to her at one time.'

'Of course I'm shocked.' He looked up at her. 'But not surprised. Not really. I don't believe in natural victims, but she wasn't an easy person to be close to. There were times when I felt like killing her. Not her fault. I saw that even then. I wanted to understand. Perhaps that's what pushed me into this line of work. But it didn't stop me feeling like strangling her.'

'Tell me.'

'I was in love with her,' he said. 'That mad, passionate obsession that you only get when you're a teenager. I wanted to write poems to her, spend every minute with her—'

'Fuck the pants off her,' Vera interrupted helpfully.

He laughed. 'Well, that too, I suppose. But in a very tasteful and romantic way. We'd been reading Lawrence. I imagined it in moonlight, on a pile of hay. Something like that. Young people are so pretentious, aren't they?'

Vera thought of Luke Armstrong and Thomas Sharp, stealing from building sites, mucking around on the quayside, standing up for each other when the bullying started. Not all young people, she thought. A plump, motherly woman walked up with their food. Vera waited until she'd returned to the bar before continuing.

'Did it live up to expectations?' she asked.

'At first.'

She wanted to ask if they'd done it outside, like his fantasy, but thought that was just prurient. She was like the sad middle-aged detectives who had their day made when they were asked to go through a mound of seized porn.

She was about to tell him to get on with it, but he continued without prompting. 'It was the autumn at the beginning of year twelve. I mean, that was when I plucked up courage to ask her out. There was a band I knew she liked at the City Hall. I managed to get tickets, asked if she'd like to go. I'd just passed my driving test and persuaded my mother to let me borrow the car for the night. There'd be no other way of getting home that late. I was so nervous before I asked if she wanted to go with me. I remember I was shaking. We were waiting at the bus stop on the way to school. We'd both got there early and I just took my chance. It was one of those lovely days you can get in October. Sunny with a hint of a frost. I stumbled over my words, felt about eight years old. She smiled. That was when I knew it would be all right. "I thought you'd never ask." That was all she said. Then some other kids turned up to catch the bus.'

'When did it start going wrong?'

'Just before Christmas the following year. We had coursework to get in for A levels. It was even more important for her than me. She'd got a conditional place at Oxford. But suddenly she didn't seem bothered about revising for exams. She expected to see me every night, even though we'd spent the day together at school. I was starting to feel suffocated.'

'So you finished with her?'

'Not at first. I suggested we should just go out at weekends. It would make the time we had together more special.'

'Did she go for that?'

He shook his head. 'I did still care for her, but she was starting to do my head in. She accused me of seeing other women behind her back.'

'And were you?'

'No! I was trying to get some decent A levels so I could get away to university.' He paused. 'We had this enormous row. We'd been to the pub in the village where she lived and I was walking her back home. She'd been drinking quite heavily. She suddenly lost it, started shouting and swearing at me. Said I'd never loved her, that I'd spent all evening eyeing up the lass behind the bar, that she couldn't bear it if things carried on like this. I'd had enough. "Fine," I said. "Let's call it a day." She was almost home, so I turned and started walking back. She chased after me, pleading with me to change my mind. "I'm sorry, Ben. I can't help it. I just love you so much." It was pissing with rain and I thought how crazy she looked standing there, sobbing, her make-up running down her face. I didn't know what to do. She was so upset. So I put my arm around her and went with her to her front door, waited until she'd got the key in the door and ran for it.'

'Quite the gentleman,' Vera said.

'It was too much for me to deal with. I should have spoken to her parents, explained why she was distressed, but I couldn't face them. They always seemed very old to me. Quite strait-laced. Anyway, things like that you didn't talk to your parents about.' He paused, played with the empty glass. 'That was a Friday. She wasn't in school the next week. Her parents sent in a message to say she had some sort of throat infection. I was relieved because I didn't have to face her. I thought that would be the end of it. She'd come back to school and everything would carry on as it had before we started going out. People were always breaking up. It wasn't a big deal.'

'But it was a big deal for Lily.'

'Apparently. Her mother phoned, asked me to go and see Lily. She wasn't sleeping, wasn't eating. I had enough sense to refuse. I knew if I gave her any encouragement, the whole thing would start over again. A couple of weeks later she came back to school. She looked dreadful, pale and ill. I wondered if there might be something physically wrong with her, had this nightmare that she had some incurable disease and I was making her worse. Really, I was sure her mother would have had her checked out. In a strange way I was flattered. To have that effect on someone I'd worshipped! Lily became very isolated and withdrawn. She'd never had real friends. I hadn't realized before we became close how alone she was. But still I thought it would be OK. She seemed to throw herself into her work. I thought she was starting to get over the separation. There were no big scenes. After a week or so she even looked a bit brighter. I mean, she started to take more notice of her appearance, she spoke to me when we met.'

'But it didn't work out?'

'I wish. Now, of course, I realize how depressed she must have been. She wasn't getting better at all. The new clothes, the chattiness, were all part of her delusion that I was about to take her back. There was a crisis over the Easter holidays. She turned up at my house all dressed up, all smiles. "Where are you going to take me?" She had it in her head that I'd arranged to take her out for the day. I didn't know what to do. In the end I took her home to her mother's. When she realized what was happening she started to sob. It was horrible. That was when the phone calls started. She'd ring dozens of times a day. I knew she was ill and I tried to be sympathetic but it wore me down. And it drove my parents crazy. We changed the number, went ex-directory. I don't know if she ever had treatment or if she just came out of it. Most of the next term was study leave before the exams. I didn't see much of her. Caught a glimpse occasionally in the distance on her way to a classroom and made sure I kept out of the way.'

'Have you seen her since then?'

'No. She wasn't even at school when we all went to get our exam results. I suppose she realized she'd not done brilliantly and couldn't face the rest of us celebrating.'

'Has she been a patient at St George's since then? Or an outpatient at the day centre?'

'I haven't seen her.'

'You must have been curious, though,' Vera said. 'You admitted she was partly why you took up this branch of social work. Didn't you check if she was in the system? I know I would have done.'

He didn't answer her question immediately. 'I still think about her,' he said. 'She was my first real girl-friend. Probably the most beautiful woman I've ever met.' Then he looked up at Vera. 'You'll have to check with the medical staff about whether or not she's been treated locally. But you're right. I was curious. And I couldn't find any trace of her.'

The landlady came to collect their plates and Ben stood up to go. Vera stayed where she was and he paused, looking down at her, realizing there was another question.

'Does the name Claire Parr mean anything to you? She was in her late thirties, depressed. She committed suicide.'

'No,' he said. She could tell he just wanted to get back to work.

'It doesn't matter.' Speaking almost to herself. 'I expect it was before your time.'

Chapter Twenty-Nine

Vera telephoned Clive Stringer's home number from her car. She'd parked behind the dunes and was looking out over the beach. An old man was walking along the shore, his head bent. Every now and then he stooped to pick up sea coal and stick it in an Aldi carrier bag. She thought he probably lived in a housing association flat now with central heating, but old habits would die hard.

She pressed the buttons on her phone. It went on ringing – there was no answer service at the other end – and she was about to give up, when a woman spoke. Her voice was faint, breathless. She gave the number.

'Mrs Stringer.'

'Yes?' She was suspicious, used to people selling things. Perhaps her son had told her just to hang up if a stranger called.

'My name's Vera Stanhope, Mrs Stringer. I work for the police. Perhaps Clive said I'd be in touch. It's about that lassie he found dead by the lighthouse.'

'I'm not sure . . .'

'Is Clive at home? Perhaps I could speak to him.' She crossed the fingers of both hands and her phone nearly slipped from her grasp. Early afternoon, surely he'd still be in the museum.

'He's at work. You'd best talk to him there.'

Again Vera thought the woman was about to hang up.

'Look, I'm going to be around your way in about half an hour. I'll call in then. We can have a chat.'

'Really, I'd rather you waited till Clive was here.' Vera thought she could hear panic in the voice. That meant nothing sinister. Plenty of old people were worried about strangers knocking at the door. They'd watched all the crime prevention ads.

'It's nothing to be anxious about.' Vera heard herself speak with Ben Craven's *You're mad and I know what's best for you* voice; she winced. 'I'll show my identification. You can phone the police station to make sure.' Then she pressed the button on her phone to end the conversation before Mrs Stringer started to protest again.

The Stringers lived in a low pre-war bungalow in North Shields. Once the street had been a main road, tree-lined, busy, with a shop at each end, but the surrounding area had been redeveloped and a new road system had left it stranded. Now Gunner's Lane ended abruptly in a breeze-block wall. Beyond that a glass and concrete sports centre threw a long shadow down the middle of the street. Vera knew the area. She'd been there a few times to visit Davy Sharp, had been surprised that he lived somewhere so unassuming and respectable. It was all part of his cover, his ability to fit in.

Mary Stringer must have been watching out for her. As soon as Vera knocked, the door opened immediately, just a crack. She was tiny, her features small, her neck so thin it seemed impossible it could support her head.

'I phoned Clive. He said he didn't know anything about you coming to the house.' Even through the crack in the door, Vera could tell she was shaking.

Vera made no attempt to get in. She fished in her bag for her identity card. 'You must admit it's me,' she said. 'Look at that picture. There can't be more than one person in the north east with a face like that.'

'Clive said I didn't have to talk to you.'

'And he's quite right, but you don't want the whole street listening to your business, do you?'

There was no reply. Vera could tell she was weakening. 'H'away, hinny, and let me in. I called at the baker's on the corner and got a couple of custard slices. Let's get the kettle on and have a civilized chat.'

The custard slices seemed to swing it. The claw-like grip on the door loosened. Vera pushed it gently and went inside.

The interior of the house couldn't have changed much since Mary Stringer had moved in. It was clean enough and tidy, but the furniture was old, a little shabby. Vera stood just inside the front door, waiting for the old woman to take the lead. Having taken the decision to allow Vera in, now she seemed almost pleased to have company. She led Vera into a small, over-filled living room and bustled away to make tea. Above the mantelpiece there was her wedding photo. Mary in traditional white and a man, as skinny as she was, looking sharp and pleased with himself in an ill-fitting suit.

Mary came back with a tray and saw Vera looking. 'He died when our Clive was a month old. An accident at the shipyard. They were good, mind. I had a pension.'

'Hard for you, though,' Vera said. 'Bringing up the lad on your own. Did you have family to help out?'

'No one close by. The neighbours were smashing. I'm not sure how I'd have managed without them. It was a friendly street in those days. Still is, really.'

'Clive said you helped out with Thomas Sharp when he was a bairn.'

'Only as a favour,' Mary said quickly. 'I mean, they gave me a few pounds to mind him when they were stretched. You know what it was like – Davy in and out of prison. I wouldn't want the pension people to know. Or the social – I mean, I was never properly registered as a minder.'

'You were helping out a friend.' Vera wondered if that was all the anxiety was about. Mary had broken a few rules ten years before and still got into a panic about it. 'Nobody's going to worry about that now.'

And Mary did seem to relax then and to play the hostess. The tea was in proper cups with saucers. There were matching tea plates and Vera prised the sticky cakes from a paper bag, handed one to Mary then licked her finger.

'Did you ever meet Thomas's friend, Luke Armstrong?' An outside chance, but worth asking all the same.

'I hadn't seen much of Tom at all recently. Not to talk to. He'd wave when he went past to get the bus into town, but that was it. You can't blame him. What would he want with an old lady?'

'Clive would have known him quite well, then?'

'He was lovely with Thomas when he was a baby.

Even changed his nappy sometimes. You don't expect it of young men, do you? He took him out in his pushchair when he was a toddler.'

Vera thought it sounded as if Mary had done more than a bit of occasional child-minding for the Sharps, but said nothing. She bit into the custard slice; the icing was so sweet she could imagine her teeth crumbling at the roots. The vanilla custard spilled out, squashed between the hard, indigestible pastry. She scooped it up with her little finger and put it in her mouth.

Mary watched her fondly. 'My Clive likes his food,' she said, 'but he never puts on an ounce. He must burn it up.'

'A bit of a nervy lad, was he?' Vera asked.

'Maybe that was my fault. There was only him and me and I always hated being on my own. Perhaps I smothered him a bit. I couldn't have borne it if anything had happened to him.' She paused, gave a little complacent smile. 'He's a good lad. I had a stroke a while back. Not major, but some sons would take their opportunity to put their mam into a home. Not him. He took time off work, brought me home and looked after me here.'

'You're close, then?'

'Aye, very close.'

'You'd know if anything was bothering him.'

'Well, that's a different thing, isn't it? He's not one for wearing his heart on his sleeve, our Clive. I'm not sure I can ever tell what's going on in his head.'

'Has he been seeing a lass lately?'

'No!' She seemed to think the idea inconceivable. 'We're quite happy here, just the two of us.' Then she added, for form's sake, 'Not that it would worry me, mind. I mean, it would be lovely if he could find a good woman to settle down with. I'd love a grand-child.'

'Has Clive ever had any treatment for his nerves?'

'What do you mean?' She was suddenly suspicious. She'd been eating the pastry with small delicate bites, nibbling away at the edges, mouse-like. Now she frowned over the cake at Vera.

'I'm just asking, pet. Lots of people do.'

'He's not depressed, if that's what you're saying. We're very content here, him and me. We don't need anyone else prying into our business.'

Vera let it go, wondered if the woman was protesting too much.

'You don't mind when he stays away?' she asked.

'It doesn't happen much these days. One time, it was every weekend. Up the coast with those grand friends of his. I didn't complain, mind. He has his own life to live. But since I had the stroke he's been a bit more thoughtful. I said to him, "How would you feel if I had a turn and I was here by myself?"'

Vera was starting to think Mary was a poisonous old witch. She could have understood if Clive had wanted to do away with *her*. 'You knew he was going to be away last Friday?'

'Of course. He wouldn't have arranged it without asking me first.'

'He prepared you a meal?'

'Like I said, he's a good lad. He usually cooks if he's here. He didn't eat, mind.' She sniffed. 'He was going to get something fancy at the party.'

'What about the Wednesday?'

'He was a bit late home from work because he went shopping on his way home. I was waiting for him. When you're on your own all day, you look forward to the company.'

'He doesn't drive much now, he was telling me.'

'No.' She paused. 'I used to quite enjoy our jaunts out in the car, but he never much liked driving. When it failed its MOT a few years ago, he didn't bother having the car fixed and sold it for scrap. He says it's better for the planet to use public transport. It would be handy for me now, though. He'd be able to give me a lift to the outpatient clinic at the hospital.' She gave a quick look to the clock on the wall. 'Is there anything else? Only the quiz I like on television comes on soon and it makes my day.'

Vera decided she'd go before she said something she regretted. She'd checked out Clive's story. She couldn't see him as Joe Ashworth's madman, who killed young people just because he was jealous of the way they looked. He might be depressed, but who wouldn't be, saddled with the self-obsessed mother?

Mary had switched on the big TV. Vera had begun by being sorry for her. Now she thought the woman had her life organized very much the way she wanted it. Vera got up. 'I'll see my way out, shall I?'

The little woman nodded. 'If you don't mind. I'm not so good on my feet, since I was ill.'

Vera closed the living-room door behind her and stood in the hall. The signature tune from the television faded. The host made a joke. Mary chuckled. Vera pushed open one of the doors leading from the corridor. It had a thick white carpet on the floor. A double bed with a pink candlewick quilt. That old ladies' smell of worn nightclothes and talcum powder. The next door she tried was the bathroom. It was very small, a shower over the bath, the blue shower curtain with a pattern of beaming fish. The smell in here slightly more masculine. Shower gel? Aftershave? She looked at the bottles on the shelf. Had Clive always made an effort with his appearance, hopeful perhaps that one day he'd find a woman, an excuse to move away from his mother?

Then she was standing at the door of Clive's room. It was firmly shut but not locked and opened with a gentle click. The curtains were drawn and she had to switch on the light. She had been expecting something dusty, full of specimens like the workroom in the museum, but it was uncluttered, anonymous. A single bed and matching pine wardrobe and chest of drawers. A bookcase with standard field guides. In one corner a mist net packed into a canvas bag. So Clive must be into ringing birds too. A few fantasy novels, an upturned book on the bedside table. A computer desk with the ubiquitous PC. A chess set. No pictures on the wall. It was as if he knew his mother had access to his room and he wanted to give nothing away. There was just one photograph, propped on the bedside cabinet, where you might expect the picture of a girl-friend or lover. This was of the group of four friends – Clive looking shy and awkward, Gary laughing, and each side of them Peter Calvert and Samuel Parr. It had been taken at the lighthouse and they were all gazing out to sea.

Vera walked back into the corridor. There was a burst of laughter from the television studio audience.

She took advantage of the noise to shut the front door behind her and walk out into the street.

She stood for a moment then walked three doors down to where the Sharps lived. Now she was here, she might as well talk to Davy's wife.

Chapter Thirty

Vera could tell that Diane Sharp knew who she was as soon as the door was opened – not her name or where she came from but that she was a police officer. She must have developed some sort of sixth sense after years of practice. She was a plump woman in her forties, with very pretty features, hair which looked as if she had it done every week. She wore a pink blouse and a white linen skirt.

'You're wasting your time here,' she said. 'Davy's inside. Acklington.'

'I know. I spoke to him last week.' Vera was trying to remember if she'd met Davy's wife before, thought she probably hadn't.

'And our Brian doesn't live here any more. He's got his own place in town.'

'It's you I want to talk to,' Vera said.

The woman seemed surprised by that, so surprised that she stood aside and let Vera in.

'I don't get mixed up in their business.' As she spoke she led Vera through to the back of the bungalow. Everything was very neat, very respectable. She opened a door and suddenly light flooded into the space. There was a conservatory the width of the building, looking out onto a tiny patch of lawn. 'Davy had this done last time he was home,' she said. She settled herself into a wicker chair, nodded for Vera to join her.

'This isn't about what your men get up to,' Vera said. She paused. 'I was so sorry to hear about Thomas.'

The woman sat very still before replying. 'That was an accident,' she said at last. 'Nothing for you to trouble yourself about.'

'Are you sure about that, Mrs Sharp?'

'Aye, it'd have been easier if there was someone to blame, but it was just lads larking around.'

'You'll have seen in the paper that Luke Armstrong was killed?'

'Yes,' she said. 'He was a smashing lad. Tom spent a lot of time at his place.'

'Did he come here?'

'Not so often. Brian was still at home then. There were things going on. I didn't want Tom involved.'

'What sort of things?'

She hesitated, chose her words carefully. 'Brian mixes with a rough set,' she said. She could have been talking about a five-year-old mixing with bad company at school.

Vera knew one of the rough set had been convicted of attempted murder, a stabbing in a city-centre pub, but she let that go. 'Tell me about the memorial they did for Tom. The flowers on the river. Whose idea was it?'

'I'm not sure who started it.' Diane was looking through the glass at the trimmed lawn. 'Someone in the street probably. Everyone here was very fond of

Tom. I don't think it was organized. At first there was one bunch of flowers. Then everybody joined in.'

'Did anyone blame Luke Armstrong for Tom's death?'

The woman looked up. 'You're thinking of Brian? After revenge?'

'Your little brother drowns, you'd want someone to blame. Like you said, we all want that.'

She shook her head. 'It wasn't Brian. I'd have heard.'

Vera thought that was probably true. Besides, Brian Sharp would have kicked the Armstrong door down, battered Luke with fists and boots. He wouldn't have charmed his way in with flowers.

'Tell me about the Stringers,' she said. 'Your neighbours.'

Diane seemed surprised by the sudden change of subject. 'Why do you want to know about them?'

'Clive's a witness in another enquiry. I'm just curious.'

'Mary Stringer was like a mother to me when we moved here,' Diane said. 'Davy wasn't around much and I was pregnant with Tom. She was on her own apart from Clive. She lost her husband in an accident. Clive wasn't like either of my boys. He was very quiet. Always had his head in a book. No trouble. Not really. He was teased a bit as a kid, but Brian soon put a stop to that. We were almost like one family. Mary looked after Tom for me most days until he started nursery. I had my hands full with Brian and she was only on a widow's pension. She needed the money and I was happy enough to slip her a few pounds. Clive loved having Tom around. Most lads wouldn't have been interested, but for a few years they were like brothers.'

'Did Clive ever meet Luke Armstrong?'

'He might have done. Tom never said.'

Vera couldn't think of anything else to ask and stood to go. Diane shut the door firmly behind her. Outside, Clive Stringer was standing next to her car. He must have left work as soon as his mother phoned him about Vera's intended visit. He was wearing black jeans, a black polo shirt, black trainers. He had the sort of complexion which easily burns and his face was red, greasy with sweat. Vera could tell he'd stood there, fuming, getting hotter and crosser, waiting for her to return to her car.

'You had no right bothering my mother.'

'She didn't seem to mind, pet. We had a nice pot of tea.'

'Anything you want to ask, you can come straight to me.'

'You look as if you could do with a cup yourself. Is there anywhere round here we could get a drink? Save bothering your mam again. Stand here any longer and we'll start gathering a crowd.'

A gang of teenagers were slouching down the road on their way home from school and they'd already begun to stare. Clive shrugged. 'There's a caff on the corner.' He set off along the pavement leaving Vera to follow.

The cafe had set a garden table and chairs outside on the pavement. Any attempt to create a continental atmosphere was ruined by the smell of greasy burgers and stale cigarettes coming through the open door, but the pavement was in the shade now and they sat there anyway. Vera drank instant coffee, Clive a bottle of bright-orange fizzy pop. She thought again that he'd never grown up.

'It can't have been easy,' she said, 'growing up without a dad.' As soon as the words were out she thought that was a patronizing thing to say, but in the short walk Clive seemed to have become calmer.

'My mother's never been easy,' he said. He looked up with a sudden grin as if he'd made a joke.

'She depends on you?' Vera was feeling her way with him. One wrong word and she knew he'd clam up again.

'There's nobody else. No relatives. She's not very good with friends. She makes demands on them, but won't make any effort in return.'

'She made an effort with Diane Sharp.'

'Diane paid her. Besides Mam liked Tom when he was a baby. She could make believe he was hers. She didn't like him so much when he was old enough to answer back.'

'You never answered back?'

'No,' he said. 'I never got the hang of it.' She expected him to smile again, but he seemed quite serious.

'How did you get on with the Sharps?'

'At one point they were like family,' he said and Vera thought that Diane had said almost the same thing. 'It would have been easy to get sucked into all that. You know, the stuff they were into. But the bird-watching came along and that was a way out for me.'

'And another sort of family.'

'Aye,' he said, grateful that she seemed to understand.

'Do you have any idea what lies behind these murders? The flowers. The water.' Of all the people, she thought he might have. He had the sort of mind which could see the patterns in things. The question came out before she'd considered whether it would be sensible to ask.

He sat for a moment, his eyelids blinking wildly behind the thick lenses of his glasses.

'No,' he said. 'Of course not.'

Chapter Thirty-One

Felicity had assumed Vera Stanhope would collect Lily Marsh's ring and was a little confused to find a young man standing at the door. He introduced himself as Joe Ashworth and, when she still seemed unsure, he showed her his identity card and explained, 'DI Stanhope's my boss.' He could have been the junior partner in a small business. He was well mannered and engaging and she took to him at once. She realized then that she'd been foolish to expect an inspector to turn out on such a trivial matter.

Almost immediately afterwards, James arrived from the school bus. They were still on the doorstep and he ran past them into the house and into the kitchen, shirt untucked, trainers unlaced, ravenous as he always was when he got in from school. Even when they followed, he took no notice of the stranger and continued pulling biscuits out of the tin, talking with his mouth full about sports day. She wished he had given a better impression, been more polite. But Ashworth seemed to understand children and smiled at her over the boy's head. He sat and made small talk as if he had all the time in the world.

'Your husband says you're the gardener in the family.'

'I suppose I am. He's very busy. And though he's a botanist by profession, his real passion is birds. He'd much rather be out on the coast.'

'We live on a new estate,' Ashworth said. 'There's not much of a garden at all. My wife makes it pretty, though. She watches the makeover programmes on the telly.'

While he was chatting about his wife and daughter and the new baby on the way, Felicity thought what a *nice* young man he was and how she wished Joanna had married someone like that, instead of Oliver, who worked in television and hardly seemed to notice that he had a child at all.

'Recently wor lass has got into making home-made cards,' Ashworth was saying. 'They had someone to speak at the WI about pressing flowers. Sarah's started growing plants she can pick for pressing. She sells them round the village. She'll do a one-off if someone wants a card for a special occasion. There's not much profit in it, but she covers the costs and she loves doing it.'

'Goodness! I wish we could attract some younger women to the Institute here. The average age must be about seventy-five and I'm the youngest by miles.'

'Maybe you had the same woman as a speaker?'

'I don't think so. But all those talks on craft become a bit of a blur. I'm not really interested. Two left hands. Any spare time and I'd rather be in the garden. I'll show you round later, if you like.'

James ran outside to play with the girls from the farm, but Felicity and Ashworth stayed in the kitchen to talk. She set the ring on the table between them.

'Such a pretty thing.' She smiled, confessed, 'I was almost tempted to keep it.'

'You're sure it belonged to Lily Marsh?'

'Oh yes,' she said. 'As soon as I saw it I knew it was familiar. It was only when I got back to the house that I remembered where I'd seen it.'

'You didn't notice Lily drop it?'

'If I had,' she said primly, 'I'd have returned it to her.'

'Of course.' He paused. She thought he was more deliberate than Vera Stanhope, slower in his thought and speech. 'I'm not clear how she might have lost it. Did she use the bathroom there? Take it off, perhaps, to wash her hands?'

She played back in her head the young woman's appearance at Fox Mill. 'No,' she said. 'No, she went to the bathroom here in the house, before we went across to the cottage. Perhaps it had just come loose. If she'd lost weight since it was bought . . .'

'Yes.' He gave a doubtful little smile. 'Wouldn't you have heard it drop, then? Unless the cottage is carpeted?'

She was starting to lose patience. She wondered if she had been wrong about this young man. Had he taken her in with his stories of his wife and daughter? Was he trying to trick her? 'There's no carpet,' she said more sharply. 'Flags downstairs and wooden floorboards in the bedroom. Does it really matter? She must have dropped it. I'm handing it back.'

'It might matter. If she was still wearing the ring when she left, it would suggest that she returned. We still don't know where Miss Marsh was killed. You do see how important these details are now?'

Felicity felt suddenly sick. She couldn't quite get to grips with what the detective was saying. 'Do you mean she was killed in our cottage? That's ridiculous. Impossible.'

'I don't think it's impossible,' he said calmly. He could still be talking about pressing flowers and the WI. 'It's not that far from here to where her body was found. We know it was her ring. We know it meant a lot to her. It was a present from someone very close to her. If we can find evidence that it was still in her possession when she left you, that would be significant, wouldn't it? It would mean she came back. Probably on the day she was killed.'

There was a silence. Felicity realized she was staring at him, that she was expected to speak. 'I really can't remember if she was wearing the ring when she left me. But she was a stranger. Why would she come back? Do you think she'd changed her mind about renting the cottage?'

Ashworth ignored the last question. 'Are you sure your husband had never met her?'

'Of course. He told you.' But while she was saying the words she was wondering if that was true. Peter knew nothing of *her* affair with Samuel. It was perfectly reasonable that he might have a life which was hidden from her. The idea was horrifying. How hypocritical is that? she thought. What right do I have to be jealous or hurt? But Lily had been so young and pretty. Of course there could be no question of her having an affair with Peter, who must have seemed an old man to her. This anxiety was ridiculous. Then she realized the detective was speaking again and she tried to concentrate on his words.

'I'd like our crime scene investigators to look at the cottage,' he said. 'Just in case. You said you found the ring there this morning. Will anyone else have been in since you showed Lily round?'

'I took Inspector Stanhope in at the weekend.'

He gave a sudden broad grin. 'Her footprints'll be distinctive enough,' he said. 'Those sandals she wears. The size of elephants' feet. The CSI won't confuse them.'

'They won't find any footprints!' She didn't mean to be defiant, but realized that was how she sounded and she couldn't stop. 'That's what I was doing when I found the ring. I was cleaning. I brushed and mopped all the floors, scrubbed the work surfaces. It's not worth bringing in your experts.'

He stayed very calm and looked straight at her.

'What about bedding?' he said.

'I washed the sheets this morning. They're on the line. I told you, you're wasting your time. You won't find anything.'

'Oh you'd be surprised,' he said, 'just what we can find. You give us permission, I take it, for us to have a look?'

'Of course.' She knew it was too late to retrieve the situation. He must be convinced now that she'd cleaned the cottage to destroy any evidence that Lily had been killed there. 'We'll help in whatever way we can. We have nothing to hide.'

From the kitchen window she watched the drama unfold. He stood at the front of the house to make his phone call. He had his back to her and she had no idea what response he was getting. From his car he took a roll of blue-and-white tape. Had he been expecting this outcome? Had he brought it with him specially? He walked across the meadow and stretched it across the cottage door. She wanted to rebuild the rapport they'd had when he first arrived. Should she go out to him, offer him more tea? But she could tell he would consider it an intrusion. They might own the house, but this was his territory now.

He walked back to the drive, sat on the bank where the crocuses and snowdrops grew in spring and waited. He brushed the pollen and grass seed he'd picked up in the meadow from his trousers. His phone rang. She couldn't hear it from the house, but she could see him answer. A sudden grin. Triumphant. More scary than when he'd been so cool in conversation with her. She thought she should phone Peter at work, warn him what was going on, but when she dialled his direct number at the university there was no reply. The raucous call of a cuckoo came from the kitchen clock. It was six o'clock. He would already have left. She struggled to remember what she had planned for supper, but the thought slipped from her mind and she returned to look out of the window.

James wandered down the drive. The girls from the farm must have been called in for tea. He was wearing shorts and his knees were filthy. The detective raised his hand in greeting and James sat beside him on the grass. He was curious now about what the stranger was doing here. They talked for a few minutes. Felicity thought they were getting on well. They seemed to be sharing a joke. *Surely he must realize we wouldn't commit murder. We have a lovely son. Too much to lose. We're nice, respectable people. People just like him.*

James got to his feet and walked into the house.

He disappeared from her view for a minute, then appeared in the kitchen. She thought, knowing the image was a silly exaggeration: He's like a cold-war spy who's come across from the other side. He might have valuable information. But he opened the fridge and peered inside as if it was any other evening. 'I'm starving. When's tea?'

'Won't be long.' She tried to keep her voice even. 'What were you and Mr Ashworth talking about?'

'Is that his name?' He was drinking orange juice straight from the carton. She restrained the urge to snap at him to fetch a glass. 'He told me to call him Joe. He was asking me about Miss Marsh. What she was like as a teacher. How she got on with the kids in our class.' His voice grew more excited. 'They're bringing in crime scene investigators to look at the cottage. Like on the television. There might be some trace in there to help them find out who killed Miss Marsh. Wait till I tell Lee Fenwick.' Lee was his best friend and keenest rival. In winter they played chess together every evening.

She heard the faint sound of a vehicle turning in from the lane. She expected it to be Peter. *Please keep your temper. Please be polite. He's only doing his job.* But it was a white van. A man and a woman jumped out, greeted Joe Ashworth as if he was an old friend. They pulled on the paper suits she'd seen in films and started lifting equipment from the back of the van.

James had forgotten about food. 'Do you think I could go out and watch?'

'No,' she said sharply, then regretted her tone. Of course he was fascinated. So was she in a horrible, frightening way. 'Won't you get a better view from your bedroom?'

James ran off and she felt a sudden relief that she no longer had to pretend that everything was normal. When he'd opened the fridge she'd seen a bottle of white wine, started the night before, and realized she was desperate for a drink. She took it out, removed the vacuum stopper and poured herself a large glass. Her hand was shaking.

Back at the window she saw Peter's car coming down the drive. His normal parking place had been taken by the van. She saw him get out and prepare to demand it was moved. Then he realized what was happening. He saw the two figures dressed in white walking across the meadow. Their weight was tilted towards each other, because of the heavy metal box they carried between them. Like James, he had watched enough television to understand what they were doing. Felicity saw Joe Ashworth approaching him, hand outstretched, but Peter hadn't noticed. His focus was still on the cottage, the androgynous figures who had now reached the door. His face was very pale and still. My God, Felicity thought. He looks guilty. Guilty as hell. If I was Joe Ashworth I'd think he'd killed the girl.

She didn't dare ask herself if she thought the same thing. The thought hovered at the back of her mind and she pushed it away, concentrated on the fish she'd cook for supper and on whether she should make sandwiches for Ashworth and his friends in the cottage. Now Peter and Ashworth were deep in conversation. They walked together towards the house.

She prepared herself to be normal and welcoming, took a deep breath as the door opened.

Peter looked at her with the expression he put on when he'd received bad news, a paper rejected, a record dismissed. Aggrieved. She knew he wanted reassurance, but she didn't have the heart to give it. In the end it was Ashworth who spoke.

'Dr Calvert's agreed to come to the station in Kimmerston to have a chat with DI Stanhope. A few points we want to clear up. It shouldn't take long.'

She forced herself to smile. 'Of course,' she said. 'I told you, anything we can do to help . . .'

Chapter Thirty-Two

Vera thought Ashcroft had made a mistake bringing Calvert in. The botanist was hardly likely to leave the country. She believed they were showing their hand too soon. Perhaps *she'd* made a mistake in phoning Ashworth to tell him that Charlie had found the antique shop in York where Lily's ring had been bought. There was still no evidence that Calvert was the lover. An older man with an attractive young woman, the owner had said. Tall, fit for his age. That could describe a lot of people, including Samuel Parr. They'd found a photo of Calvert on the jacket of a textbook he'd written, but it had been published nearly twenty years before and his hair then had been longer and dark. No wonder it had sparked no recognition. If Calvert had been the man in the shop.

The ring had been bought in January and paid for with cash. The owner had drawn his own conclusions about that. 'It's not unusual. He wouldn't want his wife finding it on his credit-card statements, would he?' And perhaps that did point to Calvert. Samuel Parr no longer had a wife to check up on him.

'Can you remember anything about the gentleman?' Charlie had asked. Vera could imagine him standing in the smart shop, looking scruffy and out of place. York wouldn't be Charlie's sort of place at all. Except for the races. He'd be quite at home there.

And then the owner had come out with the one useful bit of information they'd got from him. 'He was in town for some sort of conference. It was lunch-time and he said he had to go back for an afternoon session. The young lady didn't like that at all. She was trying to persuade him to miss it. There wasn't a row, not quite that. But a disagreement. That's why I remember. And because she was such a beauty.'

Vera would have liked some confirmation that Calvert was at a conference in York before sitting opposite him in an interview room. She'd phoned everyone she could think of, but this time in the evening there was no one around to ask. She'd set Holly onto the internet, university websites, botanical societies, but most of the sites had been updated. There was no record now of an event which had happened six months earlier.

She made sure he was treated with respect. She didn't want to waste time dealing with complaints and she wanted him to underestimate them. He'd give more away if he was feeling superior. At the last minute she asked Holly to join her in the interview room instead of Ashworth. Maybe Calvert would feel the need to show off in front of a pretty young woman. Among the rest of the team there was a bub-bling excitement. They thought it was nearly all over.

She made coffee for Calvert – from her own sup-ply, not the crap from the machine – and carried it through to the interview room.

'Sorry to ask you in before you've had time for supper,' she said. She took time to settle herself, let papers fall out of her bag when she put it on the floor, picked it up again to search for a pen. 'Still, this shouldn't take long. Just a few things to clear up. You don't mind if we tape the conversation? Standard procedure.' She looked at him for the first time. He seemed composed enough. Ashworth had said he'd almost fallen apart when he'd seen the CSIs walking towards the cottage and that was one of the reasons why he'd brought him in. She introduced Holly and Calvert nodded, gave an insinuating smile which was enough to make your flesh crawl.

'Did you attend an academic conference in York in January?'

He hadn't been expecting the question and it threw him. She saw his mind racing. He'd been so careful, paid for everything by cash. How could they possibly know? Ashworth had been right. He had been Lily's lover.

'Dr Calvert?' She kept her voice quiet, tentative. Then, when he still didn't answer, 'You do realize we'll be able to check.'

He pulled his thoughts together. 'I'm sorry, Inspector. Yes, I was there. I just can't see the relevance to your enquiries of my giving a paper at a conference.'

'You had a companion,' she said. 'Not at the conference, but in York.'

This time his response came more quickly. 'Ah,' he said. 'So my sins have found me out.' He gave the smile which was supposed to be charming. 'You must be able to understand why I lied about that, Inspector. I have a wonderful wife and family. So much to lose.

I hoped I'd get away with it, that they wouldn't have to be hurt.'

'You were having an affair with Lily Marsh?'

'Yes. At least, I'd had an affair. It was all over by the time of her death. But you can imagine the shock of seeing her body in the water. And of realizing that my son had known her.'

'You can't expect us to sympathize, Dr Calvert.'

'No,' he said quickly. 'No. But I'm trying to explain why I handled the situation so badly, why I wasn't entirely truthful.'

'You weren't truthful in any way. That has to end. I can't consider your sensibilities when I'm investigating a murder. Two murders.' She realized she sounded like a Sunday school teacher, but he seemed to respond.

'I really don't know anything about the first murder,' he said. 'Luke Armstrong. I'd never met him.'

'You had heard of him, though. Gary Wright had fallen for his mother. He was talking about it in the pub after the last Bird Club meeting.'

'Was he?' Calvert seemed genuinely confused. 'I'm sorry. I can't have been listening. Some things had been said at the meeting to which I took exception. A criticism of an article I'd written in last month's *Birding World*. I suppose it seems trivial now, but I was preoccupied.'

'Tell me about the affair with Lily. How did you meet her?'

'Quite by chance last summer. I went into the shop where she worked to buy a birthday present for Felicity. It's an awkward situation for a man. What do we know about women's clothes? She was very helpful. We talked briefly and she explained she was a student. Then I saw her at the university, bought her a coffee to thank her. At that point there was nothing more to it than that. I couldn't believe she'd be interested in someone like me. I suppose I was flattered, a foolish old man.'

'You gave her money?'

'Yes, something towards her rent. Her parents couldn't help out. My daughters had finished university. I suppose I wanted to make a gesture. Do something generous. I expect you think I was naive, that she was only going out with me for the money.'

Vera didn't answer that. It wasn't her job to reassure him. She didn't believe it was true, though. Lily had been an obsessive. Money hadn't been the object of her desire.

'So you started seeing her. Where did you meet?'

There was a slight hesitation. 'This does sound so squalid. Afternoons in cheap hotels. Occasionally in her flat when she knew her friends were away. At first I suppose the secrecy was part of the excitement. Later it all became rather unsatisfactory.'

'Did she ever come to your house?'

'Not to the house, no. That would have seemed quite wrong.'

She picked up the precise wording, the slight hesitation. 'Not to the house. But to the cottage?'

He hesitated again. 'Yes, we met in the cottage. A few times. When Felicity was at a concert or the theatre and James was staying with a friend. Lily loved it there. I found it a bit close to home. I could never quite relax.'

He was lost in thought and for the first time

Vera did feel a small moment of understanding. Was he remembering a specific evening? Winter, perhaps, frost on the grass in the meadow and a fire lit in the grate. But never really enjoying it, listening out for a car on the drive, the danger of interruption.

'Did she have a key to the cottage?'

'Yes,' he said. 'I had one cut for her. She never gave it back.'

'Who ended the relationship?' The question was peremptory. She couldn't allow herself sympathy here.

'Neither of us. Not really. We just agreed that it had to end. Before it became general knowledge.'

'That wouldn't matter to Lily, would it? She wasn't married after all. What would she have to lose?'

'She must have seen that the relationship wasn't going anywhere. I suppose she wanted all the things her friends had – a shared home, real companionship, a family eventually. She was very fond of children. I'd never have been able to give her that.'

It sounded very plausible. But Lily Marsh hadn't been like her friends.

'Why do you think she turned up to look at the cottage? If your relationship had ended amicably, it seems an odd thing to do.'

'Perhaps she was struck by the coincidence of having James in her class and came to look at the cottage for old times' sake. She might even have seen it as a weird kind of practical joke. She'd expect Felicity to tell me she'd been.'

'Was it coincidence, having James in her class?'

'Of course. What else would it have been?'

She arranged it, Vera thought. She was obsessed by

you in the same way as she was obsessed by Ben Craven. She found out where James went to school and she asked Annie Slater for a placement in Hepworth. She got to know the boy, orchestrated the visit to look at the cottage. Why? To put pressure on him? A form of blackmail? They sat for a moment in silence. Calvert seemed preoccupied, but not anxious. Was he so arrogant that he believed he could get away with murder? In the end he broke the silence.

'You are looking for the same person for both murders?'

'That's the theory we're working on just now.' She wasn't going to commit herself further than that. They'd kept the details of the Armstrong crime scene out of the press, but word got out. Friends and family talked. Police and CSIs were only human. A good story was for sharing. She couldn't rule out the possibility that Lily's death had been a copy-cat killing. Someone wanted her dead and had used the details of Luke's murder to muddy the water. The phrase stuck in her head. *Muddy the water.* She supposed it was apt.

'I couldn't have killed the boy. I was looking at the notes on my book. I made a phone call on Wednesday night. Ten-thirty. A detail I needed to check with a friend. There'll be a record, I presume, on my phone bill. It was a long call to a mobile.'

Vera didn't answer immediately and Holly spoke for the first time. 'That's very convenient, Dr Calvert. What a shame you didn't mention it before. We'll need to talk to your friend, of course. Otherwise the call could have been made by anyone in your house.'

The response irritated him. He struggled to keep his composure. He smiled again at Holly. He probably

thought he was good with young women. 'I under-
stand that I made a huge mistake not telling you about
Lily. I'd expect you to check. But please believe me,
I'm not keeping anything else back from you.'

'What will you tell your wife about the affair?'
Holly again. She even gave him a grin. Cheeky,
almost complicit. *What else do you get up to? What else
have you got away with?*

'The truth. She deserves that. She knows me well
enough to realize I'd never kill.'

'We found a card among her belongings,' Vera said.
'Made of pressed flowers. Did you send it to Lily?'

He paused. 'No,' he said. 'I don't go in for sentimental gestures, Inspector.'

'You're sure?'

'Of course I'm sure. It's not something I'd forget.'

*So who did send it? And why was Lily's card marked
with kisses while Luke's was blank?*

'You were very close to Lily? I mean, you had a
physical relationship, but you talked? You felt you
knew her well?'

The question made him uncomfortable for the
first time. He struggled to find appropriate words.
At last he answered very simply. 'I was infatuated. I
thought I loved her. For a while, at least. No, it wasn't
just about the sex.'

'Did she tell you anything which might give a clue
to her killer? Was she troubled, scared, anxious?'

'She didn't talk much about herself.'

She'll not have had the chance, Vera thought.

'Just before we separated, she said she'd met up
with an old friend. Someone she'd known from the
village where she'd grown up. It seemed to be a big

thing for her. She was a loner. She didn't have many real friends.'

'Man or woman?' *Ben Craven?*

'A woman.' He paused. 'If you give me a moment I'll remember her name. Her first name, at least. She worked as a nurse at the RVI. Kath.'

It took Vera a moment to make the link. Kath Armstrong. Wife of Geoff. Stepmother to Luke.

Chapter Thirty-Three

Vera caught up with Kath Armstrong at the hospital. Her shift had just started and she was in a meeting with the day staff. Vera waited by the nurses' station and heard muttered voices coming from the sister's office, an occasional stifled laugh. Visiting was over and the ward was peaceful. The women in the side rooms were plugged into their televisions or reading. There was a little desultory chat. Further down the corridor the tea trolley was being wheeled away. On the window sill funereal bunches of flowers drooped in the heat. Vera had never been in hospital and knew she'd hate it. Not the illness or the pain. Not even the dreadful food and going without alcohol. But giving up control. Being at the mercy of people who knew more about her body than she did.

The meeting broke up and Kath came out. She was still chatting to a colleague, didn't notice Vera sitting in the orange chairs where patients waited to be discharged. 'I'd like a word,' Vera said. 'Sorry to bother you here, but something's come up.'

'Nothing's wrong, is it?' A moment of panic. Vera knew she was thinking about her little girl.

'No, nothing like that. Is there anywhere we can talk?'

Kath turned away to whisper to a motherly middle-aged woman in a sister's uniform. 'Maggie says we can use her office.'

They sat where the nurses had been huddled in their meeting. There was a photo on the desk of two small boys leaning against a farm gate next to a bearded man in specs. The ward sister's husband and kids. A child's drawing was pinned to the wall. More happy families.

'What's this about? Have you found out who killed Luke?'

Vera ignored the question. 'You didn't tell us you knew Lily Marsh.'

'You didn't ask.'

'She wasn't dead when I spoke to you, pet. You'll realize it's just a bit important. Two murders within a week and you knew both victims.'

'I didn't know her well. I mean, I just thought: What a weird coincidence. I couldn't contribute anything to your enquiry.'

She seemed genuinely puzzled. Vera wondered if she spent too much of her life investigating crimes, making connections which were insignificant, seeing motives which didn't exist. A sort of strange paranoia, which didn't allow for coincidence at all.

'How did you know her?'

'We grew up together. I mean, I'm quite a bit older than her, but we lived in the same village. My mam was good friends with Phyllis Marsh. You know how it is in a place like that. They'd been to school together, they met up at the church, the WI. Lily and I were both only children. I ended up looking after her when we were younger. We were close in a way. She loved coming to visit. You know what children are like with older kids. Especially girls. And maybe I've always had this maternal thing. We lost touch when I moved into town and started working here.'

'But you met up again more recently.'

'Yes.'

'How did you meet?'

'She came into the hospital as an outpatient. She thought she was pregnant. She'd missed a couple of periods, but her home pregnancy test had come up negative. She wanted to check. I bumped into her in the lift when she was on her way out.'

'Isn't that the sort of thing you'd see your GP for?'

'She'd have had to wait for an appointment. For some reason she was desperate to know.'

'She wasn't pregnant,' Vera said. It was a statement not a question. The post-mortem had been clear about that. She remembered the pathologist's sadness that Lily would never be a mother, would never carry a child.

'No. And I could tell she was upset. It was the end of my shift and I took her for a coffee. The mothering thing again. I should learn to leave well alone.'

'She wanted a baby?'

'Desperately. I said all the usual things. She was young. It would happen sometime. It would be better anyway when she'd completed the PGCE. I could tell that none of it was having any effect.'

'Did she tell you who would have been the father?'

'Not in any detail. She said he was an older man. That was all.'

'Was that the only time you saw her?'

'No. I was worried about her. I knew she'd had a

bit of a breakdown when she was in the sixth form. The stress of exams. Phyllis expected so much from her. Oxford, the glittering career. She didn't have much of a marriage and was living through Lily. Nobody would have been able to stand the strain. I asked Lily if she was seeing a doctor. She lost her temper, said she wasn't ill, everything was fine. I gave her my mobile number, told her to give me a ring if she wanted to talk.'

'And she did.'

'Oh yes.' Kath took a breath. 'To be honest she became a bit of a nuisance. She'd often be waiting in the car park when I finished work. After a night shift all you want is to get home, have a long bath and a few hours' sleep. And I didn't really think I could do any good. She needed psychiatric help. Then one day, a Saturday afternoon, she turned up at the house. We were having a day at home, one of those Saturday afternoons when you just want to chill. Rebecca was in the garden playing and Geoff was watching sport on the television. Luke was staying and he was glued to the box too. I was in the kitchen, keeping an eye on Rebecca through the window. And suddenly Lily was there, in the garden. She started chatting to Rebecca, then lifted her onto the swing and started to push. By the time I got out, she had Rebecca in her arms.' She paused. 'I'm not quite sure what would have happened if I hadn't been there.'

'You think she might have gone off with her?'

'I don't know. I'm probably overreacting. She was training to be a teacher, for goodness' sake. Why would she do something like that? But I made it clear that I didn't want her coming to the house. I said

Geoff wouldn't like it. Luke wandered out into the garden and was obviously a bit anxious when he saw I was upset. She went without a fuss, said she was sorry she'd turned up when it was obviously not convenient. The next time she waited for me outside work I made an excuse not to spend time with her. I felt mean, but she wasn't my responsibility. There was nothing I could do. I told her again she needed medical help, said I'd sort it out for her if she wanted. A veiled threat, I suppose. I never saw her again. When I heard she was dead, I suppose my first feeling was relief: Well, at least she won't come bothering us again. Isn't that dreadful?'

'Was she upset when you threatened to arrange a psychiatrist to see her?'

Kath paused. 'Not so much upset as angry,' she said. 'She didn't say anything but she glared at me, then turned away without a word. It was horrible. I felt she hated me. I was tempted to go after her, just to make things right between us, but I didn't. I couldn't face the idea of her turning up at the house again.'

'You never heard from her after that?'

'No.' Kath looked at her watch. 'Look, I should go. There's a patient coming up from casualty. I need to admit her.'

'She didn't say anything which made you worry for her safety? She didn't seem afraid of anyone? The man she'd been seeing?'

'Nothing like that. She said he loved her. I wondered if that was true. Perhaps he'd rejected her and that was why she seemed so upset. If I had any worry at all, it was that she might harm herself.'

'Suicide?'

'Perhaps.' Kath stood up and led the way out of the office. 'Look, I should probably have been kinder, made more effort to see she was OK. But my family came first.'

Vera drove home, pleased to be leaving the city and the investigation behind. Turning west into the hills she was almost blinded by the setting sun. When she arrived at the old station master's house, she sat for a moment in the car, too tired even to go in. Then she roused herself, got out of her car, unlocked the door. She stepped over the pile of mail on the floor, took a can of beer from the fridge and carried it outside. Even now, in the dusk, it was still warm. She sat on the white seat, where once passengers had waited for the small local train, and looked out over the valley. Everything was in shadow and drained of colour. Here, she thought, it should be possible to rest.

But her mind couldn't leave the investigation behind. She felt as feverish and obsessive as Lily had been, turning over details, chasing connections. If I could write it down, she thought, perhaps I could let it go. But she was too exhausted to get up to fetch paper and pen. And there was something creative in this concentration, in being forced to keep all the details clear in her mind at once. It came to her suddenly that this was what it must be like to be a writer of fiction. All the characters and stories and ideas spinning around her head. How could you bring some order to them? Make sense of them, give them shape.

If I was writing a novel, she thought, Lily would be the murderer. It would be one of those psychological thrillers, where part of the action is seen from the murderer's point of view, written in a different font or the present tense. Vera borrowed books like that from the library sometimes, enjoyed throwing them across the room when they got the details of police procedure wrong. So, Lily's the central character. She's been screwed up from childhood. A repressed mother and a depressed father. An illness that's been covered up by her mother, hidden away, never diagnosed. She's become a loner. A beautiful, obsessed loner. The reader will see her fall in love with an older man. Lily sees him as her salvation, even becomes happy for a while. Then he rejects her, because she's becoming too demanding, a nuisance, and she gets ill again. Imagines a pregnancy. And everywhere she goes there are happy families. Kath, Geoff and Rebecca. And Luke. Within the fiction she might kill the boy out of anger. A twisted revenge. Not realizing that he'd had a lot to put up with too.

Without being aware of it, Vera had wandered into the house, thrown the empty beer can into the box for recycling, opened the kitchen window to let in some air. She put the last two pieces of bread under the grill, sliced cheese to go on top, looked at the unopened bottle of white wine in the fridge and resisted the temptation. Took another can of beer instead.

All the time thinking, teasing out the different strands of the plot. Lily hadn't been a murderer, she'd been a victim. So how did that work out? How did that make sense?

She'd been a nuisance to Peter Calvert. He'd been happy to have a beautiful girlfriend, sex on tap, no strings attached. That would have done his ageing male ego no harm at all. Then she'd started to make demands, intruded into his respectable life of university big cheese and happy family man. No way was their separation mutual. Lily's conversation with Kath had made that clear. There couldn't be *another* older man in Lily's life.

Had Calvert killed her? Vera couldn't see it. He was too much of a coward, had too much to lose. His wife had indulged him in everything else in his life, why not in this too? Vera could imagine the conversation in the elegant living room at Fox Mill, the windows open to let in the breeze from the sea, the view to the lighthouse. *I'm so sorry, darling. I don't know what came over me. You will forgive me.* And of course she would because she had as much to lose as he had. Anyway, where did Luke Armstrong fit into that scenario?

If Lily had been killed first it might have worked. There was a motive for Lily's death. Luke could have been an involuntary witness. But this way round it made no sense at all.

Vera sat at the kitchen table and ate her cheese on toast. She switched on the light, so the clutter on the worktops, the stains on the floor near the bin, were all illuminated. Her thoughts turned to the four men who'd been there when Lily's body had been found. All different. But all screwed up when it came to women. Clive, so dominated by his mother that it made Vera want to weep. It was too close to home. She'd spent all her life in Hector's shadow, could get maudlin, if she let herself, about the missed opportunities when it came to men. Gary, who'd persuaded himself that Julie was the answer to all his prayers. But still pining for some slender lass with big eyes and no tits. Samuel, whose wife had committed suicide. And Peter, who pretended to have a perfect marriage, but had come under Lily Marsh's spell. It came to her suddenly that there was one logical suspect. But until she knew why Lily and Luke had been killed, that insight was no more than a guess. It couldn't influence the way she moved the enquiry on.

She drank more beer, knowing it was a mistake and she'd end up having to go to the bathroom in the middle of the night. Unsteadily she went upstairs to bed, still no nearer to any sort of conclusion. She took the collection of short stories by Samuel Parr from her bag and started to read.

Chapter Thirty-Four

Gary was having a quiet time at work. The band had finished rehearsing and he'd got the sound as good as it could be. Not that anyone else would notice the difference. The musicians were Swedish. They played experimental jazz, odd discordant noises which made him wince. Now they were in the bar waiting for the gig to start. There'd have been times when Gary would be with them, matching them pint for pint. He'd got into a real mess after Emily left him. It had been such a shock. He still remembered in detail her telling him there would be no marriage. He could recreate the scene in his head – the jeans she had on, the way her hair was tied back, the perfume she was wearing.

They'd had everything planned. She'd bought the dress, sent out the invitations. They'd found a flat to buy in Jesmond. Emily worked for the Northern Rock and got a cheap mortgage. It had scared the shit out of him, the prospect of taking on a wife and a home all at once, but he'd gone along with it because it was what Em had wanted. He would have done anything to please her. Her mother had never liked him, but she *had* liked the idea of a fancy wedding. She had it all arranged – the church, the cake, penguin suits. Nothing was too good for her Emily.

Then some lad Em had been at college with had turned up out of the blue, swearing undying love. He was a thin, weedy lad, not bad-looking if you liked them underweight and poetic. And it seemed Emily did, because she dumped Gary a fortnight before the big day. She was still with the bloke, who was a teacher now in some school in Ponteland. Gary'd seen him once in a bar in town and thumped him. The bloke hadn't made a fuss but Gary'd been done for breach of the peace. He'd been drinking a lot when that happened. He wouldn't react in the same way these days.

He'd idealized Emily and frightened her away. Who could live up to that? It wasn't the skinny lad's fault.

Now Gary never drank when he was working. *If you worked in an office, you wouldn't sit there with a bottle of wine on your desk.* That's what he told the other guys who sat in the cramped bit of corridor they called an office. Behind the scenes at the Sage was more like working in a submarine than a flash new music venue. All pipes and wiring and grey gloss paint.

He took his work seriously. It had always been the one thing he'd been good at, the one thing to hold him together. When his parents had bought their place in Spain, they'd said he should go with them too. There'd be plenty of work, they said. All those bars. Lots of them would have live music and they must need someone to do the sound. But he'd decided to stay in Shields. He had his flat there and his contacts. His birding friends. The chance to pick and choose the sort of gigs he wanted to do. He'd given up that flexibility now that he'd decided to take the job at the Sage, but he told himself he didn't regret it. Not really.

He walked up the steps of the small hall and swiped his pass at the door to get into the backstage area, then made his way down to the techie office. Neil, who was in charge, was leaning back in his chair thumping away on his computer.

'That offer of a permanent job,' Gary said.

'Yeah.' Neil didn't even bother to look up from the screen. He'd asked Gary loads of times before and the answer had always been 'no'.

'I've decided to take it.'

That got his attention. He swung his chair back to upright and his hands stopped moving. When he turned towards Gary his face was a picture. He jumped to his feet, took Gary's hand, slapped him on the back. Gary found himself grinning. But when he walked away, he was shaking. He wasn't quite sure what he'd done.

Now he had this picture of how things would be. Him and Julie living together in that house in Seaton. It would be a good place to live. Not too far from the coast when the wind turned east and the migrants came in. Not too far from the tower for sea watching. He couldn't rush her, of course. Not now that she was so upset about Luke. But he thought she'd come out of the tragedy whole. She was a strong woman. She wouldn't be changed by it. And he'd be there to support her and see her through.

He wasn't sure how he would have coped with a stepson. Would Julie have expected him to be like a dad? He didn't like to admit it, but he wasn't sorry Luke was dead, not really. It would have been a complication. Julie was always going to put the boy first. It was an awful way to look at things, but he couldn't help it. That led him to think of Laura. He pictured her as he'd last seen her, standing on the pavement outside the house in Seaton, watching him drive away. Weighing him up. That was how it seemed. He saw her in the short black skirt, the white shirt. He tried not to think of her in a sexy way. She'd be like a daughter to him if he got it together with Julie, and that was just vile. But something about her – her youth or her energy and defiance had got under his skin. Sometimes he thought he was haunted by Laura as much as he was by Julie. Perhaps it was safer not to consider moving into the house in Seaton until Laura had grown up.

There was still half an hour before he needed to start work and he went outside for air, walked to the front of the huge curved building and looked out over the Tyne. His parents had left for Spain because they couldn't stand the weather, but he couldn't imagine living anywhere else. He was proud of the city. He liked telling people he worked at the Sage. To his right and down by the river was the huge bulk of the Baltic Gallery. He remembered it as a decaying warehouse, kittiwakes nesting in the cracked stonework, its facade covered with bird muck. When it had first opened, he'd gone with Samuel Parr to see the Gormley exhibition. He wouldn't have wanted to go on his own. He was only comfortable backstage. But he'd loved the sculpture, all those figures of twisted metal, fine as spun sugar. Gary had found it odd to be there with Samuel, who was recognized by some of the staff. He was part of the Tyneside arts mafia, the set Gary despised as an alien race when they came into the Sage.

The river was at full tide, moving sluggishly, almost on the turn. On the north bank people were spilling out of the bars. He heard a line of melody, which faded before he could place it, the blast of a car horn. The low sun was reflecting from all the glass and turning the water red. Would Samuel or Clive or Peter Calvert find it strange to see Gary at *his* work, sat behind the deck, in control of the sounds coming out to the audience, making a difference, a real difference to the experience they had in the brilliant space? They knew him only as a demon sea watcher. They'd been friends for years, but really they knew very little about each other's lives. They knew he'd fallen for Julie, his childhood sweetheart, with her smile and her easy, comfortable body. They'd never guess he dreamed of the teenage Laura in her short black school skirt. They believed they were the closest of friends, but they all had secrets they would never share.

His mobile beeped to show he had a text message. It was from Julie and he felt a shock of guilt, physical. His face was hot as if he was blushing. *What are you doing tonight.* He pushed away his daydreams about Laura then and answered immediately. *Working. Wont be finished til midnight.* He had to wait so long for the reply that he'd almost given up. Perhaps she'd been offended, seen it as a rejection rather than a statement of fact. He should have taken more time to compose it. He fretted, putting together another message in his head. It was time for him to go in and do the final check. He always switched off his phone when he was working. Her reply came as he was walking back up the steps, with his back to the river. *Ill come and meet you. See you then.*

Chapter Thirty-Five

Julie felt that if she didn't get out of the house she'd scream. She'd stand at the top of the stairs and fill her lungs and open her mouth and the noise would be so loud that you'd hear it at the end of the road. Her mother was still there, cleaning. All day there was the hum of the Hoover, the background stink of bleach and polish, so it didn't even feel like Julie's house any more. And when she wasn't cleaning Mrs Richardson was talking, trying to prod Julie back to life with sharp words and guilt. As if there wasn't enough guilt around already. Julie had always found it easier to get on with her father. If he'd been there instead of her mother, they could have got pissed together. He'd have sat beside her on the sofa, watching the music channels on TV, telling his old stories about the musicians he'd known, holding her when she wanted to cry.

She couldn't tell her mother to leave. She thought she was being useful and it would hurt her. Then Julie would feel guilty all over again. So all day she tried to make up an excuse to get out. She concocted a story about being invited to Lisa's house. Lisa would cook her a meal and Julie would stay over in the spare room. Julie's mother approved of Lisa, who worked as a secretary for a big firm of solicitors in town. Then Julie went out into the garden and phoned Lisa on her mobile. On the other side of the horses' field they were cutting grass. She watched the tractor moving backwards and forwards, regular and mesmerizing. She could have watched it all day, but her mam would never have allowed it. She'd see it as idle and self-indulgent and would find Julie something useful to do.

'If my mother phones, I'm at your house, but I've fallen asleep and you don't want to wake me.'

Lisa was a good mate and didn't ask questions. She *would* have cooked Julie a meal and drunk wine with her and let her cry. But Lisa lived in a smart new flat on the front at Tynemouth and it had never been the sort of place where Julie had felt able to kick off her shoes and relax. Telling all these lies made Julie feel like a teenager again. By the end of the afternoon she was exhausted by it all. But she was a little bit excited too. She'd known all along that what she really wanted was to see Gary.

She had a shower before she went out, stood in the bath where Luke had been lying. Before, they'd had an old shower curtain, with pinkish spots of mould along the hem, but the police had taken that away. Her mam had been to Matalan to get another. Julie drew the curtain and shut her eyes to wash her hair. It was the first time since Luke had died. Until then she'd used Sal's place when she wanted a bath. She took her time getting ready, make-up, a splash of perfume. It wouldn't make her mother suspicious. She was of a generation when women didn't go visiting without making a bit of an effort.

Laura was in her room. She seemed to live there these days, only came out to eat and wee. Julie thought she'd been like that even before Luke had died. She knocked, poked her head round the door. Laura was lying on the bed. Not reading, not watching television, just staring at the ceiling.

'Are you all right, pet?' Julie sat on the bed.

Laura turned, managed a bit of a smile. Julie thought she should stay in. She was reminded of Luke when he'd started to get depressed. But she couldn't quite make the decision. If she didn't get out of the house she'd go mad herself.

'I was thinking of going out. Lisa's asked me to hers. Is that all right with you?'

Laura stared at her for a moment before shrugging. 'Sure.'

Julie thought she could never tell what Laura was thinking, never had been able to.

'I might stay over. Nan will be here.'

'I'll be fine. Really.'

Julie sat in the old Fiat she'd had since Geoff had left, which was held together now with filler and paint. Each year at MOT time there was a crisis and her friend Jan's mechanic son would work his magic and pull it through. This was another first. She hadn't driven since Luke had died. She imagined the neighbours looking through their nets, waiting for her to drive away. What would they think? That she was a heartless cow or that she was brave to start putting her life together. She wasn't sure herself which it was.

It was only eight o'clock but she went straight to the town. There was the usual panic when she hit the motorway at the old BT roundabout. She never knew which lane to take for the bridge. Then in Gateshead she missed the turn for the Sage and ended up in the car park for the Baltic. She couldn't face going back and stayed where she was. She sat for twenty minutes, her mind quite blank, before buying a ticket at the pay and display machine. Nine o'clock. The light was starting to go. She realized she was relishing the sensation of being alone.

She left the car and walked around the front of the Baltic Gallery. There was some sort of reception in the downstairs bar. Through the long glass windows she saw women in long dresses, men in dinner suits. They were drinking champagne from narrow glasses. A fat woman with very short hair was making a speech. Julie felt as if she'd travelled to a new country, as if these were exotic creatures quite different from her. On an impulse she walked across the new millennium footbridge from Gateshead to Newcastle. She'd never done that before either. She stood in the centre and looked upstream at the arcs and towers of the other bridges, the Tyne, the High Level, the Redheugh, familiar landmarks seen in a completely different light. On the Newcastle Quayside, she pushed her way through the crowd in a bar, just to use the toilet. She wasn't tempted to stop for a drink. She wanted to be clear-headed when she met up with Gary. She felt a bit mad as it was.

By the time she got back to the south bank of the Tyne it was quite dark. The river was draining towards the sea. The smart people were still in the bar at the Baltic, though the speeches were over. She sat on a bench outside, watching them. It was as if the big plate window was a giant film screen and though she couldn't hear what they were saying she got caught up in the drama. There was a pretty young woman who couldn't settle. She fluttered from group to group, talking and laughing, growing more and more unsteady. When she moved away, the groups turned in and talked about her. She seemed so lonely that Julie wanted to cry.

Her phone rang. She looked at the time as she answered it: 23.38. She'd been sitting here, watching, for more than an hour. And enjoying every minute of being alone.

It was Gary. 'Hi. I've finished earlier than I thought. Where are you?'

'I'm here already. At the front of the Baltic, by the river.' She was going to add that she'd just arrived. She didn't want him thinking that she'd been sitting here for hours waiting for him. But he was talking about the gig and how well it had gone, a joy. Despite the crap music and the small audience. How some nights were like that. Smooth and sweet. And then she saw him walking towards her, still talking on his phone. He'd walked down the steps from the entrance to the Sage. She stood up, so he could see her. The phone went dead and she stuffed it into her bag, so her hands were free. They stood for a minute just looking at each other, then almost stumbled together, awkward like kids. She expected him to kiss her, but he didn't. He held her for a moment, rubbing her back.

'Where would you like to go?'

'Can we go back to yours?' she said. 'I don't feel much like company.'

'Sure.'

'I'd better follow you,' she said. 'I don't know the way.' She hoped he'd suggest something different. *Why don't you leave your car here? I'll bring you back to get it in the morning.* But he didn't, so they were only together for a few brief minutes before they were separated again. He was giving her instructions about waiting for him in her car and what to do if she lost him. She felt like the girl weaving her way through the crowd in the Baltic bar. Lost and unconnected.

But she didn't want to make a fool of herself so she did as he told her. She waited at the car park entrance until the white van drove past and she followed it all the way back to Shields. If she lost him at lights he pulled in so she could catch up with him. She drew in behind him when he parked in a narrow street. Here there was another view of the river. Suddenly she was so nervous she wished she was back at home, sitting in her nightie in front of the telly, her mam wittering on.

In the flat it was easier. He opened a bottle of wine and she drank a large glass very quickly. Sod it, she thought. She'd never intended to drive home that night anyway. He put on some music she didn't know. They both sat on the sofa, leaning back against the cushions so they were almost lying down. He had his arm around her and he was talking about the music, what he loved about it, but in a whisper, so she could feel his breath on her cheek. He put his hand on her neck, stroked it just underneath her ear.

And suddenly she thought of Luke. How someone had put their hand on his neck, pulled a rope tight around it and squeezed until he was dead. She didn't scream. The last thing she wanted was to make a fuss.

But Gary must have felt her tense because he pulled gently away.

'Sorry,' she said.

'Nothing to be sorry for.'

She told him what she'd been thinking about. Luke in her bathroom and someone strangling him. 'Sorry,' she said again. 'I'm a bit of a liability.' But she'd drunk the wine too quickly and the word came out wrong. She giggled and he joined in.

'We can do whatever you like,' he said. 'Do you want me to take you home?'

She thought how lonely she'd feel in the double bed. Her mother would have made it, so the sheets would be stretched tight, tucked into the mattress. She never bothered making it herself, she preferred the sheets soft, slightly crumpled. 'No,' she said. 'Can I have more wine?'

He poured her another glass.

She woke with a hangover, lying on the sofa, fully clothed except for her shoes. There was a strange light, coming from a different direction, so she'd known at once it wasn't her own bed. The smell of proper coffee came from the kitchen. She hadn't thought he'd be into proper coffee. He must have been waiting for her to wake because he came in carrying a mug, a plate of toast.

'You could have had the bed,' he said. 'But I couldn't move you.'

'God, I feel dreadful. What time is it?' She did feel dreadful, but only the way she always did when she had a hangover, sick and heady, and that was reassuring, a sign of things getting back to normal. And she *had* slept, without the sleeping pills.

'Ten o'clock.'

'Oh my God. Laura will have already left for school. Mam will kill me.' She swung down her legs, so there was room on the sofa for him to sit beside her. 'Look,' she said. 'About last night . . .'

'It's all right, I had a great evening.'

'Really? I don't think so.'

'You're good company. Even when you're pissed. And we've got plenty of time.'

'Yes,' she said softly. 'I hope we have.'

She took the scenic route home along Whitley Bay seafront and past St Mary's Island, singing along to one of the compilation tapes her dad had put together for her. Motown. She was trying to put off the moment of going back into the house. Here, driving the Fiat so slowly that the guy in the Astra behind her hit his horn, yelling at the top of her voice, she could almost believe that the rest of it, all the nightmare stuff, had happened to someone else.

As soon as she opened the door, her mother appeared from the kitchen. She was like a figure in one of those mechanical clocks. Not a cuckoo, of course. A peasant woman in an apron, bobbing her head and wringing her hands.

'Thank God. Where have you been? I've been so worried.'

'I told you I'd be staying at Lisa's.' And that wasn't a lie, was it?

'I expected you to be back before Laura went to school.' The guilt again.

'Yeah, well, I had a bit much to drink. Did she get off OK?'

'She didn't have time for breakfast.'

'She never has time for breakfast.'

'I don't suppose you've had anything to eat either.' And immediately she popped back into the kitchen, to put on the kettle and start frying bacon. 'I got this from that decent butcher in Monkseaton. It's not all water and fat.' And though the smell of it almost made Julie want to throw up, she sat at the table and waited until the sandwich appeared, then forced herself to eat it. To make up for lying to her mother. To make up for having a few hours when she wasn't thinking about Luke.

It was only after the plate was clean that her mother brought in the mail for her to look at. Not such a big pile. On the top, a long white envelope.

'Look,' Julie said, trying to re-establish friendly relations. 'This is addressed to Laura.'

Her mam, already in her Marigolds at the sink, turned round. 'That's nice. Some of her friends from school, maybe.'

'Maybe.' But by now Julie had recognized the square capital letters, remembered Vera's response to the last card. 'All the same, I think I'll just give Inspector Stanhope a ring.'

Chapter Thirty-Six

When the call came from Julie, Vera was in her office, reading. The night before, she'd started a short story by Samuel Parr, one she'd never heard or read before. It was in the book she'd picked up from the library on her way to meet Ben Craven, a collection published by a small press based in Hexham. The title *Jokers and Lovers* had some sort of resonance, but she couldn't remember where it was from. It said on the jacket that the anthology had won a prize she'd never heard of. The story she'd been looking for, the one she'd heard on the radio, hadn't been in it, but she'd started reading anyway. Vera had fallen asleep after a couple of paragraphs but, perhaps because of the beer swilling round in her veins, the opening image had stayed with her all night. It had described the abduction of a teenager. The abduction had been described lovingly. A summer's morning. Sunshine. The flowers in the hedgerow named. It became a seduction, rather than an act of violence. The gender of the child was left deliberately ambiguous, but Vera imagined Luke. A great deal was made of the child's beauty. This was a form which would turn heads. And Luke could have been a girl with his long lashes and his slender body.

Half child, half man, he'd been an ambiguous figure too.

In the office, Vera held the morning briefing. Joe Ashworth had checked all the car-rental places in North Tyneside.

'Nobody of Clive Stringer's name or description hired a car on Wednesday night or Friday. I suppose that lets him off the hook.' He sounded disappointed.

Vera almost felt sorry for him. She described the interview with Peter Calvert. 'We know he was Lily's lover. We know he's a lying bastard, with an unhealthy interest in bonny lasses. We know she left her silver and opal ring in the Calverts' cottage. But we can't prove she didn't drop it when she looked round the day before. And we can't prove any connection between him and Luke Armstrong.' Then she'd gone on to describe the connection between Lily and Kath. 'Is it significant that the new Mrs Armstrong didn't tell us she knew the Marsh lass? God knows. It is to us, of course. But we're living and breathing the investigation. Maybe she just wanted to forget all about it and get on with her life.'

Then Vera had retreated to her office. She knew there were more important things to do, but she told herself that her team would already be doing them. She was pulled back to the story, the strange central character. Then the phone rang.

'Julie Armstrong on the line, ma'am. She won't speak to anyone but you.'

Vera listened in silence when Julie described the envelope, the writing. 'I didn't want to bother you, like. But last time you seemed to think it was important. We haven't touched it. Well, just my mam when she brought it in from the front door.'

'Has Laura got a mobile?'

'Oh aye, they've all got mobiles these days, haven't they?'

'Phone her and tell her to stay at school. She's not to go out with anyone, not even someone she knows until you pick her up. I'll send someone in a car and you can go and fetch her. I'll contact the school. Leave the card where it is. Don't open it.'

'She won't have her phone switched on,' Julie said. Vera could sense her confusion, the onset of panic. 'It's a rule. They're not allowed.'

'Don't worry, pet. Just send her a text and leave her a voicemail message. I'll see to the rest.'

She hung up and took a moment to compose herself. She'd picked up some of Julie's panic, could feel her brain start to scramble, the eczema start to itch. Then she phoned the high school in Whitley Bay, bullied her way past an officious secretary to the headmaster. He understood at once what was needed, motivated, Vera thought, as much by the possibility of tabloid headlines – *How did they let it happen? Young girl snatched from school gate* – as by concern for Laura's safety. Then she told herself she was a cynical old bag. He said he'd track Laura down and keep her in his office until Julie and the police car arrived. He'd phone Vera back and let her know when that had happened. Vera sat, waiting. Her eyes wandered back to the book on her desk, the atmospheric jacket in muted blues and greens. The phone rang.

'Yes?'

The headteacher didn't identify himself. She

heard the tremor in his voice when he spoke, thought he was starting to panic too. 'She didn't arrive at school. She was marked absent at registration.'

'Nobody followed it up?'

'We wouldn't. Not one day. And with what happened to her brother, we could understand she might want to take some time.' Justifying himself to her, and to the unforgiving press which would want someone to blame. Already making his excuses.

'Of course,' Vera said. 'Not your fault.'

But mine? Should I have seen it coming? 'Does she have a history of bunking off?'

'No. She's reliable. A worker. One of the bright ones.'

'Can you ask around, friends, people she might have come in with on the bus? I'll send someone to take statements.' She thought she'd send Ashworth. He'd be good with young lasses.

'Can you be discreet?' he said. 'I mean, no flashing lights and uniforms. I don't want to start a mass hysteria, parents coming to take their kids away. Luke was a pupil here too.'

She was distracted. 'You knew him? I mean, as more than a face, a name.'

'Yes, I like the kids like Luke. The ones who struggle. It's what I came into teaching for. Important not to forget that sometimes. I took an interest.'

'Can you think why someone would have wanted him dead?'

'No!' The answer was immediate and vehement. 'He was bit slow, but he was a nice kid. People enjoyed his company.' He struggled to explain. 'He was completely inoffensive.' He wouldn't be satisfied with that description, but she understood what he meant.

When Vera arrived at Julie's house, the door was open and she was waiting to go. Her mother was hovering in the background. Julie turned to say goodbye to the older woman, but by then Vera was out of the car and blocking the door.

'A change of plan,' she said comfortably. 'No rush now. Let's go in. Any chance of a brew, Mrs Richardson?'

She led Julie into the living room and sat her on the sofa. 'Laura's not at school, pet. Did she definitely get on the bus?'

'I don't know. I wasn't here. I stayed last night with a friend.' She looked up at Vera. 'I was at Gary's place. Don't tell my mam. But I needed to get away, have a few drinks.'

'What time did you wake up? A bit of a hangover, was it?'

'Aye, something like that. I was out of it till ten.'

'And was Gary with you all that time?'

'We didn't sleep together. I was on the sofa.'

'So he could have gone out without you knowing.' Vera was speaking almost to herself. She didn't expect an answer.

'Where's Laura?' It came out like a scream, brought her mother rushing from the kitchen.

'We don't know. We're all looking for her. The school. My team, and they're the best you'll find anywhere.'

'What time did Laura leave the house?' Julie turned to her mother. 'Did she get the bus?'

'She left at the normal time. In a rush, no time for

breakfast as usual. I'd made her a packed lunch but she wouldn't take it.'

'Did you have a go at her, before she went out?' Julie was red and angry. 'You always have to nag.'

The older woman was almost in tears. 'I didn't have a go at her. I said she was really brave for going and I hoped she'd have a good day.'

'Oh Mam, I'm sorry. It's my fault. I should have been here. I was so wrapped up in myself and she needed me. It's like Luke all over again.'

'We've really no time for this,' Vera said. 'You can save the tantrums for later, when we've got Laura back. I need information. The time of the bus. The names of the friends she travelled in with. Favourite teachers. Teachers she hated. Boyfriends past and present. You start making a list. I'm going to look at this card.' She tore a sheet of paper from a notebook and gave Julie's mother a pen. When she left them they were sitting side by side on the settee, both with tears drying unchecked on their cheeks, but working through the problem, coming up with names.

The envelope was lying in the centre of the kitchen table. From the moment she'd got Julie's call Vera had tried to tell herself this might all be a waste of time. The woman was probably overreacting. It was a card from a friend or a relative or a teacher. Nothing sinister. But when she saw it, she recognized the capital letters at once. This time there was the correct address. It even had the postcode. The envelope hadn't been sealed. The flap had been tucked into the paper at the back. No saliva. Nor on the stamp, which was of the ready-stick variety. Vera pulled tweezers and latex gloves from her bag, put on the gloves, lifted out the card. A pressed flower. Something small and blue which she didn't recognize. The back was blank, just as the one which had been sent to Luke. No kisses.

She got on her phone to Holly at Kimmerston. 'It's definitely the same. I want it to the lab now and fast-tracked. And chase them up on the others.'

She phoned Ashworth, but heard immediately that he was surrounded by a gaggle of girls and couldn't speak. 'Call me,' she said. 'As soon as you have something.' She knew he didn't need telling that but it made her feel better to be dishing out orders.

She put on her calm, slightly daft face before going into the living room. She wrote down the direct-line number for Holly and gave it to Beryl Richardson. 'She's a nice lass. Give her a ring and give her all the names you've come up with. Julie, I'd like you to come with me. Show me the way Laura would walk to the bus stop. I've got my mobile on me and they'll call as soon as there's any news. We could both do with some fresh air.'

She had Julie on her feet and out of the house before either of the women could complain. At the gate, instead of turning left towards the centre of the village and the main road, Julie turned right. 'Laura didn't like waiting with the crowd at the bus stop by the pub. Specially since Luke died. She always felt awkward with lots of people anyway, but since then it's been even worse. She walks along the cut here and gets on at the stop nearer town.' She stopped, turned to Vera. 'I should have given her a lift in. But I was such a mess myself. I couldn't face it.'

'This isn't your fault,' Vera said, slowly enunciating every word. 'None of it.'

Julie led her down a narrow alley with allotments on one side and the backs of houses on the other and arrived at a stile. Vera heaved herself onto it and waited, perched on the top, panting for breath, looking out at the landscape beyond. The footpath followed the side of the field which had been cut the day before, along the edge of a patch of woodland towards the main road. Laura would have been visible from the upstairs windows in Julie's street all the way. Vera thought she'd get a team to do a house-to-house. It was an outside possibility that the girl had been seen, but worth a shot. If Laura had been taken, this surely was where it had happened. Once on the bus, she'd be surrounded by other kids all the way to school. She lowered herself down the other side, pulled down her skirt so she was decent. Julie followed.

'Who else would have known Laura took this path to get the bus?' Vera stooped to pick a bit of straw from her sandal, tried not to make too much of the question.

'I don't know. The other kids, I suppose.'

'Geoff? Kath?'

'She might have mentioned it. I can't see it, though. She hasn't exactly been chatty lately.'

So it was planned, Vera thought. They knew that anyway because of the card, but this confirmed it. Someone had waited and watched, followed the family's movements. Not from the street. That would have been noticed. Perhaps from here on the edge of the wood, where you had a view of the village. A good pair of binoculars and you'd see inside the houses.

Then she thought that whatever the reason had been for the first murder, the killer was now enjoying himself. Or herself. It had become a game, an obsession. A piece of theatre. Not just in the staging of the body, but in the events leading up to that. She hoped the killer would want to make the pleasure last. She hoped it meant that Laura was still alive.

Chapter Thirty-Seven

The morning Laura Armstrong disappeared, Felicity Calvert walked back from dropping James at the school bus and tried to come to terms with the news that Peter had been Lily's lover. She supposed she should feel betrayed. Not by Peter – what right did she have to judge him? But by Samuel. She was convinced that Samuel must have known about Peter's affair with Lily Marsh. Probably all four of the men who were there when James found the body had known. Peter would have wanted to boast about the conquest. It was quite impossible that he would have kept something like that to himself and he confided in Samuel about everything. Perhaps that was why Samuel had seemed so weird lately, so wound up and tense.

Peter had told her about his relationship with Lily when he'd returned from the police station. He'd arrived back at the mill in a taxi, looking drained, rather vulnerable. By then James was in bed. The boy seemed to have accepted the story that the police needed to talk to his father as an expert witness and had gone to his room without a fuss. The house seemed remarkably quiet as she waited for Peter's return. Usually she had the radio on or listened to music, but tonight she could face neither. She had opened the windows and could hear the water of the mill race, very distant.

Felicity had watched Peter climb from the taxi and gone out to meet him. He'd taken her hand, as if they were teenagers, and led her inside. Without saying a word he'd lifted a bottle of wine from the fridge and opened it. This quiet was so unlike him that she was scared. He should have been raging against the indignity of his imprisonment, the impudence of the police in carrying him off. She almost believed that he was going to admit to murder. But he was free, wasn't he? It couldn't be that.

He poured two glasses of wine and sat at the kitchen table. The kitchen was her space and he seldom sat there in the evening. He preferred the comfort of the sitting room or the privacy of his office. To sit with her was an apology in itself.

'Are you hungry?' she said. 'Can I get you something?'

'Perhaps later.' He sipped his wine, met her eyes. There was another moment of silence, then he said, 'I was having an affair with Lily Marsh.'

She didn't say she'd worked that out. There was a more pressing question. 'Did you kill her?'

'No!' Horrified. He reached out and took her hands. She found herself excited, thrilled by the touch. In their everyday routine – the family, the house, even the sex – they seemed to slide away from a real encounter. This had the charge of being touched by a stranger.

'She was very beautiful,' she said. 'I can see how you might have been tempted.'

'I was flattered.' He paused, drank more wine. 'Do you want me to tell you about it?'

She thought about that. Did she want all the details? How they'd met? Where they'd made love? She worried she might find that exciting too. 'No,' she said. 'That's your business.'

'Would you like me to move out?'

'I don't know. No. It never even occurred to me.'

'Lots of women would.' He seemed puzzled that she was taking his revelation so calmly. Was he disappointed, even, in her lack of response? 'It would be their first reaction, at least.'

'Perhaps an affair doesn't seem so important with two people dead.'

'I didn't kill her.'

She stroked the top of his hand with her finger. 'I believe you.'

Now, walking back from the bus in the shade of the elder hedge, she thought that in this short, taut exchange there had been more communication than they'd had for years. Unbidden there came into her mind a possible headline for one of the women's magazines she only read at the doctor's and the hairdresser's: *My husband was suspected of murder – And it saved our marriage!*

Even the night before, sitting opposite him, she had found the exchange melodramatic and faintly ridiculous.

'It was over,' he said. 'Ages ago. I wasn't still seeing her.'

'Who finished the relationship?' More mag speak.

'I did. Lily was unbalanced. I should have realized no normal pretty young woman would fall for me.'

Perhaps there was a hint of a pause while he waited for contradiction. She kept quiet. At least his adultery meant she didn't feel obliged to play games with him. 'She'd become obsessed. She turned up at work. Phoned me.'

'I think she called here,' Felicity said. 'Several times when I picked up the phone, it went dead.' She remembered the roses in the cottage, the sound of footsteps in the hall. 'She might have been here too.'

'She seemed convinced that I'd leave you to marry her. I never promised her that. I didn't promise her anything.' He got out of his seat to fetch the wine from the fridge again, filled her glass then his own. 'I told the police that we'd parted amicably. I didn't want them to think I had a reason for killing her. But it wasn't true. It's been a nightmare. She was stalking me. I never knew where she'd turn up next. She must have arranged the placement in the school in Hepworth, so she could get to me through James. And then that charade, turning up here, pretending she needed to rent the cottage.'

'I don't think,' Felicity said, 'that you can expect me to sympathize.'

He was apologetic again. 'No, no, of course not.' And suddenly she felt ashamed and exhilarated at the same time, because her secret was still intact. Should she confess too? About her and Samuel? There was something addictive in the rawness of the conversation and she wanted that to continue. She felt as she had when she was a student, sitting late at night with her friends, the room lit by candles, something gloomy on the record player. Then, every discussion had the intensity of the confessional. But reason took over, a sly realization that while the balance of power had shifted between them she should make the most of it. Insist that James go to the local high school, for instance, rather than being shipped off to the institution in Newcastle which had screwed Peter up. In this penitent mood, he'd agree to anything. Besides, she told herself, this wasn't her decision to make. Samuel wouldn't bear it if their relationship became public knowledge. It would kill him.

Later that night they'd made love, with the windows open so she could still hear the water outside. Afterwards they stood together looking out towards the lighthouse. I'll finish it with Samuel, she thought. No one need ever know. It'll be as if it never happened.

The next morning they got up as usual, Peter left for work early while James was still having breakfast. The boy had been full of questions about the police and the CSIs. Peter had been patient, looked over James's head to give her a wry smile. He kissed her on the lips before he drove away. It would soon be James's summer holiday and she walked up the lane with him to meet the bus, making the most of their time together. Next year, she knew, James would insist on doing it on his own.

She reached the house and let herself in. She hadn't slept well and felt restless, edgy. The walk hadn't helped. If Samuel were asked to choose between me and Peter, she thought, Peter would always come first. That was why he didn't tell me about Lily, why he didn't warn me.

She made herself coffee and stood by the kitchen door to drink it. There was still blue-and-white tape across the cottage door, and while she was standing there a car appeared in the drive. It was one of the crime scene investigators from the previous day. He waved at her, before climbing into his paper suit and walking across the meadow.

In the cool of the house she phoned Samuel. It was quarter past eight and she thought he might be still at home. He lived only ten minutes from the library. Before dialling she didn't have any idea what she was going to say to him. When the answerphone clicked in, she was quite relieved. She thought she might have made a fool of herself by demanding an explanation. *Didn't it occur to you that I deserved to know my husband was having sex with a girl younger than our daughters?* But he could have retaliated. *You were having sex with your husband's best friend.* Besides, she'd never made any demands on Samuel. It was the basis of their relationship. She replaced the receiver without speaking.

On impulse she decided to go into Morpeth for the day. She wanted people around her, the feel of fabric between her fingers as she looked for something new to wear, coffee, a good lunch with a glass of wine. She didn't even bother to change or put on fresh make-up, just picked up her car keys and her bag and almost ran out of the house. As she locked the door behind her she heard the ring of the phone inside. She paused for a moment but she didn't go back in. She might call into the library to see Samuel later, but she needed time to plan what she was going to say to him.

Chapter Thirty-Eight

Vera had left a family liaison officer with Julie, with instructions that she should be taken away from the house – to a friend's, to her parents' home, anywhere as long as it wasn't in the village where soon a team would be doing a fingertip search of the length of the footpath leading from the allotments to the main road. Now Vera was back in the station. She'd called the team together, her three closest staff, shouted them into her office from her open door. Charlie was still on the phone to the officer who was coordinating the Seaton house-to-house enquiries. Joe Ashworth had just arrived from the high school, serious, rather flustered. She realized he was thinking of his own daughter. When Katie was fourteen, would he have the courage to let her get into school, into town, on her own?

'Laura definitely didn't get on the bus,' he said. 'The other kids didn't make anything of it. They thought she just hadn't been able to face school after what had happened to Luke.' He paused. 'I had the impression she didn't really have many close friends. They were shocked that she was missing, excited even. But none of them seemed terribly upset. The teachers told me she kept herself apart from the other kids. One of them said she was a bit aloof.'

Of course she was aloof, Vera thought. Since she was young she'd had to put up with people teasing her about Luke. And for a moment Vera wondered if it was all much simpler than they'd been making it. Perhaps Laura *had* killed her brother. Revenge because he'd not saved Tom Sharp when he fell in the Tyne. Because he was always the centre of attention and he'd made her life a misery without even trying. And now she'd run away. Perhaps Lily's death was nothing but a horrible coincidence. Then she told herself that was ridiculous. The idea that there was no link between the two deaths was preposterous. And still at the back of her mind was the thought of the one obvious suspect.

Holly came in with a tray of coffee: four mugs of black liquid, a pile of plastic pots of milk on a chipped saucer. It was the first time ever Vera had seen her make drinks without being bullied into it.

Charlie finished the phone call and joined them. 'Nothing,' he said. 'Not yet. Some of the residents of the street are still out at work. I've told the team on the ground to get their phone numbers, call them at wherever they're working to see if they saw Laura this morning.'

In any other circumstances Vera would have been pleased that they were pulling their fingers out, working together, showing a bit of nous.

'I got the coroner's report on Parr's wife's death,' he went on. 'It was definitely suicide. She slit her wrists. The paper's on your desk.'

She nodded her thanks.

'This puts the focus back on the Armstrong family,' she said. 'Perhaps all the business with Peter Calvert was a distraction. Perhaps Lily Marsh was never an intended victim at all. She saw something, got in the way. Are we any closer to knowing what she was doing the night Luke Armstrong was killed?'

'The girls she shared the flat with were out that night. A trip to London to the ballet. Very classy. They stayed with friends in Richmond. They can't tell if Lily was there Wednesday night or not.' Holly had become an expert on Lily's flatmates.

'What would Lily Marsh have been doing in Seaton? An ex-pit village on the coast. I mean, it's just not her sort of place, those clothes she wore. She'd have stuck out like a sore thumb. Nobody saw her. I did the house-to-house myself.' Charlie had worked that patch as a PC and still had friends who were community police officers. 'There have been no strangers around at all.'

They sat, each of them trying to imagine Lily in her silk and her beads in the street where the kids played skipping games and the mothers sat on the steps watching them. All of them failing.

'Where do you think Laura's body is?' Charlie asked. The question they'd all had at the backs of their minds, none of them wanting to speak it.

'We don't know yet that the girl is dead.' Vera didn't shout, she kept her voice calm and reasonable. It wasn't the time for being showy. But she meant it. Or maybe she just wanted it to be true. For Julie and for herself. She wasn't used to failing and another death, the death of someone young, who'd never had the chance yet to be happy, would be the worst sort of failure.

'He didn't keep the other victims alive,' Joe said. 'Not that we can tell. Certainly not the boy.'

'This might be different.' Vera knew it was irrational, the idea she'd formed walking along the footpath with Julie, that the killer was enjoying himself, the game, the spectacle. That he might want to prolong the pleasure by keeping his victim alive.

Charlie knew better than to argue. '*If* there is a body, where will it be?'

'In water,' Holly said.

'So where should we look? Every house in Tyne and Wear has a bath.'

'No,' Vera said. 'He won't use a bath again. Laura's a striking young woman. Not beautiful like Lily, but big eyes, cheekbones you'd die for.' She caught her breath at the phrase but nobody else seemed to notice and she continued, 'She looks odd, exotic. He'll want to turn her into a picture. It'll be somewhere dramatic.'

'Then he must be holding her,' Joe said. 'Either alive or dead. He won't risk posing the body in broad daylight. Not again. He got away with it with Lily, but he'd never try it a second time.'

'Did we ever hear back from Northumbria Water?' Vera demanded. 'Weren't they supposed to have blokes working at the outfall by the lighthouse the afternoon Lily was killed? Has anyone spoken to them?'

'That outfall hasn't been used for five years,' Joe said. 'Some European directive on sewage and clean beaches. The guy I spoke to reckoned a team must have just parked up there to have a break.'

'Well, talk to him again. Get the names of all the workers in the area that day. They're the closest we've got to witnesses.'

There was a moment of silence, then Vera jumped up, stood in front of them. 'I want ideas,' she said. 'Any ideas. Crazy as you like. Places to look. Places we can keep under surveillance.'

'The Tyne. That's where Tom Sharp died. That was flowers and water. The start of it.' Charlie again. More animated than she'd ever known him.

'Eh, man, that'll be some surveillance, the whole of the Tyne.' Joe looked around at them. Not being cruel, but demanding they be more specific. Joe was always the practical one.

'He's right, though,' Vera said. 'That's where it started.' She wondered if she could justify another trip to Acklington Prison to talk to Davy, wondered if by now he'd have something for her. She decided it would have to wait. She didn't want to be too far from Julie if the worst should happen.

'Where, then?' Charlie was sitting on the edge of her desk, hunched forward. This had become personal for him too. Vera wondered if he had a daughter, realized she'd never asked him about kids. She didn't like talking about other people's children. It gave her an empty, jealous sort of feeling. 'The Fish Quay at North Shields where Tom Sharp had the accident? There's that sheltered bit of the water where the boats tie up.'

'That's busy until the early hours. Bars, restaurants. People living in those smart apartments they've put up.'

'It would be some statement, though, if he could get away with it,' Vera said.

'Does it have to be a *he*?' It was Holly. She was the most detached of them all. She's still young enough to feel immortal, Vera thought, and to be self-absorbed, untouched by another person's tragedy.

'Physically a woman could have done the strangling. Carrying Lily across the rocks to put her in that pool, that's another question. Who were you thinking about?'

'Kath Armstrong is the one person who links all the victims,' Holly said. 'She's a nurse. They're trained to carry, aren't they?'

Not the one person. There's someone else too.

'What motive could she have?' In her head Vera was trying to find an answer to her own question. Perhaps it had something to do with perfect families. Lily, Luke and Laura had all intruded on the little family in the neat house in Wallsend. Were the crimes Kath's warped attempt to protect her own little girl?

She was imagining the Tyne at North Shields late at night. The shadows thrown by the buildings, the harbour master's office, the deserted fish market, the lights from the south bank. Within the dock the water was calm and oily. She pictured the dark shape of a girl, a silhouette against the reflected light on the water. But a body wouldn't float. Not at first. Perhaps the murderer would find something for her to rest on. A pallet? A fish tray? A small dinghy? And cover her with flowers. What a picture that would make. She tried to clear her head and leave her mind open to other scenes, other places.

'So, any other possible scenarios?'

'What about Seaton Pool?' Joe said. 'It's close to where the girl must have been abducted and isn't there a hide there? The birdwatchers would know about it.'

'The locals have looked there already,' Charlie said. 'It was one of the first places they tried because it was so near to her home, and they know some of the village kids hang out in the hide when they've bunked off school. They found a pile of empty lager cans and some graffiti. Otherwise nothing.'

But Vera thought it could very well provide the sort of setting that the killer would be looking for. Seaton Pool had been formed by the subsidence of mine workings, though there was no indication now of the industrial past. It lay between the footpath where Laura had walked to catch her bus and the sea.

When she was a girl, Vera had once sat in the Seaton Pool hide with Hector. There must have been some reason for him to have made a rare trip to the lowlands and it troubled her for a moment that she couldn't think what it was. Then she remembered. An American coot. They'd waited for more than an hour for it to appear out of the reed bed. It had been a cold sunny day and the pool had been ringed with ice. She'd been bored and Hector had been characteristically offensive to the other birdwatchers. The bird had occasionally been disturbed by people passing along the footpath which followed the west side of the pool. It was a favourite place for dog walkers. During the day, Vera thought, it would be a risky place to set out the body. But the murderer seemed not to mind risk. He seemed not to care whether or not he was caught. And later in the evening there would be no danger at all.

'Are they still searching along the footpath?'

'They'll be at it all day.'

'But not this evening. Not once the light goes.'

'No,' Charlie said. 'They'll call it off then.'

'I want someone watching all night,' she said. 'From the time the search team finishes up there and all the wooden tops go home. Hidden. Unobtrusive.' It crossed her mind briefly the effect that would have on the overtime budget but really she didn't care.

'Is there any chance he'd go back to the light-house?' Holly asked.

'Or there's the stream at Fox Mill,' Joe said. 'If the cottage is significant. If Lily came back, met someone there, lost the ring Calvert had given her, the place could have a special meaning for him. It'd be risky with people in the house . . .'

But he doesn't care, Vera thought again. The risk is all part of the game, part of the performance. He's come to realize that he likes an audience.

They were waiting for her to make a decision. There was a moment of quiet which sometimes occurs in busy buildings. Outside, a baby was crying in the street and a mother was trying to comfort him.

'Three teams,' she said. 'One at the Fish Quay. Talk to the harbour master. One at Seaton Pool, camped out in the birdwatching hide. And one in the house at Fox Mill. The least the Calverts can do is let you use the house, the runaround they've given us. I can't see him using the lighthouse again. The tide's such a variable there.

'But that's for tonight. Before that I want the detail checked. Go back to the beginning. By this evening it'll probably be too late. The girl will be dead.'

Chapter Thirty-Nine

When Felicity arrived back at the mill from town she saw that there was a car in the drive. A car different from the one belonging to the CSI. She presumed it was someone else to do with the murder enquiry and wondered when it was going to end, this invasion by strangers, the prying into their business. She supposed she should be grateful that the press hadn't got wind of their involvement and wondered even if the car belonged to some reporter. When she looked at the cottage she saw that the crime-scene tape had been removed.

She'd just had time to take off her shoes and put on the kettle when the doorbell went. From the kitchen window she saw the young detective sergeant who'd come to take Peter away the evening before. She went to answer the door in bare feet and she saw him looking down at her toenails, which were painted a very pale pink. She sensed his disapproval and wanted to say something to him. *Doesn't your model wife, who belongs to the Women's Institute, paint her toenails? Or don't you like it because I'm a grandmother?* But she said nothing. She stood, waiting for him to speak.

'We've been trying to phone you,' he said. There

was accusation in his voice and something else. Anxiety verging on panic.

'I've only just got in.'

'Where have you been?'

'Into Morpeth.'

'Were you with anyone?'

She didn't answer that. It was none of his business. 'Why, what's happened?' Because she could tell that there was something serious. 'Another murder?'

He didn't answer. 'It would be very helpful if you had some proof of your whereabouts this morning. Did someone see you?'

'No,' she said reluctantly. 'I was there on my own.'

'A till receipt, then. Something showing the date and time?'

Then she began to panic too. She imagined herself being carted off to the police station in Kimmerston, sitting in a cell, being questioned. Perhaps they thought she and Peter were involved together. What would happen to James then? 'I didn't buy anything. I intended to, but I ended up just window-shopping.'

Then she had an idea and went outside, still in her bare feet, the gravel on the drive stinging her soles, to look in her car. At last she found a parking ticket for the Safeway car park under the seat. The date and the time were clearly marked and Joe Ashworth's attitude changed slightly. He grew more polite and asked if he might come in.

'A young woman's gone missing,' he said. Back in the kitchen the kettle had already boiled and switched off automatically. She made coffee for him without asking if he wanted one. 'There's a possibility that it's linked to the two murders. I've been into the cottage.

I hope you don't mind. The CSIs have finished and you weren't here to ask. In the circumstances . . .'

'No,' she said. 'Of course. You must do everything you can.' But she was shocked he still considered the cottage as a potential crime scene. Did that mean the men in white paper suits had found something? Did it mean Peter was still implicated?

'Did your husband leave for work at his usual time?' Ashworth asked. His tone was polite and lacked urgency, but she wasn't taken in. She wasn't going to tell him that Peter had left early this morning.

'Yes,' she said. 'At about the usual time. And you'll be able to check when he arrived at the university. They sign in. Fire regulations.'

He smiled so she realized that had already happened. She wondered if Peter had actually been there when they'd checked or if they'd spoken to his secretary. She would have liked to ask, but had too much pride.

The kitchen clock squawked. Some bird call she didn't recognize. She saw it was already two o'clock.

'I haven't had any lunch,' she said. 'I'd planned to have something in Morpeth, but in the end I couldn't face it. I was going to make myself a sandwich. Can I get you anything?'

He smiled. 'I'm just going,' he said. 'But if you see anything unusual – a car you don't recognize, people hanging around the cottage – you will give us a ring?'

'Yes,' she said. 'Of course.'

She was walking to the door with him when the phone went. Her mobile, still in her bag in the kitchen. She knew it would be Samuel, and was preoccupied with the thought, so she didn't take in the implication of the detective's next words.

'Will you be in this evening? In case we have any more questions?' He seemed not to have noticed the trilling of the phone. Or perhaps he didn't care if she was inconvenienced.

'Yes,' she answered. 'Oh yes. We don't often go out.' She just wanted him to leave.

He smiled again as if that was the reply he'd wanted, as if that was why he'd come in the first place. 'Excellent. That's fine, then. I'll see myself out.'

By the time she returned to the kitchen the phone had stopped. There was no message. Call register brought up the number of Samuel's mobile. She tried to ring it but it had already been switched off. She left another message, but although she tried his home phone again, she couldn't get through to him. She kept trying until James came home from school, then she gave up.

Peter arrived home from the university a little earlier than usual. It was only half past five. From the kitchen window Felicity saw him get out of his car and stand for a moment looking over to the cottage.

He's thinking about the girl. He misses her. A lump of jealousy, solid, like food stuck in the throat, making her want to gag.

James must have seen him too from where he was playing in the garden. He ran round the house to greet him. She couldn't hear what he was saying, but he started talking as soon as he saw his father. Some news about school. Peter smiled and picked the boy up and swung him over his head.

Felicity watched, thought how fit he was despite

his age, how strong. Peter put his arm round his son's shoulder and they walked together towards the house. The land line rang. Felicity went into Peter's office to answer it, glad of a chance to compose herself before she greeted them.

It was Samuel.

'Hello,' she said. 'I've been trying to call you.' She had tried several times while she was in Morpeth that morning. There'd been no reply from his home phone or his mobile. She'd plucked up courage to go to the library, but the woman behind the desk had said he'd taken a day's leave. Then she'd gone to his house and knocked at the door. There'd been no reply.

'Why? What's happened?' His voice sounded strange, a little blurred. She wondered if he'd been drinking.

'I can't really discuss it now. Peter's just come home, if you'd like to talk to him.' She kept her voice light and easy as she always did when there was a possibility of being overheard.

'No. It's you I wanted.'

'Are you all right?' she asked. 'Where have you been all day?'

He didn't answer immediately. She heard Peter calling her from the kitchen, put her hand over the receiver and shouted back, 'I'm just on the phone. Won't be a minute. Stick the kettle on, will you?'

Still there was no response from Samuel.

'Where have you been?' she asked again.

'I thought you might have worked it out.' It was the sort of thing he might have said when they were alone together. Teasing. Implying a shared understanding. But now he just sounded bitter.

'Are you all right?' she said. 'Is something wrong?'

'I need to see you.'

'I don't think that'll be possible,' she said. 'Not this evening.' She'd forgotten all about her plans to accuse him of keeping the secret about Peter's affair with Lily Marsh. Forgotten the bubbles of lust which had sustained her since they'd got together, made her smile to herself when nobody was looking. Now she wanted to extricate herself from the relationship as soon as possible and with as much dignity as she could manage. With this phone call, she was starting to consider Samuel as a liability.

'It's the twentieth anniversary of Claire's death,' he said.

Of course, she thought, that had been mid-summer too. She remembered the funeral. A still, humid day. Swarms of insects under the trees as they waited outside the church. The awkwardness, because suicide was such an embarrassing form of bereavement. She'd felt almost that they should be commiserating with Samuel for being dumped. Later they'd brought him home with them and he'd described finding his wife. 'She looked more peaceful than I'd seen her for months. Her hair floating around her face.'

She had a sudden shock, as she realized he could be talking about the recent victims, then she pushed away the picture of Samuel as a murderer. Samuel was a gentle man. He wouldn't hurt a fly. 'I'm so sorry,' she said. 'I should have remembered.' She knew he was waiting for her to agree to meet him, and for a moment she hesitated. Perhaps she should go to him. Just as a concerned friend. James had switched on the television in the living room. She heard the signature tune of an early evening soap. Peter yelled from the kitchen that tea was ready. This was the important stuff, she thought. The everyday trivia of family life. This was worth fighting for. 'Look,' she said. 'I'm really sorry but I can't. Things are difficult here. The police took Peter in for questioning last night. Are you sure you don't want to talk to him?'

Samuel didn't answer.

'Everything's such a mess,' he said at last.

'Where are you?' she asked.

'Forget it.' More bitter than she'd ever heard him. He switched off his phone.

Peter had made her Earl Grey, with a splash of milk, just as she liked it. 'Who was that?'

She hesitated for only a moment. 'Samuel. He sounded a bit upset. It's the anniversary of Claire's death. I tried to get him to speak to you.'

'I'll talk to him later.'

'That young detective was here this afternoon. Another young woman has gone missing.'

Peter carefully set down his cup, but she could tell the news had upset him. Perhaps it reminded him of Lily.

'Do they think that has anything to do with the murders?'

'That was what Ashworth suggested. He wanted to know where I'd been this morning.'

'They've been trying to track me down all day.' Peter leaned back in his chair, stretched, implying that he'd been so busy that he was exhausted.

'Where were you?'

'A meeting. Extremely tedious and abysmally chaired, which is why it went on so long.'

327

'Really?'

'You can't think I had anything to do with this abduction?'

'No,' she said quickly. 'Of course not. Not that. I went into Morpeth this morning. I tried to phone you. But I couldn't get hold of you either.'

'You suspected I was with another woman?'

'I'm sorry. It did cross my mind.'

'Never again,' he said. 'I promise I'll never do that again.' He moved his head to take in the house, James in the next room, the view of the garden. 'This is all too important.' She realized he was echoing the thought she'd had earlier, when she was talking to Samuel.

After dinner, she and Peter watched television with James. Later, they went together to put the boy to bed, then they took their drinks onto the veranda and watched the huge orange sun floating low over the hills to the west. Peter seemed anxious, preoccupied. He returned several times to the subject of the abducted young woman. What else had Ashworth told her?

'Nothing,' she said. 'Really. But if they find her and catch the person who took her, you'll be in the clear, won't you? It'll all be over.'

But that thought seemed to give him no comfort. He couldn't settle. At one point he went into the house to make a phone call. She assumed it was to Samuel.

'How was he?' she asked when he returned.

'I don't know.' Peter was frowning. 'He wasn't answering.'

The police officers arrived just as it was getting

dark. She'd never met them before. She'd locked the front door and they walked round the side of the house, a man and a woman. They seemed impossibly young to her, gauche, inarticulate, though they made every effort to be polite.

'Sergeant Ashworth said we could watch the mill race from here. You told him it would be OK?'

'Did I?' She couldn't really remember what she'd agreed to.

'Perhaps there's a front room upstairs? We could watch from there.'

'Of course,' she said. 'Anything we can do to help.'

They were still in the spare bedroom when Peter and Felicity went to bed. She saw them sitting in the dark, peering out over the meadow towards the cottage. There was a moon now. It didn't give enough light to see detail, but would be enough to make out somebody moving as a shadow. But what will they do, if someone does turn up? Felicity wondered. They're hardly more than children.

She made them a flask of coffee and some sandwiches. They thanked her, keeping their eyes on the window.

She must have fallen asleep before Peter. She was aware of him lying next to her, very still, trying not to disturb her.

Chapter Forty

It was mid-afternoon when the search team found Laura's shoe. It was in a ditch by the side of the road, not very far from the bus stop. They'd started close to Julie's house in Seaton and followed the line of the footpath, spreading out across the field which was all stubble now. The residents of Laurel Avenue watched them from the upstairs windows, saw them as black figures against the bright sunlight and the gold of the cut field. The officers moved in sequence like dancers in a slow, elaborate ballet, their shadows shifting as the day wore on.

It must have occurred to some of the team, after being at it for so long, that they'd find nothing. Vera thought that in this situation she might find it hard to keep up her concentration; she'd start thinking of home and a shower, a cold beer. But when they hit the road the team didn't stop. They moved along the hawthorn hedge and down the ditch, which was almost dry now. They were still focused. They just stood up occasionally to stretch or rub an aching back. They worked almost in complete silence. Even after the discovery of the shoe they continued all the way along the verge to the big roundabout on the outskirts of Whitley Bay.

It was clear that the shoe had been dropped by accident. It was a mistake. Whoever had taken Laura hadn't realized she'd lost it. There was no sign that it had been placed in the ditch to hide it and it wasn't there to make a point. The water was so low that it was clearly visible sticking out of the mud. Vera was sure this had nothing to do with the placing of the bodies. There were no flowers. It was just a shoe. A flat, black shoe with no heel and no back, simple, the fashion of the summer. The kidnapper would know now that it had been left. Would it be preying on his mind? Would he think the forensic team would be able to work some magic with it, that they would deduce immediately who and where he was?

Julie recognized the shoe at once and began to cry. Until then it had been possible to convince herself that Laura had bunked off school. To pay her back for being such a crap mother. For not being there that morning when she set off for Whitley High. She looked at the shoe in its plastic evidence bag and she howled. Vera couldn't bear to see her in such a state. She persuaded Julie to take one of the tranquillizers prescribed for her by the doctor. This was more for her sake than for Julie's. The sound of the crying woman got under her skin and stopped her concentrating. Even when she'd gone outside to speak to the supervisor of the search team the noise remained with her.

Of course the shoe told them nothing. It could have told them about Laura. About how tall she was likely to be, about the way she threw her weight forward when she moved, about where she'd been walking. It didn't tell them anything about the man who'd taken her. But close to the spot where it had been found there were tyre tracks on the verge. The grass was very dry there. The tyres had only crushed the grass and left no real imprint. However, just where the grass sloped down to the tarmac was a small patch of reddish builder's sand. Perhaps it had been left during road repairs or spilled from a lorry. And there a perfectly formed tyre mark remained. Only a fragment, half the width of the tyre and about ten centimetres long, but enough to excite CSI Billy Wainwright, who crouched over it, like a toddler concentrating on making a perfect mud pie.

'Well?' Vera knew she shouldn't really be there. She should be back in her office, pulling in all the information, keeping on top of things. Only she didn't feel on top of things.

'I'm not sure we'll be able to identify the make of tyre from this.' Billy stood up. She thought he looked knackered and a bit stressed. He was too old to be playing away with his new young lover. Too decent to do it lightly. Again she wanted to tell him to be glad of what he had. A wife he could talk to at the end of the day. Not to throw it all away for some mid-life fantasy, however young and however bonny. 'But if you find me a suspect vehicle, I'll be able to tell you if there's a match. Look, there are very specific marks of wear, chips and nicks in the rubber.'

'So we're not looking for a new tyre?'

'No,' he said. 'The treads are very faint. This is hardly legal.'

It was a perfect late afternoon in mid-summer. Less humid than it had been earlier in the day, when everyone had been muttering about thunderstorms.

Vera stood for a moment watching the search team inch their way towards the horizon and the swallows swooping and dipping to pick up insects over the stubble field.

'If you can get an ID on that tyre, you'll get in touch?'

He nodded briefly and, looking at him, she thought he knew already how mad he was to take up with the pretty pathology assistant. He hated himself but he couldn't help it. He didn't want to admit he was making a fool of himself, or he was too old, or that the woman was using him. He'd persuaded himself that he loved her.

In Kimmerston, the incident room was unusually quiet. A strained expectant quiet, so every ringing phone or unexpected raised voice set nerves jangling. She'd just settled into her office when her phone did ring. Not an internal call. This had come through on her direct line. She gave her name and there was a pause. In the background the sound of echoes in an enclosed space, a metal gate slammed shut and locked, rowdy men's voices. Then a different, quieter voice. 'This is David Sharp.' Davy Sharp in Acklington Prison. It would be teatime. She pictured him on the wing. He'd have had to queue to get to the phone and there'd be a line of men behind him. All listening in.

'Yes, Davy. How can I help?' Keeping it easy. Her voice low too so only he could hear.

'More the other way round,' he said. 'More what I can do for you.'

'What can you tell me, Davy?'

'Nothing on the phone. You'll need to visit. And it could be nothing at all.'

'Run out of tabs, Davy?' She couldn't leave the investigation and rush off to Acklington just because he wanted a cigarette. Not without news of Laura. 'It's impossible today. Can I send someone else?'

'No,' he said, his voice still even. 'It's you or nobody.' There was a moment of silence and she thought the phone had been cut off before he continued. 'It's complicated. A bit odd. I don't understand it. But no rush. Tomorrow will do.'

'There's a girl missing, Davy,' she said. 'I need anything you have now.' But this time the phone was dead and she wasn't sure he'd heard what she'd told him. She replaced the receiver, angry with herself. She should have handled it differently.

Despite what she'd said to him, she was tempted to go. At least it would be action of a sort, the drive to Acklington, the banter with the prison officer on the gate. An escape from the waiting. But Sharp hadn't sounded urgent. There was no way she could justify it.

The collection of Parr's stories on her desk caught her eye and she was distracted by thoughts of the writer. She had a sudden picture of him, sitting with the rest of the group in the garden at Fox Mill, the night they'd found Lily's body. The four men and the one woman on the veranda. It occurred to her now that all those men were a little bit in love with Felicity Calvert. It wasn't the birding which glued them together. It was the woman. The ideal housewife with her flowery skirts and her perfect baking. The men were all lonely, screwed up, frustrated. Like me, she thought. Just like me. Then she was taken back to the story she'd been reading when Julie had phoned, the abduction of the young person at the height of the summer, the loving description of the capture.

Vera opened her door and yelled for Ashworth. He came immediately and she saw the people in the rest of the room look up from their desks to watch. She realized they were thinking there'd been a development. A body. It might even come as a relief for them, a break from the tension, if the girl was found dead. At least then they would know what they were working with.

'There's no news,' she said, speaking to the room in general. 'Soon as there is, I'll tell you.'

Ashworth shut the door behind him and leaned against it. She thought he looked tired, then remembered his wife, the baby due any day. Things got uncomfortable the last few weeks of pregnancy. Especially in this weather. So she'd heard. Perhaps neither of them was getting much sleep.

'Read this,' Vera said. She nodded to the book on the table. 'There's this story, written by Parr. It's not exactly like the abduction of the girl, but near enough.'

Joe looked at her as if she'd completely lost it, but he picked up the book and began to read.

'I started it last night,' Vera went on. 'Now I can't get it out of my head.'

Joe looked up from the book. 'You think it's a sort of fantasy. Parr's written about it and now he's playing it out.'

'Crazy, isn't it? Ignore me.' And really she couldn't believe it. It was too theatrical to be true.

'There's no evidence he ever met the Armstrongs,' Joe said slowly. 'Certainly no motive.'

'I told you,' Vera said. 'It's a stupid idea.'

'It's pretty weird stuff. And as you said, very close to the abduction and the murders. Not all the details perhaps, but . . .' he paused for a moment '. . . the atmosphere. How does the story end?'

She was pleased he was taking her seriously. Her earlier irritation at his lack of focus in the case was forgotten. For this she would have forgiven him anything. 'I haven't got that far. I don't know. And I'm too busy to sit here reading.'

His attention was pulled back to the pages. 'What do you need to do?'

'I want to pin down where they all are,' Vera said. 'The people who were there when Lily's body was found. What are they doing today?'

'Felicity Calvert's at home. I went to look in the cottage at the mill. Just in case the girl was being held there. This morning Felicity went into Morpeth. Shopping, only she never bought anything. And nobody saw her. The only proof she was there is a parking ticket from the car park in the town centre. I phoned Calvert at the university. He's there somewhere. At least, his secretary said he signed in this morning and then went into some sort of conference which was going to last most of the day. She promised to track him down and get him to phone me back, but I've not heard anything yet. Clive Stringer's been at work. I spoke to him in the museum earlier.'

'Is he still there?'

'I presume so. It's not long since I spoke to him. Gary Wright's in North Shields. He's not working until tonight. One of the local men called on him earlier.'

'Did they look inside?'

'I don't know. Didn't ask.'

'I'm going to check Wright's flat,' Vera said. She knew it was probably a waste of time, but she was too restless to wait in her office for the phone to ring. She imagined Laura Armstrong locked in the room where she'd sat chatting to Wright, drinking beer. Even if the girl got out onto the balcony and started shouting, would anyone hear? 'And Parr? Where's he?'

'Nobody knows. He's taken a day's leave. Arranged it yesterday. He's not in the house in Morpeth.'

'I want to find him.'

Ashworth nodded. 'Look, do you want me to finish the story? I don't want to be too far away from home today anyway. Sarah had a few twinges in the night. Could be the baby.'

So that was what it was all about, she thought. He wasn't supporting her at all, just looking for an excuse to be in the office. She was about to make a sarky remark then thought it wasn't worth it. Office politics didn't matter so much with Laura missing.

'Stay in here,' she said. 'Give me a ring when you've finished the story. Earlier if anything occurs to you.' He nodded. She gathered up her bag and left the office. He was already engrossed.

Vera was in the car park when she realized she hadn't looked at the coroner's report into Claire Parr's death. She retraced her steps, ignored Ashworth who was comfortable in her chair, and dug through a mound of paper until she found what she was looking for.

'Oh Christ,' she said. 'Parr's wife. She *did* slit her wrists. But lying in the bath. Parr found her.'

Chapter Forty-One

Gary Wright opened the door to her with a sandwich in one hand and she realized that she should be starving. She wasn't, though. The thought of food made her feel sick.

'What's all this about?' He stood aside to let her in. 'One of your people turned up this morning, but they wouldn't say what was going on.' There was some music playing. Vera didn't really do music. Occasionally there was a song which stuck in her head, made her feel sentimental. Usually a tune she'd heard as a kid. Mostly she just considered it a distraction.

'Do you mind turning that off?'

He turned a knob and the music stopped. They were both still standing. 'Coffee?' he asked, then, seeming to remember her last visit, 'Beer?'

'You've not heard from Julie, then?'

'Not today.' He paused. 'She was here last night.'

'Aye, she said.' Vera sat down. 'You'll not have heard about her daughter?'

'Laura? What's happened?' He'd just finished the last of his sandwich and she had to wait for him to empty his mouth before he answered.

'Do you know her?'

'I met her once when I went to the house in Seaton.'

'What did you make of her?'

'Nothing. I don't know. We only exchanged a couple of words.'

'Interesting-looking girl.' She nodded to the photo of Emily. 'And you like them skinny.'

'For Christ's sake! She's fourteen!' But despite the bluster, Vera thought she caught something under the words. Guilt? Somehow the girl had got under his skin. 'I felt sorry for her. Being in the house while her brother was being strangled. I was saying to Clive the other day—'

Vera interrupted. 'She's gone missing. You don't mind if I have a quick look round.'

'What would she be doing here? She doesn't know where I live.'

'Humour me, eh, pet.'

She pulled herself to her feet, knowing all the time that she wouldn't find Laura. If Gary had taken her he'd be too clever to bring her back to his flat and she couldn't really see it. But now she was here she should go through the motions. She opened the door to his bedroom. The bed had been made and the room was tidy.

'What time did she go missing?' he asked.

'About eight-thirty. She never made it to the school bus.'

'I was here then, with Julie.'

'According to her she was sleeping off the effects of a bucketful of wine. Which you gave her.' Vera threw open the bathroom door. There was a row of shower gels and aftershaves on the window sill. More things to make you smell good than she'd ever possessed. No sign of Laura.

'She was determined to get pissed. I couldn't have stopped her even if I'd wanted to. And why would I? She wanted one evening when she wasn't thinking about Luke.'

Vera looked into the kitchen and through the glass door onto the balcony. Nothing. 'I know. I don't blame you.' She stood, quite still, in the middle of the room. 'You can imagine what sort of state she's in now. Are you quite sure there's nothing you can tell me? About Luke, or Lily Marsh? About any of this mess? Have you heard anything from Clive or Peter or Samuel?'

He hesitated for just a moment. Had he been tempted to confide in her about Peter Calvert's affair with Lily? Had he known about that? But in the end male solidarity took over. He shook his head.

'Sorry, Inspector. It was all just a horrible coincidence. I can't help you at all.'

At that, she lost patience with him and walked out. She'd only reached the top of the stairs when she heard the music again.

In her car she punched her own office number into her mobile, having to think for a moment what it was. Joe Ashworth answered immediately. 'Inspector Stanhope's phone.'

'Well?'

'No news on the girl. I'd have called.'

'What about the story?'

'I'm still only halfway through. I wanted to start at the beginning. It's fascinating, though, isn't it? The similarities.'

'I thought I was going mad,' she said. 'Obsession can do that to you. I'm going to see if I can track down Parr.' She switched off her phone before he could reply, slipped it onto the passenger seat. She'd never got round to fitting a hands-free set.

When she got to Morpeth, it was early evening. In the quiet street where Samuel Parr lived, his neighbour, a middle-aged woman, was dead-heading roses in the small front garden. Further away, children were splashing in a paddling pool, giggling and shrieking with delight. The woman tried not to watch as Vera got out of her car and knocked at the door. She would think it rude to stare, would hate to be seen as intruding. Vera thought Samuel Parr should be in. This was a time for preparing an evening meal, for the first glass of wine. But there was no reply.

Vera went up to the wall which separated the houses. The woman looked as if she wanted to escape inside.

'You don't know where Mr Parr's likely to be?'

'I'm sorry, I don't.' Tight-lipped, as if she begrudged the effort it took to form the words.

'It's all right, pet, I'm not selling.' Vera flashed her warrant card, grinned mirthlessly. 'I need to find Mr Parr. It's urgent.'

The woman looked up and down the street. 'You'd better come in.'

They sat overlooking an immaculate back garden. Away from public view the woman seemed to relax. 'I'm sorry, I really don't see how I can help. We've been neighbours for a long time, but never what you might call friends.'

'Did you know Mr Parr's wife?'

'Claire, yes. So sad. She always seemed happy enough. A little excitable, perhaps. We were all very shocked when it happened.'

'There was never any question that it was suicide?'

'Oh no, of course not. Samuel was heartbroken. I'm sure he blamed himself.'

'Why would he do that?'

'Well, it's a natural reaction in circumstances like that, isn't it?' the woman said. 'Guilt.'

'You don't think that he provoked the suicide? That he was having an affair, for example?'

'Of course not.' The woman seemed horrified. 'Samuel is a librarian!' As if his profession made the idea impossible.

They sat for a moment in silence, then she said, 'What are all these questions about?'

'I'm working on another enquiry,' Vera said. 'Mr Parr was a witness. His wife's suicide probably isn't relevant. I'm a little concerned for his safety.'

'Of course!' the woman said. 'It's the anniversary of Claire's death! My husband mentioned it this morning when he saw the date on the *Telegraph*.' She paused. 'You don't think Samuel's done anything stupid? That he can't face going on without her?'

'No,' Vera said. 'I don't think there's anything like that. But if you do see him when he comes in, ask him to give us a call.'

In the car, Vera realized she'd left her phone there when she'd gone in to speak to the woman. She'd had two missed calls, both from Joe Ashworth. She rang him.

'I've finished the story,' he said.

'And?'

'I think you'd better come in.'

Chapter Forty-Two

Back in her office, Joe was as excited as she could remember seeing him. 'Read the last few pages.' He moved away from her desk so she could sit down, hovered just inside the door.

Vera returned to the story. There was a description of a garden, where the kidnapped young woman was being held. It was an Eden gone to seed, a place of fleshy leaves, enormous flowers and overripe fruit. Vera found it oppressive, longed for a passage set in the hills, somewhere with lots of sky and a bit of a breeze, thought she'd been feeling like that since the beginning of the case. As the plot reached its conclusion, she grew more tense. She told herself it was fiction, wished she could throw the book aside and return to the reality of forensic tests and reason. But with Joe watching she had to continue reading. At last the inevitable ending occurred. The young woman was strangled. Parr had written the killing as if it was an embrace, a gesture of tenderness. The murderer was still anonymous; any relationship with the victim unexplored. In the final paragraph the body was placed in a pool, surrounded by water lilies.

'Well?' Ashworth demanded. 'What do you think? It must have been Parr.'

Vera didn't answer. 'I know where the story is set,' she said. 'I've been there.'

Vera's father had been part of the committee which had set up the Deepden Observatory. She wasn't sure who'd been foolish enough to ask him onto it. His brief flirtation with the birdwatching mainstream hadn't lasted for long. Hector had been too much of a loner to get on with the other committee members and his attention span had been too short for tedious meetings about fundraising events and the observatory constitution. Besides, he got his thrills from the illegal activities which surrounded his passion – the late-night forays into the hills for raptors' eggs, taxidermy carried out on the kitchen table. He wasn't really interested in the gentle and scientific study of bird migration. After about six months he sent an acerbic and libellous letter of resignation.

He had, however, been invited back to a party to celebrate the tenth anniversary of the opening of the observatory. Vera thought the invitation had probably been sent by mistake. He was on a list and nobody in authority had checked the names. The committee wouldn't have wanted him there. By that time, everyone in the Northumberland birding world had become aware of his illicit activities. He'd never been prosecuted, but it was a small world and there'd been rumours for years about his egg collection. When he was drunk he boasted about it. The best amateur collection of raptors' eggs in the country, he'd say. Probably the best in the world.

Hector, of course, had been delighted to receive the invitation and insisted on going to the party. She'd known better than to try to dissuade him. He'd always been a stubborn old sod and he delighted in making a nuisance of himself. By that point in his life he was drinking heavily and Vera had gone with him as a sort of minder, to stop him making a scene and to drive him home. It had been the same time of the year as now, another dry, still evening in mid-summer. Probably some of the people involved in the recent murders had been there.

What did stay with her was an image of the place. By the evening of the party the garden had grown up and everything was lush and green, an oasis in the parched flat land which surrounded it. There had been a conducted tour of the ringing hut, the mist net rides and through the orchard. Later, she'd stood by the pond, keeping a watchful eye out for Hector, ready to move him on quickly if he started to cause offence. But that evening he'd been on good form. A little loud, perhaps, but good-humoured, entertaining. As the night wore on she was able to relax. She even found herself enjoying the occasion.

She didn't tell Ashworth that story. 'I can't be certain, of course,' she said. 'But I think it's Deepden. Not far from the lighthouse where the girl was found and only just up the road from Seaton, where the Armstrongs live.'

'What are we waiting for, then? And if Parr's there with the girl, we'll need back-up, won't we? Do you want me to get on to it?' Now his anxiety about his wife was forgotten. He didn't want to miss out on the glory of an arrest.

'Let's keep it quiet for the moment. Low key. Any hint that we're on to him and he'll kill her. What's he got to lose?' But it was more a matter of pride for her than concern for the safety of the girl. Pride was her great failing. She didn't want a song and dance about this, in case they'd got the whole thing wrong. She hadn't got Samuel Parr down for the murders. She had in mind someone else entirely. And Laura could be dead. Vera imagined the gossip there'd be if she cocked this up publicly. *The boss got the idea out of a book. Talk about fairy tales. This time she's really lost it.* She would hardly be able to say then that it had all been Joe Ashworth's idea. She wasn't sufficiently sure of his theory to pull people away from the locations her team had come up with originally – Seaton Pond, the Tyne at North Shields, Fox Mill. Those places would still be watched.

'This'll be just you and me exploring an outside chance,' she said to Ashworth.

She could tell he believed the girl was at Deepden, he'd been seduced by the story, the flowers, the water.

She took a large-scale Ordnance Survey map from the shelf in her office and laid it across her desk. 'This is where we need to park,' she said, jabbing her fat finger onto the paper. 'If he's there, we don't want to be so close to the house that he can hear the engine.'

Before she left the station, she called into the incident room, sat on the edge of Charlie's desk, gave him her instructions. 'Then get off your backside. You could do with the fresh air and there's something I want you to check.'

As she drove towards Deepden she tried to recreate a plan of the place in her mind. The bungalow was side-on to the road, with the orchard behind it. The overgrown garden and the pond lay between the house and the flat fields running to the coast.

She didn't want anyone to know where they were, but Ashworth insisted on keeping his phone on until they got to the observatory. 'Sarah has to be able to get in touch.' She felt like screaming at him. *What will you do if your wife does go into labour? Leave me here on my own and drive off to play happy families? Or will you stay with me? Be in on the end of it and let your wife give birth without you?* She wasn't quite sure what he'd answer. Perhaps the same thought had occurred to him, because she could sense he was jumpy, sitting beside her, reading the map with his small Maglite torch, keeping his finger on the road.

'Nobody's booked into the observatory tonight,' he said. 'I checked with the secretary.' He'd told her that before. He couldn't cope with the silence. It wasn't like him; usually he was restful. Perhaps she should have left him in the incident room, so he could contact his wife every ten minutes. But Vera was used to having him with her at important times. She was glad she wasn't doing this alone. He cleared his throat. 'Apparently it was quite busy on Monday. There was some rare bird. But this time of year, people really only come for the weekends.'

She pulled into the verge, switched off the engine. There were no street lights and it was so quiet that they could hear the ticking of the car as it cooled. Outside it was almost dark, impossible to see colour or detail, but she could make out the shape of the hedge running alongside them.

'I'll walk up the lane,' she said. 'See if there are any lights on in the cottage, if there's a car there.'

Ashworth didn't answer.

The heat as she got out of the car made her think

of Spain. There should be cicadas, the smell of rosemary. Walking down the lane, keeping close into the
hedge in case she heard a car turning off the main
road, she was reminded again of her father. Until she
was old enough to protest, he'd taken her out on his
raids. She'd hidden in ditches and behind patches of
scrub and drystone walls, keeping lookout for him in
case the police or RSPB wardens should appear. She'd
hated every moment. The panic. The fear of being
arrested, locked up, of getting it wrong. What would
she do if someone did turn up? But it had been exciting too. Perhaps that's why I became a cop, she
thought. I got addicted to the adrenaline rush at an
early age.

Her eyes were becoming adjusted to the dark and,
before she came to it, she saw the five-bar gate which
led into the observatory garden, and beyond that the
matt black shape of the cottage. There was no car. Not
on the lane, at least. It was possible that it had been
pulled onto the drive and was hidden by trees and a
bramble thicket. She wouldn't see it from here. She
walked on down the lane in the hope of getting a
better view of the front of the house, where there
were windows. Would he take the risk of turning on
lights? Was he there at all?

At first she saw nothing, then there was a flicker
of light. The striking of a match or a torch being
switched on and off. So brief that she could have imagined it. If she'd been the imaginative sort. Perhaps Joe
was right after all. Perhaps Parr was here. She imagined how triumphant Joe would be when she told him
there was someone in the bungalow. She allowed herself a daydream. She was in Julie's kitchen, her arm

round Laura. *I've brought your girl home, pet.* Though she had no evidence that Laura was still alive she wanted that moment so much that it hurt.

She turned and walked back to the car, let herself in. She'd just shut the door when Ashworth's phone went, startling her so she felt her heart suddenly race.

He pushed the button after the first ring. 'Yes?' Even his whisper seemed very loud after the silence outside. Then she felt him relax and she could tell it wasn't his wife on the other end. She must still be tucked up at home with her cocoa. He wouldn't have to run back just yet to be present at the birth. 'It's Charlie,' he said. 'He wants to talk to you.'

She took the phone from Joe. 'Well, Charlie? What have you got for me?'

'I found Parr.'

'Where was he?'

'The first place you suggested. The cemetery. Next to his wife's grave. It's twenty years today since she killed herself. When I got there he was sitting on the grass. Looked as if he'd been crying.'

'You got someone to check his tyres against the mark on the road at Seaton?'

'Aye, and they're nothing like,' Charlie said. 'He drives a new car. Billy Wainwright said the tyre that left the mark was almost illegal. Besides, I don't think he's been in a fit state to snatch the girl. Sounded to me as if he'd been in the cemetery since early this morning. He puts on a good show, but I'd say finding that lass at the lighthouse brought it all back. When I got there he could hardly hold it together. I asked him about Laura Armstrong, if he knew what had happened to her, but he didn't have any idea what I was on about. Really, all he could talk about was how he'd let his wife down. I took him home, had a quick look round inside the house before I left him. There was no sign of the girl.'

'Thanks, Charlie.' She handed the phone back to Joe. 'They've found Samuel Parr. He had nothing to with abducting Laura.'

'So that's it, then. We can go back to Kimmerston.' She couldn't tell if he was pleased that his theory had come to nothing, or pleased that he could get back to his wife.

'Someone's in the cottage. I saw a light.'

'Are you sure?'

'Certain. I'm not given to visions.'

'One of the birdwatchers, perhaps. The members have keys. They're supposed to let the booking secretary know they'll be there, but they don't always.'

She saw him sneak a look at his watch, took no notice, shut her eyes to help her concentrate.

'Why don't we just go to the front door?' Ashworth said. 'Find out who's there and what's going on.'

She ignored him. It was important to think this through. Perhaps Samuel Parr's short story about the abduction of a child was irrelevant. A strange coincidence. She'd been so desperate to find Laura Armstrong that she'd allowed herself to be misled, swept along by Joe's enthusiasm. But the details were so similar, so consistent. She thought of the jacket of the anthology, the swirling greens and blues of the design, a stylized image of waves. The title in white, sharp against the patterned background. Parr's name at the bottom of the page. She'd borrowed the book in hardback from the library. Hundreds of people could have had access to it.

When she opened her eyes, she knew what had happened. She'd been right all along. It wasn't a surprise to her. She usually was.

Chapter Forty-Three

She was relieved when they found the door of the cottage was unlocked. Ashworth hadn't mentioned it again but she wasn't sure he believed her about the light. Not when they pushed open the five-bar gate, lifting it carefully on its hinges, and the place was dark. They walked across the grass to avoid the sound of their feet on the gravel drive. The grass was long and felt cool, slightly damp, through her sandals. Then a thin moon appeared and she even questioned her own judgement. Perhaps what she'd seen had been some sort of reflection. She'd wanted so much to find Laura here. She looked through the window, but could make out nothing inside.

But why would the cottage be open if the place was empty? She touched the door gently until it opened a crack, and listened. Joe Ashworth was making his way to the back of the house. She couldn't hear a thing, not even his moving. She stretched in her arm and ran her fingers over the inside wall, feeling for the light switch. Woodchip wallpaper, then the smooth plastic of the surround to the switch. She struggled again to remember the layout of the bungalow. She was sure there was no hall. This was the living room. Beyond it lay the kitchen and to the right two doors leading to the bedrooms which were used as dormitories. She gave Ashworth a few more minutes to take up position, switched on the light, pushed the door wide open.

The light came from a low-watt, energy-saving bulb which hung from the centre of the ceiling, but for a moment it blinded her.

'Police. Don't move.' She blinked as she shouted, heard a noise somewhere, a door being opened.

There was no one in the room. It was much as she remembered it. A table under the window. It might once have been a decent piece of furniture but now it was scratched and covered with rings from coffee cups and beer glasses. Two upright chairs pushed under it. A sagging sofa and two easy chairs facing the empty grate. On the walls photographs of birds and a number of paintings and drawings, mostly terrible. A few shelves with natural history books, maps and field guides. In the seconds it took to look around her, Ashworth appeared. The noise she'd heard had been him opening the door into the kitchen.

Without speaking she threw open the doors to the bedrooms. They were both surprisingly neat. Three sets of bunks in each. Grey blankets folded at the foot of each bed. A faint smell of mildew and socks.

She turned to follow Ashworth, who'd wandered back into the kitchen. It was the time to admit she'd been wrong. To get him to promise not to tell the world they'd cocked up and to let him go home to his enormous wife.

'Someone's been here very recently,' he said. 'The kettle's still hot. The light you saw could have been someone lighting the gas.'

So there was still a chance they'd find Laura before she was killed. She wanted to kiss him.

Ashworth seemed not to realize the effect of his words. 'He can't have gone anywhere. We'd have passed a vehicle in the lane. There's no car in the drive. He must have parked further down the track.'

'He knows we're here now,' Vera said. 'Switching on that light wasn't the brightest thing I've done in my career. You'll be able to see it for miles.' She ran out of the house and into the garden, stumbling on the last step from the front door. The pond was ahead of her. There was hardly any reflection from the water, only tiny patches of silver around the edges. In the centre a black shadow. She found herself praying in her head to a God she'd never believed in. *Please let her not be there. Not the girl. Not Laura.* She heard Ashworth close behind her, the sound of his breathing, the rustle of denim against denim as he walked. I hope you're praying, she thought. You're a believer. He might listen to you.

She crouched to get closer to the water. Began to make out the shape of a young woman's body, arms outstretched, when Ashworth switched on his torch. As the narrow beam swung over the surface, the image changed. She saw flat, waxy leaves, balls of tangled vegetation sucking in the light, but nothing human. Nothing dead. She realized she'd stopped breathing and took a lungful of air. She felt her head swimming.

The girl might already have been killed but she hadn't been posed. Not yet. She hadn't been used for effect, turned into a piece of art which had nothing to do with the real Laura. At least Julie had been spared that.

Vera straightened and tried to keep her thoughts clear, to remember the detail of what had happened during the Deepden party. Because she'd been determined to keep Hector on the straight and narrow, she'd been perfectly sober. The memories should be sharp. There'd been the guided tour: a walk through the orchard, sunlight sloping through the trees, a look into the cottage, which had been freshly painted for the occasion, a ringing exhibition.

The ringing exhibition. They'd stood in a semi-circle while a tall man in a blue smock reached out a bird for them to see. A yellowhammer, loosely held, the head caught between his second and third fingers. Through the door, they'd seen him weigh it. He'd slid it head first into a plastic cone which clipped onto a spring balance. He'd measured its wing with a metal rule. With his free hand he'd taken pliers from a shelf and a silver ring from a string hanging on the wall. He'd fitted the ring on the bird's leg, then squeezed it carefully into place. Then he'd stood at the door, the bird resting on the palm of his hand, until it had flown away.

It hadn't been the cottage door. She was sure of that. She dug in her memory for a picture of it. A flimsy wooden door held shut by a padlock which the ringer had unlocked when he'd returned from catching the birds. A door into a hut, the size of a big garden shed, made with stained wood panels. A corrugated iron roof. And surrounding the hut a thicket of bramble and buckthorn, so it was hidden from the garden and the house. They'd been surprised when the tour guide had led them there down a path cut through the undergrowth. The bushes had been cleared close to the front of the structure and that was where the group had stood, an audience waiting for the show to begin.

Now she tried to get her bearings. Standing next to Hector on the night of the party, while the ringer did his stuff, she'd felt her father start to get restless; he could only take not being the centre of attention for so long. She'd thought that he might escape, show his boredom by making an obvious run for it. It would have been easy enough for him to do that. The hut was right on the edge of observatory land, on the boundary with the field of rough grazing which led to the sea.

She began to move along the edge of the grass, looking for a gap in the vegetation. It seemed to her that the moon was brighter, or perhaps her eyes had adjusted to the dark. Then she found it, a narrow path leading through the bushes. She made herself walk slowly. She knew if she hurried, he'd hear them coming. If he was listening out for them he'd hear them anyway. Some noises she couldn't prevent – her laboured breathing, the snapping of dry undergrowth as it snagged on her clothing. The path was so narrow, she couldn't help that. But perhaps he wouldn't be listening out. Perhaps, locked in the hut, he hadn't seen the light from the cottage. Her fear was that if he knew they were there, he might be goaded into some grand gesture. It would upset him to be denied the water and the flowers, but he'd love a live audience.

He's forgotten why this started. He's become seduced by the glamour of it. He probably keeps a scrapbook of newspaper cuttings. Where will we find them?

The hut was just as she remembered it. Perhaps the paint had faded, the roof rusted, but in this light it was impossible to tell.

They stood on the edge of the clearing. Vera put her mouth so close to Ashworth's ear that she could feel his skin briefly against her lips.

'Wait. Until I call.'

She inched her way across the grass, aware of the weight she carried, the space she took up. As if, inside the hut, he'd sense the vibration of her feet on the ground, the displacement of the air.

At the door she stopped. There was no padlock. It had been pulled to from the inside, but she didn't think it had been bolted. She listened. No voices. Then she heard a rhythmic creaking, metal not wood, then a hissing. A white light appeared in the crack between the door and the frame.

Opening it, she tried to imagine she was visiting her neighbour. No fuss, quiet and easy. Wanting a favour. *I've run out of booze. Don't suppose you could spare a bottle of wine?*

Clive Stringer stood beside a narrow wooden table, his face lit by a tilley lamp. That had been the sound she'd heard, the creaking had been the pump as he'd primed it, the hissing the noise as it caught. Beside the lamp lay a bunch of flowers, mostly ox-eye daisies, their stems wrapped in damp newspaper. She tried not to look at them, or to peer into the shadow to look at the girl. Rolled up in bags in the corner, the mist nets used for catching migrant birds. And tucked inside, the thin nylon rope used as guys to anchor the poles. There'd been a mist net in Clive's room. She was sure now he'd used a guy rope to strangle his victims. She was glad of her size, blocking the doorway. He seemed very slight.

'It's all over now, pet,' she said. She kept her voice friendly. She didn't expect him to put up a fight, thought he might even be relieved to be caught. 'You'd just as well come with me.'

He stared at her without speaking.

She went on talking, keeping her voice even. 'You were the obvious suspect once I knew Lily was involved with Peter Calvert. You linked both families. But I couldn't work out why. You did it for them, didn't you? For Tom and Peter. Your friends.'

She thought he would answer, but he took the lamp by its wire handle and flung it against the wall. The glass smashed and the wood caught immediately; the paint bubbled and blistered and the flames licked along the line of the spilled paraffin. Stringer backed away from Vera into a corner. She ignored him, all her focus now on the girl, a still figure lying on the floor at her feet. Laura was wrapped in a blanket. Her face was covered. Vera picked her up, felt how thin and light she was. Ashworth was at the door, yelling for her to get out. Vera passed the bundle to him and turned to Stringer. He was almost surrounded by flame, though none of his clothing was burning. The red light was reflected in the lenses of his glasses. She wanted to get through to him.

'Come away out, man. Your friends wouldn't want this.'

He gave no indication that he'd heard her.

She was going to move towards him, but Ashworth took her by the arm and pulled her outside.

He'd laid the girl on the grass. Her face was filthy, her mouth covered by parcel tape, her hands and feet bound. Vera ripped the tape from her mouth, felt for a pulse. She didn't see the hut crumble in on itself, the heavy roof fall onto the man inside, trapping him so even if he'd wanted to escape he couldn't. If he screamed she didn't hear.

Chapter Forty-Four

Vera had dreamed of taking Laura back to Julie. From the moment she realized the girl was missing that picture in her head had kept her going. She'd seen herself in the kitchen, her arm around Laura's shoulders. *Look who's here, pet. I told you I'd get her back to you safe and sound*. And of course Julie had been grateful. In the dream.

It didn't happen like that. What happened was that Ashworth turned into the hero. When they stripped the tape from Laura's mouth she started choking and wheezing. The stress of the day finally bringing on an asthma attack. Or having her breathing restricted for that length of time. It was Ashworth who worked out what was going on, called for an ambulance, went with the girl to the hospital. He sat with her, holding her hand as the sirens wailed and they sped down the Spine Road to Wansbeck General. By the time they reached the hospital she was a lot calmer. They kept her in the hospital overnight, but by morning she was itching to be home. A little girl again, wanting her mam.

It was midnight when Holly brought Julie into the side ward where Laura was under observation. The woman was tense and frowning. Until she'd seen her daughter, she didn't dare to believe that Laura was safe. Ashworth was still sitting by the bedside when they arrived. He was the one to see Julie weeping and to receive her gratitude. And though Vera knew it was pathetic, she minded it. She'd wanted it to be her Julie thanked with tears in her eyes. But she'd been right about the killer. There was some consolation in that.

Instead of delivering the girl to her mother, she stood in the garden at Deepden waiting for the travelling circus which always followed a major incident. The fire engine arrived first. The fire fighters seemed disappointed that it was such a small fire, so easy to contain. She had the feeling that only the fact of a fatality made them think it was worth their being there. While she watched them she couldn't get rid of the image of Clive Stringer in the flame-red spectacles, standing quite still while the hut fell around him. He'd had his grand gesture after all. Later, when the scene of crime team searched through the wreckage, they found a couple of stems of daisies whole and undamaged.

Vera got to Fox Mill just as Peter Calvert was getting into his car. She saw Felicity watching them through the kitchen window, her face pinched with worry. The mood she was in, Vera couldn't feel much sympathy.

'I want a word,' she said.

Calvert began to bluster.

'You lied to me,' she said. 'I could charge you.' She wished she was a man. She wanted to hit him. 'We'll go and chat in the cottage, shall we? Back to the love nest. It might jog your memory. Don't worry, I've got a key. I rescued it from the CSI. We don't need to bother your wife with this. Not just yet.'

She started across the meadow, knowing that Calvert would follow. She had the door open and was sitting at the table when he came in.

'This is where Clive killed Lily Marsh,' she said. 'But then, you know that already. You suspected it, at least. Otherwise why lie about sending the card made of pressed flowers?'

He sat opposite her, gave a little smile. 'A small lie under pressure, Inspector. It means nothing.'

'You set Clive up. You were his hero. You knew he'd do anything you asked. You told him about Lily. How she was threatening to go public about the affair. When? At one of your cosy Friday lunches?'

'I needed someone to talk to, Inspector. It was a stressful time.'

'How did you put the idea into his head? "If only she were to have an accident . . ." You told him you'd sent the card. Were you worried she'd use it as evidence of the affair? "But at least I didn't sign it. No one will trace it back to me. We were very careful." But you didn't mention the kisses.

'Only Clive had a more elaborate plan than you'd anticipated. He was a chess player. He liked intricate patterns. And he had no real grasp on reality – my sergeant realized that after one meeting. It wasn't enough to kill Lily Marsh. He had to distract us from you. He had his own reason for wanting Luke Armstrong dead, so he killed him first. And to reinforce the connection to Lily, and to protect you, he sent the card. You must have known about that. Otherwise why lie when I asked if you'd sent a similar one to Lily?' She paused to catch her breath. 'When was that, Dr Calvert? When did Clive admit he'd killed Luke and Lily?'

The man didn't answer.

Vera thumped her fist on the table, so hard she knew it would be bruised the next day.

'You're quite safe, man. I can't really charge you. The CPS would throw out the case in minutes. You're bright enough to know how these things work. But tell me. Satisfy my curiosity.'

'There was a Marmora's warbler at Deepden a few days ago. I gave Clive a lift back to town. He told me then. As if I should be pleased with him. I was horrified.'

'Not sufficiently horrified to tell us what had happened, though.' Her voice was deceptively calm. 'There could have been another victim. But still you kept your mouth shut. Why was that, Dr Calvert? A warped sense of loyalty? Or were you scared Clive would implicate you in the murders?'

'I don't have to listen to this, Inspector. As you said, you can't charge me.'

He got up from his seat and walked out through the open door. Vera watched him cross the meadow, and stop to blow a reassuring kiss to his wife, who must still have been looking from the window.

At ten that morning Ashworth's wife went into labour. He phoned the office at teatime, to tell her they'd had a boy. Jack Alexander. He'd been nearly ten pounds, a real bruiser. Vera was just about to leave the station for bed, but she agreed to meet up with him for a drink. She found it hard to celebrate other people's babies but she'd rather have a few drinks with Joe than go back completely sober to an empty house. In the end, she suggested he come to the old station master's house on his way through. She knew she'd not be able to stick at a couple of halves and it'd save her having to drive. On the way home she stopped at the supermarket and got a bottle of champagne and a huge bunch of flowers for Sarah. She thought Ashworth would appreciate the gesture. Also in the trolley she put a ready-cook Indian meal and a bottle of Grouse. She'd need something to get her to sleep.

Ashworth arrived just five minutes after her. From her kitchen window she saw him leap out of the car, bleary-eyed and beaming. She'd already had a large Scotch. She rinsed out the glass and put it back on the tray, so he wouldn't know.

They sat outside. The house was even more untidy than usual and she didn't want him seeing it. She couldn't bear it if he started feeling sorry for her. She was light-headed through lack of sleep. Their conversation was punctuated by the sound of her neighbours' animals – sheep, goats, the inevitable cockerel.

'You were right, then,' she said. 'Stringer was a nutter.'

'You knew it was him, though, didn't you?'

'I thought it was a possibility.'

'You didn't let on.'

'No proof. And I met a few lads like Clive Stringer when I was growing up. Obsessives. Loners. They didn't all turn into serial killers.'

'Why did he?'

'He was a romantic,' she said. 'He believed in happy families.'

'That's no kind of motive.'

'It made sense to him,' she said. 'It had a weird sort of logic.' Looking into the distance, she thought the hills seemed very sharp and close this evening. She wouldn't be surprised if the weather didn't break soon.

'You'll have to spell it out.' Joe believed in happy families too, had done even before he got one of his own. But then he'd grown up in one. She caught him looking at her as if she was daft.

'Clive was a loner,' Vera said. 'No dad. No friends. Only that witch of a mother who tried to suck the life out of him. He had two surrogate families – the Sharps and Peter Calvert's birdwatchers. Both murders were committed to protect them. He was very close to Tom Sharp, looked out for him when he was a kid, blamed Luke for his death. The Calverts were his idea of a perfect couple. He idolized Peter and fancied himself in love with Felicity. He didn't want her hurt by news of her husband's affair.'

'We'll never really know what was going through his mind, will we?' Ashworth looked up from his glass. She could tell his head was full of the wonder of his new son, wrinkled and red and screaming. She'd had to hear all the details of the birth before he'd let her start talking about the murders. About how brave Sarah had been. 'All she had was a couple of puffs of gas and air.' He didn't care why Clive Stringer had murdered two people and kidnapped a third. Not tonight. *Nutter* was good enough for him.

But Vera cared. And she knew.

'Peter Calvert was his hero. Clive was doing what Peter wanted, saving his marriage, getting rid of Lily Marsh for good. Do you remember, we asked Clive in the museum if he'd keep quiet if he'd found out one of his friends had committed murder? He said of course he would. We should have asked him if he'd commit murder for his friend.'

She spoke almost to herself. The sun and the whisky and the lack of sleep had sent her into a sort of trance. 'If he'd kept it simple he might have got away with it.'

Joe looked up from his drink, his attention caught at last. 'What do you mean?'

'Lily Marsh was his first target. She was threatening to make life difficult for Calvert. We know she was starting to get awkward. That was why she turned up with James to look at the cottage. She assumed Felicity would tell her husband Lily had been there and he'd realize it was a threat. *Take me back or I'll tell your wife.* She was phoning Calvert at work. She'd even convinced herself she was pregnant. Calvert confided in Stringer. They met up for lunch every week. He knew he was Stringer's hero, has the sort of ego to allow him to believe a friend would commit murder on his behalf. We'll never be able to charge him with it, of course.'

She imagined Clive in the bungalow in North Shields, Calvert's words rattling around in his head, planning the murders while his mother watched television game shows in the other room. Obsessing about it, as he obsessed about birds and friendship. 'He played chess,' she said. 'He used to play with the

Calvert boy. He worked out the moves in this drama well in advance.'

'So why Luke Armstrong? And why was he killed first?'

'He had to be. Stringer didn't want Calvert implicated in any way with the murders. By making Luke Armstrong the first victim, he thought we'd concentrate on the boy in our search for a motive.'

'So the first victim could have been anyone? Stringer chose him at random to throw us off the scent?'

'No. It wasn't random. Stringer would never have worked himself up to commit murder unless he'd convinced himself that Calvert needed him, but I think he was glad of an excuse to kill Luke. He blamed him for Tom Sharp's death. Lots of people did. He looked on Tom as a brother. As I said the Sharps were his surrogate family. And he was there when Gary was talking about his plans to go out with Julie, so he knew she wouldn't be in the house that Wednesday night. Perhaps he saw it as a sign, decided it was time for him to make a move. He didn't know about Laura, though, didn't know she was there when Luke let him in. Gary told him later that Luke had a sister and she'd been in the house.'

'So that's why he abducted her?'

'Nah,' Vera said. 'He'd started to enjoy it. Being in control for the first time in his life.'

'And he got the idea for the flowers from Tom Sharp's memorial on the Tyne?'

'Maybe. He knew the best way to keep Calvert out of the frame was if the police considered the two murders as one case, the random killings of a madman.

They had to be linked. That was the reason for the flowers, the water. I don't see Stringer as naturally theatrical. The posed bodies and the dressing of the scene was part of the plan.'

'You wouldn't think he'd have that much imagination,' Joe said.

'Well, he didn't dream it all up himself, did he, pet?' Vera poured herself another drink, hoped Joe was too distracted with thoughts of the baby to notice. 'He got the idea from that bloody story. Parr's story. The one that almost had us convinced he was the murderer. In that the victim was strangled. How did Parr describe it? "Like an embrace"? And then the corpse was laid out in water. Clive had the book in his room when I visited the house. But it was in paperback. A different edition from the one I'd borrowed from the library. A different jacket. I didn't take it in at the time. He took his mother's bath oil to put in the water in the Armstrongs' house. When I looked round the Stringers' bungalow there were only male toiletries in the bathroom. I should have noticed.'

She reached out and finished her drink. Her third? Or her fourth? 'As I said, it was all planned. Very carefully. He knew Calvert had sent Lily a card with a pressed flower. So he sent one to Luke.'

In the distance her neighbour was calling her hens to be locked into the coop for the night, rattling a bowl of mash with a spoon to bring them in. The stupid woman had names for them all, cried when they had to wring their necks. Vera took the carcasses off her to casserole.

'He stole a car to get there. We checked car-hire firms, but not stolen vehicles. I was taken in by him, never had him down as a thief, but he'd knocked around with the Sharps for long enough to realize how it was done. He'd been good at it at one time, I heard today. Supplied cars for Davy on and off when he was still at school. Gave up when Calvert got him the job at the museum. After killing Luke, he dropped the vehicle back in Shields. If he'd stopped there we'd never have tracked him down. But that wasn't the object, of course. The object was killing Lily Marsh, saving Calvert's marriage, making himself indispensable.'

'Did he kill her in the cottage at Fox Mill?' Ashworth asked. Interested enough at least to put the question, drawn into the story despite himself.

'He must have done. How else would he get a woman like that alone? He wrote her a note, perhaps. Forged Calvert's writing or did it on his computer. We might never know. But I'm sure he was there. I phoned Felicity Calvert this afternoon. When I pressed her she remembered seeing a white Land Rover in the lane when she was bringing James home from school. Given long enough the CSIs would find a trace of him.'

'The white Land Rover,' Ashworth said. 'Stolen from Northumbria Water. That was how he got her body into the gully.'

'He took it from the depot,' she said angrily. 'Nobody missed it until I asked them to check. That was what Davy Sharp was phoning up for yesterday. He'd heard that Clive had been stealing again. Couldn't understand it when he had so much to lose. He'd heard that the girl had been abducted. With the Land Rover he could get all the way to the gully over the grass and rocks. That was why nobody saw him with Lily's body.'

Now, she was starting to feel properly tired, starting to relax. One more drink and she might sleep tonight. 'Clive must have gone back to Seaton, watched the house, maybe from the footpath by the pond. Seen Laura. He was a regular there. He'd been birdwatching in the area since he was a lad. If anyone saw him with binoculars it wouldn't register with them. The birders are a part of the scenery. The day of the abduction he'd have followed her almost to the bus stop, waited until the road was quiet. She was a skinny little thing, easy enough to overpower. He'd never had a girlfriend. Imagine the fantasies, as he lay awake at night reading that book. She'd have fascinated him. Especially as she was so similar to the figure in Parr's story. He'd have justified it to himself – that she might have seen him the night he was there with Luke, or he needed to throw our attentions back on the Armstrongs because we were getting so close to Calvert. But that wasn't why he went out early in the morning to take her while she was on her way to school. He kept her alive, because he liked the thought of having her there for him. He locked her in the boot of the car he'd stolen while he went into work and established his alibi. And all the time he was planning the murder, how it would look. How beautiful she would look when she was dead. He took flexi time and left early, took her up the coast to Deepden and locked her in the ringing hut.'

'But he intended to kill her?'

'Certainly. He had the flowers with him.'

Ashworth finished his drink, looked at his watch.

'I'll get back. Hospital visiting. And Sarah's mam's had Katie all afternoon. It'll be good to have everyone together at home tomorrow.'

Vera watched him walk to his car, the champagne in one hand, the flowers in the other. Thought that if she'd been married to someone like Joe Ashworth, she'd be so bored she'd commit murder herself.

Visit **www.panmacmillan.com** to read more about all our books and to buy them. You will also find features, author interviews and news of any author events, and you can sign up for e-newsletters so that you're always first to hear about our new releases.

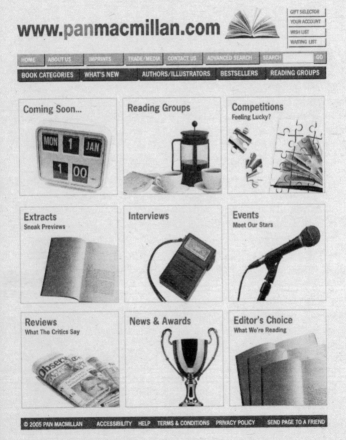